FOREIGN INVOLVEMENT

Robert E. Smith

Copyright

Cover photograph by ANDREW DICKSON

2

FOREIGN INVOLVEMENT

PROLOGUE

The large home sat high on the hill, facing west toward the Oregon coast range and the rapidly setting sun. The two intruders walked down the stairs to the basement, discussing plans. The first man turned away for an instant, and immediately the piano-wire garrote tightened quickly around his neck until life slipped from his body. The killer looked impassionedly at the lifeless heap on the floor as he removed the wire from the dead man's neck and stuffed it in his pocket. The only thought that crossed his mind---- *he's been officially dead for years ----now he really is!*

He lifted the lifeless body, moving it to a location where it wouldn't be discovered anytime soon. Although heavy, he had little trouble placing it in the dark hollow of the crawl space and then secured the small access door. He was in excellent physical condition, and took these *housekeeping* details in stride. There's more work to be done he thought, as he methodically finished wiping down every surface, checking each room for any trace of his presence. This routine came as second nature to a man that survived all these years through his cunning and attention to detail. Afterward he left as he came, through the side door----out of sight from the street.

CHAPTER 1

The young morning sun crept silently higher in the distant eastern sky. It climbed steadily over the smoky green pines, committed and undeterred by the occasional splash of a hungry bass breaking the calm lake's glassy surface. This display of nature's wonder was now my entire world, as was the reality of a soon to be scorching July day. Life for me now consisted of nothing more than watching the sunrise while drinking a steaming cup of the worlds blackest coffee, hot off the propane flame from my stove a dozen steps away. I usually sit on the rear deck of my 56-foot houseboat enjoying life in its simplest form on Shasta Lake in northern California, which in my opinion, is the world's most beautiful lake.

For the uninitiated, a houseboat is not one of those homes on floats tied permanently to a mooring, moved only by some form of tugboat---if moving was ever required. The best way to describe a houseboat is two steel or aluminum pontoons welded together under a steel deck frame with a sort of mobile home plopped on top. They're outfitted with one or two engines, as basic as an outboard, or more generally an inboard engine with an out-drive, and some more powerful than an SUV engine.

Back to my difficult life, some days I actually break the routine by casting a fat worm at the endless rings of ripples created by a hungry trout or bass. If I actually get lucky and pull one in, I usually toss it back to catch it another day.

If it sounds like I have nothing much to do these days, you're quite right and I like it just fine. After a not too fulfilling nearly fifteen-year career as a San Francisco homicide detective, my troublesome independent streak won out and I found a way to get paid for thinking outside the box. Don't get me wrong, I loved my job, I just didn't like the politics.

Finally, I figured out a way to get paid more than a human being deserves to be paid. When someone is crazy enough to shove serious money at me for a little software company I founded, I took the money and ran. As of the day I left two years ago it hadn't made a profit, and wouldn't for some time to come. What happened? About four years ago a light bulb went off in my head about developing software that researched an individual's background for criminal and other public record information, which up to that time was impossible to generate from a single source. To make a long story short, I quit my job, went into debt, borrowed every nickel I could and hired the best software genius around to work for beans at first and a generous amount of stock, with a payoff down the line----- maybe. And voila, shortly thereafter venture capitalists from the Silicon Valley threw money at us for development. Then came the offer of stock and cash for the company. I lucked out in another way and sold all the stock I received as soon as my one-year obligatory employment contract ended. I look pretty smart now with NASDAQ taking a dive, and had I not sold my stock when I did, it would be worth less than a tenth of what it was when they bought the company. How many millions can one spend? I don't know, but I do know that my income tax is paid, and for the present this huge windfall is parked in CD's, so my biggest decisions these days is whether to sit and read or snooze, on the top, rear or front deck. Then I have to decide what to pull out of the fridge for dinner, or whether to run my Cobalt over to Bridge Bay Marina and pop

into the Tail of the Whale Restaurant for happy hour and the Captains Cut prime rib. This is my second year on the lake with my beautiful Starbright houseboat, custom-built in Kentucky. I have everything I need to navigate and enjoy the more than three hundred and sixty-five beautiful miles of Shasta's pristine shoreline. My floating castle's interior is finished in magnificent teak and specialty wallpapers. Deep-pile wool carpets and beautiful hardwoods cover the floors. The kitchen is equipped with every convenience for the gourmet cook. Three TV's, a satellite dish and state of the art sound system with ten speakers individually controlled and strategically located, round out the entertainment systems. There are two bedrooms, one used as an office, and a master with a king-sized bed, granite counter-topped vanity, fantastic shower with great pressure and a walk-in closet. The front and rear decks are spacious with the rooftop more than forty feet long, with two-thirds under a canvas awning. The roof deck is furnished with a large rectangular glass-topped table and six cushioned chairs. In addition there are

four cushioned lounges along with a bar, refrigerator, ice-maker and six bar stools. Hidden below the rear deck are a huge marine engine and a 20-kilowatt generator that will run almost any electrical device one can imagine. Sounds like a boat built for entertaining and partying, but in my case it's a refuge, a place to unwind in total tranquility. I just head for a cove several miles up the McCloud River, and tie up for a week or more. I have total privacy only interrupted by an occasional family of deer or ducks looking for a handout, or on a very rare occasion I might even see a large brown bear looking for berries, or the occasional accessible fish, or garbage left behind by a trashy boater or camper. They don't bother you if you mind your own business, but they're a real trip to see in the late evening or early morning.

My only contact with the outside world is by cell phone when I'm foolish enough to turn it on. Only a small handful of friends and family have my number.

Being divorced since shortly after college and no children, my family consists of parents, Charles and Aileen Winters, retired and living on the Oregon coast, and an older sister Fran in Seattle. Oh by the way, I'm a "Junior", but I never acknowledge that, and go by Chuck Winters or C.E. Winters. I see my folks during holidays and whenever I can, or when I feel like some fresh Chinook salmon that no one prepares like my mom. On such occasions I have to endure the standard lecture from mom----"Chuck, don't you think you should settle down and find a nice woman to grow old with? Just look at your father and I, we couldn't be happier."

"OK I get the picture, but later, much later!" I never say that aloud---I just nod, smile and think it.

Today started just like every other summer day on the lake; weather forecast hot, mid to high-ninety's, cooling to mid-sixty's overnight. It was almost six A.M., and as the sun came up I could see out into the lake from my cove, smooth as glass, fish rising like surfacing subs, clearing the surface with turmoil of overlapping expanding rings and settling again. The cell phone startled me out of my natural ecstasy-induced trance, dedicated to absorbing the pure paradise of my surroundings, as I lounged, sipping coffee on the back deck----stern to real sailors. Since the phone is usually plugged into the cigar lighter to keep it charged up, I had to hustle on up to the front or bow of the boat. "Hello".

"Chucky?" This had to be Tom Claudius, CEO of One Star Venture Funding, in Palo Alto. No one calls me Chucky! I decided a long time ago that Tom could call me anything he wanted----and he has. He funded my start-up, and only because of him I can enjoy this life of independence.

"Tom, what's up at this ungodly hour?"

"I've got a real problem, and you're the only person on this earth that I can trust with it. I need to see you right away. Can you get down here for lunch-----today? It's really important." The sound of anguish was rare with Tom, and I sensed it now big time.

"Tom, you're the only person outside of my folks that could drag me away from *this*---- on a moments notice. See you at your office at high noon."

"Thanks Chucky". He hung up without another word of explanation.

My houseboat and speedboat are moored at Holiday Harbor Marina, near the O'Brien exit on I-5, about 19 miles north of Redding, CA. I picked Holiday, because I rented houseboats from them for years and they're the nicest, friendliest folks you'll ever meet. I quickly showered and shaved, dressed in lightweight slacks, polo shirt and my obligatory boat shoes.

The cruise back to the marina was uneventful and quiet, as anyone on the lake at this hour was either fishing or sleeping. I saw the big flagpole with the American flag marking the marina entrance from a mile away, and was soon in the no-wake zone, creeping along so as not to rock the other boats in the marina. I maneuvered the big boat, with my Cobalt speedboat tied alongside, into my double slip, tied them down, locked up and hopped onto the dock. The marina's shore facilities are located a half-mile down the dock walkway from my slip. My ride is a new black Escalade by Cadillac. For those who haven't heard of an Escalade, it's an SUV, and as close to a luxury car as you can get. The marina parking lot for moorage customers only, is secured and off to the side away from the distant general parking area for rental customers.

When I reached my rig, I kicked the dry Shasta red clay dust off my shoes that collected from the walk across the unpaved parking lot, pulled off the protective car cover and tossed it in the back. It was 7:00 A.M. when I pulled myself into this luxurious instrument of the roadway. The new car smell seemed unusually present this morning, however there was also a strong feeling of foreboding clinging to my sensibilities, after earlier hearing the voice of Tom Claudius. It wasn't what he said, but what he *didn't say* that bothered me.

If I hurry I'll just have time for a quick breakfast at The *Tale of the Whale* at Bridge Bay Resort, two miles south. Pulling into the lot, I couldn't help wondering what Tom wanted. I hoped it wasn't related to InfoCheckReport, my old company. I was mentally divorced from it and made a not so easy conscious effort to stop thinking about it, a process that previously consumed every waking moment since I thought of the concept.

The long and the short is, there's no way I'm giving back the close to a *hundred-mil* I received, and I'm not interested in going back to work in order to bail them out if they're having a problem. I'm done and I've moved on------period, end of story!

The *Tale of the Whale* is a charming restaurant hanging over the south end of Shasta Lake. The exterior is comprised of dark rustic wood with brass- trimmed portholes, a truly inviting nautical feeling. Upon entering and walking down a twenty-foot entry hall, you're at the currently unattended reception podium and desk, where you can peek around the corner and see a wall of glass with overwhelming views of the lake from the dining room. The tables are made of lacquered ship hatch-covers, supported by ropes and pulleys----surely from pirate sailing ships. The coveted tables are at the window, and considering I was early, I had my pick and took my favorite. The breakfast menu is definitely for sailors, as the only diet item is oatmeal and fruit. I of course considered the healthy breakfast for about half a second and went right to two eggs, sunny-side up, four link sausages, hash browns, and a huge home made biscuit, in lieu toast. I always feel good about passing up the biscuits and gravy. That makes anything else I order OK. After gobbling up my bounty while talking with a couple of old Shasta buddies at the next table, I was back on I-5 heading south toward San Francisco.

CHAPTER 2

By 11:15AM, I was on the Bay Bridge and soon would
be passing the San Francisco Airport heading south to the
Palo Alto exit. After cruising up University Avenue
under a tree-shaded canopy, I crossed El Camino Real,
made a right turn onto Arboretum Road, and then took
the first left. Tom's office was in a beautiful old Spanish-
style stucco building, which he owned, with a red tile roof,
set amongst the towering eucalyptus trees at 2760 Sand
Hill Rd. Rolling down my window, I could hear the
familiar whoosh, cachunk-cachunk sounds of the
Rainbird sprinklers watering the carefully manicured
lawns, allowing my senses to absorb the wonderful aroma
of fresh cut grass and lush, moist vegetation.

I pulled onto the tree-lined driveway along a stucco
wall of fiery red bougainvillea, rolled around to the rear
parking area and slipped into the back door with five
minutes to spare. Betty, Tom's secretary of many years
was sitting at her desk near his office and as usual looked
ten years younger than her fifty plus years. An attractive,
trim, five-foot nine inch slender woman with short black
hair, looking up, she responded, "I can't believe it, aren't
you a sight for sore eyes? How long has it been since
you've blessed these hallowed halls, Chuck?"
   "Not long enough, I thought I was through with this
business and for that matter business in general, but
seeing you darlin' is another story altogether."

"Same old Chuck, I've missed you." Betty added
smiling, and meaning it. "If only", she thought to herself.

"Tom called this morning and asked to have lunch.
How could I say no?"

"You couldn't. Tom really needs your help right now. Go on in, he's been pacing the floor since I came in this morning."

Chuck moved toward Tom's door in a casual yet graceful manner for a man six-foot-four, weighing two hundred pounds. His deep tan and somewhat longish brown hair with a hint of gray at the temples was just about right for a retired forty-five year old "boat person".

"Where in the hell have you been Chucky?" Tom Claudius shouted. He was in his late fifties, gray short hair, five-foot ten, slight build, silver wire-rimmed glasses, and a tan that was easily maintained from regular sessions on his forty-foot sailboat. Tom wore hand tailored suits, usually from Hong Kong, and looked every bit the consummate dealmaker, which he was.
"Tom, its 12:01 P.M., what's going on?"
"Let's get out of here Chucky, I'll drive." We got in Tom's silver Jag, hopped on El Camino Real and drove south a few miles, pulling into the Patio Broiler parking lot. With Tom quickly leading the way to an umbrella table in back, I ducked trying to avoid colliding with large hanging baskets, overflowing with giant ferns.

"What's happening Tom, for Gods sake tell me?"

"You remember TechX in Beaverton, Oregon?"

"Yeah, you put a lot of dough in that about a year or so ago, how're they doing?"

Tom sat there with a sick expression on his face and replied, "They're not! You remember Denton Jaxton, the founder?"

"Yeah, I recall you mentioning him?"

"He's gone!" Tom said staring at me, and before I needed to drag it out of him, he went on. "Disappeared, vanished, missing for two weeks with no
word. He isn't on vacation. No one at the company has heard from him. He just disappeared over a weekend and didn't show up on Monday. He was single, lived alone and had no steady girl friend, at least none that his people knew about."

"Have you called the police?"

A scowl crossed his face. "Are you nuts? We can't let this out. We have an IPO scheduled for next March. If the news gets out that Jaxton is missing I'm
going to lose my ten million dollars, forget about the initial public offering. Do you realize Chucky, that Jaxton hadn't completed the development work, and Phil Hampton----do you remember him?" He asked, looking more upset by the minute.

"Should I?"

"Should I?"

"You've met him, he's the number two man at TechX, and he doesn't have a handle as to what's happening product wise, mostly because Jaxton was so protective with his research and development. I was concerned about this when I got involved, but I thought when we wrapped the company around him, he would realize that he had to involve the development team with the big picture, rather than his compartmentalizing approach."

14

"So what does Phil think happened to Jaxton"?

"He doesn't have any idea. He managed to get into Jaxton's house the other day after there was no contact from him for more than a week. There was nothing unusual in the house and his car was missing from the garage."

"What do you want me to do?"

"I want you to fly to Beaverton, right away. Go through the office, his house, wherever you have to go---- just find him."

"Why me?"

"Hey, you were a San Francisco detective for a good many years, you know this software business inside and out, and I trust you implicitly. We just can't let this get out."

"Tom, I don't do police work or for that matter any kind of work anymore."

"Chucky, don't make me beg."

"OK Tom, but it's going to cost you----big time, not for me but for some charity that helps kids."

"You got it Chucky just let me know. I'll call Betty and ask her to make air arrangements right now and reserve a Town Car for you at the Portland airport. You can handle your hotel when you get there. I know you don't have any clothes, so you can run down to the mall and pick up what you need. Is your boat OK for a week or so?"

"I'll call a friend with a key, and make certain everything is secured. I'm going to need everything you have on the project, it's status as you know it, and your complete file on Jaxton *and* the deal you made with him in terms of stock options, vesting period, incentives --- everything. Also include his personnel records----and don't leave anything out."

Tom grinned for the first and said, "It's ready and on my desk back at the office."

"Real cute! Will Phil cooperate with me on this investigation? Where does he stand on this whole thing?"

"Phil's my man. I hired him and insisted he be number two if I was going to put up $10 million bucks." Tom replied. "I called him this morning and told him you'd be coming----and do whatever you ask and give you access to everything."

"How did you know I'd agree to this wild chase?"

"Chucky---- I know you."

"Too well it seems."

"Don't spare any expense. Do what you have to, go where you need to, and please keep me informed. Do you have your laptop with you? Tom inquired.
"Yeah, I tossed it in when I left not knowing what you had up your sleeve."

"Great then let's keep this an e-mail communication deal only. Chucky, I really appreciate this."

"I know." We drove back to the office and picked up the files and my flight and car reservations from Betty.

After saying our goodbyes I headed to the mall for my unexpected shopping spree.

The Stanford Shopping Mall was still busy from the lunchtime crowd. It was a large sprawling marketplace with every store one could imagine and I might need---- and more. The bay area fog had drifted down the peninsular this day but was lifting and the sun was working its way through the haze with the promise of a beautiful day. I had a little over two hours before my United Shuttle took off from San Francisco airport, just enough time to buy a suitcase, toothbrush etc., a few changes of underwear, sport coat or two, slacks that are pre-hemmed, shoes ---- come to think of it I guess I'm buying a wardrobe. Oh yes, lest I forget, Oregon rain even in the summer—I'll need a raincoat and jacket, just in case.

Upon returning to my fancy cruiser, I opened the tailgate and laid out my purchases. After all the tags were pulled off, everything was semi-neatly folded and packed in my new suitcase on wheels. I also picked up a brief case to stow the five-inch thick file Tom had assembled for me, along with my laptop.

I headed for the Bayshore Highway, turned north and cruised along at 65mph for the twenty minute drive. It was now 2:45PM and my flight was scheduled to depart at 4:00 P.M., plenty of time to drop off the car in long-term parking and check in.

CHAPTER 3

Betty booked a first class seat for me, and after the whirlwind start to this day, I was ready for a vodka martini, dry and up. Make that a double!

We touched down in Portland at 5:45 P.M., to a beautiful day----near 80 degrees. I retrieved up my checked bag and headed for the car rental area. By 6:30PM, I was rolling west on Highway 84 into the city in my emerald green, Lincoln Town Car. As TechX was located near the Embassy Suites Hotel, I called from my car and made a reservation.

I pulled into the Embassy Suites Hotel, near Highway 217, next to the huge regional mall, Washington Square, at just after 7 P.M... My room was typical, for the hotel, very comfortable with a living room, wet bar, microwave and refrigerator, and king-sized bed which I really require. First chance I had, I placed a call to Phil Hampton at his home number.

"Hello"--came the reply.

"Phil?"

"Yes".

"Chuck Winters."

"Hi Chuck, Tom said you'd be calling, how have you been – how's retirement? I hear you're the Admiral of Shasta Lake."

"I'm just fine for a retired guy. The question is how are you? And what's the latest on Jaxton?"

"I'm at a loss on this thing, and Tom won't let me involve the police. I understand where he's coming from, but there'll be a time when we have to do it. There's no clue----it's like he dropped off the face of the earth."

"Hey Phil, have you eaten yet?"

"No, I haven't had much of an appetite."

"Do you want to come down to the Embassy Suites and grab something to eat with me? It'll give us a chance to talk."

"Sure, how's a half hour from now?"

"Perfect, meet me in the bar."

I called my Mom and Dad, and let them know I was up here and promised to
sneak over to Salashan and spend an evening if I could get away.
I headed down to the bar. It was past 7:30 P.M., and I missed the evening complimentary happy hour in the atrium area. The bar was quiet as would be expected on a Monday night after the free happy hour. Only a few groups of business people were at the tables and sitting at the bar. Most were munching on the fish crackers and dry roasted nuts in the carafes on the bar and tables. I ordered a Vox, vodka martini, up with two olives, and relaxed while waiting for Phil to arrive.

I couldn't get my mind off Jaxton, and why he'd disappear. Could he have been killed, accidentally or on purpose? Was there a woman involved? Was it job related or totally unrelated or random? Did he have a problem other than business and run off, or did he have such a problem with the business that he decided to leave before it was known? Was there money missing? How were his personal finances? These were all questions that needed answering.

Phil arrived right on time wearing jeans, a white polo shirt and white Nikes, the *official shoe*---if you work two minutes from Nikes' world headquarters. He looked like a computer nerd, slender, brown hair in some disarray, and fit. He'd worked for a number of Tom's companies and it appeared that Tom was his mentor, in some way, I wasn't sure why. He ordered a Coors Lite. I was still nursing my vodka. After following Phil's lead ordering an awesome crusted herb halibut dinner, and catching up a little, we got right to business by my asking all of the questions I had been turning over in my head. Phil didn't know much about Jaxton's personal life or if he had a girlfriend. He was a loner and didn't socialize with his employees. He worked at home a lot, and as to his finances, all Phil knew was that he was cashing his $10,000 monthly paychecks. He leased a nice home in the Forest Heights area of executive homes about ten minutes north of the company offices, and drove a newer Jeep Cherokee. Phil's description of Jaxton---dark complexion, six feet tall, one hundred and eighty pounds, fit for his thirty-five years, ran occasionally, and was a member of Gold's Gym, located halfway between the office and his home.

"Have you looked at the company bank records in light of what's happened?"

"I supervise the controller and see the financial reports on a regular basis. I took a quick look after we realized he wasn't around and didn't see anything that jumped out at me."

"How far along were you on the first software release?"

Phil looked perplexed and a little chagrined. "I really don't know. It *was* my job to monitor the progress. At least that was my charge from Tom when he put me in this company. I was supposed to be his eyes and ears, and I managed to lose the founder of the company. Jaxton was never satisfied. He kept changing the parameters, re-writing programs. We were scheduled for a November release----and the last I saw, even if Jaxton *was* around and pushing, we would never make it by then. Until he settles in on the final product we can't possibly forecast a release date. Marketing is dead in the water because they don't know what the final software will do."

"Is Jaxton justified in his constant revamping of the software, or is he intentionally sabotaging the company?"

"I just don't know why he would. I thought we had a pretty good product when Tom funded Jaxton and the new company. The concept was a winner because it cuts chip manufacturer's testing process time by as much as seventy five percent and produces a product that's been tested for almost every conceivable application eventuality. This allows the manufacturer to come to market much faster, and offer a product that's thoroughly tested and reliable."

"Phil, last year you had a product that worked and was deemed by the board to be ready to produce and release. What was Jaxton doing to tweak the product that resulted in these delays for the last six or seven months?"

Phil hesitated some and replied. "He'd re-write a procedure because he felt it wasn't adequate. The design engineers didn't agree. It was like Jaxton *decided* something didn't work right so it had to be changed. Most of these design changes were actually developed and written by him personally. He wouldn't let the design or testing staff, test his product changes. He insisted on doing this personally. I can't say what was in his mind, and I don't know if he operated this way before this company was started, but I do know that the way he was operating, there would never be a product release."

"Did Tom know this was going on?"
"Yeah, I told him. He was so hopped up on the genius of this guy that he was willing to give him his head, until it disappeared along with the rest of his body. Now he's really panicked and rightfully so."
"I guess I don't understand what people were doing when Jaxton was keeping them out of the loop. Did he act this way from the day you met him, right after Tom agreed to fund?"

"Not really, we pretty much worked as a team for the first six months or so, and then Jaxton started finding fault with the product. I thought he was kind of a perfectionist at that point because he wanted the software to perform perfectly. But after a while it sort of evolved into ever increasing disarray.

Jaxton kept people busy by assigning a lot of second-generation busywork, when we didn't even have the first generation on line."

"Do you think he has a mental problem--- did he flip out or something?"

"I don't know. How the hell would I know if he was clinically a wacko? He always seemed lucid to me. I just can't read his motives."

"I'd like to meet with the key employees on an individual basis tomorrow, and then take a look at the books. Tom wants my visit to be low profile. I want you to introduce me as One Star's representative getting caught up on status, not that I'm on some big mission to find Jaxton. I also want your chief engineer to start testing the product that evolved from Jaxton's revisions. I want to know how it works right now, and if it meets or exceeds the standards that were in place when Tom funded the company. I need this right away. Also, I want to go to Jaxton's house----you have a key?"

"I'll make a list of the key people and their job responsibilities first thing in the morning, and you can interview them whenever you want. I had a key made to get into Jaxton's house, because Tom didn't want the police involved until we were certain there was a problem. Do you want to work out of Jaxton's office or do you want something else?"

"I don't want to use his office----if you have an empty office, I'd prefer that. I do want to take a look through his office though."

"No problem. Hey Chuck, I'm glad you're here."

"Thanks Phil. See you about eight in the morning?"

"You bet, and thanks for dinner."

"Thank Tom" I replied.

"Oh, right, how quickly I forget."

I signed the tab and we got up from the table, Phil headed out to his car and I went back to my room to go through the pile of information Tom had Betty put together in Palo Alto. Then, I was hoping to get some sleep, as I expect I'll be totally immersed in this thing for the next few days.

CHAPTER 4

The phone was ringing and I was unpleasantly surprised not to be floating on Shasta Lake, but in a hotel room, with a less than pleasant assignment ahead of me, one that I just didn't need. "Good morning it's 6:30 A.M." At least there was a USA Today, paper at my door to cheer me up while I tried to wake up.

I showered and shaved, dressed in jeans, boat shoes, a light green polo shirt because I don't like wearing a tie these days and won't unless I have to, and in this case I felt I didn't have to. I wanted to blend in and not play up the seriousness, my authority or mission, with the employees. I just wanted to come across as a representative of the venture company who's trying to establish where they are and what cash needs are going to be lurking around the corner in terms of a second funding.

A quick breakfast was in order at the complimentary buffet in the atrium area. The scrambled eggs, sausage, fruit, bagel, orange juice and black coffee, was just the start for cop work. I didn't see any donuts though. I ran through the plan of attack in my head during breakfast, and felt ready to get to the bottom of this, fast. I already missed Shasta. It was a good thing I threw my laptop in the car when I left the boat yesterday, because I needed the Yahoo map and driving instructions to find the TechX office complex. I'm not certain I believe all that talk about Oregon raining all the time. The sky was blue without a cloud, and the forecast was headed for the north side of seventy. I'll take it. I pulled up to a two-story flex-space type complex on Nimbus Parkway in Beaverton. The building was nothing fancy, about typical for new startups with reasonable initial funding. Construction was concrete tilt-up walls painted crisp white, with functional landscaping and lush green lawns in front. I found a parking place along the side of the building, grabbed my briefcase and briskly walked to the front door of TechX Corporation. A company was missing a President and built around a product that wasn't even a product yet, staffed with employees that might be unemployed any day, if I don't find some solution to this mystery.

At the front reception area was a young lady of about twenty-five, blonde hair cut very short, with a body that was hiding behind the high counter, but she did have a nice smile and a warm greeting. "Hi, can I help you?"

"Hi. And you *can* help me if you'd let Phil know that Chuck Winters is here."
Miss Smiley punched a few numbers on her phone console and told Phil that I was present. "He'll be right along Mr. Winters."

"Thanks." The reception area was nice with a thick dark green carpet, soft looking couches and current reading material on the coffee table.

"Chuck, welcome to TechX. Have you met Karen yet?"

"Not officially."

"Chuck, this is Karen Simpkins. Karen, meet Chuck Winters who represents One Star Funding and will be with us a few days."

We exchanged our hello's and hi's, and Phil led the way to his office which was down the hall and toward the rear of the building. As I passed by open doors I saw much the same as I had seen in numerous hi-tech firms

I'd been to in the past. People hunched over their computers doing things that made them look busy. If they were or were not, I had no idea.

Phil had a reasonably nice office. Cherry wood desk, credenza, two leather side chairs, and a small round conference table with four chairs. The best part about Phil's office was the view from the window; a beautiful forest setting with lawns and a jogging path that happened to be loaded with pretty bouncing young ladies making their way past Phil's window. No wonder he didn't know what was going on with Jaxton, his eyes were glued to the window all the time.

"Chuck, I have a breakdown of key people for you. I think I should take a minute to give you a tour and introduce you to the employees, and at the same time, explain that you'll need to talk with many of them in order to get a thorough understanding of the needs of the company. Before we meet the gang, let me show you your office."

We went past some more offices and Phil opened a door and turned on the light of a nice smaller office, furnished with a desk, table with two chairs, a computer and a window looking not at the pretty girls jogging, but the parking lot.

"This is fine, Phil". I put my stuff down and we headed out to meet the employees and see the operation. One that as far as I could tell was dead in the water at the moment. Phil continued. "First we need to stop by the coffee room and grab a cup for our grand tour, OK?"

"Fine with me, I still have room in the tank." The lunchroom was once again pretty average. It consisted of a coffeemaker, pop machine, refrigerator and microwave, along with a table and six chairs. We both poured black, no sugar and headed out.

The first office we went to was the controller, Christine Donnelly. She was easily five-foot ten or eleven in her bare feet, a body that was an eleven on a scale of ten. I checked out her ring finger and saw that she wasn't married---interesting. Easy boy! No time for fun and games or even thinking about them. Phil did the introductions and I stared and finally muttered, "Hi, I'd like to take a few minutes of your time after I have the grand tour. Would that be OK with you?"

"Sure. Do you want to come here or do you want to talk somewhere else?"

"I'll come to your office where you have your records. I just need to get a feel," bad choice of words, "an idea on where the company is on cash needs, forecasting budgets for the next twelve months if you have such a report, and maybe a look at your systems for expenditure approvals, and cash balances in your accounts. Also a copy of your operating reports for the last year."

"Great, I'll pull what I have together for you and see you soon."

"Thanks".

We moved off to the testing lab where engineers were running tests cycles on what, I wasn't certain. There were seven engineer-nerd types, four men and three women. After the introductions, I didn't remember one

of their names, but I did find out that they were not working on the current release.   After
some inquiry I learned that Jaxton had them working on a second generation test program, that was a significant deviation in concept than the product that was the basis for funding the company.

I asked the group, "What's the status of the chip test program?" The response was generally that Jaxton wanted to make some changes that would improve the product, and this meant that the engineers were assigned to the next product development while the new parameters for the original product were being developed.

Phil introduced me to Frank Bolza in marketing and Bryan Cranston Director of Engineering. I didn't feel that marketing could add much to my investigation, but one never knows when an innocent comment might provide a fresh insight into the reason or reasons that Jaxton seemed to be set on destroying this company through an apparent systematic strategy of sabotage.

I wanted to pick the brain of Brian Cranston. He was key, and I was interested in knowing what he thought the status of the project was, as well as how Jaxton caused this program to evolve virtually off the radar screen. However my main interest in Brian was to evaluate him, to determine if he could pick up the ball, run with the product and see it through to completion and release.

I headed for Christine's office with a yellow pad and my personal charm, in case the pad didn't impress her. "Hi Christine, I don't want to take a lot of your time, but I need to get a feel of how my boss's money at One Star has been spent and what the needs might be for the near future. For the moment, I can save some time by asking questions now, and look at the printouts later. OK?"

"Ask away. I may need to refer to some documentation. I don't have all this stuff in my head." She said with a tilt of her head and what could have been a *contrived* smile.

"Great, how much cash is left from the initial ten million funding from One Star?"

"Boy you get right to the heart of things." She responded with a smile that looked genuine this time. "There's in round numbers, two and half million left."

"What's your burn rate?" I asked. For those still using typewriters, it means how much is the cost of operating this enterprise on a monthly basis, or in simple terms how much do you spend for everything each month. Or more succinctly put, how much money will you lose each month.

"We spend an average of $400,000 per month".

"So you have about six months life left without any unusual expenditures." I calculated out loud.

"That would be about right." Christine replied. "If your monthly burn rate is $400,000, the numbers don't add up. You would have spent something over five million by now, not seven and a half. What happened?"

"We had some big outside consulting expenses a couple of months ago."

"What were they for? Who proposed them? What was the approval process like? Did Tom approve them?" I fired back.

"Whoa----don't kill the messenger, I report to Denton. He approves the extraordinary expenses and department heads approve their budgeted items, with an explanation of out of budget line items. Denton's signature is required on all variances, those line items that exceed budgeted amounts.

When an extraordinary item is presented, it must also have Denton Jaxton's signature on it as well as complete documentation and the reason for the expenditure. I assume he gets board approval on those expenditures, but I've never been assigned the oversight responsibility for Denton's decisions. I know the outside auditors would follow up on those kinds of issues, but not until the fiscal year ends in about five months." Christine said.

"I'd like hard copies of the files on all extraordinary expenditures approved by Jaxton. By the way, do you know when he's returning? I heard he was off on some personal business or something?"

It'll pull the files you asked for. As to how to find Denton, I don't know where he went. He didn't mention anything to me when I last saw him at the office about two weeks ago. Sometimes he gets so wrapped up in his work that he stays late at the office for a week or two and has been known to work all night. Other times he won't come in for a few days, I thought this was like that."

"I haven't met him, what's he like?"

"Denton? Oh he's a little odd, as I said in his hours. He doesn't have friends in the company and avoids company parties. I would say he's quiet, but gets anxious with people if they don't perform to his standards."

"How about girl friends, have you met any?" I casually asked.
"I don't know what this has to do with your interest in financial planning for the company, but to answer your question I've never met any of his friends, male or female." She said with an obvious coolness.

I was getting a bad vibe from Christine. Maybe I'm imagining things, but my gut tells me this girl is holding back and is pretty resentful of my questions, *and* doesn't buy my cover story. I really don't care what she thinks. I know Tom Claudius pretty well, and I know if he were getting financials that showed a big increase in monthly expenditures for consultants, he would've been storming up here months ago. Something smells and I need to find out----- fast.

Christine was sitting behind her desk with her arms crossed over her not so modest breasts, looking at me like I was with the IRS auditing her personal taxes.

"One Star gets a monthly financial report according to the funding agreement, isn't that right? Have they been getting that report?"

She continued her frosty stare and responded, "Denton told me to give him the One Star financial reports because he liked to include a written progress summary for Mr. Claudius. So, I was never involved in actually sending the reports on to One Star."

My blood pressure was rising like it was my own money at stake here. I wouldn't have two nickels to rub together if Tom hadn't had faith in me, so I kind of felt like it *was* my own. "Why don't you start by printing the financials for the last twelve months, with all explanations, foot notes, etc.? Then get the other documentation we discussed after that. How soon can you have this for me?

"Give me thirty minutes and I'll bring them to you. Where will you be?"

"I'd appreciate it. I'm using the office at the end of the hall just past the lunchroom."

CHAPTER 5

I headed back to my office, amazed at what appeared to be happening here, as well as wondering why Phil wasn't on top of this. It was time to keep my mouth shut around here, and not discuss the vibes I'm getting with anyone in Beaverton. I picked up the phone and decided to break the e-mail, secret mission rule, and call Tom direct. "Betty, Chuck, is Tom around; I need to talk with him."

"Hi Chuck, how's Oregon? Tom's in LA. He'll be back late tonight."

"OK Betty, go to the TechX file and e-mail me the monthly financial reports for the last twelve months if you can."

"No problem Chuck, but give me an hour or so, OK?"

"Perfect. If you talk with Tom, tell him I'm into this thing and will be reporting by e-mail as soon as I can---- no later than tomorrow morning if I get the reports from you."

"Chuck, I know this might sound stupid, but are you just trying to make an old lady work, or can't you just take a few steps down the hall and get it from the horse's mouth?"

"Betty, I'm getting the records from the horses 'something', I just want to see if Tom's been looking at the same horse." I told her with a chuckle.

"Chuck, you always were too smart for this girl?" She replied with a giggle.

"Right, but you're always a few jumps ahead of everyone Betty. Thanks for the help."

I picked up the phone again and called Phil in his office down the hall and inquired if there was a vehicle parking system for the building, like many landlords had to control illegal parking on the property. As luck would have it there *was* one that required registration of each employee's car in the building. They in turn where given a sticker for the backside of their rear view mirror, in order to identify legal parkers. I asked for a list of the company registrations, which I found was available from Miss Smiley at the front desk. Reaching her desk, I was handed a copy and returned to my office.

CHAPTER 6

Just what I wanted! Denton Jaxton, 1517 Blue Pointe Way, Portland, OR. 97213. 1998 Black Jeep Cherokee, license number-- OREGON 684-884.

I turned on my laptop and went to my address book and clicked open Roberts & Levy Investigations in San Francisco. Art was a former partner of mine in the San Francisco Police Department. He left the force abut five years before me, and along with another ex-cop, Jimmy Roberts, formed an agency that was the very best in uncovering sensitive information, that as a cop, I couldn't access without court orders and red tape.

I dialed Art's direct line at Roberts & Levy and heard the familiar "Levy".

"Art, Chuck. How are you doing? Been a while, huh?"

"Well I'll be go to hell, Chuck how the hell are you? I didn't think Mr. Money Bags had time for us poor folk."

"Let me tell you Art, Shasta is fantastic. I really love the peace and solitude up there. It isn't lonely. I've met a lot of house-boaters and we've got a pretty
tight group there. You guys need to drive up for a weekend----you'll never want to leave."

"Sounds great, we just might do that."

"Not only do I have time for you poor folk, I have some business for you. This of course is top secret. By the way, how's Jimmy doing, did he ever get married to that little Italian girl?"

"Are you kidding? Jimmy's in love with a Swedish airline hostess. It works well for him, he only sees her every couple of weeks. It's hard for him to screw up to much that way, and she can't get too possessive when he has so much free time." Art chuckled as he spoke.

"Art, I'm helping out the venture company that funded my deal. They've got a problem with one of the companies they put a lot of money in, and asked if I'd snoop around. It's in Oregon, Beaverton----a suburb ten miles west of Portland. The CEO of TechX, Denton Jaxton, spelled D-E-N-T-O-N J-A-X-T-O-N, has disappeared and we don't know under what circumstances yet. The investor doesn't want to make this a police matter until there's a solid reason to do so. I'm at their offices now and want to hire Roberts & Levy to chase down some things for me. First, I want you to use your affiliates to check airports in Portland, Seattle, Vancouver, B.C., San Francisco, and Los Angeles, for his car----in that order. This includes private lots and airport parking. Next I want a credit report run, and a list of his credit cards and banking relationships. I need a list of his credit card expenditures for the last twelve months, as well as copies of checks written during the same period, front and backs, plus bank statements. I know the routine, this kind of information isn't available, and if it were it would be expensive, but that's OK, I still need this yesterday." I said with sufficient emphasis. "I'll e-mail you in the next few minutes, all of the personal data I have at the moment. You e-mail me back as soon as you have anything. And Art, this is really a rush."

"You've got it Chuck. We'll get right on it----and you're right, this is expensive."

"I know that. Oh, I almost forgot. If you have a way of checking with customs to see if this guy left the country that would be very helpful too."

"We'll be in touch Chuck." Art said in closing.

"Thanks, I can't tell you how much I appreciate this."

CHAPTER 7

The file that One Star gave me regarding the personnel information on Jaxton had enough details for Art Levy to get started. Jaxton was born in Denver, Colorado, 36 years ago. His father is deceased, and his mother who retired as a school teacher, still lives in Denver, as does his older sister who's married to a doctor and has three children. Jaxton grew up in Denver and went to the prestigious East High School, graduated with honors and received a scholarship to Stanford, where he received a Bachelor of Science degree in mathematics. From there he studied at Cal Poly, earning his masters in computer science. He worked for a number of major companies in the computer field. The last being The Harris Corporation, who specialized in computer chip consulting, where he formed the genesis of his product idea. Jaxton, on the personal side was married when he graduated from Stanford, a union that lasted less than a year, with no children. The reference checking conducted by One Star didn't turn up any red flags as to irresponsibility or trouble. On the contrary, he received high marks for work productivity, and was promoted in every company he worked for. Reading between the lines however, one might conclude that Jaxton possessed an opportunistic bent in that the product idea he developed, could arguably be the property of Harris Corporation, his last employer, as the company was deeply involved in working with chip manufacturers, with the objective of improving their design processes, which include testing and bringing their new products to market.

The important information needed by Art Levy to immediately get started was in the files, such as social security and drivers license numbers, work history, personal references and necessary address details. I summarized the pertinent data and e-mailed the information to Art in San Francisco.

For the moment, I can skip the rest of the personnel except Brian Cranston, Director of Engineering. I need a few minutes to get an overview from him as

to what happened to the first product that had been completed, and was supposed to be in the final test stages necessary for release to the market for promotion and sale.

I found Brian's extension number on the list by my phone and punched in 318.

"This is Brian."

"Hi Brian, Chuck Winters. Could I spend ten or fifteen minutes with you to just get a quick overview of your department?"

"Sure", he replied, "do you want me to come to your office or do you want to come here?"

"I'll run down to yours. Is now a good time?"

"Come on down."

He sounded like a guy with nothing to hide, but I've been wrong before I thought, as I picked up my yellow pad and headed down the hall.

Brian was much more relaxed when I came in, than when Phil and I stopped by to see him. He looked to be about forty, five-foot ten and slender. His hair was a little longish, with a trimmed beard and traces of gray mixed in the brown whiskers. He wore chinos with a light blue sport shirt and had the standard nerdy penholder in his shirt pocket. I was quite surprised at his change in demeanor and body language. He came from behind his desk and suggested we sit at his round table.

"Coffee?" –he asked as he motioned to a pitcher and mugs on the table.

"Why not, I think I'm starting on my second gallon."

Brian laughed heartily. This was getting weird however his change of attitude was cleared up with the next words from his mouth.

"I thought your name sounded familiar, and it dawned on me after you left. I had no idea you started ICR or InfoCheckReport. I read all about it when you went public. That was an incredible task bringing together all the diverse information into a single server. I have to say, I'm impressed. Let me tell you, your experience would be very helpful here. I'm amazed that you're here in the first place, I thought I read that you retired."

"Thanks for the kind words Brian, I *have* retired, however Tom Claudius at One Star was short handed and asked if I'd give him a few days to bring him up to date on TechX. As you might expect, I owe Tom a great deal for funding my company, so the fishing can wait for a few days."

"I understand, how can I help you?"

Boy did I luck out with Brian. I hope his awe of my legendary genius in the software field is not tarnished when I open my big mouth.

"I'm sorry I missed Jaxton, I really need to talk with *him* as well, in order to make my report as complete as possible for Tom. Where the hell did he go?"

"I have no idea. He didn't report to me of course, but when he left work two weeks ago Friday, he seemed OK. It's really weird. I hope he's OK. I understand Phil went up to his house and he wasn't there, so he obviously wasn't sick in the house somewhere."

"Could he have gone somewhere on business, maybe to some chip manufacturer--in order to solve some glitch in the product design?"

"He could've, but I don't see him going somewhere like that without telling someone here."

"Has he ever left before without telling anyone?"

"Well, occasionally after a weekend, he might not come back until say Wednesday. We just assumed he was working at home, which he did a lot. But this time he didn't call in like he normally did when he worked at home, wanting information, or something faxed or e-mailed to him."

"Well, lets get to my little report needs. Where are you, and I'm speaking as *in the company*, not you personally, on the product finalization and release?"

"Well, we were almost ready six months ago, and Denton wanted to make changes to the program. Were they necessary? I'm speaking out of school, but it has to be said. I didn't think we needed to move to a second-generation product before we released the first product that was unique and provided significant benefits for the chip manufacturer. I just assumed that the board had approved the direction we were taking, and I was doing what I was told by Denton."

"Brian, I really appreciate your candor, and let me assure you that anything you say "out of school" as you put it will not be held against you. Tom

Claudius is the man with the clout in this company. He'll respect your straight talk, because that's exactly the kind of guy he is." I answered.

"Thanks, Chuck, what would you like to know?"

"Where's the original program, right this minute? What will it take to polish it up, finish the testing and release it?"

"The problem is that the development disks are missing for the original program. I was looking for them last week to get an insight on a second- generation development problem, and the master file is just not there. All the protocols are gone, the hard copy work files are gone---- everything. I didn't panic because I thought Denton may have taken them home to verify the protocols for the new generation product."

"Let me pose a hypothetical to you. If the board walked into your office tomorrow and asked you to resurrect the original product, do you have enough notes and assorted files laying around to get it ready for release, and when?"

Brian scratched his beard and said, "My people have significant work product in their own offices, as do I. If someone has the test disks in their office files, we jump ahead significantly. Even without the test disks, we've experienced the product in its substantially completed form. I think we could bring it back in maybe ninety days or so, if we stopped everything else."

"I'm going to be busy and hard to reach over the next day or two, so when you speak with your folks about raising the Phoenix from the ashes, just e-mail me at this address what you found and think you can do. From there, either Denton if he's around, or the board, will make some decisions and issue the order for direction of the product development effort."

"I'll do it Chuck. It was great meeting you."

Brother do I have you fooled, I thought. When it comes to program design I barely know enough to be dangerous. I just hired the best people to make my ideas happen, simple as that. Oh right, I guess I had to have the ideas to give them in the first place. Maybe there is a redeeming quality here after all. It sure is easy to like a guy like Brian who thinks I walk on water.

CHAPTER 8

It was nearing lunchtime, and I was about ready for my gumshoe cop stuff. Office work was always the crap part of being a cop. I stopped by Phil's office to get Jaxton's house key. The door to his office was open and he was actually looking at a file on his desk rather than at the honey's running by his window. Maybe Phil *is* more interested in files than fillies. "Hi Phil, I thought I'd run over to Jaxton's house now and see if I can pick up a clue. You know, boring old cop stuff."

"Great, I'll come along and we can grab lunch on the way." Phil said.

"I think I'll skip lunch today, I had a little too much all you can eat buffet breakfast at the Embassy Suites." I told him hoping he'd take the hint that I wanted to go alone.

"No problem, I wasn't that hungry anyway, let's go." Phil said as he reached in his center drawer for Jaxton's key.

"Phil, I'd prefer to go alone. I want to do a modified crime scene search, which doesn't work if someone else is walking around possibly contaminating
evidence. Do you mind?" I asked, not knowing what a *modified crime search* even was, but it sounded good, and by Phil's expression I think he bought it.

"Oh, no problem makes sense to me. Here's the key, do you know how to get there?"

"Yeah, I used Yahoo map directions." I replied, and headed out and towards Miss Smiley's reception desk, and recalled that I hadn't received Christine's financial reports she promised me 'in a half hour'. I turned back and went to her office. She wasn't there, and I asked an accounting-type person sitting in front of a ten-key, if she knew where she was. I was told that she's in the copy room around the corner. I found her running copies and surprised her a little.

"I'm sorry I'm late with these, I got sidetracked they're about copied." She said as she retrieved the stack from the tray of the copy machine, stapled and handed them to me.

"Thanks, when do you think you'll have the rest?"

"Later this afternoon, I have someone pulling the files together now." Christine indicated with a fake smile.

Once again, I headed for Miss Smiley at the reception desk. "Hi, see you later." I said with a big smile.

"Bye."

CHAPTER 9

Employees from TechX and surrounding offices were streaming out of their buildings into this beautiful sunny day, where their senses were experiencing the best of Oregon. The sweet aroma of cedar, pine and fresh mowed lawns, as well as flowering shrubbery together with the wafting cloud from a Marlborough cigarette, made the afternoon just about complete. I told Phil I wanted to go through Jaxton's office, but that'll have to wait. In my opinion his house was a priority. I'll work in the Jaxton office search as soon as time permitted. Cop work doesn't usually involve driving a new Lincoln Town Car with a global positioning system, but it does in this case. Sitting in the parking lot I checked out the map from Yahoo, and realized that the screen on my dashboard could show me the way as well. I probably won't or can't get lost, but don't count me out on that one. First, I need to check my e-mail, which I can do from my newfangled cell phone. A quick speed dial button push, a couple of double-clicks and I'm on line with my e-mail. The screen comes up and I'm scrolling through the junk mail. Delete, delete, bingo, a response from Betty on the financials. I better swing by the hotel and print a set before I tour the 'Jaxton estate'.

Since I was almost driving by anyway, I swung into the parking lot and left the car in loading and headed with my trusty laptop to my room. Surprise, surprise, the maids hadn't cleaned up. I went in and printed the financials on my mini-printer. I knew I wouldn't run out of paper. I pilfered a ream from the TechX copy room before I left the building.

Without looking at the documents, I put the freshly printed financial statements into my briefcase, and headed out of my room to the elevator. The hotel was bustling with activity, and I worked my way through the crowded lobby to the entry and my car. I was soon on Highway 217 heading north to Barnes Road then west on Miller Road and north again to Cornell Road. Then I needed to go north on Skyline Blvd. When I arrived at the intersection of Skyline and Cornell, I saw the Skyline Restaurant. All of a sudden I was hungry. Sorry Phil. Besides, I have some reading material I wanted to go over in private before I searched Jaxton's house.

Pulling into the parking lot of this relic from the past, it was clear to me that this restaurant has been around for at least fifty years. The restaurant was busy, and I was lucky to get a booth when I walked in the door. I checked out the menu, and since I was starving, ordered the large Skyline burger, fries and a chocolate, malt.

I had a large booth, which was convenient for spreading out my e-mail financials I just received from Betty in Palo Alto, and compare them with the 'official' record from Christine at the company. I lined up the two sets side by side, arranging the documents so only the total monthly expenses were lined up for easy comparison. "Son of a bitch" I muttered under my breath, as I looked at the groupings, Jaxton walked away with what looks like more than two million bucks. I pulled out my calculator and totaled the variance between the two sets of numbers, $2,687,050.00----not exactly chump change. Jaxton was clearly doctoring the books so One Star wouldn't know the money was missing. Christine could either be part of this fraud or an innocent party, unaware of Jaxton's activities and phony financials. My question is how would Phil not know unless he was getting phony financials as well, either from Jaxton or Christine? Could Jaxton provide Phil with an identical set like those that went to Tom at One Star

48

without discovering that something didn't add up? Shouldn't Phil know where the bank balances stood? What motive did Jaxton have? When the company went public, with his options he stood to make millions. I was ending up with more questions than answers. But it was clear to me, someone stole almost three million bucks and it looks like Jaxton.

Maybe my breaking and entering, with a key of course which was next on my agenda would help to clear things up, but for some reason I doubted it.

After gorging myself on the 'not on my diet' lunch, which I might add was fantastic, I paid the tab and was ready to start my 'modified crime scene search'.

CHAPTER 10

Before I made my grand entrance at Jaxton's house, I wanted to make sure no one was home. After calling his number on my cell phone and letting it ring at least twenty times, I felt confident that no one was going to answer. Interesting that he had no voice mail or recorder.

I pulled out of the Skyline Restaurant parking lot and headed west on Skyline to Hawkins Avenue and south until I reached Blue Point Way. Jaxton's rented house was on the right at the end of the street. It was a large home with a three-car garage. I pulled into the driveway and parked----after all I had nothing to hide. The company was concerned about Jaxton's welfare and wanted me to check on him. The house was large with stucco siding and a red tile roof, more reminiscent of California than Oregon. There was a large front lawn with numerous plantings along the walkway. This was truly a grand home and costly by most standards.

I made my way up the curved brick walkway to the massive and impressive front doors. Out of prudence and being somewhat of a coward when it comes to invading strange houses, I rang the doorbell. Not once but several times just to make sure I wasn't going to get shot in the line of duty.

No answer, so I guess I was OK. I opened the front door with the key Phil had given me and walked in. If I've ever had a bad vibe before, it didn't equal what I was feeling here. I stood in the entry and just looked around. The house felt eerie, although I had no reason to think that Jaxton's disappearance would generate such a feeling. The home was sparsely but professionally decorated. From where I stood I could see into the living room with floor to ceiling windows, cream carpet, complimentary wallpapers and furniture that fit the space with a professional expertise. I called for Jaxton just in case and heard no reply which I expected, but wanted to be sure I announced my 'innocent' presence in his house before I moved forward. Hearing nothing, I ventured into the living room. Nothing seemed unusual so I moved on down the hall to the family room. I found a large screen television, VCR, sound system and CD equipment. I checked the VCR which was empty. The wall unit had no tapes just a grouping of CD's----nothing notable. I moved into the kitchen. The cupboards were filled with the usual dishes, and the pantry was also stocked with standard items. I walked to the small built-in desk against the wall next to the refrigerator. The drawer pulled out easily and I found kitchen appliances pamphlets and menus from local restaurants indicating he preferred Chinese. Pulling the drawer out, I looked inside and underneath, again nothing. I opened the refrigerator and found milk with a pull date, or 'use before date' that expired ten days ago, leftover Mexican food in a carton that was growing green hair for a science project. The lettuce crisper had rotten, black lettuce, and soft moldy tomatoes. There were oranges and apples in the fruit drawer, which obviously managed to hide their age, although they appeared to be as old as the vegetables. As in the movies, I looked in the freezer for diamonds or drugs, and only found Haagen-Dazs ice cream, which was still looked pretty good. My assumption from the refrigerator was he hasn't been home for two or three weeks.

Moving on, I was quite certain the door ahead of me led to the garage. Opening it gingerly, I found the three-car garage with a garbage can, debris barrel, and a power lawn mower which probably was never used by Jaxton. Gardeners use their own equipment. I checked the boxes piled in the corner and found nothing that could help me. The garbage can was another matter. I dumped the contents on the floor of the empty garage and scrounged through the garbage looking for paper scraps that might give me a clue as to who this man Jaxton really was. After sorting through rotting vegetable waste and coffee grounds, I came across a copy of a druggist's instructions for a prescription, with no clue what it was for. I did however have the druggist's and the doctor's names. That went into my 'evidence bag', which was nothing more than a brown envelope I brought from the office this morning. I was looking for a newspaper or grocery receipt with a date, in order to help tie down the timing of his disappearance, but couldn't find anything. After further sorting, I found a number of opened billing statements, with evidence that the portion that was to be included with the check was missing and presumably sent along with the payment. They were related to utility payments, lawn care and the newspaper. These were also added to my "official brown evidence bag". Hopefully there are more complete records of Jaxton's life in other parts of the house that might provide a hint into his personal make up.

I was unable to find his old newspapers. I noticed a newspaper box by the mailbox on the street, but it was empty. I hadn't wanted to look in the mailbox until I was certain no one was in the house. From the garage I went back into the house and walked into what might be considered a den or office. There was a desk and computer near the window facing the door I entered. Walking up to the desk, I could see that it was clear of what might be considered work product. I started by lifting up the blotter and found nothing. The edging of the blotter was a little over two inches wide and didn't

expose a card or note or any kind of evidence or knowledge or insight into this man. The top center drawer looked like it had been sorted and replaced. I emptied the contents, which included a stapler, city map, ruler, paperclips and empty writing pads. I looked in the other drawers for his banking and paid bill files and found nothing. It appeared that either he left with everything pertaining to his private life, or someone already searched this place and removed any helpful information.

Considering that I'm such a computer whiz, the little I know might be helpful in just this situation. That being that there are ways to follow ones tracks in a computer that most people would never suspect. I turned on his computer and got the desktop. My fingers danced over the keyboard and finally reached his 'trash can', or deleted files, file. The thing to remember about deleted files is they just *look* like they're gone, but in reality you might still find them lurking around in this file, it depends on when the file is programmed to finally empty or delete what's there. I found dozens of files that had been deleted and were still 'available'. Most were the normal duplications or other useless items the average person would delete, however, one of the files related to Chinese computer chip manufacturing, a company called Knowledge Resource Ltd., based in Hong Kong. I opened up additional

files and found page after page of engineering drawings and other specifications written in Chinese characters. I needed to copy these to a disc before the 'trash can' emptied on some timed basis. Looking around the room I found a bookcase with a shelf that held miscellaneous computer supplies including a box of new floppy discs. I did know enough to download the entire 'trash can' to disc so I could go through this stuff at my leisure if I was going to have some, which I doubted. This little snooping process turned out to be endlessly time consuming, but I felt it extremely important.

The next thing a good or even bad detective would do was to try the re-dial on each telephone in the house to try and determine the last calls made from each particular phone. I hit the redial on the desk phone and tried to count the dialing sequence. I never could do that, however it wasn't necessary in this case because the phone was answered by of all people, Miss Smiley herself, "Good morning, TechX, may I help you." I hung up without comment.

Since I was on a roll with the telephone redial program, I headed back to the kitchen where I remembered a phone on the small desk next to the refrigerator. I picked up the receiver and punched re-dial. The call was answered on the third ring. "Hi, you've reached Victoria, I'm not available,
leave a message at the beep". I hung up and collected my thoughts as I was going to leave Victoria a message that needed to be interesting enough to get her to call back. I tried it again and said after the beep, "Victoria this is Chuck, I'm in town and staying at the Embassy Suites. Give me a call it'll be great to catch up, 555-1893 extension 835, see ya."

The family room also had a wall phone next to the wet bar. I pushed the re-dial and listened for the answer, which was a Mexican restaurant, the name I couldn't make out, but was undoubtedly for the take out order I found in the refrigerator. I went back into the kitchen to see if there was a name on the take-out carton. No such luck. I decided not to bother calling the restaurant.

The bathroom on the main floor was clean and the wastebasket empty and the medicine cabinet contained only an aspirin bottle and an air freshener can.

I headed up the carpeted staircase to the second floor. The first door on the right was a guest bedroom, furnished but empty, not a personal item in the room. I checked the closet, dresser and wardrobe drawers, nothing, and without a phone. The next room was about the same, it could just as easily been a room from a model home, empty of personal effects and probably never used.

The master bedroom was the last door on the right, at the end. I opened the door and found a king-sized bed, bathroom and walk-in closet where I started. There were men's clothes, both casual as well as suits and sport coats. It was by no means full. He had a decent selection of shoes. I started by searching the pockets and found nothing of consequence, except in a shirt I found a matchbook from an Indian casino located about an hour west of Portland. There wasn't an apparent trap door or hiding place in the closet, nor was there any obvious place for hiding anything that one wanted kept secret. I pulled up the mattress and found nothing there. The wardrobe had nothing other than drawers of underwear and socks. Except there was a brochure from a travel agency, that highlighted Hong Kong, which found its way into my brown envelope. On each side of the bed there was a nightstand and lamp. One table had a telephone. I opened the drawers and found a couple of mystery novels by authors unknown to me. Also, nasal spray and cough drops. There was nothing really personal and no condoms, not that there should be. I pushed the redial on the phone, and heard a voice identified as that of the international operator. I hung up and made a notation in my notebook of the call and the phone used, as I had for the other three phones.

I started over, searching the house for anything of interest, but after another hour of detailed searching, it was clear that for now I had more questions than answers, and a lot to mull over before my next move. I also needed to get my first report from Art Levy. On the way out I wanted to check the mailbox and see if I could 'borrow' or better put, keep secure Jaxton's mail should there be any. I wonder why there wasn't mail on the kitchen table or office desk if Phil had looked over the house a week or so ago. I strolled down the walkway to the street and mailbox and casually opened it like it was my own and found nothing. This could only mean that Jaxton notified the post office as well as the newspaper to hold deliveries. I need to check this out. It sure would be nice to get an invoice from a credit card company to see where he's been lately and what he's been up to. 'Art, I need your report, now!' I thought.

I pulled away from the house with a sigh of relief. It felt much better to be in the rental car. At least I belonged there. I guess I've been away from cop work too long.

CHAPTER 11

It was 4:30 P.M., I decided to skip going back to the office and instead headed to the hotel to sort out the information I had. The traffic was getting heavy as people headed home from work this Tuesday afternoon. I backtracked toward the hotel with my mind spinning about the apparently misapplied funds at TechX. I needed to look at the extraordinary expenses and track the money. I assume it ended up in a Jaxton account, but I don't know for sure. Also, I don't think I can share the results of my investigation with Phil or anyone else at the company. There's too much going on with no whistle blowers. 'Why was that?' I wanted to know!

I pulled into the Embassy Suites at 4:45 P.M., just in time for the complementary cocktail session. It'll have to wait until I check my e-mail and look over the details if any, in the financials that Christine gave me this morning. I managed to park fairly close to the door and went into the lobby which was abuzz with activity. People were checking in with golf clubs and skis. Courses were close by and skiing was popular, forty five miles away on Mt. Hood----even in the summer. The glass elevators overlooked the atrium side and offered quite a view of the cocktail party on the ride up to the eighth floor. As I entered my room I was happy to see that the maids had arrived and everything looked neat and clean. My red message light was blinking on the phone, so I dropped my stuff and settled into the swivel chair in the living room next to the phone. Pushing the message button, I listened to the voice mail. There were two messages, first from Phil wanting to know if I could join him for dinner. 'I don't think so!' I said aloud. The second call was from Art, he just wanted to remind me to check my e-mail.

'Thanks Art, you must have something for me.' I thought.

I put the laptop on the table, connected it to the phone jack, dialed up the Internet access number for Portland and clicked into my Hotmail. Aside from a half dozen junk mail pieces, I saw the <u>Artlevy@r&l.com</u> e-mail. Clicking on Art's mail, I opened his three-line report. *Jeep found at Portland Airport, Long Term Parking, Section 108, space B34. Everything appeared normal. Ticket on dashboard indicates car parked on June 28, 2:00PM. Waiting for results of other requests. Good Luck, Art.*

I took the disk I downloaded from Jaxton's computer, inserted it into my laptop and started cruising through the 'trash' or recycle bin. I came upon a Windows Word document with a list of Internet accounts and passwords, Jaxton obviously wanted to keep only a hard copy for security reasons and not in his computer. This was like winning the lottery. It had his e-mail address and password, along with his Amazon.com password and a host of others. I printed this out and punched in his AOL e-mail account. It worked and I went through his mail. Aside from the junk mail, he opened but had not deleted an e-mail from <u>bw@kresource.com</u>, dated the Monday after he disappeared. It was the same Hong Kong company I found in his computer trash bin. It said that 'the requested payment arrangements for the software partnership were being made and would be funded in four weeks'. I closed the file after printing a copy. Feeling that I was finally pulling away a few layers from this onion, I thought I'd amble down stairs, pick up a glass of wine, a plate of whatever and make my way back up to my comfy swivel chair and ponder my next move.

That included dissecting Christine's financial reports. I needed to pinpoint the extraordinary expenses listed on the reports, although I was confident they were inaccurate. It was approaching 5:30 P.M. when the phone rang. I picked up. "Hello".

"Is this Chuck?" she asked.

"Yes it is."

"This is Victoria Danville, you called this afternoon and I must confess I can't place you. The only reason I ----."

I interrupted her in mid-sentence with, "Oh hi, Victoria, I'm on a long distance cell phone call, could I call you back in about two minutes, I should be through by then?" I said. "Would you mind giving me your number again so I don't have to go down to the car?"

She answered, "555-8297".

"Thanks, call you right back." I said with a cheerful, friendly voice.

Now I had her name *and number*, and I can find out more about her if she brushes me off on the phone. Two minutes later I placed my call to the number she gave me. It rang about five times and she picked up, "Hi this is Victoria".

"Victoria, this is Chuck Winters, I was calling because I wanted to know if you've heard from Denton."

"Mr. Winters, the only reason I called you back was that my caller ID indicated that you were at Denton's house, and I couldn't figure out what was going on."

So much for cleverness, I better brush up on my approach. "I'm sorry for not being upfront with you. I was asked to look into Denton's absence from TechX, by one of the company's board members. It seems that Denton, whom I've never met, hasn't contacted the office in almost two weeks and they were getting quite concerned."

"How did you get in?"

"Phil Hampton let me in."

"I haven't met him, but Denton would mention his name occasionally. For that matter I never met anyone at TechX. How did Phil end up with a key?"

"I'm not sure." I answered, or better put I stretched the truth a little as I really didn't know what locksmith he used.

Victoria said in a worrisome tone, "I'm concerned about Denton, did you know he is diabetic? We share the same pharmacist. The other day he asked me where Denton was because he hadn't picked up his insulin prescription. It just wasn't like him. He really needs it and I doubt if he has a different pharmacist now."

"This doesn't sound good."

"I've been calling four or five times a day. He hates answering machines and voicemail. I haven't left a message about his prescription because he wouldn't pick it up anyway."

"Could you come down now to the Embassy Suites and have a glass of wine with me in the Atrium area? We can try to pool our information and see if we can find him."

There was a hesitation and, "Sure why not, but I can't stay long, say twenty minutes."

"Great, I'll find a table. I'll be wearing a green polo shirt and jeans."

I looked in my address book and called Art Levy at home. "Hello," he answered with typical gruffness.

"Art, I got your e-mail, great work! Now, I need something e-mailed tonight if possible, a complete as possible dossier on a Hong Kong company, Knowledge Resource, Ltd. I need names and phone numbers of the main players as well as something about their business, what they do and where they stand in the market place, and if possible their credibility."

"It's a good thing I have no life and it's also a good thing that it's tomorrow morning in Hong Kong."

"I know that, why would I bother you at this hour otherwise? You still have active contacts there don't you?"

"Only the best and I might add the most expensive." He replied in a devilish tone.

I promised Tom at One Star I would regularly update him by e-mail. Thinking I better get off to a good start, I sent him a *'laying the groundwork, busy, nothing noteworthy yet, will keep you informed, Chuck'* type of e-mail.

CHAPTER 12

I just had time to click on Travelocity on the web, and check available flights, made some notes and dialed a number that was technically Redding, California, but actually Shasta Lake area. After a couple of rings she answered. "Hello".

"Do you hear my heart pounding?" I asked Valarie Austin, the love of my life for oh, the last year or so. She was a fairly successful painter, bright, beautiful and very independent as well, living in a house high on a hill in the Jones Valley area with a sweeping view of the lake from her studio.

"What do you want now, I checked out your boat yesterday, what am I your little gopher?" She responded with her typical caustic jab. "And where are you?"

"I'm still in Beaverton, however I was calling to see if you were busy for dinner tomorrow night, or make it the day after tomorrow, Thursday." I asked with a private grin on my face.

"You are lucky, on both days." She replied. "I'm free as a bird, where are we eating?"

"On a little floating restaurant in Aberdeen Harbor, Hong Kong----OK?"

"You're kidding of course."

"Nope, you can pick up your tickets at the Redding Airport for the 1:00 P.M., United flight tomorrow. I'll meet your flight in San Francisco at 1:25 P.M., and we catch the 3:30 Delta flight to Hong Kong. We'll return on Sunday. OK?"

"OK," she said, "what's the catch?"

"Bingo. There is one small catch. You need to go down to the houseboat and get my passport out of my sock drawer. I know yours is still good from last summer, OK?"

"Done deal. Love ya----see you in San Francisco and don't be late." She demanded.

"Love you too, I won't be late and thanks." I said as I placed the phone on the receiver, grabbed my briefcase and went down the elevator to the happy hour, or I should say hours, in the atrium area. I found a table and saved it by leaning my chair against the edge and went to the bar for a glass of merlot. Upon settling in at the table, I saw a very attractive, thirty-something lady, smiling and walking toward my table. Her hair was medium length and dark brown. She was tanned and appeared to be taller than average, and slender like a model. She wore sandals and a sexy sundress that clung to her curves.

"Victoria"?

"Chuck!" She responded with a continuing smile.

"Please sit down. What can I get you?"

"A dry white wine please." She indicated still smiling.

I returned with a glass of chardonnay and sat down. "How long have you known Denton?"

"Excuse me for sounding rude, but I don't know you and I'm not too comfortable discussing my private life with a man that calls me from a house where the occupant is who knows where, and has never met him. What's really going on here, and just how do you fit in?" She asked, with a hint of an edge in her voice.

"Fair enough----the company that provided the venture capital for TechX, One Star Venture Capital, namely Tom Claudius the principal called me from my retirement on my Shasta Lake houseboat to do him a favor and check this situation out. Besides being a good friend, he was the person that funded *my* company. I couldn't refuse him. That's my story in a nutshell."

"Well that does tell me a little more, but I still don't know if you're being straight with me. Show me some identification. California drivers license, a photo of your boat, credit card, you know the sort of thing to make me more comfortable." She replied, now serious.

I just happened to have a picture of my boat in my wallet, along with the other requested identification. She wrote down my address and asked for my phone number, "Just for the record", she said.

"It's obvious you're night job's a lawyer, what's your day job?"
"The same!" She grinned and we both laughed. "I'm really worried. It's not like Denton to leave without calling me. We talked every day, even if he was traveling."

"Do you mind if I ask you a personal question?"

"It depends on the question." She fired back.

"Why is it that when I asked Phil about a woman in Denton's life, he said he knew of no one?"

"Simple. Denton thought his private life was private and didn't mix it with his business life. I feel the same way and appreciated the fact that we weren't pot-lucking and going to endless company parties."

"I have to say I don't blame you."

"What's he like? I mean on a personal basis, what kind of guy is he, what does he like to do for fun?"

"He's a very sweet and thoughtful man. He would bring me flowers and remember important dates. He loves his work and loves his free time. We like to ski at Mt. Hood Meadows, not far from here every chance we have."

"How long have you known Denton?"

"Almost two years. We're planning on getting married when the product release is finished."

"Do you have any idea where he might be? Did he say anything about traveling somewhere?"

"No not a word. As I said, this just isn't like him." She responded with a distraught look on her face.

"Does he have anyone close that he might confide in, like a male friend or anyone other than you?"

"For some reason he wasn't close with his sister, and his mother has been sick and has a form of dementia. He has casual friends from the gym, and executives in the industry, but really no one close that he would tell instead of me."

"This is another personal one but needs to be asked, how were the two of you getting along recently? Could there be another woman?" I asked sheepishly.

"No way! We were getting along famously, and I'm sure you're aching to know----our sex life was terrific!" She said with a grin.

"Thanks for that, I know this is hard for you. It is for me and I never met him. Now that we're being totally candid, how are his finances? Is he hurting for money?"

"Denton? He still has every nickel he ever made, and he's very judicious in his investments. He bought every share of stock he could from his previous employers, and of course exercised every stock option that made sense. When he started TechX he was a wealthy man, and not motivated by the money potential. He's a perfectionist, that's why he was so frustrated at work. The software engineers couldn't quite get the performance he expected from the software, and close enough wasn't acceptable to Denton. That's why he took it upon himself to shift gears so much and do the majority of the design work himself. He told me that he had them involved with the groundwork that was necessary for the second-generation software. That way, he'd have a 'leg up' as he called it, on the competition for a second generation of the program, when the first release was ready. He loves to talk about his work, and since I had a degree in mathematics before going to law school, he found a willing ear in me. I'm fascinated by it."

"Victoria, I can't tell you how much this insight helps me in getting to know Denton. I'll do everything in my power to find him. In the meantime, I'm going to be hard to get a hold of. But, if you need me or have an idea or some information, here's my e-mail address." I handed her one of my old business cards from my wallet. "I check it regularly and will get back to you by e-mail or call you."

"Oh, one last question, what did Denton think of Phil?"

"Truth?" She asked with a piercing stare.

"Of course!" I replied with a half-smile, half-frown.

"He thought he was weird. He only worked there because One Star wanted him."

Victoria stood and I jumped to my feet like any good gentleman in the company of a beautiful woman. "I have to run. I have to file a motion in court first thing, and have a few things to check out yet this evening. It was really nice meeting you Chuck, and I'm glad you called so we could 'catch up', after all, it's been a very long time!" Smiling, she held out her hand, warmly shook mine and was gone.

CHAPTER 13

I decided to head up to my room. I wasn't hungry, only very confused about what was going on. The freeloaders were still enjoying the free drinks, and I'm certain a good number were not guests, or guests of guests of the hotel. Not my problem, though. While waiting for the elevator, I perused the menu from the main restaurant, which was conveniently posted nearby in an attempt to snag the paying guests. My previous experience with Embassy Suites was that the main restaurant was usually very good and generally not so busy that a reservation was required. What do I care? Valarie and I will soon be bobbing around on a delightful floating restaurant somewhere in Hong Kong.

I reached my room about 8:15 P.M., and inserted my card key into the lock slot. The green light came on and I pushed on in, finding total destruction. The cushions and drawers were overturned and on the floor, as was my two-day old suitcase and wardrobe. Considering I had the foresight to grab my briefcase when I went to meet Victoria, everything that counted, including my laptop was with me when this bomb-like intrusion occurred.

I turned around and walked right down the stairs to the front desk, forgoing the elevator. "Excuse me. May I speak with the manager?" A moment later a short, stocky man in his mid-thirties, with a black handlebar mustache came forward. "There seems to be a housekeeping problem in 835. I'd like two adjoining rooms on another floor. I want only one room of the two registered, and I need to know which room it is. For security reasons, I don't want anyone knowing that the other room is involved. Can you handle this?"

"Sir, Mr. Winters, can you please tell me exactly what housekeeping problem you experienced?" He asked with a, you know what kind of grin on his face.

"Mr." I leaned over and almost toppled over the desk trying to read his name- tag without my bifocals, "Rivera, my cushions are on the floor, my mattress and box springs are half way over the balcony, I have socks hanging from the draperies, and shoes in the sink. The only thing that is still in place is the wallpaper, probably because they couldn't figure out how to strip the stuff off. Now, if you need a further description, I suggest you shag up the 137 stairs to Room 835 and have a good look for yourself."

"Yes sir, we'll send someone up right away to your room, pack your belongs and move them to room 414 and 416, which along with dinner in the hotel dining room will be complimentary. You will be registered under Room 414; however that number will also remain confidential, even to the hotel staff." Mr. Rivera replied. I wonder if he has a brother named Geraldo, I pondered, and headed up to Room 414, with my briefcase and a bit of apprehension, and not much else. After entering room 414, I closed the door and opened the door to room 416 using the special key the night manager gave me to lock and unlock the adjoining door. I turned out the lights in 414, locked the adjoining door and went inside. Now that I was ensconced in a room within a room, sort of, I decided to call Phil at home, returning his call and responding to his invitation to dinner. It seemed late enough to properly decline without seeming too rude, not that I gave a rip. I searched around for his number in my overflowing briefcase and dialed.

"Hello." Phil answered.

"Hi Phil, Chuck here, sorry I didn't get your message earlier. I think I'll try to turn in early, how about a rain-check on your dinner invitation?"

"Sure, no problem, how did it go this afternoon at Jaxton's?"

"Well, the place looked pretty darn devoid of human touches. It felt like a model home in a new subdivision. Did you notice the same thing?"

"Yes it did look a little unlived in."

"I'm curious did you see any newspapers or mail? It looked like deliveries had been held."

"Come to think of it, I didn't see any either. What else did you notice, any clues?"

"The only clues I found was that he wasn't there. His car was gone and he liked Mexican food. There was no sign of a woman visitor, frequent or infrequent to the house. Have you ever known Jaxton to date?" I asked once again just to be sure.

"No not even at an office party."

"Do you suppose he's gay?

"Could be, I just don't know."

"I won't be in the office for the next few days. I've some business to attend to but will be back up the first of the week and ready to hit it again. If you hear anything or Jaxton shows up you can e-mail me. That'd be simplest. You do have my e-mail address don't you?"

"Yeah, it was on the card you gave me."

"Hold down the fort and thanks again for the dinner invite. Oh by the way, I'll need to hold off on going through Jaxton's office for a few days until I get back up here. Did you find anything that'd be helpful when you looked through it?"

Not really. From my perspective I didn't." He added as we finished up, "See you soon."

I sat in the swivel chair and rocked, trying to figure out who might have tossed my room. They must have been looking for something I might have discovered in Jaxton's house. First I wondered how they knew I was there. Only Phil and Victoria knew I was at the house, and of course whoever they may have told personally. What could they think I might have found? If they wanted me off the case, I could have been shot or eliminated between Jaxton's house and the hotel----or for that matter in my room. If they feared I might have found something, it might indicate that they were concerned that they didn't sufficiently clean the house of incriminating evidence. Or maybe Jaxton didn't go anyplace and just wanted to throw off his pursuers, and in reality was lurking in the neighborhood and followed me from the house. Nah----, so it's either an inside deal at TechX and a joint venture with Jaxton, or an independent deal with Jaxton and others, or Jaxton alone. The *others* could have been watching his backside and wanted to make certain I found nothing important.

These mental games are not too productive. The best advice I could give myself is to 'watch my backside and be very alert on a twenty-four-seven basis'. Now that I'm totally depressed, I think it's time to check my e-mail one more time.

I plugged the extension into the phone-jack, double clicked my internet icon, and then my mail box. There was another e-mail from Art Levy. I quickly opened it and read the report on KRL in Hong Kong. It seems that they're a chip manufacturer and distributor, with a dubious reputation. They've had a number of scrapes with the law, in terms of dealing in stolen computer chips. They have sales exceeding a billion dollars, modest for the industry, but large in terms of potential profit. They're headed by a reputed, Chinese Mafia fellow named Ho Chi. He went on to say that he had a contact that has the ability to set up a meeting with Chi and his top lieutenant Billy Wong, a former San Francisco thug. They're interested in buying anything in their field whether it's stolen or not. They just care if it can be acquired at a steep discount, like 60 to 70%. He went on to say "let me know about setting up a meeting. I'm assembling the information on Jaxton's financials, bank and

credit cards etc. as well as credit reports. Will advise. Good luck. Art."

I responded to Art by asking for a meeting with his contact Friday morning and possibly a meet with Chi and Wong on Saturday. Also to see if his contact could discreetly inquire about TechX software for chip testing, and whether they know of or are dealing with Denton Jaxton. I suggested that maybe these questions would be best asked of an underling in the company that could be paid for information and silence, and closed by thanking him for his terrific work.

It was time for my free meal in the dining room offered by the night manager. I unlocked the adjoining door to room 414, moved into the room, re-locked the door to 416 and walked through the darkened room to the outside door. I cautiously walked out the door, being alert to what was going on in all directions, a far cry from my carefree boat days three days ago. On the lake the only danger I was exposed to was getting nipped on the toe by a hungry turtle, which never happened, as opposed to a big-money caper with a foreign influence. I walked carefully and somewhat paranoid to the elevator, pushed the button and waited. The free drinks in the atrium were over and guests that were not leaving the hotel, congregated in the bar and dining room. Others could choose one of the many excellent restaurants within a few minutes of the hotel.

I was the only passenger in the elevator, and upon reaching the main floor I walked to the dining room carrying my briefcase, not willing to leave it in my new 'room within a room'. I was wondering if my suitcase with my *flying shoes* will be in the room when I return.

At my request I was seated in a location against the rear wall. The restaurant was about half full, with guests seemingly enjoying themselves, by the sounds of their laughter and conversation. The waiter was a pleasant man in his early fifties who demonstrated his years of experience. When he inquired as to a cocktail order, I decided this was a double vodka martini day, stirred, shaken, I didn't care, just so it came quickly with adequate olives and onions, and if possible----make it Vox from Finland.

The waiter brought the martini, and described the specials of the day, which were tilted toward seafood. I decided on Caesar salad, crusted halibut, garlic mashed potatoes and asparagus. The martini was just right and the dinner was excellent. No desert, thanks.

I picked up my briefcase and thought about the impending journey back to my rooms, hopefully uneventful. I reversed my steps with the exception of using an elevator on the other side of the atrium to throw off any lurking bad guys. Seeing no suspicious people along the route, and hoping that the perp or perps were long gone and not hanging around to make another attempt at grabbing my briefcase, I waited for the elevator. When it arrived, there was a small man wearing a dark brown suit standing inside when the door opened. I stepped aside for the man but he didn't get out. Considering this was the ground floor and the last stop, I stood and looked him over carefully. Without knowing his ability or armament, I decided to walk back toward the restaurant. Glancing back, I saw he was still standing in the elevator. Thankfully, someone on an upper floor called the elevator and the door closed. He moved near the glass window craning his neck, watching me walk back toward the restaurant. When I was certain he couldn't see me I moved back toward the front desk and the stairwell that led to the upper floors. I carefully walked up the four flights and exited onto the landing that surrounded the floor overlooking the atrium. There was no one on the floor and I moved to room 416 instead of 414 and listened for a moment before inserting the card key. It was quiet but that wasn't very assuring. I slowly opened the door, standing aside to be out of a line of fire if any, reached for the light switch and flipped it on. This room had also been tossed. It was a total mess, carried out even with more vengeance than my first room. I inched my way into the bedroom and slipped into the bathroom. No sign of anyone. I then went to the adjoining door leading to room 414 and again listened for a minute or so and took the key from my pocket, slowly inserted it and turned the latch. The door was now unlocked and I pushed it slowly. The room was dark as a moonless night. A chill of foreboding swept over my body. I slowly pulled the door closed and left the room the way I entered. The landing was clear except for an older couple heading my way after exiting the elevator. I went toward them and said hello on the way to the elevator, which thankfully was empty when it opened. I rode down to the main level and walked to the front desk where I hoped to speak with Rivera the night manager. He came out with his normal look of disdain for my interrupting his routine watching of the Dating Game or something as elevating.

"Hello again, I think I'm going to let you have your two complementary rooms back, however I did enjoy the complimentary dinner----it was excellent. I have just one more little favor, would you send a few of your large staff people up to my room 414 and bring down the same suitcase that your people previously placed in there." I asked with utmost courtesy for a change.

He smiled and left to round up some poor hapless bellman to hightail it up to my room and get the suitcase back so he'd never have to deal with me again. Ten minutes later a bellman showed up with a ripped jacket, torn shirt and a bloody nose----without a suitcase. He must have run into his ex-wife or my intruder. Now I felt bad about my lack of candor with Rivera. Since I'm not fluent in much more than take out I assumed the bellman didn't think he was getting paid enough for this action and walked out the door saying something about Rivera's sister, I suspect.

I guess I should have gone in there myself or warned them about the potential tiger lurking in the darkness however I felt I had squeezed enough life out of one day and didn't want to complicate things further with a police confrontation. That of course could create a very difficult situation in trying to honor my agreement with Tom Claudius regarding keeping the Jaxton situation under wraps. The last vision I had of this scene was that of the large-framed night manager wheeling around the corner and heading toward the elevator to confront the tiger that tore the bellman to shreds a few short minutes before. My option was to leave now and avoid any further discussion with him upon his return, which of course meant I could forget all about the strong attachment I had to my clothes that I've owned for oh, about two days---- and just buy some more in the morning.

As I was weighing this option, Mr. Rivera returned with a look of concern on his face, most likely regarding the condition of the room, for which he was responsible, rather than for my things.

He started, "Who is after you? The room is a total mess just like your room on the eighth floor? Are you sure you had nothing to do with this? Someone is going to have to pay for the damage."

"Mr. Rivera, I had nothing to do with this and I have no idea who is involved. I'm afraid however that I'm not safe here, as someone is able to find my room number and gain access even though you've promised to keep it confidential. From what I saw the first time there wasn't any physical damage, just some major straightening up. I assume the fourth floor break-in, which didn't appear to be a forcible entry is similar, and therefore we are probably about even----considering you can't keep nasty people out of your guest's rooms. As a result, I'll check out and pay for my first night and restaurant charges, even my 'complimentary dinner' you offered for tonight and leave immediately. Are you all right with that?"

Mr. Rivera looked as though he had won the lottery---- since his 'problem guest' was about to walk out of the building----never to return. A little straightening was a small price to pay. "That will be fine."

"One more request Mr. Rivera, would you mind calling me a cab, and while I'm waiting, will you please go out to my rental car, a new green Lincoln Town Car parked in space number 26 and let me know if it's been broken into?"

He returned and indicated, "The trunk's been forced open and the driver's side door is open a little."

"Thanks, the car rental company will pick it up in the morning."

A few minutes later a Yellow Cab pulled up at the front door. I asked Mr. Rivera if he would ask the driver to pull around to the restaurant back door, and also if he would be kind enough to escort me through the kitchen to meet the cab.

The night manager was only too happy to jump through these little hoops to once and for all get rid of his biggest headache.

The cab was at the back door, as I was traveling light with only my briefcase, I hopped in and we headed out. "To the Sheraton at the airport" I indicated, as I checked around for suspicious people or cars on our tail. None that I could see. We headed North on Highway 217 for five or six minutes while I continued to watch out the rear window for any possible following vehicle. We turned onto Highway 26 and headed east toward downtown Portland and over the Marquam Bridge onto Highway 84 and then on to the airport. We turned onto the main entry drive into the airport general area and pulled up at the Sheraton Hotel entry. While I paid the driver I continued to be vigilant in surveying the vehicles that were pulling onto the hotel property after we arrived.

The night air was humid and the sky at this hour was a streaking progression of landing and departing aircraft, each with an anonymity associated with the lives that are linked in a close single-minded commitment to a safe arrival for an hour or hours, and then for the most part never again to cross paths or have such a common interest. For that reason The Sheraton Airport Hotel was the best solution for trying to 'hide in plain sight'. It was large and busy enough that I might get lost if someone was looking for me, particularly if I could successfully entice the front desk clerk to somehow give me the privacy that 'big name' guests have.

I casually strolled through the glass front doors and made my way across the large foyer to the front desk carrying only my briefcase. There were a number of people in the lobby with assorted piles of bags waiting for the shuttle to the airport that ran every few minutes. Others were walking from elevators to the restaurant or lounge. I continued to be as alert as possible for
any sign of trouble that might be following me. The desk clerk was a tall thin young man in his mid-twenties, wearing a gold Sheraton nametag of one
Jerome Figgens. "Jerome", I said with my friendliest persona, "I would like a room for tonight, but I need your help. Do you read?"

"Uh, you mean books, or do I understand? He responded with hesitation.

"Well yes, novels," I said, adding my friendliest smile.

"Well sir, I'm going to college and working, so aside from my assignments I hardly have time for recreational reading."

Perfect, I thought. "Jerome, I just left a hotel which I won't name but I am an author and have a book signing tomorrow in the city. Who let the word out at the hotel I don't know, but I had at least a hundred of my fans knocking on the door of my hotel room this evening, trying to get an autographed copy of my new book 'Villain by Starlight'. I don't even have a copy with me or I'd give you one. My publisher is bringing the books tomorrow. Jerome, what I need from you is to somehow keep my name out of your computer system. Every hotel has an employee that for twenty bucks will give out my room number." I explained in the hope that he will rise to the occasion, which was accented by the hundred-dollar bill I slid across the counter with my American Express card.

Jerome palmed the Ben Franklin, sliding it into his front pants pocket and responded, "Mr. Winters, you will be registered as Mr. Frank, as in "Frankly my dear, I don't give a damn ---- as to who you are----sir." I registered as John Frank, signed my credit card charge correctly, and was given a card key. Jerome asked me if I needed help with my luggage and I politely declined the assistance of a bellman to carry my briefcase. He assigned me room 315, and I walked into the lounge hoping there was another exit, which there was that led into a side hallway where the restrooms and phone banks were located. There was a lady speaking in a loud and animated fashion at a pay phone, and aside from her the hallway was empty. On the right were conference rooms and other assorted offices, which at this time of night appeared to be unoccupied. I worked my way down the hallway----my antenna up, trying to find a stairwell or some secondary method of reaching my room. I continued walking past the kitchen area and came to housekeeping. Near the laundry and maintenance doors I saw the 'maintenance elevator'. This was the extra insurance against being followed, which I was almost certain I wasn't.

It was nearly 11:30 P.M. when I finally reached my room. I opened the door this time without apprehension for a change and walked into quite a nice room for requesting just a king. Undoubtedly Jerome was using his apparent authority to upgrade a guest for merit, i.e. notoriety of some sort, which a hundred dollar bill residing in Jerome's pocket would certainly justify such standing if to no one else but Jerome. The room was without question first class. It was a suite, with full living room, dining area, powder room and a huge master bedroom with a marble bathroom, complete with telephone and personal bathrobe. Jerome was not a reader but he would get along just fine. He understood how things worked in the real world, and was probably, except for pocketing the hundred, operating within his authority at the hotel.

I set up my laptop and plugged into the phone line in order to check my   e-mail. There were two, one from Art Levy regarding a meeting arranged on Friday in Hong Kong, with an informant that's willing to discuss Knowledge Resource Ltd.'s possible involvement with TechX. The second e-mail was from Mr. Sun, Art's contact who set up the meeting, indicated that he would meet me at the Royal Imperial Hotel where he had taken the liberty to arrange a reservation for me. He provided his phone number that was good on a twenty-four basis, as well as his office address.

I quickly fired off a confirming e-mail to Mr. Sun, with a copy to Art, thanking him for his assistance and asking if he could provide as much additional background about the key players as possible, as well as if he could in fact schedule a meeting on Saturday with one or both of the principals of the Hong Kong Company, under the guise that I had something of value with questionable ownership credentials to sell at a bargain price. I asked him to talk with his informant and determine what type of product Mr. Ho Chi and Billy Wong, of KRL, would find enticing enough to meet a stranger on Saturday at the Royal Imperial Hotel. My next e-mail was to Art, bringing him up to date on the 'close scrutiny' I'd been receiving this evening, and to

see if he could have his local Portland contact nose around a little to see if he could uncover something without being too obvious.

I signed off the web and picked up the receiver, dialing the 800 car rental number from my reservation, which was my only choice as the telephone book listing had the same number. Now I'm speaking to a very interested agent, located who knows where telling me, "Sir, you must return the vehicle to the Portland International Airport per your agreement."

Coming from a somewhat amused position, I tried to explain, "Madam, my car is at the hotel address I just gave you, because the car has been broken into and I fear for my personal safety. I understand there's an additional charge for this extra request, but I'm not going

83

to return the vehicle to the airport." I tried to explain as clearly as possible

"Is there any damage to the vehicle?" She persisted.

"Madam, I don't know, all I want is a confirmation number that demonstrates I have informed you of the location of the car, and that I request that you have it picked up and checked in for me." I politely requested.

"But sir, we don't have a confirmation number for this kind of thing, we only request that you return the vehicle to the place it was rented unless you have an agreement to drop it off at another location." She insisted.

"May I ask your name, so that I will be able to verify that I have informed the company?" I asked.

"Mary" She said.

"Mary what?"

"We are not allowed to give out our last names."

"What's your extension number?

"We can't give that out either sir"

"Mary, you have the present location of my car, you have my first and last name, you have my date of birth, you have my address, you have my credit

card number, you have my telephone number, you have my drivers license number, you have my rental agreement number, you have so much information about me, you could marry me, divorce me, hire me, fire me, audit me, and last but not least bury me, which may be the objective here.

"Good night Mary." I placed the receiver back on the phone and set the clock radio for a 7:00AM wakeup, and crashed in my luxurious bed, in my luxurious suite.

I awakened before the alarm, stretching and still emotionally drained from the exhaustion of the previous evening's experiences. I felt I should exercise some before I started another new day of *un-retirement*, but thought better of that it, went into the bathroom and made a pot of coffee, not wanting to risk room service or go to the restaurant. For the moment and until my flight left at 9:50AM flight, I would stay in the room as long as possible trying to make sense of the facts I now knew.

Denton Jaxton was missing and his car was found at the Portland International Airport, parked there on Saturday of the weekend he disappeared. He had a girlfriend named Victoria Danville, which appeared to be concerned and indicated that he was a diabetic. Ms. Danville seemed convinced that Jaxton was not financially motivated and had a substantial amount of wealth accumulated throughout his career. She was also convinced that he was a perfectionist and would not release his product until he was satisfied with its performance.

It didn't appear that Christine, the controller, was trying to cover because she willingly sent me financials that were different by a substantial sum from that provided to One Star.

Phil appeared to be cooperative and didn't seem to hinder my efforts. To the contrary, he seemed willing to assist in every way.

Bryan in engineering, was also very cooperative and didn't talk poorly about Jaxton, but did think that they could have gotten a product out the door a lot sooner if they'd been willing to put one out that worked well, but could have been more advanced, as industry technology improvements occurred almost

on a daily basis. The primary files on the first product effort were generally missing from the engineering department and not available in one place at TechX. This could demonstrate a concerted effort to sabotage the product development, or a reasonable policy direction that concentrates the latest staff engineering effort on second generation development, with the initial product release final engineering work being finished by the CEO, founder and inventor of the product idea----Jaxton himself.

On the other hand, KRL in Hong Kong definitely has agreed to the 'requested payment arrangements' for the software partnership. Now this could be innocent and a first sale of the TechX software release orchestrated by Jaxton himself, or a clandestine arrangement to line the pockets of Jaxton, and he disappears forever to a tropical island.

I checked my e-mail and found a response from Bryan Cranston. "Chuck good meeting you today. I checked with my people as well as my files, and determined that we have virtually all of the supporting documentation and could pull this together and do the last of the testing in the next eight weeks, barring any unforeseen problems. All we need is the official go-ahead from the board or Denton, and we'll crank it up. Let me know. In the meantime,

I'll pull the present documentation together in one place and outline a final testing procedure. This won't interfere with our present work that Denton assigned us to concentrate on. Best regards, Bryan."

I sent a short response back to Bryan. "Bryan, great news I'll be back to you. Thanks, Chuck."

I thought it was time to pick up the phone and have a one-on-one with Tom Claudius. "Hello." He answered at his home number.

"Hi Tom,"

"Chucky, what's happening up there?"

"It's been a little dicey, someone doesn't like me I can tell you that. Who it is, I don't know yet, but I expect to know soon. Jaxton's car's been parked in long term parking at the Portland International Airport. It's been there since Saturday of the weekend he disappeared, but I don't know where he went yet. I talked with Bryan Cranston, chief engineer, and he's informed me

that his department can have the product ready for release in about eight weeks after the go ahead from the board or Jaxton, with or without him."

"I'll call Cranston. Where in the hell *is* Jaxton? What's he trying to do with this company----ruin it?" Tom asked acidly.

"Tom, I don't know what the story is yet, but I will very soon. I need to tie up some loose ends and get to the bottom of this. I'll be in touch, and don't worry too much. I think this'll all work out. You've got some good people in the company, so hang in there until I get back to you."

Next, I called Betty in Tom's office. "Betty, you're looking lovely today."

"Hi Chuck, what do you want now?" She asked with a twinkle in her voice.

"Do you have a copy of the TechX insurance policy?"

"I'm certain I do, it should be part of the package we require in all of our funding. You should know that Chuck."

"I thought so, but I wasn't certain you hadn't singled my company out for extra harassment." I chuckled. "Can you e-mail me a copy----please?"

"Chuck, do you know what a pain that is?" She asked in a semi-miffed response.

"I do, and let me tell you I wouldn't ask if I didn't really need it." I answered, doing my very best to pacify her.

"All right, but this will cost you Chuck, big time." She said with a phony sharpness to her voice and hung up.

I was in my shorts. It was the best I could do about creating a different look that most likely wouldn't 'play too well' with the airline crowd. I needed my bag back from the Embassy Suites, where last night's exit through the back door was not too conducive to an orderly retrieval. Night manager Rivera was probably holding it for me, and considering he was off duty, *I'd* need to track it down myself.

"Good morning, Embassy Suites." The answer came.

"Good morning, can you connect me with the manager please?"

"One moment sir."

"Dorothy Harris, how can I assist you?" She replied with a sweet as honey voice, one that for certain would turn to vinegar when she found out who was calling.

"This is Chuck Winters, I---" before I could finish she jumped in with a----.

"Well *you* left quite a mess last night when you bailed out of here."

"Ms. Harris? Is it?" I questioned on purpose.

"Yes." she replied, coldly.

"Let me tell *you*, for a supposedly secure family facility, I was a little concerned when my rooms were broken into twice, as was my car. I think you should be happy I'm not currently planning on filing a lawsuit for mental anguish, emotional distress, and whatever else my slick attorney might throw
at you. However, I just might forget about this whole distressing incident if you find my bag and have it ready for my cab driver to pick up." I strongly stated to Miss Manners, or the lack of same, with my best seething tone.

She responded after a moment's silence. "Your bag will be at the front desk."

"Thank you. A cab will be dispatched immediately."

The Yellow Cab Company agreed to pick up my bag and bring it back to the Sheraton in forty minutes, induced by the promise of a generous tip to the driver for meeting the time frame.

Upon calling United Express I confirmed that my flight to San Francisco was departing as scheduled at 10:25AM. As I was just five minutes from the terminal, there was plenty of time for the bag pickup and delivery. If they didn't come through I was no worse off than I was at the moment, sitting in my shorts with a pair of jeans and a polo shirt tossed on a chair. Since I didn't have time to shop for another travel wardrobe in between planes in San Francisco, I'd just have to pick up a few things in Hong Kong.

I called the gift shop and ordered a "ditty bag". Something to toss my shaving gear, toothbrush and stuff like that in, and asked the young lady to fill it up, as my bags were lost. She could understand that a lot better than some unknown terrorist type tore up my two rooms as well as my Town Car in a matter of two hours last night. "I'll send them up to your room right away Mr. Frank", she replied. Not a bad use for my new alias, I thought.

"Thanks, as soon as possible, oh by the way, do you have any sport shirts in your shop?"

"Yes we have short sleeved prints, polo shirts and sweat shirts, but you may want to take a look at what we have."

"I want you to pick out something in extra large, like you might for your father as a gift, just use your own judgment and don't forget, I'll be flying in it----in public." I jokingly replied.

"She said OK, but you'll be sorry, my father never wears the shirts I buy him."

"I'll take that chance, and hurry I need to shower and have a plane to catch."

"I'll have it all to you in ten minutes----OK?"

"Perfect."

While I waited for my stuff, I had a few minutes and thought I'd check in with Art Levy to see if he could cheer me up with something. "Hi Art."

"Chuck, I'm glad you called. I have a bit of news. There's nothing too exciting about Jaxton's finances, just substantial, nothing new. He's been growing his wealth for a number of years. His credit is good, pays his bills and has no debt. He's a good solid guy on paper. No problems with the law in civil or criminal matters in his past. I got a hold of his credit card information. As I said, this will cost you, because it wasn't easy to come by. He hasn't been charging on his cards since before the weekend he disappeared. He either is using cash to eliminate a trail, or he ain't going to leave a trail because he can't----and maybe never will." Art reported in his usual somber style.

"I can't say I'm totally surprised, after talking with his girlfriend Victoria, she pretty much said the same thing about his financial status. The non-use of his credit cards is another story altogether. After flying somewhere, he might not be using his credit cards if he's the guest of someone else."

"That's true." Art replied.

"Art is there any way at all you can find out where he might have gone when he flew out of Portland? I know it's almost impossible, but can you somehow check with each airline that flew out of Portland that Saturday afternoon and evening?"

"I know a guy that might help on that score, but I think he's out of the country on vacation. I'll check."

"There's someone knocking at the door, just a second."

I cautiously looked through the peephole and saw two men, a man in a white shirt and one that appeared to be a bellman.

"Who's there?" I called out.

"Yellow Cab."

"And bellman."
"Ok!" I guess I hit the jackpot.

After giving the cab driver a big tip, and paying the fare in exchange for my bag, I asked the bellman to step in for a minute while I opened my suitcase and found what I expected, a jumbled mess, designed by my dear friend Mr. Rivera, the night manager at Embassy Suites who retrieved the contents of my bag from the hurricane-like explosion my room encountered at the hands of my personal terrorist last night.

Then I took a look at the effort made by the nice young lady in the gift shop, and decided the shirt didn't look half bad and I could squeeze another ditty bag in my suitcase. I signed for the purchase with my best John Frank signature, gave the bellman a tip and asked him to take an envelope with a twenty-dollar bill in it to Mary my personal shopper whose name was on the billing statement from the gift shop.

I forgot I had Art on the phone, but quickly remembered when I heard growls coming from the bed where I set the receiver. "Sorry Art, I had to clean up some loose ends from my fiasco last night at the other hotel. Have you got a lead on my intruder yet? I know someone had to be paid off to get the room numbers."

"Not yet, but I have a man discreetly working on it."

"Thanks for your help in Hong Kong.

"Not a problem."

"I assume you noticed from my e-mail that I'm meeting with Mr. Sun, and I think with his contact on Friday. I asked him to set something up with the top guys in the company on some guise that I can sell them some hot material. If I do this right, I might be able to learn something about their TechX relationship."

"Be careful, Chuck. These guys would have no problem cutting you up and dropping you in the harbor if they sense any odor in your deal."

"I know that Art, I'm a big boy. That sort of goes with the territory, I'll be careful."

"I'll be in touch by e-mail." Art said as he hung up.

Time was running short before my flight, but I had enough for a steaming hot shower amongst the marble luxury of my lavish bathroom, thanks to my new best friend Jerome the ambitious front desk clerk. I showered, shaved, and threw on some foo-foo stuff to kill the odor of fear emanating from my pores – just kidding, maybe a little apprehensive. I'm too old for this cops and robbers stuff. I find I'm really missing Shasta Lake.

The Sheraton's shuttle ride to the airport terminal was uneventful and with no apparent tail following me. After checking my newly found bag at United, I made my way through the throngs of travelers. It's easy to get lost in a busy airport, and conversely, it's easy to follow someone unnoticed, in such a place ----oh well.

I made my way to the United Shuttle flight 2380 to San Francisco, departing at gate E-6. The rolling walkway was moving at a slower pace than the foot traffic along side, but it gave me a good opportunity to casually glance around to see if I could spot someone that *had to have* my beautiful briefcase.

Flight 2380 boarded at 10:05AM, and considering I had a first class ticket, I was the second person to board. The gate attendant greeted me with a broad smile and a 'Good morning' as I made my way through the tunnel walkway to the plane. I always have to duck my head as I enter the plane. Experience dictates that if I make conversation with the attendant at the door and lose my concentration, I end up with a large goose egg, square on my forehead. This is particularly true if the attendant is an attractive young lady, not that I'm interested. This time the attendant is a man, which insures that my cranium will remain unscathed.

Seat 2-B was a second row aisle seat and an excellent location to see every face boarding the aircraft. I was looking for that little suspicious man I encountered in the elevator last night, since he was my best and only suspect at this time. After checking out every passenger, there wasn't one *little suspicious man*. 'Maybe in San Francisco' I thought, but hoped not.

CHAPTER 14

Flight 2389 arrived at 12:10 P.M. and I was pleased to see that I wasn't greeted by my *little man* at the gate. The San Francisco Airport was bustling as usual, and I kept an eye out for someone that might be following me, however when I walked in any direction I found that half the people were following or leading me anyway----so that theory goes out the window.

I went down to the baggage claim area to retrieve my bag, not that I didn't trust United to transfer it to Delta at the International Terminal. I just wanted to relieve them of that responsibility. It arrived as I had hoped and I grabbed it from the belt and went back to the United Shuttle gates and checked on Valarie's flight that was scheduled to arrive at 1:30 P.M. The monitor showed it arriving on time at Gate 84. Since it probably hadn't left yet, I thought, 'how would *they* know it would be on time?'

I had about forty-five minutes to kill before she arrived, so I decided to slip into the bar across the way and have a beer and use my cell phone to check on messages as well as touch base with Art and Tom.

I hadn't checked my voice mail for a couple of days so this was as good a time as ever. I had five messages. One was from the marina wanting to know if I wanted to schedule service on my boat. I called them and said it was a good time to do it, with my real motive to have someone actually check on it while Valarie and I were both gone. Two calls were Shasta buddies wanting me to meet them at some cove to go bass fishing. One was a hang up and the final was from Phil Hampton at 9:00AM this morning, asking that I give him a call at the TechX office.

Interesting, I wonder what's on his mind----best give him a call.

I dialed TechX and of course got Miss Smiley. "This is Chuck Winters returning Phil Hampton's call". I said with my own smiley voice.

"Just a moment Mr. Winters", she said as she beamed me up to Phil.

"Hi Chuck."

"You called?"

"Oh, right, I was just checking in to see if you knew anything more about Denton. I understand that Brian is doing some work on the first-phase procedures." He offered with a tentative tone. "Right, I asked him to update me on the progress----and I don't know anything new on Denton, do you?"

"No not a thing."

"Is there something you need, your message gave me the impression there was some information you had or something was new?"

"No, not at all, I just wanted to know if there was something I could be doing to assist you while you're gone. Where did you say you were going?"

"I didn't, but if you need something or have some information, please e-mail me. I often forget to check my voice mail."

"I sure will." Phil said as he hung up.

What a weird call, I thought.

I ordered a beer and a turkey sandwich on what else--- - San Francisco sour dough bread. The snack bar was busy with travelers grabbing a late lunch between flights, and it felt relatively safe as I saw no little man looking at me.

I called Tom Claudius, and he was out. Betty was her normal friendly self, even after she went to the trouble of e-mailing me the entire TechX insurance policy, which I hadn't even opened yet. "Hi Chuck, did you get my e-mail insurance policy, you know the one that is one hundred and forty two pages long?"

"Betty, besides calling for Tom, I wanted to thank you for that. I know it was a lot of work----."

"Do you Chuck?" She asked with a fake flavor of vinegar in her tone.

"Betty my sweetheart, you know I'm doing none of this stuff for me, I'm only doing it for Tom. You also know me well enough that if this assistance to Tom wasn't very important, I would never ask for it. I also know what a pain in the butt, scanning into the computer the number of pages involved was. I wouldn't know where to start if I were doing it, but it was very helpful and I really appreciate what you----"

"Chuck, knock it off. I get the picture. I know you appreciate it and I was out of line by making a big deal about it. Truce----OK?"

"Betty there's no need for a truce. I wasn't listening to your bitching and moaning in the first place." I said, chuckling.

"You just never change, do you?" She responded, teasingly. "How do you keep that lovely Valarie? I don't see how she puts up with you?"

"Betty, she loves me just like you do, and why wouldn't she?" I popped back.

"Chuck, you're absolutely right, although I hate to admit it----particularly the part about me. I'll tell Tom you called and will be checking in when you get a chance. Be safe."

"Thanks Betty, as always you're a doll----see ya." I said and punched off.

CHAPTER 15

It was time to order another cool one, and call Art for my information fix. I dialed Art's back line, and just my luck his recording said he was out for the rest of the day and to leave a message.

"Art, Chuck, sorry I missed you. You must be doing something important for me----like saving my rear. I'm at the San Francisco Airport and will be leaving for Hong Kong in a couple of hours. If you pick up, before say 5:00 P.M., call me on my cell."

I was watching the clock for Valarie's flight to arrive----another five minutes. I really missed her, not so much from the time apart standpoint, which has been less than a week, but more for the events that have occurred in the last couple of days that made it seem like months since I last saw her. She's always good company, and fun to be with. She's very bright, with a personality that's a combination of caustic and loving, both in the right measure. I just hate to bring her into this mess and have to give her the opportunity to back out of this trip, considering that things have become
much more dangerous than when I first asked her to travel with me to Hong Kong.

Her flight was announced and I anxiously pushed my way to the front where the doors would soon open and the passengers would deplane. Since I booked a first class seat for her little hop down from Redding, I expected her to be first off the plane, which she wasn't. Not first, second or at all. Everyone was off the plane and no Valarie. I checked with the ticket agent and got nothing. I quickly went to Security and gave the guy the retired San Francisco detective routine, which always works in the brotherhood, even with security cops. He walked me over to the counter and inquired about Valarie. The agent glared at me for pulling rank, but told us that she was a no show at the airport.

I called the Redding Airport and spoke with Aaron Jackson, an ex-NFL football player and head of security. He and I met several times when Tom charted jets and landed at the Redding airport. He also knew Valarie. "Aaron, Chuck Winters, I've got a problem. I'm worried. Valarie was supposed to fly out on the 1:00PM United flight to San Francisco. She didn't catch the plane, and since this little job I'm working on for a friend is becoming very dangerous, I hope and pray it hasn't spilled over to her. She'd call if she missed the plane for any reason. Can you check it out from your end and also see if her green Porsche is in the parking lot?"

"Chuck, I'm on it----your cell the same? I'll call you in fifteen minutes, glad to help." Aaron said firmly.

"Yes it is, and thanks Aaron." I said and punched off.

'I can't go and leave her now. I'll have to take another flight, she's more important to me than this deal or anything else.' I thought to myself. I called her home-studio, with no pick-up after a dozen or so rings.

What a helpless feeling, however there was one more thing that I could do and that was to call Chief Marino in Redding, and ask him to send someone over to Valarie's house and see what they can find there. Maybe she's sick or hurt herself. After checking in with the Chief, who Valarie and I met last summer when his fishing boat motor stalled near my houseboat. I received his assurance that he would also put out a description of her car and plate number, which he said he could get from her name and address on the police computer network. I gave him my cell number and he hung up. He probably was using my software, I thought.

My cell phone rang and I hurriedly pushed a button to answer. It was Aaron, with negatives all the way around. No check in at the terminal, and no Porsche in the parking lot. A few minutes later, Chief Marino called. He had a car out at Valarie's house and it looked in order. Her car was gone. I asked him if I gave him the location of her hidden key, could his man go through the house and see if anything was amiss. "No problem, as long as the key belongs to you and you're authorizing entry to the house."

"It's my key," I said, playing this little technicality charade.

"Ok, he's going in." The chief said.

"Call me back when he's done?"

"Sit tight a couple of minutes----you can have your report right now."

He came back on the line and said, "Everything looks ship shape in there. Are you sure she just didn't change her mind about meeting you?"

"She would have called me."

It was approaching 2:30PM and no word from anyone, and my cell rang again. I grabbed for it and hit the button.

"Chuck what in the hell is going on?" Valarie yelled into the phone.

"Oh my God, I've been worried out of my mind. What happened? Where are you? Are you all right?"

"I'm fine. I just crossed the Bay Bridge, so I'm a few minutes away from the airport. I just thought a high-speed run down I-5 would be more fun." She said in her normal caustic manner.

"Come on, what's really going on?" I asked with a not unmistakable sternness in my voice.

"I was leaving the house to head to the airport----when a car, a white Ford, looked like a rental car, tried to block the road just a couple of hundred feet past my driveway toward I-5. He was definitely looking for me, because when I pulled out of my driveway and headed his way, he pulled from the side of the road into the center, blocking the entire road. So you know me, I won't put

up with that shit, and shot off the road and up the hill and around him. I threw the little green monster into second and laid about fifty feet of rubber on that old potholed road. By the time he turned around, I was ripping down the windy road toward the highway doing about seventy, with him several hundred yards back. When I got to I-5, I headed south toward Redding about 90 MPH, never a cop when I want one. I turned off at Airport Road and he saw where I turned. After I crossed over the overpass, I skidded into that little surface road that runs next to the highway, pulled over and waited for him to go over the overpass and head east toward the airport where he thought I went. Then I jumped back on the freeway when he was out of sight, and barreled down to San Francisco. I didn't call the police, because I didn't think it would do any good, and besides I'd miss our flight. Anymore questions?" She asked. I would guess with that typical smirk on her face.

"I guess that pretty well covers it, you're one gutsy lady."

"Hey---- do you think you're going to get out of taking me to Hong Kong that easy? Are you sure that wasn't one of your buddies trying to discourage me?" She teased.

Ignoring the comment, "Did you see who was in the car? Was he alone? What did he look like? Was he a little guy?" I peppered the questions at her-----now that I knew she was OK.

"Hold on there fella, I didn't see anything, I was more interested in getting the hell away. Can you possibly understand that?" Valarie asked with her normal direct approach.

"Park your car; I'm going to head to Delta at the International Terminal and meet you there, is that all right with you?

"That's fine, I'll see you there."

"Hey, I'm sure glad you're OK, I was really worried *before* your escape story. If I had known what you were really going through, I'd have probably had a heart attack."

"See ya soon." Valarie said as she signed off.

I grabbed my suitcase and briefcase and headed for the nearest terminal door, looking for the International Terminal shuttle. The sun was shining, the air was fresh and you could smell the sea rolling in from the bay. The shuttle bus came within a couple of minutes and I was rolling toward the terminal. It was packed and a third of the passengers were standing in the aisle. When we reached the Delta terminal I went to the ticket counter and checked in so I would only have to deal with Valarie's ticket when she arrived.

I went back outside to wait for Valarie and stood among the smokers. After about ten minutes of pacing, the shuttle pulled up in front and out stepped the most beautiful woman. She had streaked blonde hair, blue eyes, nice even tan, five foot nine, a beautiful figure, dressed in a green silk blouse with the first three buttons unbuttoned, a long white skirt with a slit up the side and green heels. Every eye was on her, and yes her name is Valarie.

I kissed her with a passion that I think even surprised her. It came partly from missing her and partly from almost losing this woman that I truly loved. Picking up her bag in my left hand I put my right arm around her waist and we moved toward the ticket counter. She smelled like a dream with a fragrance that had become part of my life after wandering into that little art gallery in Mendocino more than a year ago. Valarie had a show of her paintings that weekend at the prestigious White Lilly Gallery. I didn't know at the time that her work was good, very good, but never the less, I bought three of her paintings because she was so beautiful and I wanted to get to know her. After buying the paintings I looked at them really for the first time as she was wrapping her artwork for me. "Isn't that Ski Island on the Pit River on Shasta Lake?"

She was impressed and surprised, and said, "It is! How did you know?"

I said something cool like, "I live there".

"On Ski Island?"

Knowing that no one lived on Ski Island, I must have sounded very stupid to her. "No, I live on a houseboat----on the lake.

"You're kidding, so do I."

"You live on a houseboat on Shasta too?"

Then she laughed. "No, I didn't mean that, what I meant was I live near the lake----in the Jones Valley area."

The next day it was Sunday dinner at the Tale of the Whale Restaurant on "our lake" at Bridge Bay Resort, and then I cooked on my houseboat, and then she cooked at her home, and on and on----.

"Here" She said, handing me my passport. "At least something went according to plan on this exercise."

The timing worked out fine. The Delta flight was running late by about a half hour, we weren't rushed and had a chance to unwind and catch up on the break-ins and other events of the last two days, while sipping cold beer in the small bar near the Delta gate.

I couldn't disregard the seriousness and commitment of the people behind the attacks on my belongings and the attempt on Valarie this afternoon. There was a very sophisticated on-going effort with a depth and breadth I had no way of evaluating. I've clearly been lucky, and my timing and that of Valarie's, has been way too close for comfort. A misstep surely would have proven to be disastrous.

My concern for Valarie's safety is such that I just don't know if she is safer at home or with me. I don't want to let her fend for herself at home and I recognize the danger associated with being in a foreign country facing unknown adversaries. There's no easy answer, but *she* needs to make the decision.

Further discussions with her underscored her desire to go forward with this Hong Kong trip and she didn't demonstrate any fear or concern about going, so we made that our final decision. At least while we were waiting for the flight to board ---- it was.

Delta called our flight and I downed my beer while Valarie left a third of hers on the table. Picking up my briefcase I slipped my arm around the familiar curves of Valarie's waist and threaded a route across the now even busier concourse to the Delta gate. We were able to board immediately and upon entering the first class cabin we were greeted by a smiling, very attractive Chinese flight attendant dressed in a red mandarin styled jacket and tailored black slacks. She seated us in 2 A & B and offered to take my briefcase, which I politely declined, "No thanks, I'll need it", and slid it under the seat in front of me.

"Would you care for a cocktail before we depart?"

"That would be very nice," I said as I deferred to Valarie.

"I'd like a Bloody Mary, no salt, please."

"Vodka martini, up please." I answered with a smile.

Remembering my detective days when I had to fly on the job somewhere, I sat in 'last class' and had to search my pockets for cash before I ordered a beer. I was last to board and last to depart. My how things have changed in a few short years.

We received our drinks, which of course were served in crystal glassware, and toasted each other on a safe and wonderful trip. We laughed and agreed not
to use the word exciting, as we've had entirely too much excitement in our lives lately.

The big Delta 747 took off to the east over San Francisco Bay and circled toward the Golden Gate Bridge. To me, the grandness of this view is without equal. The deep azure blue waters of the bay shimmering from the sun's rays dancing over the white caps rolling in from the sea, is a sight I and most observers never tire of. It causes me to reflect on how proud I am of my country, and represents to me a symbol of how strong and resilient our democracy has been during its history of trials, tribulations and amazing success and progress.

"I never take off without feeling a sense of awe when I see that sight, isn't it beautiful, almost as much as you?" I added with my normal subtle charm.

"Yeah, right, what do you want now?" She asked with her typical response to a compliment----from me. "Seriously, I'd really love to paint this view, from this very spot."

"No problem, all you'd need is a helicopter to hang you here in the flight path, while you do your canvas magic. Of course, you'd have to duck now and then when the San Francisco Air Traffic Controllers take pot shots at your chopper." I laughed.

I could not forget about the difficult position we were in, where who knows who is after us, in two states, with a strong suspicion that the chase will not end at the Golden Gate Bridge. Either we're too close to the answers or someone thinks we are. Or they think I already have the answers and need to stop me or divert my effort by abducting Valarie----causing me to stop my investigation and find her. Maybe she's better off with me rather than being alone. It was clear today she's an easy target, although quite to their surprise, a slippery one.

The first class cabin was about half-full, and with heightened alertness I didn't sense any problems with fellow passengers in this section. Since I couldn't see the boarding passengers in the coach section, I had no way of knowing if the 'little man' was aboard, and wouldn't have any way of identifying any other conspirator that might be working with him. I did however bring a group picture of TechX's management team in order to try and get the Hong Kong informant to pick out Jaxton from the group. I could pick out *Jaxton* easy enough if he were on the plane, but doubted that would even be a possibility.

Valarie was looking out the window. The sun was very intense and the blue sky clear, with only an occasional scattered pink puffy cloud passing by. I sat there mesmerized by the profile of fresh honest beauty she presented, when the flight attendant came over and jolted me to my senses asking, "Would you care for another cocktail?" We politely accepted as she handed us a dish of snack crackers and assorted nuts.

"Are you tired,"

"No, although I should be exhausted after the Indy 500 race I ran this afternoon." She grinned and reached for my hand resting on the center armrest. "Do you think we're really in danger? That was quite scary --- right by my house. Who would know about me and how would someone find my house up in the hills? I'm not in the book you know."
"Sweetie I don't know, but I promise you I'll find and catch the bastards." I replied with conviction. "I think the guy or guys that broke into my rooms are trying to either scare me away or find out how much I know. There

are millions missing from the TechX accounts, and the obvious suspect, Jaxton, doesn't necessarily fit the evidence I have. But that doesn't mean he couldn't. I think we're dealing with more than first-time amateur crooks. This isn't a one-man job, and the information tentacles they appear to possess reach effectively wherever they want."

"I hate to admit it but I'm a little scared." She said, looking at me with obvious concern.

"I need to call Art Levy and update him and also see if he knows anything new on this thing before we leave telephone range." I ran my credit card through the slot on the seat phone and dialed Art's home number. He answered and I filled him in on the recent events with Valarie. He was very concerned how conditions had worsened. He was calling Mr. Sun in Hong Kong and having him assemble a security team to meet us at the airport, and stay with us the entire time we're there. He said he was still waiting on the research, and would keep moving forward on the investigation of the break-ins. Add the accosting of Valarie today to the equation. He instructed me again to be careful, because in his opinion 'these people aren't going to back off'.

Valarie excused herself and went to the restroom. The restrooms in the front were all occupied so she went to the restrooms in the rear of the first class section, which were also occupied. "Well, I guess I'll take a stroll to the economy section and see how the other half lives", she mused to herself. She walked down the right side, about half way back and found a vacant restroom and went in. She maneuvered into the tiny stall and turned to lock the door, as someone was pulling on the door handle trying to get in. Valarie grabbed the handle and pushed the door open with her shoulder and shoved a small man against the opposite wall. He quickly scrambled to his feet while several people stood by and scampered around the corner and out of sight. She made a mental note of his description and headed back to first class with a full bladder and an anxiety that wasn't with her twenty-four hours earlier. She wanted to tell Chuck what just happened, but the cry from her bladder won out. The first class restroom visit was a non-event in terms of anxiety, thankfully, and she returned to her seat.

"I thought you went home, are you all right?"

"Well, considering a----how did you describe him----a 'little-man', tried to break into the restroom that I entered. I had to get rough and bounced him
off the wall and onto the ground. He then scampered away like a cockroach in sunlight." She said, describing the events with a hint of glee, now that she was safe again in her seat.

I listened to her recounting of the 'little man' episode, and became a bit concerned, thinking that a friendly stroll through the coach section might give me an appetite for dinner.

"I'm going to take a little walk to the rear and work up an appetite, OK with you?"

"Enjoy your walk. By the way, he's wearing a brown knit shirt and brown slacks." She commented with a slight smirk.

"Who is?" I said, with my own look of gotcha.

I walked down one side and up the other, and didn't see the 'little man' I saw in Oregon, or the man Valarie described during her kickboxing match. Her 'little man' may be in a restroom, or slouched down in a middle seat somewhere, or better yet getting medical attention from his beating by the pretty lady.

I returned to our seats and Valarie was resting her head on a pillow propped against the window, sound asleep. She looked like an angel, exhausted from conflicts large and small that made up her day.

I gently sat down next to her and ordered another drink, explaining that we'll wait to eat dinner. Before long I fell asleep and awakened about an hour later feeling refreshed and a bit hungry. I turned to Valarie; she was awake and smiling as I came to life after my little rest.

The flight was about thirteen hours, and we'd be arriving in Hong Kong around 9:00 P.M. Thursday, the next evening after time-zone changes. Since our internal clocks are going to be upside down and backwards, and considering the unknown threats we may face in Hong Kong, any sleep we can get on the trip over should be considered a welcome bonus.

"Hi Honey, how are you feeling?"

"I feel much better after my little nap, how about you?" She asked.

"Great, after I walked, I slept like a baby."

As we were heading west chasing daylight in a race we could never win, we could still enjoy the beautiful blue sky and bright orange sun a bit longer.

"Are you hungry?" I asked.

"Absolutely, I haven't eaten anything but the snacks served with our drinks, since yesterday." She said as she readied her tray table.

I caught the eye of our attendant and she quickly went about describing our dinner choices. Caesar salad, filet of salmon with rice pilaf for Valarie, and for the gourmet himself, Caesar salad, filet mignon, medium rare, and a baked potato. The nice selection of California wines would wait for later.

We savored our dinner, and afterward Valarie tried to read but was soon nodding off on her pillow against the window. I took a light blanket handed me by the flight attendant and covered her. This was a good time to start evaluating where we were again and what my plan of investigation would be from this point on.

I started by re-thinking what the game plan might be for those involved. If it's Jaxton, and should be by the appearance of the current evidence, he could only be doing this for money. From everything I've learned at this point, it just doesn't fit. If it isn't Jaxton working alone, then the other option is he's partnered up with someone on the inside or not, maybe someone that's forcing him to do this, perhaps blackmail. It could be someone on the inside that's trying to set up Jaxton and make him take the fall for whatever's being done, which I'm not certain of at this time. Aside from the problem with the books, my gut tells me nothing. Could Christine who did the accounting and paid the bills be the responsible party for the missing funds? Or could Christine be working with Jaxton, and planning on meeting him on some far away beach for a cool one with an umbrella in it, while living in obscure luxury for the rest of their lives? Maybe Phil and Christine or Bryan and Phil or Bryan and Jaxton, or Jaxton and Victoria, or----? This is stupid there are too many possibilities. I need to narrow this investigation down a bit, or a lot. I think a clear head would help, maybe a little nap. I pushed in my seat-back control button and leaned back with a pillow and a blanket, setting out to let my sub-conscience solve this caper. What I really need is some *cop stakeout donuts* to make the juices flow.

I awakened around midnight, my time, and noticed that Valarie was awake and reading her mystery novel. "Hi," I said, rubbing my eyes, "are you hungry or thirsty?"

"Well, I hadn't really thought about it, but now that you mention it, can you rustle up some Chinese?" She requested with a little smirk.

"I thought you'd never ask my dear, that's right up my alley." I stood up and stretched, then ambled up to the first class galley and asked, "Do you have take out?"

The young ladies hanging out in the galley area broke into laughter and played along with my lame attempt at midnight entertainment by asking if I had coupons for the half-price combination dinner. At least they hadn't asked me for my senior citizens AARP card.

Our smiling attendant said, "Let's see if we can find a nice assortment of Chinese delicacies for you and your lady. Are you real hungry?"

"I'm always hungry when I see Chinese food, and this looks fantastic." I told her as she opened the steam table covers and displayed at least a dozen different containers. I had no idea what most of the serving pans contained, but the aromas were reminiscent of my many delightful forays into the finest restaurants in San Francisco's Chinatown. Two platters were expertly assembled with an assortment of most of the mysterious, wonderful delights from the steam table.

She suggested that I return to my seat and promised to appear shortly thereafter with my special, surprise *take out order.*

"Your special order sir," she said with a flourish, as she and her associate uncovered the trays and placed the gourmet delight before us on red linen tablecloths, along with matching napkins, sterling silver, and crystal glassware. A small crystal bud vase with a red rose was the fitting final touch for each tray.

Valarie was speechless with delight. The attendants were standing alongside smiling and I just sat there and shrugged. "This is so wonderful, I can't thank you enough for this treat it's just perfect." Valarie responded with her most appreciative smile.

"How did you arrange this, no one else has it?"

"Who me? I said with a smirk, "I don't know a thing about it."

With that, she slugged me on the arm and said, "Don't deny it!"

CHAPTER 16

Art Levy dialed Frank Hixon on his personal line at Hixon & Frontier, Private Detectives in Portland. They've been consulting since they first met in Miami in 1985 at a seminar on high-tech investigative equipment. He brought Frank into Chuck's case when they were trying to find Jaxton's car at the airport. "Frank Hixon."

"Frank, Art here, how goes the Portland battle?"

"Well if you're talking about your case, I don't have anything new. But if you're talking about life in general----not too bad."

"Actually both. I'd like you to do a couple of things for me on this case. One is a hunch that I want you to confirm or deny. I'd like you or one of your technicians to go back to the airport and dust Jaxton's door handles for prints. Don't go inside, this thing may escalate fast and I want us to be as clean as possible if the police are brought in. Second, I'm going to fax you a master list of TechX employees which includes pertinent information including college degrees, etc., and I'd like you to do a quick check on them.

Credit, civil and criminal, and verify education. I just want to know if these people are true or false. I know the employee check will take a day or so, but can you get the car dusted pronto?"

"Art, we'll get on it right away. I'll have the print information to you before noon tomorrow."

"Thanks old buddy, I knew I could count on you."

CHAPTER 17

HONG KONG

The conference table at Knowledge Resource Limited, or KRL as it was known in the community, was occupied by Ho Chi and Billy Wong, the principals of the company, along with Mr. Lee, a rather non-descript small man in a dark suit who was orchestrating the acquisition of a breakthrough, integrated circuit testing software program, that could be worth in the billion dollar plus range in the marketplace. Mr. Chi, dressed in a conservative three-piece gray suit, was in his late fifties, with thinning gray hair and a short trimmed beard. He was a contrast to the quite rotund and short Billy Wong, who in his forties, appeared to be much older. He was bald with a fringe of graying hair ringing his large head. He wore a small gray goatee and was dressed in a gold, silk long sleeved shirt and black slacks.

"Mr. Lee," Chi spoke, "When will the final software protocols be provided by TechX? Your Mr. Jaxton insists on getting his ten million U.S. dollars wired to that Cayman Island Bank----now! I don't trust this deal and I don't want to lose that kind of money. I still don't know why the president of a company, with a breakthrough product that he himself developed, would be willing to sell out his company for ten million dollars when his stock could be worth many times that if the product is as good as everyone says it is. Or, maybe it doesn't work and we are buying a losing deal. What is it Mr. Lee?"

"Mr. Chi, I have told you that Mr. Jaxton is unhappy with the deal he has with the venture capital people. They took most of the stock, and when the company does go public, he'll get such a small portion that he's willing to sell the program now and get his fair share. It's really that simple."

Mr. Chi, stroked his gray trimmed beard and contemplated what he had just heard----and said, "I still don't like this deal, something is wrong."

Billy Wong spoke up for the first time and said, "I understand how the guy feels----he's getting screwed, and this is a way to get his money and screw them while he's doing it. Our people tell me that the tests are complete and the final protocols are being sent, along with the assurance that all of TechX's records will be destroyed, prohibiting them from gearing up and competing with us. When we announce our new product 'breakthrough' in Hong Kong, and take the new company public, our valuations will be worth billions."

"When will we have final assurance from our engineers that we have the complete software program and all protocols we need for this product?" Mr. Chi asked Billy Wong.

"I would say that we'll have everything done by Monday, and then we'll have to wire the money to Jaxton's accounts in the Caymans."

Not trusting anyone, Mr. Chi asked when TechX was going up in flames.

"Jaxton is using that as a little insurance. He won't destroy the remaining records until he knows the money is in his account." Billy Wong said.

"Yes, but what if he doesn't destroy TechX, our potential competition? What can we do if we pay him the money and he doesn't perform?" Mr. Chi inquired as he raised the steaming cup of tea to his lips.

Mr. Wong said emphatically, "He's dead, and he knows it."

CHAPTER 18

FORTY THOUSAND FEET
APPROACHING THE SOUTH CHINA SEA

Valarie awakened after her midnight snack nap. The sun was up and the sky was a brilliant blue. I turned to her and asked if she was ready for breakfast.

"I can't believe it, all we've done is eat since we took off." She answered with an impish look. "Of course I'm ready for breakfast."

We were offered a choice of a Chinese or American breakfast. After breakfast, I felt I should be jogging around the coach section looking for the "little man" just for exercise, but thought I might need my energy and didn't want to risk losing a single calorie.

I pulled my briefcase from under the seat in front and started to review the Jaxton file, provided by One Star. I might have missed something when I glanced through it in Beaverton a couple of days ago, which seems like a lifetime now. The file included Jaxton's resume, which was very impressive. He always progressed in his jobs and was responsible for developing new software as well as improving existing products. The rest of the file was similar in terms of consistency in his career progression.

I only wished that we were about to land for purely a pleasure trip. My only previous trip to Hong Kong was about ten years ago while a detective with the San Francisco Police Department. I was investigating a drug case involving a homicide and interviewing a material witness being held on other charges by the Hong Kong

Police Department. I was in Hong Kong for a week, and thoroughly enjoyed the experience. I discovered the city to be beautiful, alive, bustling with activity, and steeped with history. A city I definitely wanted to return to and thoroughly wanted to explore.

CHAPTER 19

Hong Kong was occupied by the United Kingdom in 1841, and formally ceded by China the following year. Various adjacent lands were added later in the 19th century. Pursuant to an agreement signed by China and the UK on December 19, 1984, Hong Kong became the Hong Kong Special Administrative Region (SAR) or China on July 1, 1997. In this agreement, China has promised that, under its "one country, two systems" formula, China's socialist economic system will not be practiced in Hong Kong, and that Hong Kong will enjoy a high degree of autonomy in all matters except foreign and defense affairs for the next fifty years.

Hong Kong is divided into four main areas---- Kowloon, Hong Kong Island, The New Territories, and about 234 Outlying Islands, consisting of about 750 square kilometers of land, with a population of over 7 million people. The name Hong Kong, originally known as *Heung Gong,* usually translated as "Fragrant Harbor", had its origin in a small settlement now called Aberdeen, and eventually gave the entire island its name. Aberdeen, which was named after a British peer, is a sight any visitor to Hong Kong will consider unforgettable. It is comprised of brightly decorated trawlers, which double as floating homes for Aberdeen's fisher folk. They fill a sheltered harbor whose hillsides are decked with woodland, Chinese cemeteries and residential towers. Visitors can charter sampans or join guided tours for close-up views of the fishing fleet, and Aberdeen's famous, multi-decked floating restaurants. I'm anxious to show Valarie the "Imperial" décor and thousands of colorful lights with gilded dragons and carved wood that are incorporated into the floating restaurants. The restaurants are, from my first hand experience, as attractive as their Cantonese cuisine and fresh seafood is delicious.

Victoria, commonly known as Hong Kong Island, is one of the most densely populated areas on earth. Its business hub is Central District, on the north side across the bay from Kowloon. Just east of Central is Wan Chai, once a sailors playground and still a great place for dining and nightlife, not to forget the cultural parts of life encompassed in the Museum of Chinese Historical Relics. Causeway Bay is to the east of Wan Chai, home of the beautiful Victoria Park, replete with weekend performers, lantern and flower festivals and a variety of free entertainment. The high rises that have risen from the island provide beautiful views of the harbor but have taken away much of its picturesque residential quality. Right next to Central to the west is the Western District, the first area settled by the British. This area has a significant amount of Chinese influence and is the home to many Chinese artisans. Here you can buy everything from herbs and ginseng at roadside shops and stalls, to furniture and jewelry. I'm certain that the artist in Valarie will be drawn to the Western District and in particular the Western Market, a reconstructed Edwardian building that sells specialty items like fabrics, and Hollywood Road where Chinese porcelain, rosewood and blackwood furniture can be found.

The New Territories are to the north of Hong Kong Island, or Victoria, and situated between the Kowloon Hills and the land border with Mainland China. More than three million people live in the New Territories, many in handsomely landscaped 'New Towns', many with performing arts, sports and community centers. Much of The New Territories remains an unspoiled rural land dotted with ancient villages and fishing harbors, duck farms and fishponds, in keeping with an abiding sense of harmony with nature.

My first visit to these beautiful surroundings was with Virgil Duncan, a British police sergeant major in the Hong Kong Police Department. Virgil and I drove through this magnificent countryside early one September morning. We encountered many scenes that will forever remain in my memory, one of which was that of an elderly Chinese duck farmer, wearing loose dark ballooning pantaloons and a large flowing shirt, carrying a walking or herding pole, half again as high as his slight body, while he maneuvered the quacking and swaying waddling ducks, perhaps fifty or more toward another pond or field. I had to think that this same sight had repeated itself for a thousand years or more with little variation. It made me and my activities seem very insignificant in the greater scheme of life.

CHAPTER 20

With a squeal of tires, the big Delta 747 touched down at Chet Lap Kok, the Hong Kong airport. Just prior to touchdown the pilot announced the time at 9:15 P.M. Thursday evening and the temperature, after my mental centigrade gymnastics, was the equivalent of about 75 degrees Fahrenheit.

Valarie and I gathered our belongings which consisted of her purse and my briefcase. We stood and headed toward the first class exit door where our favorite attendant stood smiling in her handsome tailored Chinese outfit. We expressed our gratitude for the kindness she showed during our flight and particularly for the extraordinary 'midnight snack' she assembled for us.

After clearing customs and passing into the general terminal area, we were approached by three Chinese men dressed in suits and two of them looking for the most part, menacing. The smallest of the three walked forward and inquired, "Mr. Winters?"

"Who's asking?" I asked with some trepidation.

"Mr. Sun," he said as he extended his hand. "Art Levy asked me to meet you and provide around the clock security during your stay in Hong Kong."

"Mr. Sun, how did you recognize me?"

Mr. Sun reached in his pocket and retrieved a photograph that appeared to come from my California driver's license. "Art e-mailed this to me this afternoon."

I looked carefully at the e-mail. It appeared to be authentic and contained Art's correct e-mail address. "Mr. Sun I really appreciate your help on this case as well as the security. It looks like I'm in good care." I said as I looked at these obviously former or present power lifters, with twenty-inch necks and shaved heads. I guess the shiny heads reduce airflow resistance when chasing after the bad guys. I'm sure their loose fitting suits hide more weapons than their arms and legs.

"I must inform you," spoken by Mr. Sun in perfect English, and nodding to his associates, "that Mr. Lee and Mr. Hong speak little English, but make up for this deficiency by their many talents." He finished his statement with a very wide smile. Picking up on their boss's grin, my 'trained nurses' broke out in smiles that proved to be infectious to us. Here we were, five fools, blocking traffic at the gate and grinning from ear to ear for no apparent reason. Oh well!

Mr. Sun said he would accompany us to our hotel and see that we are checked in. He would leave our care to our new best and closest friends, Mr. Lee and Mr. Hong. The cab ride over from the airport on Lantao Island to the Royal Imperial Hotel in the Central District of Hong Kong, took about thirty- five minutes. The right-hand drive cab, moving through the busy traffic on the left hand side of the road, could be a bit confusing for first time visitor/drivers to the country. During this ride, which would have been more cramped, Mr. Hong followed in a second cab, not only for comfort but for security reasons.

I asked Mr. Sun what the Friday schedule was in terms of interviewing the informant. He indicated that he was taking extra precautions, and would contact Mr. Hong in the morning and give us some notice on a meeting time and place that would not be fixed until that time. He also explained that Mr. Hong knows enough English to communicate the basics, so not to be concerned.

In hushed serious tones, Mr. Sun said, "Art called me just before we left for the airport and wanted you to know that he had Mr. Jaxton's car dusted for prints at the Portland airport, and found that the door surfaces and handles had been wiped clean. There was not even a smudged print to be found in any place where there should have been. He also spoke with Jaxton's doctor who called his pharmacy and found there was no insulin picked up, nor was there a request to him from any other pharmacy. This is why he is so concerned about your safety, as this case has taken a serious turn".

I looked at him and was stunned by the information. It was clear that the chance that Jaxton was responsible for the events that have transpired had been substantially diminished. Of course, it would be perfect cover for Jaxton to wipe clean his car, and use cash for everything as well as a different name and a new doctor to treat his medical needs, but somehow it seems a bit much to swallow. "Well that sure changes my thinking. The meeting tomorrow morning takes on an even greater importance."

"Art feels that there may be so much at stake in this case for the perps, that murder may already be a foregone conclusion, and may already have occurred. He feels that you have been given enough warnings without backing down, and that from here on out the warnings could be of a permanent nature for you, and now Miss Austin." He sternly indicated.

I looked at Valarie and saw the look of concern on her face. "Chuck, are we in serious danger here in Hong Kong?"

"I don't know honey, but I'm not going to take any chances." I replied, with half-hearted conviction in my voice. "I'm sure glad that Mr. Sun's two men are going to be around."

"Art suspects that somehow they'll be tracking you down here in Hong Kong. We better be prepared. You'll need a gun while you're here, and I've already cleared this with my contact at the Hong Kong Police Department. You have a permit as a temporary employee of my firm. I had to provide him with your SFPD resume and a reference at the department, which Art was kind enough to provide me, so you are all set. I have a nice 9-millimeter for you, with a shoulder holster, your permit, two clips and a box of shells." Mr. Sun took the items from his briefcase and handed them to me.

"Thanks so much, I can't tell you how much I appreciate the job you're doing."

"Glad to do it. Art is a real good friend and has never let me down."

Both Red Taxis pulled up to the front door of the Royal Imperial Hotel. Mr. Sun arranged for two rooms, one for his team and the adjoining one for us. He insisted that our room be at the end of a hall and his men next door. His schedule called for one to be out in the hall at all times, and the other in the next room, either sleeping or spelling the man in the hall as needed. There would be no room service, and anything needed to be brought to the room would be picked up and delivered by the off duty man.

Valarie and I were getting hungry about 11:00 P.M. and went down to one of the hotel restaurants for a late dinner with our 'nurses', who sat at another table with good all around visibility.

The dinner menu was extensive however for us non-linguistic folks, the pictures next to the menu items saved the day. Valarie selected a dinner that had green vegetables, fried shrimp and what appeared to be a fried rice dish and some kind of noodle bowl. I in turn had what appeared to be a Kung Pau chicken dish, along with maybe egg-foo young, and fried rice---I guess. In any event, after we assured ourselves that the waiter didn't speak English, we pointed and ordered. Since we weren't certain about how to order a cocktail, we sort of used sign language and both ordered vodka on the rocks.

I nodded to Mr. Hong and Mr. Lee, and they smiled and nodded back. Amazing, this communication indicates that we've broken the language barrier. I did notice that they were able to order dinner without looking at the menu, and with what appeared to be telepathic communication.

"Well, here we are in beautiful downtown Hong Kong. Me in my duster and you with your 9 millimeter." Valarie joked. "Do you really think the harassment will follow us here?"

"I don't know, but what Art just found out doesn't make me want to let my guard down. These people, or this person, is serious, and has already stolen two and a half million bucks. Considering there's potentially a lot more money involved here in Hong Kong, the action just has to shift here. Or maybe the action is really concentrated where *I am* at any given moment. My guess is, the only reason to harass or silence me is to buy time, and then after money is transferred they don't care.

I'm amazed that they have such an intelligence network when it comes to staying on top of my activities. I don't think they know about Art, and that really helps."

The drinks came and were soon followed by the dinners. I've heard that the finest restaurants in Hong Kong are located in the hotels and not for the most part in independent stand-alone operations. In this case what I heard is true, the food was exceptional and the service was the same. We truly enjoyed our dinners.

We finished our meals, and before our check came, Mr. Lee disappeared and Mr. Hong sat smiling at us while constantly surveying the room. The waiter brought our check, and I was about to sign my name, and hesitated when I saw the $450.00 dinner tab, then realized that it was Hong Kong dollars which equate to about $7.50 per one dollar US, which was a little more like it, approximately $60.00, plus tip.

We left the table and strolled out into the lobby, which was ornate in gold and red, with abundant carvings of lions, snakes and other wild things. The walls were mirrored and the ceilings were perhaps thirty feet high with a very ornate, gold painted mezzanine balcony surrounding the large room. The floor was carpeted with beautiful oriental patterns and looked very expensive. The room was busy with activity, however, the noise level was muted, perhaps due to the plush carpets and high ceilings, or maybe because the beauty of the surroundings caused a decorum that was in keeping with such splendor.

All this time, while we were gawking at the lobby rooms, Mr. Hong, appeared to be having a difficult time assimilating the various people crossing our paths from every which direction, and making judgments as to friend or foe. As a result, I nodded to him that we were going to take the elevator back to our room and rid him of his discomfort.

We pushed the elevator button and one of five doors opened in the lobby. Mr. Hong walked in after we did, and nearly filled the space to capacity, which was fine with me. Two other men also squeezed in and faced the front. Mr. Hong gave them his trained eye and was positioned to knock their heads together if they even looked sideways. Luckily for them and us too, they exited at four and we continued our ride to the tenth floor. The doors opened and we moved to the right, but not so far that Mr. Hong hadn't brushed past us like a bull moose, and surveyed the hallway ahead. We turned the corner and followed him to our wing, where he stopped suddenly. Mr. Lee was not standing by our door where Mr. Hong apparently expected him. He motioned us to stand against the wall and held his hand out for our card key, which I easily understood and handed to him, as he moved toward the door. He listened with his ear to the door and apparently hearing nothing. He carefully slid the key into the slot as the green light lit indicated the door was unlocked. With gun drawn he quickly pushed the door open and stood there blocking our view like a wall. He then, with an appearance from our perspective to be at the ready, swiftly moved into the room swinging his gun arm back and forth while surveying the space. I moved into the doorway, catching the door before it automatically closed and saw what looked like Mr. Lee, crumpled on the floor, blood pooling around his head.

I motioned to Valarie to stand back, and entered the room with gun in hand, surveying the situation. The room had been searched or was in the process of being searched when Mr. Lee apparently came back from the restaurant ahead of us, and using the cardkey I gave Mr. Hong at check in, was about to inspect our room before we returned. He apparently encountered the person or persons responsible for his death, the moment he entered the room, less than fifteen minutes earlier. Upon examining Mr. Lee, he had one small caliber wound in the back of his head, apparently from close range, and probably died instantly because of the lack of significant blood pooling on the carpet, indicating that his heart almost immediately stopped pumping.

Mr. Hong had a look of anger interspersed with sadness. It appeared that he and Mr. Lee had been the closest of friends. He pulled out his cell phone and called someone, spoke in Chinese and handed me the phone. It was Mr. Sun, who said he was calling the police, and wanted us to stay there until he arrived, and he'd move us to a safe location.

Valarie appeared to be in a state of shock, but kept up a good front by saying, "I just feel so bad for Mr. Lee, I wonder if he has a wife and family."

"Mr. Sun is on his way and has called the Hong Kong police; everyone will be here in a short time." I said in an attempt to bring some order to the chaos I was beginning to feel. This thing was spinning out of control fast, and needed to come to a conclusion.

Mr. Hong pulled himself together and carefully looked around the room without walking around disturbing evidence. He was truly a professional, and had gained my respect. Drawers were pulled open and clothes were strewn about the floor. Within a couple of minutes, the hotel security arrived at the room, perhaps informed by Mr. Sun or the Hong Kong Police. The security man asked everyone to wait in the hall while he pulled the door closed. We just stood there not being able to really communicate, however I went over to Mr. Hong and touched his arm, looked him in the eyes and said I'm sorry about Mr. Lee. He understood and nodded with a sad face.

The Hong Kong police arrived en masse, with an Inspector in command and at least ten other officers including their forensics crew. They went to work in the room where Mr. Lee's body lay, while we were taken into Mr. Hong's room for questioning. Valarie stood by my side while the Inspector spoke in elevated tones in Chinese with Mr. Hong. After a minute or two, apparently Mr. Hong was able to get his story across. Things appeared to calm down as the two continued talking until Mr. Sun arrived. He immediately moved toward the Inspector, who seemed to know him quite well. At that point the mood in the room lost the sharp edge of tenseness that usually accompanies a fresh homicide scene.

Mr. Sun walked over to us, looking Valarie square in the eyes, asked, "How are you holding up?"

She looked like she had her emotions under control and replied, "I'm doing fine. I'm really sorry about Mr. Lee, did he have a family?"

"Mr. Lee was not married, however Mr. Hong was his cousin, and he's naturally very upset with this situation."

I asked Mr. Sun if the Inspector wanted to speak with us, and he said "I don't think it's necessary at the moment. Inspector Li was previously aware of you and your reason for being in Hong Kong. He was the friend that helped me secure your temporary gun permit. They're going to want to know a lot more about this case before long, so if you intend to keep this somewhat quiet in order to get some answers, we have to move fast with our investigation before the police get too deeply involved."

Valarie turned to Mr. Sun and said, "How can we be safe, anywhere? These people seem to know where we are at all times!"

"I'm about to get to the bottom of this, and that's why I have two technicians waiting for me in the hotel lobby. But first, I need another word with Inspector Li, a moment please." He said as he moved toward the Inspector, who was speaking with Mr. Hong again. They whispered a few words. Mr. Li shouted something to one of his people and Mr. Sun turned to us and said, "Please come with me."

We followed him to the door of our room, where he asked us to wait. A minute or so later, he and the policeman were carrying our two bags out the door. Valarie turned to me and said, "Where's your briefcase?"

"I guess you didn't notice, when I checked in I asked the clerk to put my briefcase in the hotel safe. I didn't want to worry about it until tomorrow."

Mr. Sun appeared pleased with my foresight and said we would go to a private room he had arranged before he came up to the tenth floor. The elevator arrived and the three of us stepped in along with our bags and proceeded to the Lobby floor. When we walked off the elevator, two men moved toward us. Mr. Sun nodded and with his head silently directed them to follow us to the rear of the lobby and down a hall to a closed door. He took a card key from his pocket, inserted it in the slot, and stood aside while we stepped in. The room was about thirty feet long and had a conference table in the center surrounded by red velvet chairs.

"Please place your personal bags on the table, and stand back for a moment." We did so, and his technicians opened their briefcases and removed some equipment with gauges and a wand device. They did some initial calibrating and moved to the closed suitcases. First they swept the wand back and forth above Valarie's suitcase, with no apparent response from their equipment. As they were doing this, I said to myself "how could I have been so stupid". They then moved to my suitcase, and a high pitch developed as the wand passed back and forth. They then looked at me and I signaled with my facial expression and extended open palms to go ahead and open the suitcase and go through my things. The signal honed in on the lining of my new suitcase on wheels, near the inside top where the handle was attached and secured. After further examination they removed a small device, half the size or a dime that was attached with a sticky substance in a fabric tear of about one-half inch long. The next device was in the cuff of a pair of pants that I purchased and hadn't worn.

Mr. Sun's technicians explained that this was the very latest global positioning system transmitting devices, so sophisticated that they transmit in buildings and can be picked up by satellite wherever they are, world wide. The CIA hasn't even equipped their people with these devices because they're so new as well as expensive.

"I guess this explains why I've been tracked everywhere I went except the Sheraton Airport Hotel in Portland, because my suitcase spent the night at the Beaverton hotel." I said, with disgust for my total lack of insight into the possibility of a GPS device tracking me.

"I'm going to disarm one of the two and see if I can trace it back to the purchaser. The second device is being sent out in the morning by Federal Express to the US embassy in Zurich, Switzerland to throw them off the scent. The embassy will be so confused that they'll probably send it to the CIA in Langley for them to inspect. Over night, it will be stored in a lead box to capture all signal transmissions. Whoever is responsible will think that your suitcase is in a basement two hundred feet below ground level and not effectively transmitting. When the transmissions start again in the morning on the Federal Express plane, they'll feel they are in control again." Mr. Sun explained.

"I should have known." I said to the group.

Mr. Sun responded, "It's unlikely that anyone would have known about the capabilities of these GPS devices, unless they're involved in the latest cutting edge surveillance techniques." He said as he kindly bailed me out of my stupidity.

"Where to now?"

"I think I'll take you to my home. I have a guest suite that should suit you, and I'm no longer worried about eyes in the sky. But before we go, I'd like to have my technicians sweep your persons to be sure you're not carrying a third device. Also, let's retrieve your briefcase from the safe and check it out just to be certain."

The sweep on our persons was negative, as was my briefcase. We left the hotel at 1:25 A.M., through the rear door and got into Mr. Sun's new right hand drive Jaguar, along with our non-threatening luggage.

We drove through the Central District and headed south toward Victoria Peak. We'd driven for about five minutes, and during this time Mr. Sun was continually looking in the rear view mirror. He made a sharp right and after a few blocks turned left into a residential area. He drove down street, and I was thinking how close in he lived in the Central District. He pulled into the driveway of a modest home, halfway down the long block and electronically opened a garage door and drove into the darkened garage. We sat in the dark for a moment, and then silently the back of the garage opened up and Mr. Sun drove out onto the street in the rear, turned right and continued on his way without a concern of someone following.

He continued south up into the hills and then turned west toward the sea. On a wooded hillside, Mr. Sun pulled off the narrow road onto an unmarked gravel road, through the trees and suddenly emerged onto a concrete drive that wound around the hillside and finally onto a large brick apron offering sweeping views of the harbor below and the lights of Kowloon in the distance. Mr. Sun's home was indicative of the success he has achieved in his highly respected business. The harbor side was three stories of glass dropping down the mountainside, with the top story, and front entry, nestled into the hillside. A large brick plaza leading from the entry-drive encircled an illuminated pool featuring a spouting lion surrounded by abundant flowering plants and trees.

When Mr. Sun pulled onto the beautiful plaza area, lights automatically were illuminated. As he stepped from his car, the front door opened and a white- jacketed older man walked over, bowed subtly to Mr. Sun, and listened to his obvious requests to welcome us to his home and deliver our bags to the guest room.

Mr. Sun said we'd be safe, not because the sensors were removed, nor due to his evasive action, but because of the fact that he had a highly trained and armed security staff, operating around the clock, seven days a week at his home.

We walked up to the ten-foot high double doors finished in a lustrous Chinese red lacquer. The doors contained a four-foot circle of glass, split in half by the joining doors and offering a clear view through the home at the twinkling lights in the harbor below and Kowloon beyond. The home was truly breathtaking, however Mr. Sun's professionalism witnessed so far, causes me little surprise that his personal achievements reflected in part by this truly magnificent symbol of success would be anything less.

Mr. Sun's manservant led us into the entry, where the teak walls were enhanced by the cool jade green marble floor. We followed him down a hallway of thick white carpet and continued on to a wide staircase that took us down to the next level. The hallway had dozens of small soft lights imbedded in the ceiling giving a look of stars, which lighted the hallway like moonlight on a white sandy beach. He stopped before a door, turned the handle and allowed Valarie and I to walk in. The wall ahead was nothing but glass, at least twelve feet high, and the décor scheme from the hallway continued into the suite with white carpet and teak paneled walls. The bed was king-sized, with an elegant peacock blue silk bedspread, placed on a pedestal surrounded by steps of white carpet on three sides, and was truly the most beautiful bedroom suite I had ever seen. The furniture was minimal but elegant, and in the bathroom, the floors were dark emerald green veined marble, with white marble fixtures and gold hardware. The walls were also teak, except that the shower and separate tub faced a floor to ceiling glass window that overlooked the harbor below and in the distance the outer islands.

Valarie and I stood in awe as the small man bowed while backing out of the doorway. Mr. Sun then appeared and asked, "Is everything acceptable?"

"Your home is magnificent, as is this suite. I know we're intruding and I apologize."

"You're not intruding, you are my guest. I feel terrible that you were subjected to such a horrible event this evening at the hotel that I selected, and in the company of my handpicked security people." He stated with seriousness.

"We'll make arrangements for other accommodations first thing in the morning."

"Nonsense. You will stay here as my guest. It's the only place I truly feel I can protect you. Enough of this, you must be exhausted and need to get some sleep. We'll meet the informant in the morning. I have yet to decide where it will be. Do you need anything? Food, drinks?"

"Mr. Sun, we have everything we need. Thank you again for your kindness."

"Good night, then." Mr. Sun said as he closed the door behind him.

After events this evening and the last day or so, Valarie was tired and if the truth were to be known, so was I. Therefore our magical opportunity for lovemaking in these surroundings would wait for another time.

We stripped to the skin, tossed our clothes on a nearby love seat and climbed the stairs to our luxurious bed. She slid into my arms, kissed me and said she now felt safe. A minute or so later she was softly breathing and in a deep sleep.

CHAPTER 21

The next morning I awakened at 7:30 A.M. local time and couldn't believe the storybook picture unfolded before my eyes. Chinese junks of all sizes, colors and designs, and sampans of every variety were effortlessly making their way around the harbor below the property. The sky was blue with a scattering of high puffy clouds dancing above the nautical ensemble. Rays of sunlight caught the brightly colored junks as they danced on the soft easy waves, pushing them endlessly to and fro as they went about their purpose.

There was a soft knock at the door and I modestly drew the covers to my chest. "Come in."

Valarie was just stirring as the door opened and an older Chinese woman, who I was certain, was not bilingual, and smiled cheerfully as she pushed a cart into the suite. She pointed toward the veranda with a questioning look, and I nodded in agreement. She slid the large sliding glass door open and pushed the cart before her on to the wide, partially covered porch. Wheeling up next to the round glass table with four comfortable looking padded chairs surrounding it, she placed platters with silver lids in the center. The china plates, cups and saucers were properly positioned, as was the silver. In the very center, she placed a tall crystal vase containing a beautiful red flower. Valarie slipped on a robe and I pulled on a pair of my recently acquired sweats and we walked out onto the veranda. The pleasant sounds of singing birds, combined with the fragrant aroma of a multitude of flowering vines, created an atmosphere that almost allowed us to believe we were enjoying a memorable holiday in a far away land, instead of direct involvement with mayhem and murder.

The breakfast was obviously a result of Mr. Sun's desire to make us feel at home after all that's happened. In addition to the hot and steaming Chinese tea, there were sweet rolls, fresh fruit and scrambled eggs. Valarie seated herself and gazed out at the panorama beyond and said, "I can't believe how beautiful this is here. I had no idea that Hong Kong was so wonderful. All I need is my sketch pad and pencil, which I brought along for the boring times ------ hah, like we've had some, and I could be satisfied right here on this deck for a long, long time."

"Are you sure you'll be all right here alone? Mr. Sun and I need to interview that informant."

"Are you kidding, as I said last night, this is one place *I do* feel safe. I believe Mr. Sun about his confidence in his full-time security force at the house, and I'll be just fine while you two are gone. I'll keep very well occupied sitting out here and sketching this unbelievable collage of activity and beauty. You boys go play cops and robbers, but don't get hurt----ya hear?"

"I hear ya!" I replied with a chuckle, and went about devouring my vittles.

The shower was another thing I wasn't used to, standing naked in a ten-foot high window before a population of millions. Not that they were looking or if so would be interested in what they saw. Now it would be a different matter if Valarie were showering in this window. I'm almost certain that half the population below would be staring at her natural beauty. Well maybe somewhat *over half* of the population.

I dressed in a casual short-sleeved yellow shirt and a pair of light tan slacks and brown moccasins. Wearing a shoulder holster over my short sleeved shirt might be somewhat intimidating to anyone I encountered, including the police should they happen to see me, so I placed it in my briefcase, which would be close by at all times.

"Valarie came in and kissed me *bon voyage* with an intensity that was either *desire* or encouragement for me to survive the day and not being sure about that happening. Of course I interpreted her actions as that of total desire and intense longing for me to return into her outstretched arms as soon as possible. The truth however lies somewhere in the middle, although in reality, probably heavier weighted toward a safe return. Holding her with a thin, loose robe separating us, although fully clothed myself, I had visions of needing another shower *before the world again*, only this time a cold one.

I came to my senses, recalling the purpose of our trip, and smiled while saying "See ya, be careful," as I released her and walked toward the door carrying my briefcase and glancing back over my shoulder, seeing her waving good bye.

I walked into the hallway and climbed the stairs to the main floor and found Mr. Sun sitting in a small library that I assumed served as his office at home. He was on the phone and motioned me to come in and sit. I chose a dark red leather, high backed chair, one of two opposite his large, dark, hand carved desk. The room was lined with bookshelves, mostly full, from floor to ceiling. Behind Mr. Sun's desk was a window-wall from floor to ceiling with the same breathtaking harbor view as in our suite.

Mr. Sun was speaking English and I soon realized he was talking with Art Levy, where it was 1:00 A.M. in San

Francisco the previous day. After a moment he said, "He just walked in, hold on I'll hand him the phone."

"Hi Art, a little late for an old guy to be up isn't?"

"Not that old, buddy. Well, I heard about last night. You were lucky that you didn't walk in on that. It's a shame about Mr. Sun's man."

"It really is. What have you learned since we last talked----anything new?"

"I did some background checks on the TechX management people and didn't find anything to sink our teeth in. Phil Hampton has had a few credit problems, but seems to be OK now. He has no arrests or civil problems. His parents are dead, as well as an older brother that served in Viet Nam. He died about eight years ago, from what, I don't know. Christine, the controller was busted for pot in college and put on probation for a few months, no big deal. Nothing since then----good credit, parents living in southern Oregon. She has two sisters, married and in southern Oregon. The rest of the management was pretty much the same, nothing notable, nothing new on Jaxton. I have a bad feeling about *his* status though. There's still no credit card, bank, or prescription trail. I'm going to do some more nosing around on him."

"Great work Art I really appreciate your assistance. I haven't been able to do much from here yet. I haven't even had a chance to check my e-mail yet."

"Disregard my e-mail to you. It's just what we're talking about here. If you've got nothing more, I'm going to try and get some sleep."

"You do that and thanks." I said as I hung up the receiver.

Mr. Sun told me I could download my e-mails from his computer that was always on line. I went over to the small table holding the computer, brought up AOL, and punched in my address and password. I saw an e-mail address that I didn't know, with a message subject of "Denton". I quickly opened the mail and discovered it was from Victoria, Jaxton's girlfriend. She said, "Went to Denton's house today to water plants like I always do when he leaves town. Found a terrible odor in the house, and looked no further. I called the police and told them that he was missing and that I'd give them permission to enter and search the house, since I was given a key by Denton. Regards, Victoria."

Mr. Sun was reading the e-mail while I placed a call back to Art Levy. He grumbled a----"Hello".

"Art, Chuck."

Not waiting for a nasty comment about his lack of sleep, "I just opened an e-mail from Jaxton's girlfriend Victoria Danville. She said she was at Jaxton's house watering plants, smelled a bad odor and called the Portland police. I know the e-mail was sent about 8:00 P.M. your time last night, so the police, if they took her seriously have been there or are there right now."

"Chuck, I thought you searched the house."

"I did, and there was no cellar, this was a newer home. There was a lower area with a utility room and a game room, leading out to the back through a glass sliding door. I glanced in the furnace room, but didn't spend much time there."

152

"Chuck, I'm going to roll my Portland guy out of bed and get on top of this. I'll call you back within fifteen minutes, will you wait?"

"You bet."

Mr. Sun and I discussed the latest events and concluded that if Jaxton is dead, and judging by the apparent odor he is, and has been for a time, then he's not the one negotiating with KRL here in Hong Kong. In our conversation, I complimented him on his excellent English, and wasn't surprised to learn that he was educated at Stanford University, and went on to receive his Law degree from Stanford Law School, then returned home to Hong Kong where he practices law on a limited basis and spends most of his time in his investigation business. Art previously told me he is the most respected and successful investigator in Hong Kong, with many contacts and a large staff.

The phone rang and Mr. Sun answered in Chinese. "Oh, Art, let me put you on the speaker."

"Well, Victoria was correct, there was a body in the house, but it isn't Jaxton's, it appears to be a dead man."

Mr. Sun and I turned to each other with a quizzical look on our faces, perhaps both thinking the same thought that it was late for Art or perhaps he'd taken leave of his senses.

"Art, bodies are usually dead----aren't they?"

"Chuck, it's late and I'm not nuts, but the police ran the prints and this body died six years ago in Europe."

"Well, why do you suppose he just started to smell?" I asked, attempting humor.

Moving on, Art continued, "This guy was named Peter Duvinchy, born in Chicago in 1949, does that do anything for you?"

"Should it?"

"No, I just wondered if you've run across the name."

"What's his physical description, did the cops get anything on that?" I inquired.

"He was about average size, in excellent physical shape for a guy that would be in his fifties now."

"How did he die?"

"Someone was stringing their piano around his neck." Art said tossing in his own bit of levity.

"Where did they find the body, and did Victoria know him?" I shot back.

"The body was in a crawlspace with access through the furnace room, and I don't know if Victoria knew him or not."

"Has this hit the street yet, Art?"

"If not already, it will for certain in the morning."

"I need to make some calls and do some damage control." I told him.

"May I use your phone again, Mr. Sun?"

"By all means, and please call me John----that was my Americanized name while I was at Stanford. May I call you Chuck?" He politely asked.

"Sure, I would like that, John. Now, I have to get to work and keep this from causing a problem for TechX." I looked up Phil Hampton's home phone number in Beaverton, and called him. While it was ringing, I looked at my watch and calculated it to be close to two in the morning in Oregon.

"Hello." Phil said with a half angry, half-awake voice.

"Phil, this is Chuck Winters, and we have a sort of emergency that you need to prepare for, because it'll hit in the morning."

"What's happened? What's wrong, tell me?" He asked with a wide-awake intensity.

"A friend of Jaxton was at his house watering plants last night and smelled an odor that was bad enough to call the police. They came and found a body. The body was not Jaxton, but some other guy originally from Chicago."

"Who was he, was he a friend of Jaxton?"

"His name was Peter Duvinchy, did you know him?"

"No, never heard of him. What happened, how was he killed? Why was he there?" He asked.

"I don't have a clue, and right now it isn't as important as effecting some damage control for the company. First I want you to make a statement to the press. Call the Oregonian newspaper, ask for their City editor, or whoever is responsible for this kind of story, and read them the following statement;

'*There was an unfortunate discovery in Mr. Jaxton's home in Forest Heights last night, while he was away on business. Neither Jaxton, nor his company knew the person that was found dead in his home, which has been unoccupied during his absence. A friend he asked to water his plants discovered the body and called the police.*' Also, call the police right now, offer any assistance they might need, and do what you can to keep this under control. Explain that Mr. Jaxton was finishing up on a major project, and as was his normal custom as CEO, his specific itinerary was not provided to the company. He seldom kept his staff informed as he traveled on business." I said. "Phil, are you clear on this?"

"Yes, I'll make the calls right now."

I looked at *John* and saw that he had turned his chair and was gazing at the harbor activity in the distance. "Any thoughts?"

"This only serves to further complicate the case, and may be carefully calculated to do just that. Let's take a cursory look at the surface of this investigation. Conflict one: There is a missing man, with a likely explanation of a money motivation. Yet there is no apparent reason for his actions, nor is there hard evidence at this point. Conflict two: We have a dead man in the missing person's house. Not only is it not the missing person, it is a man that has been dead on the official record for years. Conflict three: Someone is after you and Miss Austin, by association, and committed murder, yet have not attempted to kill you and must think that you possess something they want, but to your knowledge you don't. Why? Conflict four: We

156

don't have time for that. If we don't hurry we'll be late for our meeting in Aberdeen with Miss Tang our KRL informant." John said, all of which caused me to focus on the complexities that were suddenly before us.

"I want to leave a quick voice mail on Tom Claudius's office phone, and then say goodbye to Valarie. I'll be ready in about five minutes, will that be all right?"

"Go right ahead, I'll get the car ready and meet you out front." He said, as he rose and moved toward the door.

I called Tom's number at One Star, which was the middle of the night in Palo Alto. "Tom, just a quick update, I'm in Hong Kong working on a lead that may put this situation in perspective. I don't want you to worry too much, as I think we can work this out for the company. In the meantime, I'll tell you that the police found a body in Jaxton's house last night, not him, and I don't know where it fits in. I have Phil doing damage control with the press and he's cooperating with the police. I'm trying to keep this incident away from TechX as much as possible. As I said previously, the engineering department can bring the product on line in a reasonable time as originally planned. The status of Jaxton as to complicity in any overt activities, or by others has not been determined at this point. I believe that if for some reason Jaxton proves to be unavailable in any way, the company should be able to continue with its original mission. I'll talk with you in person later today, and will try to have a status update that hopefully will add some clarity to this matter."

I retraced my steps back to our suite and found Valarie dressed in a pale green blouse with loose fitting white cotton pants. She was assembling her art supplies on a table. "Hi."

"Hi yourself, I thought you were long gone on your secret mission." She said with a broad smile on her face.

"Well, I got hung up with some news from Oregon." I went on to explain what had happened, my conversation with Phil Hampton, as well as my message to Tom Claudius.

"It seems to me that since there's an opportunity for big money, those involved had little difficulty in crossing the line from larceny to murder, and at this point there are no holds barred, and the tempo of danger without boundaries will do nothing but increase. Be real careful." She said with a seriousness that's not often displayed.

"Boy, you really have a way of summing up." I added with a grin.

Valarie fiddled with her sketching pencils and pads for a moment and then looked me square in the eyes and said, "I love you and don't want to lose you over something you don't have to do. Can you understand that?"

"I love you too, and I know you know that. I promise I'm going to be careful, but I wouldn't feel right about walking away from this now at this stage. Can you see that?"

"I didn't ask you to walk away, I just want you to think before you risk your life, that this is not your battle, and you're not obligated to engage in it. Is that too hard to accept?" She said with a logic I could understand. Her comments underscored the reason she so attracts me. She

158

has a great mind and can assimilate a set of facts and condense it down to a real *zinger*, one that makes me think in a way I sometimes don't take the time to do.

"You are coming in loud and clear as usual, and you're right!" I said as I drew her close and gave her a warm hug, along with another kiss, making me want to chuck the whole thing and spend the day with her in our room.

As I turned to leave, she said. "Where's your piece copper?"

"In my briefcase, where did you think?"

"Just wondering," she said with a devious grin, "I wasn't quite sure".

CHAPTER 22

I stepped out into the hallway and climbed back up the stairs to the front door. John, he doesn't seem like a John, was parked at the front door in what looked like a fifty-two rusty, faded red Chevy pickup, or the Chinese equivalent of one. Two fenders were red, one was painted with a gray primer, and the left rear one was missing entirely. John was wearing a straw farmer's hat and a loose white shirt and similar pants. He said, "Hop in, sorry about the mess."

I looked in as I was opening the door. The floor was covered with old newspapers, bits of straw, and an assortment of gravel and dirt clods. "Nice, is it new?" I asked, sporting a stupid grin.

John burst into laughter and replied, "I didn't think you'd notice. This is my camouflage vehicle. Don't let the looks fool you. It has a 357 big-block engine with dual carbs and a shaved head. It can run from zero to sixty, in seven seconds. It's equipped with a heavy-duty suspension, and bulletproof glass and doors. Other than that ---- it's stock."

"You amaze me. I kind of like your summer look too." I said as I gave him the once over.

"I don't want these people that are after you to know what we are doing. If they see this old *bucket of bolts*---- that is the term isn't it, then who would suspect it was you?" John said with a smug look on his face as he reached behind the seat and retrieved a straw hat similar to his, only older and more beat up. "Here, this is yours."

I put on the hat and looking like a couple of hayseeds we pulled out of the drive and onto the narrow road toward Aberdeen. There were no cars on the road, only an occasional truck until we came closer to the city. This quaint old city is a tourist must when visiting Hong Kong, as it's this old fishing village whose harbor holds the most amazing floating city you'll see anywhere in the world. As we approached the city and before we reached the harbor, we encountered a rural population living in small shacks along the way. Chickens and ducks along with peasants and their children roamed the country dirt roads that joined up with the main road we were traveling on toward the harbor area.

"Where will we meet Miss Tang?"

"Due to the heightened activity surrounding your investigation, I decided to change the meeting place to a small park near the water. It's not on a regularly traveled road, nor is it often used, except by the occasional old timers for family gatherings. It's mostly a forgotten place, exactly the way we want it to stay."

"Tell me about Miss Tang. How did you find her and why is she willing to talk with us?"

"Miss Sue Tang's name was given to me by a contact in the Hong Kong Bureau of Labour. It is required by law for a company with more than six employees to file a report with the Bureau, when an employee is hired or their employment terminates for any reason. I secured such a list of employment changes for KRL and began working it. I would call potentially appropriate people from this list posing as a researcher on software companies and determine by a series of questions if I could secure a candidate for our purposes. As I was offering to pay for their assistance with my survey, it didn't take long to find someone familiar with TechX that would be willing to help me with my work." He explained.

"How did you explain this clandestine meeting situation to Miss Tang?" I asked.

"I told her that my research is starting to look like the TechX software sale may not be authorized by the company, and I'm checking it out. I don't want KRL or TechX to know about my research because I could be all wrong and I don't want to get sued." John explained, sort of.

"Well, I have to say you have a real talent for this kind or work John, you're truly amazing. It sounds like the only thing you left out was telling Miss Tang that you were a private investigator. Now that I think about it a researcher is a private investigator, and a researcher must keep their work private while they're researching or their work could be compromised. So I guess such an admission was unnecessary and totally inappropriate." I concluded smiling.

The park was as advertised, overgrown and isolated. We lumbered down the dirt road, which was laden with ruts and potholes. The dust was rising in clouds behind the old red truck, causing it to partially disappear from view from time to time. The vegetation was overgrown. However the untrimmed shrubs and bushes offered an array of flowering beauty that was truly unexpected.

Miss Tang was sitting on an old splintered bench at the end of a dusty parking area, overlooking the harbor. The sampans she surveyed were beautiful and graceful, some tired and faded, others shiny and bright, most lashed together, each playing a role, each important to their occupants and to one another this day and every day in the harbor.

"Sue, thanks for coming, I hope you'll excuse my gardening clothes, it's good seeing you again. And thanks for coming so far out here. This is Chuck Winters, my associate from California." John said in his polite, charming manner, which was essential in this situation.

"Hi John, I hope I can help you, but as I said before I'm not sure I can." Miss Tang replied in perfect English and in an apologetic tone. She was about thirty years old, tall for an Asian and quite pretty. She looked comfortable in her white long sleeved dress shirt tucked into a pair of moderately tight jeans and wearing white sneakers without socks. Her manner was that of easy confidence and didn't project an outward appearance of intimidation. Her only hesitation was that of wanting to be helpful and not oversell her possible contribution to this 'research'.

"Before we start, I don't want to forget your fee, a thousand (Hong Kong) dollars for this first one hour session." John said as he handed her an envelope with the equivalent of about $140.00 US dollars.

"Thanks, but it seems like a lot of money for a little help."

"Any way you help us will be appreciated." I said.

John, with the pre-approved use of his tape recorder, would ask the questions and I would handle specific clarifications as well as those questions that were not asked but necessary.

"Sue, when did you join KRL and what was your position?" John asked.

"About a year ago, I was an administrative assistant to the engineering manager, Mr. Cho."

"When did you first hear about TechX and their software? John asked.

"I attended a meeting in the corporate conference room to take notes for Mr. Cho, when he was told by Mr. Wong, one of the owners of the company, that they were going to buy a software program that was not yet on the market, and would revolutionize the testing of computer chips. He went on to say that it would substantially lower manufacturing costs while speeding up product development time. They were basically going to buy the entire intellectual property of this Oregon company, and own the product outright and exclusively."

"Who was selling this software for TechX?" John casually inquired.

"He was the founder and President Mr. Jaxton."

"Did you ever see him at KRL?" John asked.

"I believe I saw him once on a weekend when I had to catch up on some work." She said as John and I glanced at each other.

I broke in and said, "Miss Tang, I have a TechX company picture, and I'd just like to be sure we're talking about the same person. Can you identify the man from TechX?" I said as I handed her the picture of Jaxton and the engineering staff, all wearing jeans or similar casual pants and short sleeve shirts, standing

164

around a computer in the testing lab. There was no indication by looking at the picture, of the senior man in the group.

"He is not in this picture. I am positive."

John and I sat on the bench in total amazement. She had no reason to mislead us or intentionally lie that we could think of. Since she didn't identify Jaxton, I had nothing to lose by pointing him out and ask if she's ever seen him.

I handed back the picture and pointed at Jaxton and asked "have you ever seen this man before?"

She looked carefully and turned to me and said, "No, I have never seen him. If you think I might be confused, Mr. Jaxton, I am sure is shorter than that man who looks taller than the others in the picture, and doesn't look anything like him. I saw Mr. Jaxton for at least ten minutes that Saturday." She added.

"Do you know how much KRL was going to pay for this program?" I asked.

"I didn't know on an official basis, but I once overheard Mr. Cho say in his own office to someone, that if they were paying ten million US for the software, had KRL been a little more generous with *their* salary money, we could have developed it our self."

"When, was the money going to change hands?" I asked.

"It was my understanding it would as soon as KRL was satisfied that they had the entire software and it worked under their test protocols. I know the in-house testing was not finished when I left, and the department was being pressured, because TechX was getting anxious about getting their money."

"Let me understand this, the man selling this TechX software, Mr. Jaxton, is not in the picture I showed you, and is selling it for ten million US. He also is getting concerned about getting his money, is this correct?" I asked.

"Yes, as I know it." She said firmly.

"Miss Tang, you have been very helpful. Will you be available for another session, same fee, in this location?" I asked.

"Yes, but when?"

"Maybe tomorrow morning, but I need to check."

"John can call me and I will meet you tomorrow if you like." She said. "Just let me know."

Miss Tang said good-bye and walked to her car parked at the edge of the parking lot and drove away.

We just sat there saying nothing, and reflected on the latest surprise, but not totally unexpected after learning about Jaxton's car and the body in his house. "Well Chuck, what do you think now?"

"I think that Jaxton is not the person we're looking for in this case, and someone is using his name and credibility in order to make a quick ten million dollars. I also get the impression that time is their enemy and this better come together fast before someone like us uncovers the truth and ends their scheme."

"I completely concur with your analysis." John added.

"My question is who's using Jaxton's name in this? Who would have the access, except someone from the company?" I asked, thinking out loud and not expecting a response from John.

"Considering I don't know the employees, I need to leave that part to you."

They drove back to the house mostly in silence, thinking about what they had learned and where to go now, with a trail of murders stacking up and no end in sight.

"How often do you use this fancy rig?"

"Not often, but it does serve to remind me that I'm no better a man with my big fancy Jaguar, than the man driving an old red pickup. Since my wife died a few years ago, in reality, I'm a lot worse off than a happy man driving an old red Chevy. I drive it not because I have to, but because I need to, sometimes just to find my direction."

We reached the house and pulled around the circle to the front door. John turned off the motor and one of his people came from around the side of the house, greeted John and jumped into the pickup after we got out, and drove back down the driveway turning toward the road that led around the side of the house and presumably to the garages. We walked to the front door, which was opened by a maid, and when we were inside, John said, "How about some lunch? If that's acceptable to you, please ask Miss Austin to join us on the upper deck."

"Great, I'll check with her and be back shortly."

I walked down the stairs to the second level, and had to admit that the surroundings were beginning to feel quite comfortable. It certainly beats the hotel option, with potential terror lurking around every corner. Upon reaching our suite, I found the door open and could view the porch from where I stood. Valarie was sitting at the table, with what looked to be a large sketch pad, maybe 16 by 20 inches propped up before her. It was obvious that John had instructed his staff to take good care of her, seeing that she had beside her a large bowl of assorted fruit and a pitcher and glass of what looked like ice tea. I just stood there a minute admiring her natural beauty, as she almost magically transferred the harbor below onto her sketchpad. I quietly moved through the room and not wanting to frighten her, said "Hi", a few feet from the open door to the porch area.

"Hi to you, how did it go?" She said in a way that clearly convinced me she felt very safe and comfortable in these surroundings.

"May I see your work?" I said as I walked toward the glass table.

"Sure, if you promise not to laugh."

"You are too cute, like your work isn't always outstanding!" I said while leaning over her shoulder and taking in her fantastic talent. "That is more beautiful than the subject matter." I added, with my hands gently resting on her shoulders.

"Enough about my work, tell me about your day."

"The meeting with Miss Tang was quite revealing. It seems that our Jaxton, is not her Jaxton. In other words, someone is impersonating the real Jaxton, as she couldn't pick him out of a company group photo of the engineering staff, with him standing there."

"She said she's met him?" Valarie asked quizzically.

"Yes, on a weekend when she had to come in to catch up on some work."

"Wow, this is really getting wild. Who do you think is behind this? Obviously someone in the company, don't you think?"

"That's my guess, but I don't have evidence that ties anyone to it, yet. John wants us to have lunch on the main deck, OK with you?"

"Perfect."

"Before we go up, I need to call someone at TechX, it's about 8:00 A.M., yesterday in Beaverton. Sounds funny doesn't it?"

"You make your call and I'll let Mr. Sun know you'll be along." She said as she closed her sketchpad, gave me a passing kiss on my cheek, whirled around and was gone.

I went into the suite and dialed Christina's direct line at TechX. I had a hunch she'd be there, because numbers people, in my experience, usually wanted to be in place when business commenced. "This is Christina."

"Hi Christina, this is Chuck Winters, how are you doing?" I asked, trying to break the ice.

"Fine." She said, as I thought this isn't going well.

"A couple of things, first, did Denton return yet?"

"No, and to my knowledge, no one has heard from him either."

"Sorry, secondly, have you had a chance to get the copies of the cancelled checks to the consultants that made up those recent extraordinary expenses that we talked about?" I asked casually, hoping not to place a lot of importance on the request.

"Yes, when will you be back?"

I didn't want my excitement to come across, so I casually asked if she would mind faxing the copies, front and back to my fax number in San Francisco, which happened to be Art Levy's, a point she didn't need to know. She said they would be there in a couple of minutes. She warmed up and was actually pleasant when we signed off.

"Art, I know 8:00 A.M. is not your favorite office hour, so I'm leaving this voice mail, instead of calling you at home and getting yelled at for keeping you up half the night before. Here's the latest, Jaxton is not the one negotiating in Hong Kong. It seems that someone else is using his identity in this matter. Most important, while I'm leaving this voice mail, your fax machine is receiving some copies of cancelled checks, both sides, representing the two and a half plus, million bucks that were in my opinion siphoned off from TechX in the last several months. The fax is directed to me from Christina at TechX, so you'll know what it is when you get it. I'd like you to find out everything you can about who got those checks as fast as possible. Call and or fax me at John's house. Thanks Art, you're the best."

I went back upstairs and joined Valarie and John on the upper deck. Considering that it was fifteen or twenty feet higher, and faced a bit to the north, it offered a slightly different perspective and of course a delightful view. They were deep in conversation about Hong Kong's history I think, and unfortunately interrupted them as I approached.

"Hi ----" I paused, "John you are too kind, this looks wonderful." As I gazed at the lunch table, which resembled a grand seafood buffet, accompanied by tropical fruit varieties most of which I couldn't identify, carefully placed among a fresh floating flower arrangements.

Valarie was in her element. This beauty was such that only an artist could truly see each element, from every dimension, and appreciate the bounty that was laid before us as well.

However, from my basic perspective, John's kindness was overwhelming me, and I felt like such an imposition in his home, yet he seemed to ratchet up his gracious friendship, the longer we were together. Perhaps with his wife gone, he enjoyed the rare opportunity to share some of his lifestyle with people he may perceive to be interesting. Whatever----, the crab legs looked outstanding, and fresh lobster and melted butter, I'm in heaven. Need I say more?

"I am not doing anything special, this is how I live." He said with a sly grin, which didn't allow me to know if he was truthful or teasing. Valarie just sat there with a big smile on her face looking up at me and thoroughly enjoying this little dance John and I were engaged in.

"Well, I didn't think anyone lived like *I* do. It's nice to know I'm not alone." I responded with a stone cold expression that I could hold only for a moment, and then, everyone broke into an infectious laughter.

What amused me most was that John didn't have any idea that I could live like this every day of my life, and in a much grander scale if I chose. That was the fun part of my life, as I delighted in allowing people to think of me as an average guy, and was careful not to intentionally do anything to dispel that image. Making the kind of money I did, was never my goal in life, nor has it changed me, other than I don't worry about bills anymore, and I can help people, quietly now, when before I could only think about how nice it would be to do something for someone.

"Chuck, Valarie was telling me about her interest in art. I saw what she has done so far today, and I was thinking that perhaps she would like to bring some to Hong Kong and have a showing in a gallery I am involved with." John said with the enthusiasm of a man with a new hobby---- or girlfriend.

"That sounds great, she's a wonderful artist and her work is in great demand in Northern California."

"John is much to kind, I'm not certain my Shasta art would be in much demand here, although I did enjoy working on the harbor life today." She said with a casual reference to John on a first name basis. Now we all are getting comfortable here. I of course am just kidding around. I hope I don't sound jealous ----of this debonair man of the world, for whom I personally have a great deal of respect.

172

We finished our lunch, Valarie returned to her sketching on our porch and I filled John in on my call to Oregon and my message left for Art. He updated me on his conversation with the Hong Kong Police Department and his friend the Inspector. "It seems that Mr. Hong was murdered by an unknown assailant, who was careful not to leave prints, a shell casing or any other evidence. The crime lab recovered the bullet from the wall, and did determine that it came from a .38 caliber revolver. They did have one break, in that each floor has a security camera pointing down the hallway, and they were able to get some film of the suspect from behind, however, when he left your suite he managed to step in closely behind a group of people, that mostly obscured his likeness. They do know that he is Caucasian, and taller than average, short hair, and wearing a dark suit in order to blend in with the crowds. I know this isn't a lot of help, but from my perspective, it eliminates about 95% of the people in Hong Kong." John reported with a slight smile.

"I don't think the KRL group is involved any deeper than knowing they are buying something that *Jaxton* as they know him, probably doesn't have the authority to sell. I need to know who's talking to them, however, I'll probably know that when I find the recipient of those consulting checks for two and a half million." I said.

"Do you want to talk with Sue again tomorrow?"

"I need to get my hands on some additional employee pictures first. I can't ask TechX to do that without casting suspicion at the Company. I'll get Art to e-mail me driver's license photos of each employee, since he already has a list. Better yet, I could use the entire license with physical descriptions so Sue can better determine if she knows one of them."

"It sounds like the right approach. You call Art, and I will see if Sue can make herself available when you receive the e-mails."

I called Art, and caught him in his office. "Do you think I have only one client----- and it's you? Art barked, when he heard my voice.

"Come on Art, this thing is moving fast and I really need your help, *today!*" I pleadingly, demanded, if that's possible.

He grudgingly agreed and indicated that it was time consuming and would hopefully be done by the end of the day. At the same time, he updated me on the status of the checks. He was talking to a banker contact that was getting him details on the *consulting company* that cashed the checks. He hoped to have it in his hands in the next hour or so, and put together the entire dossier of who was who, and where etc., for me also by the end of the day, but reminded me that this could always slip into tomorrow if there were any hang ups.

I left the small sitting room, off the hallway near the main deck where I was using the telephone, and walked toward the front of the house and John's office. He was just finishing up a call and motioned me to come in and sit down. The conversation was in Chinese, and moved at a much faster pace than English generally does. The expression on his face was generally stern, however, it's always folly to try to read anything into a telephone call when you don't know the first thing about it, and chances are it's none of your business anyway.

John hung up the receiver and said, "I was just speaking with my friend the Inspector about this case.

174

He informed me that after a careful examination of the film of the suspect in Mr. Hong's murder, their video technicians discovered an error he made as he turned the corner in the hallway. It seems that he touched a door jam when he turned toward the elevator. They sent their lab team back to the hotel and dusted the door jam, retrieving several prints. Since the suspect was Caucasian, it was simple to discard the three prints that upon record checks, proved to be Asian. This left only one print, the suspects. The Hong Kong Police Department crosschecked the fingerprint with every known resource world wide, and so far, they came out without a match. It is not too unusual for someone to be without a fingerprint record. It is extremely unusual for someone that knows how to handle a gun, to not have a fingerprint on file----anywhere. The type of person that handles a gun, is generally in a lifestyle that would for one reason or another have a print record. As an example, this would include ex-military, law enforcement, local, state or Federal governmental agencies, various types of licenses, or just simply being in trouble with the law, even on a minor basis. What I am really getting at, is that something is very wrong here. You have a man in Oregon connected with this that is "dead", and has been for five or six years. You have a man that commits a murder in Hong Kong, who does not have a fingerprint on file anyplace in the world. You have a man selling software to a Hong Kong company, that is not the man he claims to be." John summed up a very intriguing story leaving questions and no answers.

"This sounds very complicated and difficult, but my experience is that clarification comes from a small breakthrough, and a pull of the string, usually unravels the largest mystery. We just have to look for that breakthrough and pull the string, don't we?" I said in all seriousness.

"You really know how to summarize a problem," he said with a smile, "maybe you are right. Let's find that string."

"John, I think we can find the string, and it just might be in the identity of the Jaxton impersonator. When Art e-mails the licenses, we can show Sue and see if she can pick out our man."

"I agree, let's wait until Art sends his files and we will go from there."

"If you don't mind I think I'll go down and check on Valarie."

"By all means, I will let you know if Art calls, and you can continue to check your e-mail." John said as I waved and headed toward the staircase leading downstairs.

The mid-afternoon sun was warm, and the breeze off the South China Sea, gently moved the trees, siphoning off enough degrees to make sitting on the porch in the brilliant sun quite tolerable. Valarie, perched before her sketch pad, was focused on a large junk in the near harbor, as it attempted to navigate through a flotilla of sampans lashed together as one. Her concentration was such that she didn't notice me coming through our room and out onto the porch. I stood there watching the boat, and then her hand guiding the charcoal effortlessly in directions that transformed the ghostly white sheet into a living organism of sea foam and wood with angles and shadows that captured the smell of the sea and the creaking of timbers, tossing and straining under the waves as the craft worked its way through and around the flotilla before her.

"Oh hi, how's it going?" Valarie asked, as she looked up.

"I'll know pretty soon. Hey, you really have a knack for capturing the essence of this harbor. Your sketches are so alive they're absolutely wonderful. Are you going to do a show here? You would wow 'em----really."

"I don't know, it's a long way from home and I wouldn't want to be here unless you were with me."

"Who said I wouldn't be here, it'd be fun after we get this thing behind us. Just think about it, OK?"

"OK". She said smiling, and looked back at the harbor, picking up her pencil and sliding it effortlessly across the paper like water sliding over a smooth rock in a stream of endless possibilities.

I could see that she was enjoying both the opportunity of being in such a historic artistic locale, as well as being the obvious center of attention among two very successful and totally different men.

"I need to check my e-mail and see if Art's made any progress on the TechX pictures. Be right back."

"OK, I'll be right here waiting for you." She reached out and touched my arm as I walked away toward our room.

I plugged in my laptop, and signed on to AOL. Soon I was into my e-mail and didn't have anything from Art, but did have one from Christina, which was a shocker. "Another problem, now Phil Hampton has disappeared, just like Denton. He's not home and he hasn't called in. He's been missing almost two days, and it's not in his character to act this way. Two of our guys went to his house and found a way in. There was no clue. He's just gone. We have no one in charge. I thought I'd contact you before the board. Please let me know what to do. Christina."

I picked up the phone, and using the employee list called her at home. She answered, "This is Christina."

"Hi Christina this is Chuck, got your e-mail. Is there any explanation for Phil's absence that you can think of?

"No not all. This is making me nervous and it's starting to have an effect on our people. It almost seems like we're on a ship and people are starting to disappear---- for no reason at all. It's scaring me."
"Don't be scared. There's a logical explanation for all of this and we'll have it soon. Just go about your work and I'll be checking in with you. If you need me, be sure to e-mail, and I promise I'll get right back to you. OK?"

"OK, but when will *you* be back?"

"I'm not certain, but it won't be long, and if necessary I'll come back right away. Are you all right with your work, do you need anything, or does anyone else?"

"No, everyone is pretty much doing their thing and has enough to do." She said in a more relieved tone, as if she just needed to talk with someone that represented a different authority than those presently at the company.

I didn't want to get Tom Claudius all stirred up, but had to call him with an update as he's been out of the loop. I was hoping my next contact would be a solution to the problems and that I was heading home.

"Hi Betty, Chuck. Is Tom around?" I asked in my normal cheerful voice.

"Where have you been? He's getting worried about what's going on." She asked with a sense of urgency.

"Everything is moving ahead. I'm on top of things. Love to chat, but I have an appointment. Will you put me through to him----please?"

"Sure, hold on." She replied as Tom's phone was ringing.

"Chucky, have I lost my dough?" Tom asked in his smooth manner.

"No you haven't lost your *dough*. You asked me to help you because you didn't want that to happen----right?"

"Right, but what's going on, I've only heard bits and pieces from you." He said in an impatient tone that wasn't unfamiliar to me.

"In a nutshell, Jaxton is still missing and I don't believe he's done anything wrong. Phil Hampton is missing as of yesterday and I haven't formed a conclusion about that. I've had a few close calls and one of my bodyguards was murdered in the last thirty-six hours. Valarie joined me on Wednesday and has been involved in a kidnap and possible murder attempt in two different countries, all related to this case. Aside from that, I'm eating well and have clean underwear." I answered, sure to get a rise. "Oh, I forgot, I think I can save your dough for you".

Tom came back sputtering, "What did you say, murder, where in the hell are you, what bodyguard, are you nuts? I just asked you to check on something, not to get into World War Three!" He stammered.

I couldn't help laughing at him, "Tom, cool down. This is just a simple run of the mill, oh----before I forget, speaking of "mill", someone stole two and a half of those "mills" from you, but not to worry, I'm on top of it-----."

"Hold it right there," Tom broke in, "what in the hell are you talking about two and a half mills? Are you talking about money?"

"Yes, Tom, I think so. It seems that you haven't done a thorough enough job staying on top of this company, and some money just went out the door in payables that I think was stolen. I'll have a lot more information by tomorrow, but as I said don't worry, I believe you and the company will come out of this thing in one piece."

"How can you assure me of that, when I have a big question about *you* coming out of this thing in one piece?" He sarcastically threw in.

"Remember what I used to say when you doubted me about something----*just trust me*, and everything always worked out" just trying to needle him a little.

"Yeah, yeah, yeah, stay in touch, will ya?" Tom added and hung up the phone.

I went back on line and tried my e-mail again, and sure enough Art pulled through with the employee licenses, complete with color photos. My small, portable printer wasn't good enough to print the file, so I saved it to a disk and went upstairs to fill John in.

180

"Art sent the file of driver's licenses, so we can ask Sue to see if she can identify the person she saw at the company that weekend. I couldn't print them on my small portable, would you mind printing them on yours?"

"Not at all." John said, as he held out his hand for the disk and prepared to print the file. "I'll call Sue and see if she can meet in the morning."

The pages were coming out of the printer in excellent shape, and John was on the phone now speaking in Chinese. A worried look came on his face as he hung up the telephone.

"I was talking with Sue's father, it seems that she has not returned home from a job interview she had in Kowloon several hours ago. He said it is not like her to worry her family like this. I told him to check back with me and I left him this number. I also assured him that I would arrange to get some help from the authorities if she has not returned in the next hour or so. I hope this is unrelated to our case. It could only have happened if she spoke with a friend that still worked at KRL, and then word reached the wrong ears. She had no idea this was a dangerous assignment, and only thought it was a research opportunity. She would not necessarily have been guarded with her comments."

I could see that John was concerned as it was he that contrived the scheme to obtain an informant without them knowing their role, thinking only that it was a research project.

"Anything new on Mr. Hong's case?"

"I spoke with the Inspector a short time ago and they had no new information, however they were checking arrival documentation at Customs to see if they could find some help there."

"I'd like to take you to dinner tonight, would that be OK with you?" I asked.

"It would be an honor." John said. "What did you have in mind?"

"I promised Valarie when I asked her to join me on this trip that I'd take her to dinner on a floating restaurant in the harbor."

"That is a fine idea. She can have an opportunity to see the harbor up close, rather than just the hillside view. If you don't mind, I can recommend an excellent restaurant, one that is owned by a close friend, The Black Orchid." He said with pride.

"That would be terrific. I'm sure Valarie will be thrilled about it."

"I'll call and make the arrangements."

"Thanks, and if you hear anything about Sue please let me know." I added as I was walked back to our suite with the printed licenses that Art forwarded.

Upon returning, I found Valarie sleeping lightly on the bed. I didn't want to disturb her so I went quietly to the porch to enjoy the harbor. Sitting at the glass table, I began thinking about everything that's happened in these few short days, and how people and events may all fit together. It was difficult to concentrate with the endless tide of boats, large and small, moving to and fro on the green surface, seeming to be going somewhere and yet nowhere actually in the larger scheme of things. At about 5:30 P.M., I quietly walked past Valarie, still sleeping and walked up to see John and find out what time we were going to dinner, when he met me in the hallway coming my way.

"I just received a worried call from Sue Tang's father. It seems that she is more than five hours late returning from her appointment, and it is totally unlike her. I told him I would call a friend at the Hong Kong Police Department and put him in touch. Mr. Tang promised to call back with any news. It is probably a case where she has missed a train or met a friend----she isn't a child" He said, probably with wishful thinking.

"I hope that's all."
"Oh, I almost forgot with all this activity I spoke with my friend at The Black Orchid. I am happy to announce that the owner was delighted to entertain my friends from America and will have a special table reserved for us on the deck with the best view. Is it alright if we leave here at 7:30 P.M. It takes about fifteen minutes to get to the harbor, and another ten minutes by launch to the restaurant?" He asked with a smile that attempted to mask his concern about Sue Tang and the events that were unfolding.

"That's perfect."

"What did Valarie think about going to dinner?"

"She was sleeping so I haven't mentioned it to her yet. But trust me, she'll be excited. I better tell her now because she'll want time to dress." I said, as I left, wondering if there was a connection between Sue's lateness and this case.

Valarie was up and back outside, not sketching but reading a book she'd brought along. "Hi, what's up?"

"Well, do you remember the basis for asking you to join me on this adventure, that's turned into foreign intrigue, murder and mayhem?" I asked with a straight face.

"You mean that old come-on about a romantic dinner on a floating restaurant in Hong Kong Harbor?"

"That's the one, how about tonight?"

"Tonight is wonderful." She said, her face lighting up with an expression of excitement and anticipation.

"Now comes the best part, you will have two dates, John and me. OK?"

With a straight face, she replied. "I don't know about you, but John is great."

After her normal pause for effect----she added, "Just kidding", flashing a grin.

"By the way, what happened to the more formal, *Mr. Sun*?" I asked teasing.

"While you were on the phone and I went upstairs earlier, he addressed me as Miss Austin and I insisted that he call me Valarie. He then insisted that I call him John. That's what happened----end of story." She concluded with a beautiful smile and an impish tilt of her head.

"Oh, I almost forgot, he said we need to leave here by 7:30 P.M. OK with you?"

"Great, this will be fun. This is paradise here. But to see the harbor up close will be a *real* treat."

"You packed your camera didn't you?"

"Are you kidding, I never leave home without it. I'll take it for sure and try to capture some close ups of the sampans and the people who live aboard."

"Also," I said, "the father of the girl we met this morning said she is hours late returning home from a job interview she had this afternoon, and he's quite worried. John brought in his Inspector friend. I sure hope it isn't connected to the case, but the way things are going who can say?"

"That's terrible, should we be going out with her still missing." She asked in a concerned manner.

"John has the police involved and there's really nothing we can do at this point except hope that she returns soon. He'll have his cell with him tonight."

I started to look through TechX's employee licenses while Valarie went in to decide what to wear for dinner. Sitting on the porch with the harbor beyond, the distraction from any effort is hard to explain. But if one could imagine a virtual travel film, it would only start to explain how amazing this view is and how difficult it is to concentrate on anything.

After flipping through the pages and seeing familiar and not so familiar faces, my boredom finally led me to checking the women employees I met, to see how much they actually admitted they weighed. I checked on Miss Smiley first, and she said she weighed 125 pounds. I think she was honest. My guess would be 115. I need to give her extra credit for being honest or maybe less credit for being honest. I need to think that one over. My next subject was Christina, thirty-four years old and admits to 127 pounds. I would say Christina, from my first hand observation you have Miss Smiley beat by ten pounds---- bad girl! That doesn't mean that you stole two and a half million bucks though. It only means that it's a lot easier to lose ten pounds on paper than on a diet, and I doubt it's about being carded.

Valarie decided to take a shower before dinner. So while she was bathing I headed back upstairs to check in with John. He was sitting in his office talking on the phone as I came down the hall. As usual he waved me in and I sat down while he finished up.

"I just stopped by for an update. Have you heard from Sue's father?"

"Yes I have and I just finished talking with the police about it. It seems that Sue missed her job interview altogether and is still missing. Knowing the other factors, I feel there is a strong possibility of foul play, and I am encouraging the police to investigate. They should be at Mr. Tang's house right now."

"Should we cancel our reservations tonight?"

"I am concerned, but I don't believe there is anything we can do by staying home. Also, if they learn anything, my staff knows how to reach me at all times, so I don't see a reason to remain here this evening. Are you all right with this?"

"Yes, there's no way we can help tonight, and the police are now involved. While we have a few minutes, I think I'll check my e-mail and see if Art has the information on those large TechX checks that concern to me."

"Use my computer you don't need to go down for your laptop."

"Thanks, let's see what we have here." I replied while settling in John's chair. "He sent something." I clicked on the line and read the letter. "The checks were made payable to Pacific Software Consultants, a Belleview, Washington, corporation. They were not deposited in a bank account bearing that name, but stamped pay to the order of Caribco which had a bank account in Las Vegas, Nevada. It seems that Caribco is not a U.S. Corporation, but is registered in The Bahamas. I tried to check the Bahamian registration but that's always a difficult effort, usually involving someone on site with a packet of cash in a plain envelope. I'll follow up in the Bahamas, but I have to say Chuck, your hunch appears to be on target. I'd bet this is a major scam. My guess is that we can get the answers in the Caribbean for a couple of thousand, at most. So, unless I hear otherwise from you, I'm on it. Regards, and be careful, Art."

I printed the letter and handed it to John, then opened the attachments, which I assumed were the check copies. They were----front and back as Art described. I sent an e-mail to Christina asking her to e-mail me back the supporting file documentation for these expenses, and see how they were justified to her----and by whom.

"It appears that this case is very likely an inside job. Is there anything new, on the location of Mr. Jaxton or the now missing Mr. Hampton?" John inquired.

"Nothing at all, but my guess is if we follow the money represented by these large checks back to the end, we'll find the answers to murder and grand larceny there."

"You are so right"

"I think I better change for dinner."

"Why don't you and Valarie come up when you are finished dressing and we can have cocktails on the deck?"

"That would be wonderful."

I returned to our guest suite. Valarie had taken her shower and was sitting on the porch in her robe brushing her hair. "Hi, you look beautiful, all fresh and clean." I said as I stood before her admiring her natural beauty unassisted by makeup, which she used sparingly when the occasion called for it. Just a touch of lipstick was enough to suit her.

"Why is it you always say the right thing? Make that almost always." She giggled.

"John asked us to join him on the main deck for cocktails when we're dressed. Is that OK with you?"

"Wonderful. I imagine he'll serve something yummy if lunch was an example." She answered in delight.

"We walked upstairs just prior to 7:00 P.M. Valarie wore a long dark blue straight-side silk dress and a string of pearls. I was wearing a white short-sleeved shirt, open collar, and tan slacks. To me the contrast was elegance and Burger King. A lady on John's staff politely directed us to the deck where John was standing against the railing, gazing across the harbor with a cocktail in this hand. He turned as he heard us and said smiling, "Good evening Valarie, you look lovely and Chuck----you look like a man with a beautiful lady on his arm."

I couldn't help thinking what a smooth operator John was when he gave a double compliment to Valarie and sidestepped quite deftly, the awkward position of saying something nice about my attire, which of course there wasn't anything nice to say. I have a great deal of respect for John, both professionally and personally. My turn for compliments!

"John you really look great in that white silk suit. I think I'm underdressed for dinner tonight. What do you think?" I asked with a straight face. Valarie knows me so well and knows my fun little mind games. I'm sure she's ready to kick me right about now, if she thought I wouldn't fall through the railing and into the bay.

"Thank you. I think you look fine. You will not be out of place at all. It is I who may be a bit out of place but I think this white suit is fitting for a Black Orchid, don't you agree?"

"I think it looks wonderful on you." Valarie jumped in smiling.

"What would you like to drink? I think we have just about anything you would like."

Valarie asked for a dry white wine and I asked for my usual vodka martini---up. I didn't think specifying my preferred Vox brand would be too polite. The table was loaded with everything from fruit to giant shrimp, as well as a variety of egg rolls and other delicacies I couldn't name.

190

"John, this looks fantastic. The Black Orchid is going to have a difficult time competing." I managed to say as I was stuffing the third jumbo shrimp into my mouth,

"I have to agree with Chuck, everything is lovely. We really appreciate your hospitality."

"It is my honor. I am really enjoying you two being here with me. Although I have a number of people here on the staff, it is still quite lonely. So let me assure you, the pleasure is all mine." He graciously replied. We made the normal cocktail party small talk until Valarie asked if he knew anything more about the 'missing girl'.

"I spoke with her father a few minutes ago and he said the police are investigating, but he doesn't think they will learn much. He thinks the city is so big, that finding her among almost eight million people is a difficult task. I cannot say that I disagree with his conclusion. If she was in an accident, they will know soon. If something else happened----that would be different. I do feel that any chance of identifying Mr. Jaxton's impersonator will be more difficult unless we can find Sue in good health. I did not find another ex-employee of KRL that ever saw the person posing as Mr. Jaxton of TechX. We can't bring in the Software Piracy Division of the Hong Kong Police Department, because that will immediately alert KRL to the TechX situation, and the real culprits are likely to flee before they can be arrested. The only plus side to *that* concept is that they will interview the staff and may find out who this person is----not necessarily how to arrest him. At the very least they should find out who this person *is not*. The decision is yours Chuck." John concluded dropping a heavy weight on the conversation.

"If you think we can do Sue some good by investigating KRL now, I'm for it. We can work around the difficulties that it might present. If we can find Sue it would be worth it. I'll get the Oregon people later. Let's report the KRL connection to the police tomorrow and try to identify who's behind this activity. If nothing else we can prevent KRL from getting access to stolen property, and have all of the TechX files removed and held as evidence by the police. I'd like to have the police pick up any outside consultants that may have represented the Oregon people in any way. I think they could be responsible for Mr. Hong's death and now possibly Sue's, and lead us to our Oregon people. Maybe the owners of KRL would make a deal with the police to avoid prosecution for piracy as well as possible complicity in murder, by turning on the local contact as well as the Oregon people?"

"You are right Chuck." He said as he pulled his cell phone out of his jacket and made a call, speaking for a minute or so in Chinese and then putting his phone away. "As a courtesy to us Inspector Li is coming here tomorrow at 8:45 A.M. to interview you, and then if necessary we will go to his office. Tomorrow looks like a busy day. Shall we leave for the Orchid and enjoy the evening?"

"Sounds good to me, how about you honey?"

"Fine with me, I'm ready,"

192

CHAPTER 23

BEAVERTON, OREGON, USA

The ringing phone caused her to jump. She was deep in thought about the future. "Hello." she tentatively said, as she had been continually pestered with questions from the police in the last twenty-four hours.

"Hey, Victoria, how are you doing honey?" He said warmly.

"I thought you'd never call. I've been worried about you. I'm fine, but tired of the incessant interviews from the police----and the calls from reporters. Are you sure this little dead body distraction idea of yours was the right one? I thought there wasn't going to be any killing?"

"Absolutely, we needed the extra time to get the last materials to Hong Kong. And besides that we had to---- because he decided a hundred grand wasn't enough and wanted a third of the deal. On the positive side, I think we've finally solved their testing problem. I shipped it off today. The police are mired down in this new mystery and won't be thinking about software or even *know* about Hong Kong." He said with a chuckle, obviously proud of his brilliant diversion scheme.

"What about Chuck Winters? If he's in Hong Kong, he knows about the sale and he'll be blowing the whistle on this whole thing----won't he?" She asked in a concerned tone.

"There goes your legal mind again honey. I'll take care of Winters----you just think about your part of the job. And most of all think about lying on a beach with those little umbrella drinks and ten million bucks. Have you worked out the wire transfer details from the Caymans to Switzerland yet? We need everything to work like clockwork."

"I think it's handled. It's costing another ten thousand in The Caymans, to lose all traces of the funds coming in and going out. To the Swiss, we already look like a research company opening a lab in Europe. Particularly since I bought that shell medical testing corporation for a thousand dollars, and transferred the headquarters to Zurich, as well as deposited $100,000 US in the Swiss Bank from the money you gave me last month. I have all documentation and registrations going to an attorney in Zurich who's respected, but like many others likes his fee and does not question a thing." Her response was in a much calmer voice now that her legal mind was operating, rather than her more emotional side of being a woman in love.

"Great work, I knew I could count on you. We make a terrific team----don't you think?" He said testing, rather than complimenting her.

"Yes, but I still think you underestimate Chuck Winters. He's very smart, even If he seems a little laid back. How are you keeping him from our buyers? He has to know or he wouldn't be in Hong Kong."

"He does know, but not about any details because his link to our buyers has been broken, and it'll take some time to develop another with my *wild man* running all over Hong Kong causing trouble. Thanks to our contact with the police department, we know he's staying with the Hong Kong Detective, Mr. Sun. He has an appointment tomorrow morning to cause some trouble for us, but we

194

have some plans for him. I just received word he's on the road as we speak."

"When can I see you? This is really hard on me staying behind alone and not knowing what to expect----who's calling or knocking at my door?" She said in a whiny sort of way, one that he didn't appreciate.

"I told you before that we can't see each other until we meet in Europe. In the meantime get a grip, and I'll check back with you as soon as I hear that the test is completed and the money's about to leave Hong Kong, OK?" He said, hoping she'd tone down her bitching and agree to sit tight.

"OK, but where are you now?"

"I'm flying to Las Vegas to hide out for a day or two until we get the news from Hong Kong. Then I'll call you and you can follow through on your plan to drive to Seattle and fly to Los Angeles then on to London where I'll meet you at that little hotel. OK?"

CHAPTER 24

HONG KONG

"I can't believe this weather. It's wonderful." Valarie commented as they snaked their way down the narrow road from John Sun's home to the harbor below. It was just about dusk now and visibility was slowly evaporating from another beautiful day. The small dark car that followed was not apparent to those in the Jaguar as they pulled onto the main road leading to Aberdeen. The driver was Chinese and in the passenger seat sat a fairly tall man with close cropped hair, who couldn't be much over fifty. He was toying with the pistol in his lap, which was equipped with an extra long silencer. In his briefcase, sitting between his legs, was the broken-down sniper rifle, complete with a night vision scope. The passenger was silent as was the driver, obviously intent on their mission. They wore similar clothing----dark pants and black pullover shirts, nothing notable, except for their efforts to *not* be notable. They tried to follow with a car between, successfully blending with fast coming darkness.

"How does The Black Orchid ferry their guests to the boat?" I asked John.

"They have their own launch that carries about fifteen passengers. Most other floating restaurants use one of the several for-hire launches that make regular rounds to the restaurants. That takes a little longer as they stop at each restaurant, picking up and letting off. The trip to The Black Orchid takes about ten minutes including loading and unloading, since it is for their exclusive use. It is really a very short run, but interesting as you go by the people on sampans cooking dinner, just living their lives as usual. It is hard to realize how those people could live their entire lives floating on a little boat about the size of your bathroom."

The Jaguar reached the city of Aberdeen, which was named for a British Peer in the mid-eighteen hundreds. Even then it was the most active fishing village in the entire area. The streets were still narrow, reflecting the same village ambiance that reportedly was present a century and a half prior. John expertly negotiated the twists and turns of the village roads that would easily confuse a tourist to the area, but not the little dark car following discreetly at a distance down the same narrow roads.

After a final twist and a turn, John pulled up to the waterfront on a small dock with parking for a number of cars. "Here we are, The Black Orchid Dock. I don't see the launch so they are out on a run and should return within ten minutes or so." He said as he got out and walked around to the trunk and retrieved a large flat package wrapped in brown paper.

The little dark car pulled up on the street where they could still observe the occupants of the Jaguar. A crowd was gathering at the passenger dock, therefore an opportunity to complete the taller man's mission would have to wait. The driver now knew that the destination of the Jaguar's occupants was The Black Orchid. He left the taller man and went down the stairs of the adjoining public dock and spoke to a man about renting a small motorboat for the evening. This done, he returned to the taller man, and waited.

John with package under his arm was standing near the edge peering out toward the jumble of boats lashed to one another in an endless anchoring system rolling with the gentle waves, when he suddenly announced, "Here it comes, the Orchid launch. Do you see it over there?" He pointed to a beautiful shiny black boat, methodically working its way through the sampans toward the dock and perhaps a dozen anxious diners.

We stood by as two couples climbed the steps of the launch and onto the deck, helped by a dockside Orchid employee. Our anxiously awaiting group then boarded the launch and the powerful vessel eased back into the gently rolling bay toward The Black Orchid.

The occupants of the little black car rushed back to the dock where their newly rented small outboard boat was waiting. They climbed in and the taller one gave the starting rope a pull, receiving only a pitiful cough for his efforts. After four or five more pulls, the little motor choked to a bumpy start, and finally pulled it together, chasing after the big muscle boat with little success. The larger launch easily pulled away, churning through the dark water toward the restaurant. As the gap widened between the launch and the small outboard, frustration increased as the taller man cussed and kicked the side of the little boat, watching the much faster Black Orchard launch move away. The only salvation for the followers was they already knew the destination of the Jaguar passengers, considering the launch was owned by The Black Orchard restaurant and only serviced *their* dining customers.

Meanwhile, Valarie looked down from the main salon observation window on the starboard side of the luxurious launch and saw the multitude of sampans below. From her close vantage point she could easily see their occupants as they cruised past. She saw a man fishing on a small boat, his three children playing with a stick while mom cooked over a kettle on the deck, and at the same time sold fish to other boats as they pulled near.

This was a typical scene on the sampans as the launch carefully threaded its way through the flotilla heading toward the restaurant. "This is truly a sight. I have to get some pictures. I've got to paint this," her hand rummaged through her bag for her camera. With eyes fixed on the small boat she was watching as they passed by, Valarie quickly raised the camera and started shooting as fast as possible and at every boat she passed.

Watching her enthusiasm, I couldn't help saying, "Wow, you sound like one of those photographers shooting models for a fashion magazine----click----click----click."

"I wish I was that good," she laughed. "I hope a few turn out so I can paint from them and try and do justice to their reality."

"Valarie, based on what I saw of your harbor sketches, I do not imagine you will have any trouble doing justice to what you are seeing." John said smiling.

"John you're too kind. I only wish it were true, but thank you I really appreciate it."

"Do they serve Martini's on this tub?" I asked with my silly, just kidding expression. Only I was serious.

"They tried to serve drinks on board, but ended up spending too much on cleaning bills from the jostling. They really had difficulty keeping a martini in the glass." John kidded.

"I'd agree with that concern." I said, grabbing for a handrail after a sudden lurch.

The occupants of the other boat made their way through the floating humanity, whose lives of daily survival were far removed from the deadly intent of the two dressed in black. Losing sight of the Orchid launch was frustrating to the leader although the smaller man, an Asian, knew these waters well, and the anchored location of the floating restaurant. Suddenly the Orchid launch came into view as they swung around a dozen-boat flotilla. It was tied to the port side of a beautiful black and white craft that easily measured one hundred and fifty feet, the leader observed. He looked inquiringly at the smaller man, nodded and continued on, pulling up next to an anchored fishing trawler, equally large, with only the obligatory warning lights lit for a boat that was either presently unoccupied or occupied only by a small crew left aboard for security. The starboard side of the trawler, about a hundred feet away, presented an unobstructed view of the launch gangplank leading onto the restaurant deck. They tied up to a rope ladder hanging from the trawler's side reaching almost to the lapping water----and waited.

John led the way, turning to take Valarie's arm as they walked across the wide gangplank with posts every few feet and strung with heavy rope railings for safety and confidence while crossing. The walk could make some people uneasy especially when the harbor was boiling, which was not the case this evening. The gangplank extended from a large opening in the middle of The Black Orchid on a lower deck. It was low enough that the launch could come along side, and from its top deck be at almost the same level as the restaurant entry. "This is really beautiful----all of these carved gold dragons. Such great detail, I can hardly wait to see the rest of it." Valarie said with great anticipation.

At the end of the gangplank was an alcove type porch area carpeted in a rich blood red that led to ten-foot high, red enameled doors carved with a huge medallion in the center. We were greeted by a man in a tuxedo who immediately said something to John in Chinese, and then spoke in perfect English, "Welcome Mr. Winters and Miss Austin, we are looking forward to serving you and have reserved a very special table overlooking the entire harbor."

I whispered to John as we followed another staff member, "Is that your friend the owner?"

"No that is Lee a trusted assistant, he's worked here for many years and knows thousands of Hong Kong residents by name as well as visitors from other countries that come here only infrequently."

We walked through the entry, down a short hall that opened to a grand curving staircase that was easily twenty feet wide, with a beautiful black and gold banister and a continuation of the plush red carpet. Twenty feet or so above the staircase was a huge crystal chandelier, loaded with prisms, and providing the effect of thousands of diamonds, glistening off the polished black enamel of the banister and the mirrored walls on either side. All this beauty was accompanied by the soft muted background tones of
Chinese music, that seemed to be coming from every direction through invisible speakers. We came to a large landing and our escort led us past what appeared to be the main dining room. The room looked filled and there appeared to be no available tables. The diners were mostly Asian, and from the tone of their banter seemed to be enjoying the evening. At the rear of the dining room there was another hallway the led to yet another stairway.

This was smaller than the former and led to what seemed to be the top deck. We followed another hallway that opened up to a large dining room table under a twenty by thirty foot white canvas canopy and illuminated by red glass lanterns. Completely enclosing the space were white planter boxes filled with shrubbery that grew to about thirty inches in height. Propane heaters were positioned above and on the corners of the space for those evenings that required warmth. Happily this one didn't. Upon looking around we saw that we had a 360-degree view of the harbor. This outstretched scene contained a microcosm of life, each participant facing daily challenges of existence, some easier than others as has been the case over the centuries.

"John, this is fantastic." I said. "Have you ever eaten in this beautiful setting?"

"Oh, yes, as I said the owner's a dear friend whom I've known for many years. This is the owner's private dining room and only used for special situations."

"Well John, whatever your influence I could never have arranged such a   spectacular setting. This is unbelievable."

Valarie was so taken by the view that she was speechless for a moment before saying, "John this is the most beautiful place and an experience I could never imagine. Thank you for bringing us here."

"It is one of my favorite dining spots as well. I believe the owner will stop by for a glass of wine shortly, I'm looking forward to introducing my two new American friends."

Valarie and I were standing under the canopy taking in the distant view as the gentle warm breeze from the South China Sea caressed us. There was a sound of the hallway door opening, and in the doorway stood a tall, striking Eurasian woman, dressed in a black and white wide striped satin evening gown, with her black shiny hair pulled into a chignon. She appeared to be somewhere between the age of thirty and who can say, it was just impossible to tell. She wore a large emerald pendant on a silver chain that lay suspended in her cleavage. Her makeup was simple yet effective, and as she moved she emitted a hint of fresh jasmine, which in its context on her carried an almost erotic aroma which reminded me of walking through a tropical island garden in the summer moonlight. It brought back a recollection of a special time, which has remained fresh in my memory all these years. For some reason I assumed that the owner John referred to was a man as opposed to this beautiful mysterious woman. Valarie's eyes immediately fixated on this person, just like any woman might do, or for that matter any member of any species that encountered a possible challenge for what they had----or wanted. This is not to say that Valarie felt threatened or that she had something at risk. It was more a combination of respect for a woman that she could rationalize to be more beautiful than she. As well as that territorial protection, instinctive in any woman or man for that matter as much as I hate to admit, about protecting what is theirs regardless of whether they want the prize or not.

John smiling, walked toward the woman and comfortably slipped his arm around her waist as he faced us and said, "This is my very close friend May Lee." Looking to her he said, "May Lee, I'd like you to meet my good friends, Valarie Austin and Chuck Winters from the San Francisco area."

"Mr. Winters and Miss Austin, welcome to The Black Orchid." John continued to hold his arm around her waist in a way that strongly demonstrated an affection that transcended that of a customer-owner relationship.

"We are truly impressed with your beautiful restaurant."

"Thank you Mr. Winters, John told me about you and your experience in the computer industry. I told him that I really have a need for someone I could trust with that kind of knowledge."

"Well. I don't do that kind of work any longer, but if you have a specific need, I could probably point you in the right direction." I answered in my usual boyish, charming way, while Valarie tossed me a cool look----oh well.

"I think my problem is personnel, what is it they say, *garbage in garbage out*?" She responded as she walked over to the sideboard at the end of the room.

"It sounds like your people need some training. People all too often think that when they buy computers for their business, their personnel will be able to pick it up. But it isn't as easy as the computer companies lead you to believe. I'm certain there are well-qualified computer training companies here in Hong Kong that can assist you. A good source is your local banker. Find out who they use as an out source for training." I responded, this time actually sounding like I knew what I was talking about.

"Wonderful idea----thank you, drinks?" She said turning toward us as she opened the double door cabinet, exposing a well stocked liquor and wine assortment along with a silver bucket full of crushed ice.

She expertly mixed our drink orders and poured a glass of California white wine for Valarie and herself.

CHAPTER 25

The taller man in the small boat had been patiently looking for an opening to complete his assignment. He positioned himself under a tarp he found in the little boat and was mostly hidden from view. Working in the darkness beneath the tarp cover, he carefully assembled his high-powered rifle with the night vision scope and silencer. He then methodically began searching from window to window, hoping to get lucky and find his target within his field of fire, rather than as they boarded the launch for the return trip. An approach he viewed to be more dangerous with a greater chance of getting caught.

He studied the faces he saw through his powerful scope, comparing each with the visual memory he made from the photograph he had been given, and at the hotel when he watched for a while in the restaurant while they were ordering dinner. He didn't expect to be lucky enough to find his target at a window, particularly one that faced in his direction, however if they had to wait he might as well see if he could shorten the process and guarantee a safe getaway, along with a morning flight home on the next flight to Lisbon. He methodically searched each window in the dining room, but saw no sign of his quarry.

Out of sheer boredom he though it could be productive to check the boat over to see of there might be some form of security or cameras visible from his vantage point. In doing so, he aimed his scope at the top of the boat and planned on working down. He noticed a white canopy with walls of green shrubbery in white planter boxes. The canopy was lighted and there appeared to be a group of people inside. He re-focused his riflescope in order to get a sharper picture, and immediately saw the Austin woman, "*bingo*" he thought. He straightened up to get a better look into the space that was at least one hundred and forty feet away and elevated at lease thirty feet. The woman moved from sight and an Asian woman moved into view.

'Damn it', he thought, 'where in the hell is he?'

As usual, Valarie struck up a conversation by complimenting May on how lovely her boat was, and like the student of human nature she was, she quite deftly moved the conversation back to Valarie. Knowing exactly where she was going with this, she asked her about her *work*. May had been briefed by John when he called earlier. She was quite aware of what an excellent artist Valarie was, and the fact that aside from being serious about her art, she was quite modest and unassuming as to her talent.

"My work?" Valarie asked, and continued to answer. "I'm an artist, actually still learning, but I do work on it full time----or try to". She responded, while glancing at me, perhaps from some embarrassment about this focus on her. I was listening with one ear and carrying on a conversation with John, mostly about politics in Hong Kong----or somewhere.

"That's not what I heard. John simply raves about your work." May said with a warm smile.

"John is too kind. I believe he's just trying to be polite." She replied with her own version of a gracious smile.

John, who was also listening with one ear, was answering a question about something that he forgot---- and interjected, "That is just not true, her work is outstanding and I took the liberty of bringing along an example." He picked up the package he had brought aboard and proceeded to remove the wrapping. Valarie turned with a stunned look and John continued, "I retrieved this when one of my cleaning people asked if this belonged in the trash. I of course replied absolutely not, this belongs in a frame. So that's exactly what I did." He added as he held up the pencil sketch of a flotilla of sampans in the harbor below his home, rolling with the waves from the wake of a freighter passing by. The sketch was affixed to a dark green matting, about a quarter of an inch larger than the sketch paper, and further placed on a white linen matting that filled the frame measuring fifteen inches by about twenty. The frame itself was worth about two hundred dollars, which John had only last month ordered for a favorite sailing ship print he had just purchased.

Smiles appeared all around, and John added, "This of course is your work and therefore your property, but when we decided to go to dinner tonight and were going to May Lee's place, I could not in good conscience pass up this opportunity to show your castaway----which would give anyone an idea on how excellent an artist you are. Besides, May recently told me she was looking for more art for her restaurant. I think you are the answer." He said with an infectious grin.

"What can I say, other than this flattery is undeserved and embarrassing." Valarie gushed with a modest smile.

"This work is wonderful. I want to buy it right now. How much do you want for it?" May asked.

"I won't sell it, you can have it if you really want it but I don't think it's very good." She said with some seriousness and added, "The frame is beautiful, and not mine. I can't give you that----it's John's."

"Then it's settled, the sketch is now going to be displayed in The Black Orchid, and the frame is my gift to both of you ladies." John added, demonstrating his suave demeanor.

"May I call you Valarie?" May asked, and added, "Please call me May.

"Of course May."

"I'm serious about your work, I would like to commission you to do a series of sketches and paintings of the harbor scenes and whatever else you think might be appropriate here at the restaurant." She said, and added. "And let me warn you, the exposure here may cause you to become busier than you want, however you can control that with your pricing. But my guess is, even high prices might not slow down the demand for your work if this is representative." She said, admiring the framed work.

"Thank you. I'm so flattered that you feel this way, but let's see what I have after I see my pictures and try to capture this beauty on paper and canvas. If you give me your business card, I'll be happy to send you something for your opinion."

"Here you are." May said producing a card as if by magic, considering her dress barely had room for her---- let alone pockets.

All this time John and I were enjoying the interplay between these two beautiful women, competing perhaps unknowingly in a very personal way, each taking something away from the encounter, and feeling good about themselves for it.

"Well Valarie, be prepared when all of May's influential Hong Kong regulars see your work prominently displayed. They will insist on buying them off the wall and May will insist they are not for sale. Then the capitalistic dance of supply and demand occurs and May is calling you for more." John outlined her already ordained success with obvious delight in doing something nice for her.

I walked over with John to the side of the room that looked out on Aberdeen and the sampan flotilla when the hanging lantern above my head exploded, shattering into a thousand pieces of red glass shards. The canopy material had been ripped into shreds as the bullets and flying glass caused a large gaping hole above my head. I instinctively pulled John to the ground while looking for Valarie and May. They were standing near the sideboard talking and were ten feet away from the exploding lantern. They looked unharmed and were taking cover on the carpet near the sideboard.

"Stay down, I yelled." Just as John handed me a gun from the shoulder holster under his jacket and pulled another from the holster strapped to his belt. I now know why he wore the suit jacket on this warm evening. I looked at John, his suit streaked with blood from his bleeding face, not from the bullets but from flying glass shards. The cuts appeared to be superficial but obviously painful. My face was cut as well, but my eyes were spared and it appeared John's were as well. Seeing that the girls were not injured, I pulled the cord that fed the lanterns and inched my way to the now darkened edge of the room and peered carefully through the shrubbery. I couldn't see a place on this deck where anyone could have

210

fired, as the trajectory was up through the lantern and further through the canvas canopy. It had to be below and from another boat. As I looked for a prospective sniper location I saw the muzzle flash from the small boat tied at the base of a large old cargo ship anchored in the harbor. The canopy exploded from a hail of bullets and with continuous fire the planters began breaking up, causing shrubbery and dirt to rain down on us, and this once beautiful and private dining area.

"Let's get out of here." I yelled, and May started crawling, with Valarie following close behind, toward the opening that led to the door and hallway to the stairs we came up.

When we reached the hallway, May stood and shouted, "This way." And we followed her through a beautifully carved black door and into an area that was obviously her private quarters. She went to the phone on the large glass table that served as her desk, pushed a button and shouted some orders in Chinese. Before anyone had a chance to collect their thoughts and comment on the events that just occurred, two large Asians dressed in dark suits with guns in their hands rushed through her office door. After a quick glance, I was getting ready for the next world war, or more accurately the end of the world----when May announced that two of her security force had arrived and the balance were outside looking for the "terrorists" as she chose to call them.

I was holding Valarie who assured me she was all right though still shaking some, and when the 'security forces' arrived in such a bluster, she *really* started shaking. She reassured me she was fine and told me to do what I needed to do, but be careful. Turning to her security men, I told them I knew where the fire was coming from and suggested that I show them the last known location of the shooter. Happily, one of her "strike force" members spoke reasonable English. John picked up the phone and called someone, probably the Hong Kong Police department. May came out of the bathroom with hot towels for John and me to clean up our faces and assess the damage done by the glass cuts. She announced, "You're both going to live." as she wiped our foreheads and cheeks, while smearing stinging disinfectant over our wounds.

"We need to see if we can find them. John, would you mind keeping the ladies safe, I'll be right back?"

Tong, the body guard that spoke English, listened as I described where I saw the muzzle flash. He then led the way as the three of us went down what was probably a service stairwell, through the kitchen and to the starboard side of the Black Orchid, away from where the shooting occurred. At the bottom of a ladder stairway that led to a small opening out the side of the ship, sat a sleek, black, maybe twenty-foot long speedboat. We jumped in and Tong started the surprisingly quiet powerful inboard, and we silently purred through the black water around the bow and headed toward the darkened cargo ship. Our course took us around the stern of the ship. The Orchid and another smaller anchored boat gave us total cover from observance as we approached the last known location of the shooter. Tong turned off the big engine as we reached the bow of the cargo ship, and he turned on a silent five horsepower, electric trolling motor that he had swung over the bow and into the water on an arm. Silently we stole around this huge creaking and rusting ship that had been serving as cover for the shooter. When we reached the spot where I saw the muzzle flashes, the boat was gone. We pulled up where I thought the other boat was tied up and were able to verify that the field of fire was a perfect match for hitting our deck dining room.

"I told you they'd go to our last location." The taller man whispered to the other. "This is even better." He said as they crouched in their boat about two hundred feet from the old cargo ship. This time hidden among several unoccupied boats anchored to a buoy.

The rifle fire was unrelenting as the maniacally grinning taller man held his finger on the trigger, causing a hail of bullets, ripping the luxury boat to splinters. Blood was flowing and forming in large pools, mixing with the foaming sea in a ghastly soup of death and destruction. "That does it." He said as his final barrage was aimed at what he hoped was the fuel tank. A fiery explosion resulted as the last remnants of the once sleek and beautiful craft shot into the air like a fourth of July fireworks display, then falling back into the ocean with a sizzle and a quiet, swallowing the evidence of mayhem and death that just occurred.

Everyone on the Orchid heard the explosion. The blast and ensuing turbulence caused the restaurant to roll violently until the water calmed. Almost everyone on board came to the port, or the left side to see what had happened. Only those diners seated by the windows facing the old cargo ship could see the explosion and fiery inferno that followed. The others caused even more confusion and heightened anxiety, by questioning those that had seen it.

John, May and Valarie stood in the darkened window in disbelief and shock as the explosion surely meant bad news for Chuck, and May's two security men. She reached for the phone and punched what must be a security number, and began a fast banter in Chinese and hung up. "My people are taking the launch over to the where the explosion occurred to search for survivors." She said, as John was holding the uncontrollably sobbing Valarie. "We don't know what happened or if Mr. Winters or my men were even on the boat when it exploded." May added----in an attempt to ease Valarie's worst fears.

John added, "I don't think we're in danger now, too much has happened. The police will soon be blocking the docks and roads and will be in boats checking everything and searching for Chuck and the security men."

"I don't see how anyone could survive such an explosion, and if they did, they'd drown for sure." Valarie sobbed.

"Let us not count Chuck out yet, from what I have seen, he is a very methodical thinker and I am quite certain he knows how to take care of himself." John said trying to calm her.

The taller man grinned with a triumphant look as they calmly motored away, being careful not to alert anyone or do anything unusual. The police would soon be on the case, if they weren't already. His escape carefully thought out would soon be put in place. He told the other man to take the boat to the far side of the harbor away from the restaurant dock, over where the large ships anchored. The smaller man questioned his logic but the taller man prevailed and they motored on. When they reached the docks where freighters unloaded their cargo day and night, the taller man motioned to a dock ladder that extended down the side of a piling to the water. It was dark and the ladder could barely be seen as the other man went to work tying up the small boat. The bullet went through the back of his skull, and the smaller man,

214

silently, with barely a murmur, slipped into the dark cold sea after participating in his final act of malice. The taller man checked the boat for evidence, packed away his gear and climbed the ladder.

The truck he selected, its motor running, was loaded with bolts of fabrics as the tag said and destined for a factory in Kowloon. They would soon be transformed into clothing, most likely for the American market and loaded back on another ship for yet another journey. The tarp was loose as he climbed into the back, which was easily hidden from view and from curious police who probably were searching cars leaving the harbor from the restaurant dock road, and not likely from the freight terminals on the west side of Aberdeen Harbor.

Mon Yee struggling tried to lift the near lifeless form he had discovered after the explosion, floating near the boat where he and his family barely eked out a living, mostly fishing. And whenever the opportunity presented, Me Ko his wife would sell a woven straw hat to tourists passing by on hired boats. This evening Mon Yee was thinking only of saving this man wearing nice clothing. It had barely been a minute or so after the explosion near the Black Orchid when he discovered him. Mon Yee felt this man had to be on the boat that blew up in the water. His mind, out of necessity turned to thoughts of a possible reward for saving his life, but he could never tell Me Ko such a thing. She would never think of being paid for helping another human being. The important thing was helping others and others would be there to help you. Mon Yee had been waiting for the help for a very long time. Although their boat was not large, they had managed to feed and cloth, in one fashion or another, their four children. Maybe Me Ko's philosophy was right, but Mon Yee wasn't sure they had received the good returns for thinking of others. He called to her. His frail body was aching from pulling heavy fishnets into his little boat all day long and with little success. The small boat was now carefully secured to the side of their modest sampan.

"What is it?" Looking at the lifeless body, she asked in horror, "Is he dead?"

"No he is still breathing and I think he was on the boat that just blew up."

"Let's get him inside." She said as she gently helped Mon Yee pull the bleeding, unconscious man out of the boat. As soon as he was on their deck, their oldest son Ho, thirteen, came out of the back to see what was happening. He was immediately put to work helping to carry this hurt man into the back living area. The other three children gathered around and Me Ko quickly sent them away while she went to work.

Valarie was frantic as the launch crew returned with the news that there were no survivors in the area and it appeared that the boat went down immediately in the near two hundred feet of water. John said, "Come, let us go back to the house. The inspector has all of his resources working on the search for Chuck and the security guards, and has assigned a team to protect us as well. He has a full task force dedicated to apprehending these criminals and I am in constant touch should anything come up, all right?"

Tearfully she sobbed an assent as John put his arm around her. In the company of one of May's security guards they headed down the stairs to the waiting launch.

John waited until they arrived at his home and after trying his best to comfort Valarie, went into his office and called Art Levy in San Francisco at his office. It was early afternoon. "Art Levy."

John paused to collect his thoughts, and said, "Art, I have some bad news. There has been an explosion near a floating restaurant where we were about to have dinner. Chuck was investigating a barrage of rifle shots aimed at us from a small boat nearby. I'm sorry to say he was on another boat with two restaurant security men looking for the shooter, and it was totally destroyed. No survivors have been found."

"What about Valarie?"

"She is fine and with me at my home. The police are searching for bodies as well as the people who did this. I knew you would want to call his people and let them know."

"John, are you sure he's dead? Is there any way he might have survived?" Art asked hopefully with a shaky voice.

"Art, I really do not see how. There is nothing left of the boat. The shooter hit the gas tank and it exploded into a million pieces."

"Well, I hesitate to call his family until I have absolute proof of his death, but I'll call Tom Claudius. He worked for him on this assignment. John, I'm coming to Hong Kong. I'll be there tomorrow. I need to get to the bottom of this and will need your help."

"You know I will be here for you, any way you want."

CHAPTER 26

Mon Yee and Me Ko worked hard to nurse their patient and save his life. It had been almost three hours and he was still unconscious, yet breathing evenly and unlabored. Me Ko washed his face and nursed the scratches that looked like brambles or thorn cuts. His face was badly bruised and he had a large lump on the right side of his head, which was probably causing his lack of consciousness. Mon Yee took off his wet and torn clothes and put on some loose fitting pajama style peasant clothes that belonged to his late uncle who was much larger than he or he would have kept them for himself.

John received a call from Sue Tang's father and heard that Sue had been found dead near the office building where she was scheduled to have a job interview. She had been strangled and not robbed or raped. This murder had an altogether different motive than the usual, if there was a usual. John expressed his sorrow and offered to assist in any way possible and although none was asked for, a check would be sent to her father in the morning.

"Mr. Claudius, this is Art Levy, an old friend of Chuck Winters and an associate of his on the case he's doing for you. I wanted to tell you that I have some news that doesn't look good, I----"

"Wait, Art is it?"

"Yes."

"Are you telling me something's happened to Chucky?"

"Yes. I just had a call from Hong Kong. It looks like he was blown up on purpose in a small boat. There were no bodies recovered. I told them I'm leaving right away for Hong Kong. I won't call his parents until I know if it's true."

"Art, this is my fault. I sent him on this wild goose chase. If you are willing to go to Hong Kong, it's on me, your time, expenses, everything. This is just nuts." Tom added.

"Mr. Claudius----", Art tried to add before being interrupted.

"It's Tom, call me Tom." He insisted.

"Tom, it isn't necessary to pay my expenses, Chuck is my friend----"

"Dammit, he's my friend too and I want to do this, OK?" Tom insisted.
"Art, do you think I should come, I'd come in a minute if I can help? You know, spread some dough around----whatever it takes to find out about Chuck, and who the hell has done this crap."

"Thanks for the offer Tom, but I don't think it's necessary at this time, but if I need some muscle while I'm there, you can bet I'll be calling you. OK?" Art replied.

"You got it, whatever you need, and don't forget this one's on me. You understand?"

"Thanks Tom, I'll keep you informed." Art said and hung up the phone and began booking his flight. While doing so, he was feeling a big pain in the pit of his stomach and in his mind started replaying in fast forward, all the good and bad times they've had together over the years.

CHAPTER 27

LAS VEGAS, NEVADA

Sitting in his luxurious complementary suite provided by the casino, he was about ready to head down to the high stakes poker game when his cell phone showed a message from the answering service in Los Angeles. He arranged this clever firewall to avoid any direct contact by anyone involved in the operation. If someone wanted to speak to him, they'd call a number assigned to him in a Los Angeles answering service and leave a voice mail message. The presence of a voice mail message would automatically ring his cell phone and he'd call and retrieve the message. The number and message was from the taller man. He placed the call from his blocked cell number to the man's cell phone. Upon hearing hello, "It's me." He said.

"It's done you don't have to worry about him any more. That girl's gone too. I'm flying back to Lisbon in the morning and I want the money transferred into my account when I arrive, you understand?"

"I don't know if I can have it done that fast. It takes time to arrange the wire transfer."

The taller man replied, "I had extra expenses, a local I had to hire, and he expects to be paid before I leave. Do you hear?" He said grinning to himself and knowing the *local* is nothing more than fish food in the harbor right now.

"Can't you pay him from the money you already have in your account?"

"Yes, but I'm not going to carry your expenses. After all you're making the big bucks on this deal. I've been thinking this has gotten a lot more involved than you planned, and a lot more killing. I'm taking all the chances. I think I need a boost in my share----say another million." He said, cautiously waiting for the explosion.

"Listen you bastard, you're already in for one-point-five, and now you want another million bucks. Are you crazy? Better yet do you think I'm crazy----do you?" He asked in anger.

"Calm down, let's just call it an even two mill." The taller man said.

"I'll consider it when you finish the job and my money's in the account. Do you understand that?"

"OK, just get that money in my account so I can pay my bills, do *you* understand?" The taller man asked.

"You'll have it sometime tomorrow----fifty thousand."

"Right", said the taller man as he clicked off his cell phone.

The poker game was about to start and he felt certain he was going to be lucky tonight. The Arab was in town and would be in the game. He always livened things up, as he'd sometimes drop two or three million. The phone rang again. "Hello."

"Hi, this is Lisa do you want me to come over again----
like right now?"

"No Lisa, I have a meeting. I'm leaving right now. I
have your number. I'll call you when I can." He said, as
he thought, 'Once those whores latch on to you, sensing
dough, they never let go.'

He left the suite, which he felt represented the life he
should become accustomed to, and walked to the elevator
for the trip to a world he created from desperation and
greed. He reached the lobby floor and took the familiar
turn to the right, past the rows and rows of machines and
crap tables to the elevator marked "Private". Upon
entering, an operator in front of a computer had the
name of every 'special' customer registered with the
casino, and inquired, "your name please". He responded,
"John Foster", and was permitted to press the button to
the twenty-fourth floor. He thought how clever he was to
have established a new identity, complete with credit
cards and bank accounts. In reality he was protecting
him from himself, a man with a deeply flawed moral and
legal compass.

"Good evening Mr. Foster." Said the swarthy man
with slick, greasy black hair and wearing a tuxedo.

He was taken back and then believed that he must be
such an important customer that everyone knew him in
the high stakes room, although he'd never seen the man
before tonight, and didn't know that the girl on the
computer called ahead into the man's ear piece with the
name of the arriving guest. Foster, as he called himself
was ushered to a chair at a table occupied by four other
players, including the sheik from an oil rich Arab state

and three others. All were regular high rollers at the casino who flew into the city in their private jets, and all playing for 'pocket money' as compared to their net worth. Foster was the exception in the group. The only reason the casino allowed him into this elite circle was that he demonstrated he had the cash to cover his losses, which seemed to be his playing style. Over the last several months he had lost over a million dollars playing poker, covering his losses without apparent trouble. On the surface, to the casino, Foster acted like a well-heeled guy representing new money, either dot-com or the street. But raising cash through phony consultants at TechX was a little more difficult. As a result his gambling losses and subsequent embezzlement scheme forced him to plan a grand exit from the company. He'd expected to become rich when he exercised his stock options after the company went public. But since he had to cover his gambling losses earlier in the year, everything turned upside down in his life, starting the wheels in motion for an early retirement. He had to bring in people that could help him, like Victoria and others, but ten million wasn't a bad number to start with, plus the two and a half already taken from the company, which was mostly all lost in his gambling forays.

"Mr. Foster, how much would you like tonight?" The man asked.

"I'll start with a hundred." He said as the man counted out one hundred thousand dollars in assorted chip denominations.

"Here you are sir." He said as he handed Foster the receipt for his initial starting bank.

Foster thought, "this is when I get even. I feel lucky tonight".

As usual he started with a new confidence----a man in full control. "I'll have a tall, double scotch and water----your best." He said. The long, long evening was about to begin---- again. The first hand was not to his liking. He invested twenty thousand on three deuces and lost to the Arab with a full house.

CHAPTER 28
HONG KONG

John Sun met with Inspector Li the next morning as previously planned. Valarie was thoroughly distraught with heartache over Chuck, but was unwilling to give up and insisted on attending the meeting to find out what was being done to find him. Or, in the back of her mind and unable to admit, find his body.

"John, Miss Austin, I am sorry to report that I have no further information on Mr. Winters. We have had the Harbor Police searching the area around the explosion and have commenced a dragging effort in the vicinity as well. We have also contacted the residents of the flotilla and have had no success. It appears that all three men were lost in the explosion. It is not likely that their remains will ever be found. I have told our men to continue their effort until they hear otherwise from me. We do feel confident that we have found the boat and what we believe is the body of one of the assassins. We can only assume at this point that the man was shot in the back of the head and dumped into the harbor to eliminate any witness to the attack, as well as to the attacker. The dead man was Asian and had no print record. We have been unable to identify him. My opinion is that the shooter has in his mind, completed his assignment and left the country. I am saying this not to encourage you to drop your guard, which I don't think you should, but because he killed this partner, which tells me his work is finished here. But one can never be certain."

"I'm wondering," Valarie went on, "how can someone in a small boat at least ten minutes from land, escape the police that were on the case before he could even reach the dock?"

"Miss Austin, we found the boat on the other side of the harbor near the big cargo wharves. It appears this is a very professional contract assignment by someone from America or Europe. My guess is Europe. He either had a car parked near the dock or hitched a ride on a truck heading into the city, probably unknown to the driver. Everything about this was very carefully executed." The Inspector said.

John thought a moment or two, and responded, "I can only think of one way the shooter found us, and that's from inside the Hong Kong Police Department. I was absolutely scrupulous in the tight security surrounding Chuck and Valarie's whereabouts. I have told no one that they were living at my home, yet it seems that the killer waited on the road and followed us to the Black Orchid. Who knew about this morning's meeting that was scheduled only yesterday?"

The Inspector answering with a slight offense considered the question a challenge to his integrity. Although understanding that the department was the likely source of such a leak. A number of people were working on the Sue Tang murder, which was appearing to be related to her meeting with John Sun and Chuck Winters. Such investigation required exploring any connection with KRL. "Let me assure you that the department keeps its information confidential and would not be the source of such a leak." Listening to what he had just said, he knew that it sounded preposterous. He could never control intentional or unintentional leaks within the department, so he added, "It's possible that someone working on the Sue Tang case could have mentioned the fact that Mr. Winters was being interviewed in the morning at John Lee's home, and it accidentally got out."

John nodded and said, "Art Levy of San Francisco, another associate of Chuck's was flying in. He probably still will want to press KRL for theft or attempted theft of intellectual property, namely the chip software owned by TechX, in order to open this up and find the killers of Chuck and others involved with this case. As soon as he arrives, I'll call you for a meeting. But rest assured, the meeting will be at the police station, and please under no circumstances let Mr. Levy's name leave this room until I bring him to your office."

CHAPTER 29

Me Ko gently raised the head of her patient as she had done for the last dozen or so hours, squeezing a little water into his dry mouth. The lump on his head had receded somewhat after applying continuous cold compresses throughout the night. This time she tried to get him to take a drop or two of warm broth, to as she thought, sustain him and help him out of his unconsciousness. He was unable to take the nourishment, but the water squeezed from the cloth seemed to stay in his mouth and must have been some comfort to him. They had talked about going to the authorities, but hesitated as Mon Yee had come to distrust them. This was particularly true of a harbor patrolman who used to extort fish from him in exchange for, as he was told, violating the laws on his fishing net lengths and where he could fish in the harbor. Mon Yee moved to a different area in the harbor because of this man, and felt if he reported the sick man he brought aboard his boat, he might be blamed in some way for his condition by the patrolman who seemed to have influence in the harbor. He also continued privately to think that if they saved the man's life, he himself would be forever indebted to him---
-which is the Chinese way. He felt so fortunate that he had this problem with the police, because if he hadn't, Me Ko who was a very honest and proud woman would have made life miserable for him until he called the authorities----a very un-Chinese way for a woman to act. She privately enjoyed this new duty thrust upon her. It was some time since her children or anyone for that matter really needed her. Me Ko sat in her blue lounging-type, loose cotton pants and large white shirt, the dress of choice for the flotilla residents. It could turn quite warm in the summer hurricane season and the loose clothes in a variety of colors were very comfortable. She

was thirty-seven and quite attractive. Although her figure was hidden under her baggy clothes, her black eyes seemed to come alive and sparkle when she smiled. She took great care in maintaining her beautiful black hair.

There was a warm breeze coming off the South China Sea that slipped through the flap she had opened in the side of the boat. She sat close to her patient on a bed made up especially for him, tending his every need. Stroking his temples and hoping his eyes would soon open, she had looked earlier and knew were brown. She only wished she had learned more English in school, which she assumed was his language. She did not finish school because she had to work to help support her family. But felt when he did come around she would be able to know what his needs were. As long as he was breathing steady and easily, she felt he was improving and did not need a hospital. His facial cuts had stopped bleeding and after examining his body, as much as possible, mostly when her husband was gone and the children were not close by, she found no evidence of broken bones or other problems that could be major. Just the big bump on his head causing his deep sleep she felt.

Art Levy had never met Valarie. Chuck often spoke of her in a way that he knew she was *the* special person in his life. John sent a driver to the airport to pick him up and return to the house. Upon arriving, John came out on the porch and greeted Art, his friend of many years, first meeting at a seminar on electronic surveillance in Honolulu. "Art, good to see you, although I am sorry it is under these circumstances."

"Thanks me too."

"Come in I want you to meet Valarie. But first let me show you your room. If you want to freshen up, please do so." The suite John led Art to was on the main floor and identical to the one occupied by Valarie----and previously Chuck.

"This is beautiful John. I'll just drop my jacket and take off this tie----be right with you. I want to see Valarie and get started right away."

Art walked into John's office while he was calling Valarie's room on the intercom, telling her that Art had arrived. She rushed upstairs to meet the man that might she hoped could push things forward and find out more about Chuck. Not she thought that John wasn't doing everything possible. It was just that she felt more comfortable with someone from home that was a close friend of Chuck's.

"Valarie, please meet Art Levy." John graciously said.

"Mr. Levy----"

"Hi Valarie----and it's, Art." He interrupted with a smile and held open his arms for a hug that they both needed. He sensed her tenseness and thought he heard an understandable sob.

Valarie stepped back a bit and said, "Then----Art, I really appreciate you coming. You have no idea how much this means me. Chuck thought very highly of you."

"Chuck would do the same for me. Let's get down to business. John, is there any chance that he was plucked out of the water by the shooter or a well meaning citizen that doesn't read the news or know anything about this?" Valarie immediately knew her anticipation of his arrival was not misguided. This was exactly the approach she was hoping for.

"I do not know. But of course nothing can be ruled out. The police continue to search for him----and for answers."

"John, I want to launch a private parallel search with reward money for information that assists in locating Chuck or his remains----as well as finding the shooter. Can you help me organize this effort?"

"Of course I will. There are several good investigating organizations with trained manpower to undertake such a search. Let me make some calls and get this started. If you like, we can also get some input as to what kind of a reward would motivate the people they'll be talking with, which I imagine will be primarily flotilla residents and dock workers."

"Let's get started now, please make the calls and see who would be interested in starting this operation----today." Art said. "As soon as we know what we'll need, I'll make arrangements to have funds wire transferred to your trust account and you can guarantee payment to the investigators, as well as make certain that we get what we pay for."

John picked up the telephone as Valarie and Art sat impatiently, with expressions that reflected the somber mood of the meeting, and did nothing to disguise the preconceived outcome that neither was willing to utter. Her eyes were red from tears. With this tragedy she realized just how much she loved this easy going man who was thoroughly comfortable in his skin and whose great wealth was not visible, nor was it used in any way to magnify his image. He did however find ways to help people with his resources---- accomplished without fanfare of any sort or discussed in any manner.

John finished his conversation regarding mounting the private search. "I am happy to say that my first choice is willing to take on this matter. I just spoke with Preston Hobbs, a former British intelligence officer who retired two years ago after being stationed here in Hong Kong for ten years. He has a combination of British and Asian staff, and is well respected. He also has a thorough knowledge of every aspect of Hong Kong. He will meet with us here this evening and can start tomorrow morning----if that's acceptable to you?"

"He sounds fine."

"Valarie, what do you think?" Art asked.

"If it's OK with you, I think Mr. Hobbs sounds great." She said, and thought privately that she felt more comfortable with a Westerner leading the search. Not prejudiced against anyone, but she observed during her short stay in Hong Kong that the Asian culture was different----and maybe not as understanding of her desire and optimism in finding Chuck.

"Then it's settled. If it's all right with you, ask him to come over right away."

"Fine, I will ask Preston to come over now and join us for dinner to save time."

CHAPTER 30

Mr. Lee was home enjoying his weekend, in anticipation he hoped of receiving a nice payoff next week for the sale of the TechX software to KRL, when his cell phone rang. "Hello he answered in Chinese."

"Cut out that crap, speak English."

"It's you!" He said, not expecting a call from the taller man until Monday.

"Have you talked to Wong, and are they satisfied with the final tests?" He asked sternly. Mr. Lee was quite frightened of the taller man, as he preferred to deal with Mr. Jaxton on this transaction. He walked to the window of his tiny apartment and looked at the wall across the alley. This would all change after he made the sale to KRL. He couldn't help wondering again why he was selected by TechX to handle the negotiation, considering the problems he had with the law in the past. One would think he thought, that Mr. Jaxton would have made the call himself or would have hired an experienced Hong Kong software agent rather than someone such as himself.

"I talked with Mr. Wong on Friday and they have everything they need, and should be finished early next week." He answered in a timid voice.

"What's this crap about early next week, you said Monday for sure!"

Mr. Lee cringed, making him appear smaller than he already was, leaning against the wall next to his window. He replied, "Mr. Wong said that he would wire the money when they were totally satisfied, and not to count on Monday." He said waiting for the temper tantrum he fully expected from the taller man.

"You tell Wong if he doesn't wire on Monday, the deal's off. You hear me?" He yelled into the telephone.

Shaking, Mr. Lee said, "I will." Knowing that things were so shaky with Ho Chi, the KRL President that he may say fine the deal is off.

"Lee, forget about telling Wong the deal is off." The taller man said, thinking that his quick temper was about to get the best of him----yet again. "You call him Monday and ask him when he'll be finished and ready to wire the funds. You hear me? I'll call you Monday morning, your time." Before Mr. Lee could respond, the line was dead.

CHAPTER 31

BEAVERTON, OREGON

"Hi Honey." He said, as Victoria picked up the phone at her home. "How are you? I've really missed you."

"Where are you?" She asked in an anxious tone.

"I don't think it would be safe for either of us to be discussing that sort of thing on the phone----do you?"

"If this transfer is supposed to be Monday their time, then I need to know, because I'm not going to hang out here. I need to get my reservations. Can you understand that?" She asked.

"Sure honey, from what I know Monday is the day but I'll need to confirm that and will call you. I can't wait to see you."

"Me too."

"I'll call you tomorrow."

"I love you."

"I love you too." He said and hung up, just as Lisa came out of the bathroom.

CHAPTER 32

Preston had the look of an English squire, Valarie thought as she sat across the dinner table observing him. He was in his early fifties, tall and fit with light brown eyes, gray, medium length hair and a handlebar mustache. He had a ruddy complexion and was handsome in that unique, non-threatening way of being a man's, man, as well as quite obviously a woman's man. Preston Hobbs was careful about showing his sense of humor in such sober times, but momentarily allowed it to slip through, showing a hint of his laughing eyes and broad smile. She felt comfortable with him.

"I think we have an understanding." Art said. "I'll arrange to wire into John's trust account enough to fund the reward of $25,000 US, and enough to pay the search effort for the next two weeks. And if required will wire sufficient additional funds to sustain the investigation for a longer period. This will include funds for your investigators to encourage the flotilla people to talk---- where they might not feel comfortable with the police. I'll leave that for you to control with your team. Now let me re-cap. You'll have approximately ten men starting as soon as you know John has received my wire----"

Preston Hobbs interrupted, "No, we'll start now, as soon as I get back to the office and run copies of this photo of Mr. Winters. I trust John with the money. If he say's it will be here, then it will."

"Thank you. To continue, you'll have your teams go out in boats to the flotilla and talk to the residents to see what they know about the explosion as well as the shooter. They'll talk with people at the cargo docks to see about the shooter's escape, and if Chuck could have possibly been kidnapped. You'll also put the word out about trying to find the shooter throughout Hong Kong. I'll meet with the police on Monday and see if we can get some additional information by pressing KRL."

"In the meantime John, can you assure Valarie's protection for a few days until I've done what I need to do here and can escort her back to San Francisco? Sorry Valarie, I'm getting ahead of my self, does that work for you?"

"As far as John protecting me, I hate to think that he has to worry about baby sitting *me*."

"Nonsense Valarie, it's a pleasure having you here, and it's not baby sitting in any way, all right?" He said smiling.

"All right," she said with a fleeting smile at John, then turned to Art and said, "I just don't know if I can leave before we find Chuck."

"I better get started, here's my card with all of my numbers, including my cell that will reach me anytime. Don't hesitate to call----please. John, the dinner was wonderful as usual, and Valarie, Art, it's a real pleasure meeting and assisting you. Cheerio!" Preston said as he rose and left for his car.

After Preston left, Art asked John if he could arrange for someone to take him to The Black Orchid dock to go to see the accident scene. John wanted to go with him but didn't want to take Valarie, or leave her home without him being here. They agreed to have one of John's security men drive the armored pickup to the harbor.

"Art, I want you to carry a gun and a cell phone." John said as he rose and walked back to his office to retrieve the items. "Also, I want you to call me and check in every half hour. If I don't hear from you, I'm sending in my own little army."

Art chuckled, and said, "John, you've been reading too many mystery novels."

"Art, I've been *living* a mystery novel."

"Agreed, and thanks." Art said as he went to his room to change his clothes.

"Valarie, I will do everything I can to find Chuck if he is alive, and keep you safe too. I am so sorry you have experienced such a difficult time. Do you want to sit and talk here on the deck----or go back to your room? Whatever you want just let me know." John said to her.

Standing, Valarie said, "I really appreciate your hospitality, but I'm tired. I think I'll go back to my room and try to rest. It's been another long day. Please call me when Art gets back. I'd like to hear his thoughts on the situation after seeing things first hand."

"I will do that, and will be in my office waiting for Art's calls if you need me."

CHAPTER 33

LAS VEGAS, NEVADA

The man known as Foster in Las Vegas, picked up his cell phone and called the taller man in Lisbon, Portugal. The man's cell phone rang a dozen times and finally picked up. "Yeah."

"What have you heard about the transfer?"

"Christ sake, you're calling me in the middle of the night to ask me that?" He said. "You know I'd call you when it was wired because I want my money, and by the way, where's my fifty grand? I checked with the bank and it's not there. What's the deal, huh?"

"The bank isn't open until Monday, so I couldn't wire it. Just keep your shirt on."

"See that it gets done, and don't count on the big wire on Monday because it won't go until their satisfied. It might be Tuesday instead, so don't bug me." The taller man said.

"I need to know, there are plans that need to fall in place. You call me Monday, their time and let me know. Do you understand?" He said.

"OK, but get my expense money in the bank, and don't forget my cut is two million now." The taller man said and hung up before he could hear a response.

"Shit." He thought. "That bastard never gives up."

Foster's high roller results at the casino were not kind to him. He lost his first hundred thousand and dropped another twenty-five. His poker skills were draining his embezzled funds. He needed to send the fifty thousand, fly to Europe and get ready for a life of leisure.

CHAPTER 34

ABERDEEN HARBOR

The evening breeze was cooling from the heat of the day. Me Ko had very little sleep the night before while tending to her patient. She monitored him constantly to be certain his breathing was normal as well as any signs of consciousness. After the second full evening she noticed a murmur from his lips and thought she saw his hand move a little. "This will take close watching." She thought. She squeezed a bit more water into his mouth and moved her head close to see if she could feel his warm breath on her face. His breath was strong enough to touch the fine hairs near her ears, and cause a shiver of both surprise and excitement sweep her body as she held her head close to his mouth. She hoped that no one of her family would come into this small enclosure where she kept her patient. She had grown quite fond of him and prior to his arrival had felt like she was neither important to her husband who had become distant, or her children who had long since decided they did not need mothering.

Mon Kee came in and she jumped from the surprise of his appearance. His mother who lives in Sheung Shui, in the New Territories, had become quite ill and might not live. "I need to see her before she goes and she wants to see the children. What will we do with the sick man?"

"Your mother didn't ask for me, did she?" Me Ko asked.

"Well no, but I am sure she wants you to come."

"You know that she never liked me, and doesn't want me to come. Besides, who would take care of the patient? We can not turn him over now at this late time."

"I will take the children. Will you be all right alone?"

"Of course. I will see you upon your return. Tell your mother I will pray for her." Me Ko said, hiding her joy that she would be alone with someone who actually needed *her*.

CHAPTER 35

A gentle westerly breeze was blowing off the South China Sea, as Preston Hobbs, dressed in white cotton dungarees, a blue short-sleeved shirt and white deck shoes, was perched on the twenty-foot cruiser's bench seat as it rode the gentle swells out to the flotilla of sampans. His was one of three identical boats manned by his team of investigators. Each boat consisted of the hired skipper and a crew of three investigators, two men and one woman. The combined fluency of investigators on each boat covered the majority of dialects spoken in the flotilla. In addition, Hobbs always used women in his investigations, because they were able to obtain information from both men and women that men alone were often unable to do. There would be another hour of daylight and Hobbs felt it important not to let this day go by without alerting the residents of the flotilla that there was a substantial reward for successful information in this search effort. He would also provide small financial incentives for pointing his teams to someone that may have information. Armed with two hundred computer generated pictures of Chuck Winters, the teams started canvassing the boats at a time when most of their inhabitants were finishing dinner meals, or relaxing after a day of fishing or activities in town to provide for their livelihood.

The investigative work was tedious as was the majority of work in their field, but rewarding when the effort turns into results. "Good evening." With a smile, Hobbs said in a popular Chinese dialect as his boat slowly edged up alongside a sampan, where a man and woman in their later years sat in low- slung canvas chairs. "We are looking for a man that may have fallen in the harbor after the explosion near The Black Orchid. Or maybe you saw someone speeding off afterwards. Do you know of anyone who might know something about the explosion, or who was involved? There is a reward of $180,000 HK, for helping us find this missing man, or the one causing the boat explosion. We are not the police and are only here assisting his family."

"No," was the consistent answer. Some didn't even look at the photo. Others were scared and thought they really *were* the police.

Prior to commencing the evening's activities, Hobbs sketched out a search area fanning out from the explosion site, assigning each team a specific sector. He was hoping for a quick hit on this first night. He was starting in what he felt was ground zero and moving out. If Winters was recovered, or seen for that matter, this would be the area.

"Jimmy? Hobbs here." Hobbs spoke into his radio transmitter to his team leader in boat #2.

"Preston, anything from you end?" James Andrews III, asked.

"No, how about you?"

"Not yet, it seems no one seems to have even heard the explosion, which can't be true. I get the distinct feeling they're afraid of someone or something." Andrews said.

"Are they actually looking at the picture?" Hobbs inquired.

"Not at first, but I found I had to put it in front of their eyes. They're hesitant to offend us so they look and then say they haven't seen him and don't know anything about

246

it. It's just a lot of shaking their heads. The money doesn't seem to turn them on at all, but when we hit the right one, I'm sure it might be a whole different story." Andrews said.

"How many resident groups have you interviewed tonight?" Hobbs asked.

"About ten I think, I have notes on each one."

"Are you experiencing the same thing?" Andrews asked Hobbs.

"I think we're both experiencing the same response. Since your sector was the closest to the explosion, what do people say that live within two hundred meters? Do they also disavow the entire event?" Hobbs asked.

"Well they could hardly say that they didn't hear it. Those close by admitted they heard it but said they didn't see anything." Andrews answered.

"Well it's getting late, let's see how much we can do in the next hour, and decide then if it's time to call it good for tonight and come back tomorrow."

"Billy, do you read me?" Hobbs asked.

"I hear you Preston, and I heard your conversation with Jimmy. I concur with what you both of you. I did find a close-in sampan where no one answered my knocking, or you might say my calling, although I was sure I heard someone move around and saw a dim light inside. I think I'll try that one again."

"Good Billy, give it a go and report back to me----all right?"

Billy Sang motioned to his skipper to turn back and head toward the medium sized sampan where they previously stopped and received no response from the occupants. The sea was quiet as the powerful engine idled up toward the darkened boat. As they pulled along side, Billy held the side of the other boat to keep theirs from drifting away and asked if someone was there. Through a small flap in the dark brown canvas, he could barely see a form moving ever so slightly in front of an oil lamp in the cabin area. "Hello, is someone there? I'm only trying to find a man that may have fallen into the water after the explosion. Please come out and talk with me." He said in the most generally used dialect. There was no response. He then said, "There is $180,000 HK reward for the man. Can you help us? His family wants to find him." He continued in a pleading tone, although he and his fellow team members felt there was no chance this missing man could be alive after such an explosion. But----he was being paid to do a job.

Me Ko heard the man and was terrified. Maybe she was breaking the law by keeping this man. He should have been turned over to the police and taken to a hospital. What if he has a wife and children? What would they think of her hiding this man in the back of her boat----like a prisoner? If only they would go away. The man persisted. And finally, with a plan, she went through the drape and moved onto the open deck. Billy smiled and asked again, this time to her face if she knew something about the missing man, at the same time handing her a picture of her patient. She was shaken, and hoped that her trembling hands would not betray her misdeed. She took the picture and held it carefully in her small hands----staring at the eyes she had previously only momentarily seen when she carefully lifted his eyelids.

She drew a hand to her mouth and quickly to her ear and then extended it outward with upward palm, offering a quizzical look on her face as if to say, 'I don't understand your language', or 'I am unable to speak for some reason,' and then motioned she would keep the picture and the business card he offered in his outstretched hand. Billy watched with some trepidation as the non-speaking woman moved back through the flap and into the darkened private covered area of her boat.

As their boat pulled away from the sampan, Billy turned to his team and said, "What do you think?"

"I think she knows what happened, she's faking with that deaf mute act." June said.

"I agree. She has information and we need to get it. Let's talk to her neighbors and find out about her. Probably tomorrow, considering she's most likely watching us as we speak." Henry Lee said.

"I'm calling Preston and filling him in. We'll come back tomorrow in another boat and a disguise, talk with her neighbors then have another session with her." Billy said.

CHAPTER 36

Inspector Li arrived at 8:30 A.M. to meet with John and Art Levy. He had hoped to speak with Chuck Winters about both Sue Tang and KRL, but due to the tragedy he needed to do the best he could without him.

"John, let us spend some time on how Sue Tang became involved with this case." Inspector LI stated.

John continued to feel extremely remorseful about bringing Sue into the case under false pretenses. She had no idea the assignment could be dangerous, and ultimately become fatal. "I learned that Miss Tang had recently left the employment of Knowledge Resource Limited, and might be willing to talk about the negotiations involving the acquisition of American, TechX software. As it turned out she could and would assist us. I suggested due to the danger following Mr. Winters that we meet in a lightly used park near the harbor." John explained, omitting the fact that she was working as a research consultant, and that he had led her to believe that he was a researcher, not a private investigator.

"What did you learn from her about the KRL dealings?" The Inspector asked.

"We found out that the person representing that he was the president of TechX, Mr. Jaxton, was not who he represented to be. It was also apparent that this person was trying to sell the company's intellectual property, the entire basis of the company, without their knowledge. They were asking ten million dollars, US. This software loss would probably bankrupt the company." John explained.

"That means that the real decision maker at KRL most likely was not aware of the scheme. Mr. Jaxton was represented to be the negotiator, when they were probably, in actuality dealing with a thief and killer. It also means that if we can identify the impersonator, we will be identifying the killer or a conspirator. I need to meet with the KRL management and explain that they can be charged with theft of intellectual property and accessory to murder. That should generate some cooperation, unless they are more involved than it appears." Inspector Li stated.

"Mr. Levy, will you provide me with the supporting documentation as to exactly what it is that you believe KRL is attempting to buy from this unknown person, and come with us when we visit KLR and make our charges?" The Inspector asked.

"I'd be happy to." Art said. "I think you have a good grasp on this case. This is the way Chuck wanted to approach it also. More important to me at the moment is the current status of the investigation into the attack on Chuck. Where are you on that?"

"I wish I had more to report. We have the boat. Forensics has thoroughly gone over it and found little. There were many prints, but the operating controls had been wiped clean. It is clear to us that the prints we found were from prior to that night however we are still following up on that.
We interviewed the boat owner, and he only saw the dead man we found floating at the foot of the pier near the boat. We have nothing new on the dead man. He was probably hired by the shooter to drive him, and make a

little money. We are still looking for the car they came in. It should be abandoned at the site where they parked it when they rented the boat, unless the shooter doubled back after killing the driver and drove off in it. Our harbor police unit interviewed the residents of the nearby sampans and found no one who saw anything. This is not unusual. It is difficult at best to get people involved---- particularly in something as dangerous as this might be." Inspector Li answered.

"Do you think there is any chance Chuck could be alive, considering the type of explosion?" Art asked the Inspector.

"In all honesty I don't see how, unless he jumped off the boat anticipating this kind of problem. However the concussion would have caused him to lose consciousness, and he would have drowned unless someone pulled him out right away, which does not seem to be the case as he has not turned up."

"Well what if the shooter fished him out and kidnapped him, do you see that as a possibility?" Art inquired of the Inspector.

"Not really. He wouldn't have killed his driver when he did, because he would need his help to carry him and get the car." Inspector Li surmised.

"I want you to know that we're doing some checking on our own in the harbor, and will keep you informed should something materialize." Art said, hoping to keep a good working relationship with the Inspector. He'll probably hear the same from the harbor police soon enough he thought.

"That is fine; perhaps talking with someone other than the police might do some good with those people."

Art was beginning to like the inspector more and more as they made arrangements to meet at his office later in the morning and try to schedule a trip to the KRL offices later in the day.

CHAPTER 37

Me Ko spent another night watching and waiting and occasionally touching her patient, dreaming of what life might be with this man she didn't know----but did know. She had seen and touched every part of his body, actions that would cause her terrible embarrassment should anyone discover, yet she felt almost entitled----as he was her responsibility, much like that of a child but different. This morning she bathed him where he lay, watching his strong naked body. She had never before seen a grown man naked other than her husband, and her eyes drifted to his privates, with which she became fixated---- why she was not certain. They looked different than her husband's and for some reason unknown to her. Her heart started pounding and her face became flushed. She watched for a period of time that she could not measure, and then managed with some difficulty to put fresh clothes on him. Not quite as well fitting as the others she had for him, but still acceptable. She tried once again to provide a little nourishment with fresh broth cooked just for him. Her small hands dipped the end of a clean cloth in the bowl of chicken broth. And ever so carefully above her cupped hand, transported the dripping cloth to his lips, placed her small fingers around the base of the dangling cloth and squeezed. The broth was hot and almost burned her fingers. When it entered his mouth it caused him to cough and spit the hot liquid from his burning mouth. Me Ko leapt from surprise, almost toppling over onto her back when she observed the first sign of life from this sleeping man, who admittedly she had become so infatuated.

Chuck Winters' eyes opened, head throbbing. He looked around through a fuzzy haze seeing Me Ko, then the drab small enclosure he was lying in. He tried to think but the pain from his head was overwhelming. He tried to talk, but was able only to emit an unintelligible squeak. Noticing the pain on his face, Me Ko rushed to the chest in the corner behind his head and sorted through the various vials, selecting a powder that acted much like aspirin in curing headache pain. She poured perhaps a tablespoon into a glass of cold water from a large clay pot kept full of fresh water. As a girl, she remembered her mother serving up this strong potion for her aches and pains, and it always made things better. Me Ko walked back to her patient with a warm smile and an outstretched hand, holding this mystery elixir designed to chase his troubles away. He looked at it and then at her and said, "Where am I? Who are you?"

Me Ko, didn't know a lot of English, but she did understand what he was asking----if only by the circumstances.

"I, Me Ko." She said with her warm loving smile.

Chuck Winters replied, "Who am I, what am I doing here, with you? What happened to my head?" He asked as his hand reached around to the still large bump on his head.

Me Ko did not understand what his words were but thought that he was asking about her and what happened to him. "I no know." She said, still smiling and reached out for his hand, which he hesitatingly allowed her to hold.

She seemed to think he had lost his memory or he would have tried to get her to contact someone or get help of some kind. But he lay there, apparently thinking about what was going on for him----and without answers.

Me Ko suddenly thought of the reward and the fact that this man in a conscious state, no longer provided her with the simple pleasures she was enjoying before he came around. Mon Kee would be furious with her if she lost the huge reward by being dishonest and keeping the man on the boat when she knew the police and his friends were out looking for him. She had the card of the private detective and she should contact him and inquire about the reward. She needed to keep him here, or she would not get the money, she thought. Some of the flotilla people owned cell phones. She and her husband did not. How could she contact this man, she thought? She decided she would call to a close neighbor and see if she would call this Billy Sang Investigator.

During the time Me Ko was contemplating the reward, Chuck Winter's system was absorbing the white-powder ache reliever just given him by this woman he had never seen, in a place he did not know, wearing clothes he could not imagine, trying to communicate with someone that could not communicate with him, and feeling like he just finished wrestling with a tiger. Aside from these facts and the fact that he didn't know who the hell he was, life was pretty much perfect he thought.

Billy Sang and June were dressed as a couple out fishing, wearing the typical peasant attire of loose fitting shirts and baggy trousers. Putting along in their tiny boat, they headed for the section of the flotilla where they had encountered the woman the night before that they felt was holding back information about this case. They slowly edged near a boat that was two boats away from their target-suspect. Billy cut the engine and June held out her hand to steady their boat as it glided up against a sampan. They baited their hooks and dropped their lines in the water. For the first time ever while fishing, Billy hoped he wouldn't catch anything. He didn't need the bother of dealing with a fish. After a few minutes, no one appeared on any of the boats and he thought they were gone but he wasn't sure. He decided to tap on the side of the boat next to them and see if someone was home. He tapped with the wooden end of his net against the bow of the boat, and finally an elderly woman poked her head through the canvas doorway from the back of the boat. "Good morning, we left our watch at home, can you give us the time please." The old woman turned without a word and looked like she was ignoring them, then reappeared with a wristwatch and showed him the time without a word spoken. He tried to ask another question and she again turned away and disappeared through the canvas flap.

"That was informative." He said snickering to June.

"No one said this job was easy, particularly since you know I hate fishing." June said, giving him a friendly poke in the ribs.

"No fish here, let's move toward our favorite lady's boat." Billy said.

They pulled in their lines thankfully without a fish, started the little engine and moved around the two nearest boats and went right to Me Ko's boat. Billy knocked on the bow of the boat in the same way he did with the other boat----no response. Me Ko was huddled in the corner watching her patient as he struggled to a sitting position. She moved toward him and propped him up with a pillow behind his back. He smiled at her and nodded. The headache was subsiding and he was trying to make some sense of his situation, when a loud rapping on the boat caught his attention. Then he heard Chinese which he did not understand, sprinkled with various dialects he surmised, then French, which if pressed he seemed to think he could translate, and finally English; "Is anyone in there?" Billy yelled.

Chuck grabbed the side of the canvas drop wall and pulled up enough to see daylight, and yelled as strongly as possible in his weakened state. "Hey can you hear me?"

Billy was shaking from excitement, and yelled, "Can we come in?"

"Come in, yes whoever you are." Chuck said as loudly as his body permitted.

Me Ko cowered, knowing that her desires would cost them the reward, and maybe get her in trouble as well. Billy and June quickly lashed their rope to the sampan, and with guns at the ready, pushed aside the canvas flap leading to the living quarters. They quickly recognized Chuck Winters and stood in the doorway, speechless, in total amazement of their good fortune in finding him.

CHAPTER 38

Art Levy and John Sun left Valarie in safe hands with two of John's security men, who were assigned to keep a close watch on her as they drove in the Jaguar down the winding road from his home to the main road heading into the Central District and Inspector Li's office. The air was still and the hot sun was squarely overhead as John, dressed in light cream slacks, white shirt and a silk pale blue sport jacket to cover his shoulder holster, chatted casually with his long time friend. Art, with a much greater emotional investment in the outcome of the events occurring, had a difficult time with casual conversation and found himself saying "excuse me" or "what" on more than one occasion during the ride to the main road. Considering that Art didn't pack a tropical wardrobe he wore a dark gray suit, white shirt and green tie. He preferred to look as professional as possible in the later meeting at KRL.

Earlier, after Inspector Li left John's home, Art called his partner Jimmy in San Francisco. After receiving an update on conditions in Hong Kong, he gave Art a report on their efforts to track the more than two and a half million dollars that went to "Pacific Software Consultants" in Bellevue, Washington and then into the account of "Caribco" in a Las Vegas bank. It turns out the majority of the funds in the Caribco account were withdrawn by its President, John Foster. It seems that he had the balance in the account changed into unregistered and untraceable *bearer bonds*. The interest and principal goes to the holder of the bearer bond. This means he can cash or deposit the bonds without a trail. Jimmy further reported that of the approximate two-point six million dollars, close to one and a half million was withdrawn in cash over the last ninety days, leaving a little over a million dollars going into the bearer bond. The account was just closed with the final transaction being a fifty thousand dollar wire transfer to a Lisbon bank. Art considered that things were moving fast and he needed to get to the bottom of this quickly. If for nothing else for Chuck's sake in terms of the long shot of finding him alive, as well as the satisfaction of finding his killers and knowing that he completed something that Chuck started and was committed to resolve. He asked Jimmy to find out who was the account holder in Lisbon and to pay what was necessary in order to get that information---- fast.

CHAPTER 39

Billy Wong, V. P. of Knowledge Resource, Limited, cigarette smoke curling up around his puffy face and continuing up to the elaborate black metal embossed ceiling, waited impatiently for Ho Chi to come into the corporate conference room. This day was important to Billy, as it would be he thought, the start of realizing the substantial net worth increase he felt he needed to effectuate his early retirement. The TechX software could put hundreds of millions of US dollars into his pocket, a tidy sum for any retirement package. He was worried that if the deal was further delayed it could fall through.

Mr. Lee was announced by the secretary. He walked in wearing a confident face and his best suit. He asked Billy Wong if everything was ready, and Billy informed him that the tests were completed and Mr. Chi would be in soon to authorize the wire transfer to the Cayman Islands. Mr. Lee could not believe his life was about to change from that of a second rate conman to a man of wealth and importance. A few minutes later the door opened and they were joined by Mr. Ho Chi, Chairman, President, CEO and controlling shareholder of KRL.

Billy wanting to move this on and finalize the deal reiterated what he had previously and privately informed Ho Chi; that the engineering tests were complete, as was all of the supporting documentation for the product. Ho Chi said, "I am still concerned that we are dealing with someone that I do not know or trust. I am concerned that TechX will take our ten million US dollars, and treat us just like another software *licensing* customer and go out and market the product to the rest of the chip manufacturers at a rate that is a fraction of what we are asked to pay for exclusive ownership of this product."

Mr. Lee's face dropped. He was at a loss for words with Mr. Chi being such an important man he just couldn't reach deep into his soul and come out with a point to save the moment----that wouldn't appear to be argumentative. Instead, he sat silent and turned to Billy Wong for help. Billy, sensing the teetering condition of the deal, repeated his earlier argument that the entire TechX facility would be torched when the ten million was received. Ho Chi sat, looking at the ceiling and then said, "We will wire half, five million US, and upon our verification of the facility destruction we will wire the rest. Otherwise the deal is off. Do you both understand?"

The room fell silent and finally Billy Wong said in the spirit of compromise, "I think that is a fine idea we need to be protected, if all parties are sincere then the deal works."

Mr. Lee looked horrified. When the taller man called later today and he had to report this change in the deal he would be blamed for certain and was afraid of what he might do to him. The two turned to Mr. Lee and he said, "I will inform the TechX people. When will you wire the first half?"

Mr. Chi responded, "With your concurrence, and I assume you speak for the company."

Mr. Lee nodded, thinking that he was in so much trouble already he better keep the deal together or he gets nothing.

"Fine, five million US will be wired to the Cayman bank you requested in the next thirty minutes and the balance will be wired when a party close to us in the States makes a personal visit and assures me that the building no longer exists. How do they say it in the U.S., *the ball is in your court?*" Mr. Chi said with a smile. Mr. Lee made his exit as quickly as possible and called the emergency number of a "clean, untraceable" cell phone that the taller man had given him for emergencies. The phone account had been paid for with cash and had a pre-paid credit of one thousand minutes of calling time from any place, worldwide.

CHAPTER 40

Art Levy and John Sun reached the main road and drove approximately twenty minutes to the Central District arriving at Inspector Lee's building shortly after noon. He had indicated he would send out for lunch and they could save time by working straight through. The building, located on Queensway near Chater Garden, was a beautiful example of British architecture at the turn of the century. There was a newer parking garage next to the building, which they entered after receiving the parking ticket. The garage was quite full even at the lunch hour and caused them to wind up to the third floor, where they squeezed the Jaguar into a compact parking stall. The elevator carried them back down to the garage lobby entrance where they entered another elevator that carried them to the fourth floor and Inspector Li's office. Art noticed that the activity reminded him of his days with the San Francisco Police Department, noisy, busy and smelly. John announced their presence in Chinese to the receptionist and they were promptly escorted by an aid to a conference room overlooking the beautiful and lush Chater Garden directly across the street.

After a few minutes Inspector Li appeared with a staff of four. Two were detectives working on the Sue Tang homicide and two were from the white-collar crime unit working on piracy of music CD's to counterfeit Nikes and everything in between. In English he said, "Gentlemen, I appreciate your cooperation in this matter and wish to introduce----" he stopped at the ringing of the cell phone in John Sun's pocket.

"My sincere apologies, I must take this." He said as he quickly moved toward the door, answering in Chinese.

"Perhaps we should wait for a moment as Mr. Sun is materially involved in the case before us." The Inspector said.

In no more than three minutes, John returned to the room and apologized again. He indicated it was a call of utmost importance. "I wonder if we might take a two hour break. Something has come up that I must deal with immediately. I am afraid that I also need Mr. Levy's assistance. He has expertise that I do not have myself. My utmost apology, we can return by 2:15 P.M. if that works for you." John said to the group. All, including Art Levy having looks of astonishment on their faces.

"We had hoped to move this along and be of assistance to you Mr. Sun." The Inspector said with a tone of irritation.

"I appreciate that, but it cannot be helped. It will all be clear to you in short order." John replied.

With that John stood, picked up his briefcase and quickly left the room, followed closely by Art Levy.

"John, what in the hell is going on? I thought you felt this was important for us." Art asked in a terse manner.

John was silent and deep in thought as he waited for the elevator. When it arrived and they entered the empty elevator, John turned to Art with a smile on his face and said, "Preston's people found Chuck and he is all right----mostly."

Art looked in total disbelief and at the same time like he had just won the lottery. He could not reign in his emotions enough to ask coherent calm questions. "He's all right? You're not playing with me? You're serious? Honest---- where is he?"

"Calm down Art." John said with a hand on his shaking shoulder. "Chuck was rescued by a woman in a sampan and she nursed him back to consciousness. He has a lump on his head, which caused him some mental confusion, but the doctors at the hospital in Aberdeen feel he will have a complete recovery. We are going to see him now."

"Why so secretive in front of Inspector Li, don't you think they should know?"

"Art, I don't know the men in that room and the last thing I want is another deadly leak in the police department, which has already caused Sue Tang's death and almost Chuck's. We could easily have these killers heading for the hospital right now if word got out that he was alive." John said calmly.

"You're right I was so excited I couldn't think straight. John, that's why you make the big bucks." Art said, and they both laughed for the first time since Art arrived in Hong Kong.

CHAPTER 41

John and Art left the building as quickly as possible and headed back up the hill toward Aberdeen. As they were driving, John called Preston Hobbs in an attempt to learn more about Chuck's miraculous survival.

"John, last night two of my best people, Billy Sang and June Lee, attempted to interview a lady living on a sampan very close to the explosion. They felt she responded in an unusual manner and was hiding something. So as a result they disguised themselves as fishermen, or fisherman and fisherwoman," he said with a chuckle, "and went out this morning to see if her neighbors knew something. To make a long story short, they became frustrated and went right up to her boat and tapped on the stern with no response. Finally they started shouting in every dialect and language they knew to communicate with her. But instead of her responding, your man Chuck answered. It seems Me Ko's husband fished him out of the harbor, where he apparently jumped before the explosion. He was unconscious from a blow to the head caused probably from hitting the boat. Me Ko nursed him back to health, staying by his side day and night, forcing water into his mouth, kept him bathed and in fresh clothing. She also carefully monitored his breathing, cleansed his cuts and applied continuous cold compresses to his head in order to reduce the pressure and bring him back to consciousness. I think she was afraid and didn't trust the authorities. She was left alone to care for Mr. Winters when her husband had to leave with their children to be with his dying mother. In regard to the reward, she and her husband definitely saved his life, and if I were making the decision, which I am not, I would say they earned it. One thought, a hospital bill for the same care would make the reward look like a pittance. I'm not Me Ko's agent, but I do know that she saved his life, and she's still frightened that she didn't turn him over to the police when they found him. She deserves a medal." Preston said passionately.

"Preston, this is Art. You were on John's speaker, sorry we didn't mention that before but I didn't want to miss a word."

"No problem Art, I'm just so pleased it worked out."

"Well let me say this, I was responsible for formulating this reward and making the decision. My decision is that she gets it with no question. I want to run it by Chuck if he's able, because he may feel he wants to do something more for this lady."

"Art, I'm so happy you feel this way. The whole rescue on their part was a miracle in the first place, and Mr. Winters was so lucky to fall into their hands. I'm very anxious to meet the man who has friends like you two." Preston graciously stated.

CHAPTER 42

LISBON, PORTUGAL

"Hello." The taller man said, hesitantly.

"This is Mr. Lee, we----"

Interrupted by the taller man, "Hey Lee, where's the money?"

"They just wired five million----"

Again, the taller man interrupted. "They wired what? They wired only five million? What in the hell are they trying to do?" He screamed into the receiver.

"They wired the five million now and will wire the balance when the building is burned down." Mr. Lee said with trepidation. "They have someone that will look at the building to see if it is done, then they will wire the balance."

"Why did you let 'em pull that one on us? That wasn't the deal----you fool?" The taller man shouted back.

"There was nothing I could do----Mr. Chi was about ready to cancel the whole deal. Do I get my money now?" Mr. Lee said with hesitation.

"Hell no, you'll be lucky if you get your money when the rest comes the way you screwed this up Lee." The taller man said, as he punched the end button on his cell phone.

The taller man then called the Los Angeles answering service number to reach "Foster", leaving the message, "call me immediately, it's an emergency."

Within a few minutes, his cell phone rang and Foster was on the other end, "What's the emergency? Did the money get wired?"

"Only half damn it!"

"What did you say---- half? What in the hell are you talking about?"

"Listen, he doesn't trust you, so he wants to wait to wire the other half until his man sees the smoking ashes of TechX----first hand!"

"Great, that's just great----how's that going to happen? Now what do we do?" Foster asked, as he recalled his plan never intended to do this part of the deal in the first place. He would just disappear after he got their money and never do it.

"Well I guess you'll just have to burn the damn thing down." The taller man exclaimed.

"What do you mean me? You're getting paid to do the dirty work."

"Wait a minute I have no intention of spending another day in Oregon. I think you better get your ass back there pronto and do it yourself.
If you won't, I want my money now----all of it, do you hear me?" The man in Lisbon shouted.

"I've never committed arson. I wouldn't know where to start. I'll pay you the two million if you do it."

"Bull, you'll pay me the two and a half now and I'll do it. Otherwise, I'll find you and you know it, do you hear me?"

"Make it two." Foster countered.

"Keep it up, and won't need *any* money."

"When can you get there and get it done? Leave today and burn it tomorrow night!"

"I want the two an a half in my account before I leave."

"What's to keep you from taking the money, and saying----see ya?"

"Nothing, you just need to trust me. What's to keep you from keeping the money and not paying me after the fire?"

"Why would I trust you?" Foster asked.

"I can't believe you said that? I'll take two million now and the rest when the money is wired." The taller man said.

"OK, but leave today, do you understand? I want this done by tomorrow night. They can wire from Hong Kong when the fire is burning tomorrow night in Oregon, because it'll be the middle of the day there.

How do we know that their representative will be available to see that the building is burned, or will we have to wait until he's damned good and ready?"

"I don't know, I'll have Lee ask them how soon they can verify the fire." The taller man said.

"OK just get it done. I'll check the account and see if it's been transferred yet, and if so I'll wire you two million." Foster said.

"I won't leave until I know the money is in my account."

"No, travel right away, check your account if you want before you do the job, but don't waste precious time waiting to verify.

"I'll call Lee and catch a flight. In the meantime, you have just one job and that's to get the money in my account, do you understand me?" This might work out just right, he thought. It's a perfect way to dispose of the contents of that storage unit, which was a loose end that spelled trouble down the line.

CHAPTER 43

BEAVERTON, OREGON

Victoria was in her office thinking of the life ahead. No more work or court cases, no more judges or snippy clerks, just spending the rest of her life in luxury with the man she loved. Her direct line rang and she picked it up. "Hello".

"It's me, how are you my love?" He said.

"Hi, is it done yet? I've missed you. I can hardly wait." She said.

"There was five million wired earlier today, the balance in a couple of days. Can you check to see if it's there?"

"I'll call right away, but what happened to the ten million?"

"It's a long story, check on the five and I'll fill you in."
"You call me back in fifteen minutes, OK?"

CHAPTER 44
HONG KONG
THE ROAD TO ABERDEEN

"Valarie, John. Can you be ready in about ten minutes? Art and I are swinging by to pick you up, is that all right?"

"John, what's wrong? Tell me! I thought you and Art were supposed to be at the police station?" She said, feeling her stomach knotting and her temples tightening.

"Valarie, trust me it isn't a problem. We just want you to be with us now. We will fill you in. Everything is all right----really!"

"I thought it would be better if we picked her up and then explained what we know. She'll be so excited----I can not wait to tell her."

They wound up the long road to John's house after alerting security to be on the lookout. Valarie was waiting on the front porch when they drove around the circle entry. She had a look of apprehension, as things have been horrible for her the last few days. John stopped in front and stepped out to help her in. Art moved to the back seat so she could sit next to John while he filled her in.

"What is it John?" Valarie demanded before he had a chance to say a word.

"Valarie, we're going to see Chuck----"

He started as Valarie interrupted. "He's dead! I knew it---- they found his body. What do you mean everything's all right?" She blurted out in tears.

"He's alive, and in the hospital being checked over---- in Aberdeen. He's fine and we should be able to take him home, to my home soon." John said as his face lit up with a huge smile.

She started sobbing, "I can't believe it. You're not kidding---- are you?" She asked still sobbing, and turned toward Art who sat smiling in the back seat, in an attempt to get confirmation.

"No. I'm telling you the truth. He is going to be just fine."

John went about telling her the story as he knew it, on the way to the hospital. When they arrived, they parked and went first to the information desk where John inquired in Chinese as to the room. The lady said they have no one registered by that name, and her records indicate there never has been. John was getting visibly upset at the gross inefficiency of the hospital and their staff.

John turned to Art and Valarie who were waiting with quizzical looks after hearing his tone elevate and said, "He is not registered here. I know Preston told me the hospital in Aberdeen. And this is the only one. I'm going to call him."

John called Preston from his cell phone. "Hello, Hobbs here."

"Preston, John. I am at the hospital and he is not a patient they say----never was."

Hobbs broke out in laughter and said, "John, do you think I was born yesterday? Maybe you don't know that term. How about, do you think I'm stupid?"

"Of course not, why would you ask?"

"Do you think I was going to check *Winters* in as *Winters*, with all this going on?"

"I am sorry, of course not. I should have known better. Who is he?"

"He's my brother Milton Hobbs. Who else would he be?" Hobbs broke into laughter again, and finally so did John.

John went back to the patient information desk and asked for Mr. Milton Hobbs' room. He was directed to the nurse's station on the third floor, where he repeated his request for Hobbs' room. She said that he was unable to see anyone, and asked his name.

"Oh, Mr. Sun, you *are* authorized access. It seems that his brother, Mr. Preston Hobbs is very protective of him." The nurse told them.

John continued to be impressed with the professionalism and clear thinking demonstrated by Preston. They followed the nurse to Room 414, a private room with a man sitting outside the door. He stood up blocking the door, and spoke to John in Chinese. An exchange occurred and both shook hands and smiled at one another. It seems, John whispered, that this is one of Preston's men, making certain that no uninvited guests appear after what has happened. Art and Valarie were truly impressed with the security that Preston put into

276

place to protect Chuck, and Valarie indirectly, as she could become a possible kidnap target or worse if it were known that he was still alive.

The room was dark, curtains drawn. They quietly walked into the rather large space and saw me lying in bed, eyes closed. My face was covered with scratches caused by being hit with shattered glass while on the top deck of The Black Orchid. I had a bandage on my head that secured an icepack, presumably for the swelling that was caused when I hit my head on something just before or after the explosion. My nurse motioned them to step outside for a moment and she spoke in Chinese, with John interpreting. It seems that the doctor gave me a mild sedative, and some medicine to reduce the swelling. I also was given a shot to fight any infection that might occur from either the cuts I received or the bump on my head. As a result, she said I'd be out for a while and won't be able to carry on much of a conversation.

John asked if my memory had returned and she said that she wasn't certain but the doctor felt my disorientation was a direct result of the swelling, and it should return soon, if it hasn't already.

"Hey, what's going on?"

I had awakened, although still a bit groggy. They returned to the room. I was sitting up in bed now, with a smile as large as I could muster, arms extended toward Valarie. She rushed to my bedside and gave me as much of a hug and a kiss as she dared under my apparent condition.

"Art, what in the hell are you doing here?" I asked, still smiling. "We *are* in Hong Kong aren't we, because I see John over there?"

"We're in Hong Kong, Aberdeen Hospital to be accurate. Do you know what happened or how you got here?" Art asked.

"Well I did think I had lost my mind when everyone around here started calling me Mr. Hobbs. But after a while a Mr. Hobbs came in and introduced himself and explained a little to me. It's kind of nice to have a long lost brother." I said grinning. "I don't remember a thing. My first recollection is waking up in this room earlier today, and my last was approaching that boat with May's security guys."

"I'm shocked," Valarie said, "you can't imagine what I was thinking when they couldn't find even a piece of your body after that explosion." She started crying and looked like she would totally lose it, when I reached out and pulled her to me saying "everything's going to be all right honey."

Valarie calmed down and sat on the edge of my bed just holding my hand, while Art explained how he happened to come to Hong Kong, and about Tom Claudius' concern and all-out financial commitment to finding me.

"John, I can't thank you enough for helping me and keeping Valarie safe. I'll never forget it. And Art, I know you. You'd have been here with or without Tom's involvement. You're the greatest friend a guy could have. Valarie, you went through hell and kept the faith, never giving up. I love you so much." I gave her a nuzzle. She finally smiled, and I probably looked as happy as a man possibly could under the circumstances.

"You need to rest, Chuck", John said, "and when you feel up to it, you come home and my staff will treat you like royalty."

"John, I've imposed enough. I don't need special treatment, but what I do need is to get out of here and back on the case. Where are we right now?"

John looked at Art, who nodded for him to explain that they were starting a meeting with the police when Preston Hobbs called with great news. Inspector Li was setting the stage to go to KRL and push them to cooperate, using the information about the TechX software sale and what had been learned from Sue Tang before her death. He also explained that the police did not know about finding him alive, and they would have to get back to the station and either give a cover story or tell the truth about his status.

"I have a great deal of difficulty withholding information through omission to my friend Inspector Li, even though I know the leak from his department caused Sue Tang's death. My only thought is that we take him and him alone into our confidence and keep the rest of the department unaware of your status. We could make the case for this by saying that the currently unidentified killers are under the impression that you have been taken care of, and as a result may be somewhat less cautious in their final activities, which could increase opportunities for apprehension." John said.

"You're right," I said, "tell the Inspector, but let him know how important it is that my surfacing be kept secret. It will be a lot easier for me to move around without constantly looking over my shoulder. I do think that the less he knows about my whereabouts the better."

"Then I will call him right now and fill him in. I won't tell him that you are here Chuck, only that you are safe and recovering from the explosion." John said and added, "Art, are you willing to go back with me and meet with Inspector Li and his people this afternoon?"

"Sure, but let's let Chuck map out the strategy we want to see occur at this meeting, and how to handle the people at KRL." Art said looking at me.

"I think it's time to let the principals at KRL find out that we're onto their dealings on TechX, and that they're in serious trouble, not only for theft of intellectual property, in this case software, but murder and conspiracy to commit murder. We need to get them to pick out the person from TechX that they're dealing with and turn over the local contacts if any to avoid prosecution. Of course everything depends upon Inspector Li agreeing to this. If we can identify the person responsible from TechX, then we can be close to accomplishing our mission." I said.

"Fine, let Art and I work on this.

Where are the driver's license photos? We need to take those to our meeting with Inspector Li to use at KRL."

"They're in my briefcase in our room. Valarie can find them for you." I answered.

"Not on your life, Valarie is not leaving your side." She sharply responded. "The last time I let you out of my sight, I thought I lost you for good. Can you understand that?"

With a broad smile on my face I said, "OK, you win, Art can dig through my briefcase, but I need to get out of here. I have work to do."

"Chuck, you concentrate on getting the doctors to release you, and then we will ask Preston to see that you get to my house. No one will be following a dead man. I will call Preston and have him use his influence to release his "brother" to his care."

John and Art left the room. Valarie continued sitting on my bed, holding my hand and just looking very happy.

I asked Valarie for her cell phone that was always in her purse----this being no exception. I dialed Tom Claudius's home number in Atherton, California, just a few minutes from his Palo Alto office. I estimated the time to be about 9:00 P.M., one day earlier than Hong Kong time. "Hello." Tom replied.

"Hi old buddy, what's up?" I said teasingly, and thoroughly delighted in making this call.

There was dead silence on Tom's end of the line.

"Do you think *you* might have died and we're talking as dead men?" I asked, chuckling.

"Chucky? I don't believe this. Is it really you?"

"In the flesh, old buddy."

"I sent Art to find you----did he?" Tom asked.

"You bet he did, he hired a local PI agency headed by a Brit, ex foreign- service or something, a fellow named Preston Hobbs. He's one smart cookie. I guess you know the last time I was seen was just before the boat blew. Well, I don't remember a thing after that, but I'm told a sampan man fished me out of the harbor. He had to leave to see his dying mother and left me in the care of his wife on their boat. She took care of me and didn't trust the police. Hobbs' people found me with her and took me to the hospital in Aberdeen. The smart son-of-a-bitch checked me in as Milton Hobbs his brother, so no questions were asked. The cops were looking for me, and the bad guys would be too if they thought I was still alive. I want to do something nice for the folks that saved me, but first I need to finish this job."

"Chucky, as soon as you are well enough to travel, get your butt on a plane and get back here. I don't want to lose you over something as stupid as money. I've got more than I'll ever spend. This just made me mad----that's all."

"Tom, don't you worry about me, I'm a big boy. I'm going to finish what I started. These guys have kind of made me mad too."

"Chucky, don't worry about doing something nice for the folks that helped you, Art and I already worked out something for them." Tom said.

"I can't thank you enough for jumping right on this, and sending Art over here to find out what happened to me. I'll bet you never thought he'd bring me back alive after what you heard the last time anyone saw me."

"Well, in all honesty I thought your number was up. I couldn't imagine you coming out of that deal in one piece."

282

"From what I heard I'd agree, just a lucky break that guy fishing me out. For your information, I'm going to stay *dead* for a while, at least until I find out who the bad guy is for sure. I guess Jaxton hasn't shown up alive or dead, and neither has Phil Hampton. To the rest of the world, Valarie is grieving at John's house, but in reality she's sitting on my hospital bed and doing just fine. I'll be in touch----and Tom, thanks for being such a great friend. Oh Tom, I forgot to ask, did anyone tell my folks that I was a goner?"

"Chucky, Art and I discussed it and he suggested that we wait until we could tell them something with surety. As far as they know you and Valarie are having a ball in Hong Kong----spending my money."

"Now that's not a bad idea. How are you going to explain these expenses made by a dead man to the IRS?"

"See ya Chucky." Tom said as he hung up.

CHAPTER 45

BEAVERTON, OREGON

The man called Foster sat in his Las Vegas Suite, waiting for her to pick up the phone. "Hello."

"Hi sweetheart, what did you find out? Is it in the bank?" He asked.

"Yes, darling, I just received confirmation----verbally of course, no paper trail. Do you want me to ship it off to the other account? You know where they make cheese?" She giggled as she responded.

"Victoria, this is serious stuff, and the answer is yes. I don't want it sitting around there because too many people know where it went."

"I was just trying to lighten things up. Are you going to be a constant stick in the mud----even when I get there?"

"I'm sorry this has been a big strain on me. I'll mellow out, just you wait." He replied.

He thought, "I have to cut the ties with this bitch. I don't want her in my life, nagging me in paradise, wherever that may be. There are too many sweet young things out there that would appreciate a multimillionaire a lot more than her. She's almost served her purpose, which will occur when the building is torched and the last five million is wired. If I could only screw *him* out of the two and a half, I'd be free and clear of these people. He'll be checking on the two million I'm supposed to wire to his account. I wonder." His mind trailed off considering the possibilities of conning him into torching the building without the money in his account.

Foster's cell indicated a message at the L.A. answering service. He dialed the number and found that the taller man wanted him to call back. "What now, he's in Beaverton and he checked his account and it's still two million light." he thought, "I have to save the money he expects. It's just too much of the pie. After all it was my idea and I have the money." He concluded, and started to dial.

"Hello." The taller man said.

"Returning your call, are you there?" Foster said.

"Yeah I'm here, but it's doing you no good, because I'm not moving until I know my dough is there. And it's not, I just checked."

"I just talked to Victoria, and she said the money's too easy to trace form Hong Kong to the Caymans. And if it goes direct to your account from there, it'd lead the authorities to you and to me ultimately. Besides, she's afraid it'll lead to her and she just refuses to do it that way----she just told me. She's transferring the money to Zurich, and it'll be wired to you from that special account we set up. It's cleaner that way, and safer for both of us. OK?" Foster asked.

The taller man paused and said, "Bull shit, you're screwing with me."

"No I'm not. It's the only way it'll work for all of us." Foster said.

The taller man thought for a moment and finally said, "Fine, I'll just sit in this hotel room until it gets into my account. There'll be no flames in Beaverton until then. Do you hear me?" He said----his tone angry.

Pausing to think, Foster decided to try a different approach, one with a touch of logic. "Listen, the longer we wait the greater the opportunity we have of this blowing up in our face and getting nothing more. You know my word is good. Did you see that I wired the fifty grand to you as we agreed?"

"Yeah, you did." He said, softening some.

"Well what do you think, should we get the rest of the money from Hong Kong?" Foster said, in an easy challenging way.

"Let me think about it. Call me back in an hour, OK?" The taller man said, and hung up.

He pulled out his small hand-held computer that held Victoria's number, as well as that of everyone else involved, including Foster's cell number, which he was so secretive about. He made it a point to know everything about a mission and everyone involved. He did so in order to assess the chance of success and in turn determine the value of his services. He maintained a sophisticated tracking system in Lisbon, one that allowed him to know numbers and locations of calls being made to him, even blocked numbers, along with the capability of monitoring the numbers called from any phone in the world, both incoming and out-going if it was programmed into his tracking computer. He knew who "Foster" called, as well as the duration, date and time. He regularly checked his computer from his small hand-held, for updated information.

CHAPTER 46

"Hello." Victoria answered.

"Hi, I just talked to him and he told me about your concern over wiring the money to me. What's your concern?" The taller man asked.

"What do you mean, and why are you calling me at home----on this number?"

"Well I didn't have a choice. Maybe you should tell me about him wiring money from the Caymans to me. Do you see a problem with that?"

"No, that's why I had to pay the bank vice president so much money for him to lose the documentation on this account after we empty it. I thought we were going to do that, I just talked with him and he never gave me the instructions. *I* need to do it, not him! He told me to transfer all the money to Zurich, and I forgot to ask about wiring yours from the Caymans. I guess I assumed you two worked that out."

He thought for a bit and finally said, "You're giving up everything, your reputation, career, profession as a lawyer, your home, even your country, on this scheme. Isn't that true?"

"Yes, if it's any of your business, I happen to love him." Victoria said in an almost uncertain tone. It was all true, she thought. What if things fell apart, what if they got caught? After all, she wasn't in on the planning. She just did what she was told.

"Do you trust him? I'm in Beaverton right now. Do you want to have a drink? I have a car. I can swing by and pick you up. We can go someplace and talk." He said in a smooth calming tone. She didn't even question how he happened to have her address, or why he was in Beaverton. She certainly didn't know he was about to cause a fiery inferno in the town she was about to leave----forever.

CHAPTER 47

HONG KONG

I called Preston and thanked him again for the miraculous detective work in finding me----as well as keeping it quiet. "I need your help once more, and that's to use your obvious influence to get me released from this place so I can get back to working out of John's home."

"How do you *really* feel?" Preston asked in a fatherly manner.

"I'm fine, the swelling is down a lot and my memory is back. I'm ready to go." I replied, convincingly.

"I wonder if it makes sense to go back to John's place. These people are not operating in a vacuum. I would guess they're watching his house, if for no other reason than to find out whose coming and going. They probably already know about Art and his involvement. If you suddenly popped up on John's doorstep, all hell might break loose again. Do you really want to take that chance with Valarie here in Hong Kong?"

"I suppose you're right, what do you suggest?"

"Well, I have an apartment overlooking the harbor. It's not too fancy, but it is quite secure in terms of cameras and locks, as well as an elevator that goes to a service basement with a ramp leading to the street running behind the building. I have an arrangement with the apartment association allowing me to park several vehicles there, as well as have a key to the service elevator. I guess in your country they call them condominiums. The bonus is on the rooftop; one of the finest, yet to be discovered Cantonese restaurants in town. Oh yes, they deliver to your apartment. I would be only too happy to have you as my guest. With your permission, I'll call John and see if he concurs. I know you'll want to talk with him about it, but let me break the ice as they say. Is that acceptable to you Chuck?"

"I keep on having to thank you. It sounds perfect, and wise as well. Valarie is sitting here with me. Can you hold a moment for me to discuss this with her?"

"Of course, take your time."

I explained the proposal Preston made and was surprised at her quick agreement. She felt she had been imposing on John enough, and would love, as she put it, for a chance for us to be alone.

"Preston, we are in agreement. John and Art are meeting with Inspector Li. If you call him for me, I won't need to leave word with his staff, and I don't want to break up his meeting."

"Chuck, or I should say Milton, I'll make the call to the hospital, it's much better for you to be at your brother's home recuperating, don't you think? I'll be there in thirty minutes----pack your bag!" Preston chuckled.

"Now that you mention it, there is a matter of my clothes and Valarie's things as well, how do you suggest we handle that?"

"I'll leave a message for John to call me and with his approval and a quick call to his staff. I'll have one of my people run over to his place, pick up your things and take them to the apartment. It's a good idea that Art continues to stay with John, in order for things to look as normal as possible under the circumstances. As far as anyone knows, Valarie went back to the States. John and Art can come to the apartment for meetings with you as required. John is very familiar with the apartment and the rear entrance ramp."

CHAPTER 48

John Sun called Inspector Li on the way back to the Central District, informing him that he and Art would be along shortly and apologized for the rude departure they made from the meeting. He asked for a few private minutes upon their arrival to explain everything, which the Inspector graciously granted his long time friend. During his cell phone conversation, he was beeped with another call, which he returned to Preston Hobbs after finishing with Inspector Li.

Preston's kind offer to Valarie and me made good sense to John, although I believe he truly enjoyed our company. John followed up with a brief call to his chief of staff at home and arranged for our personal belongings to be carefully packed and placed by the front door for Preston's man to pick up.

After a quick greeting in Chinese and another deep apology for his behavior, John Sun satisfactorily explained to his friend, Inspector Li, the reason for his absence as well as the need for ongoing secrecy in terms of my status. He also briefed him on the hoped for results of a confrontation with the people at KRL. All of this seemed to be logical to the Inspector and he was prepared to adopt such a direction with his staff when the meeting was resumed at the station. The group reassembled and put together their game plan after Art and John explained the steps that brought them to the present. Art provided the TechX employee photos they picked up after leaving the hospital. They decided on a time to make their "raid"----1:30 P.M. the next day. An inside source at the company indicated that the weekly executive meeting was scheduled for the next day, and that Mr. Chi and Mr. Wong would be conducting the meeting. It was decided that John and Art would not be involved and only police officers would attend the KRL confrontation.

Preston arrived promptly in thirty minutes with the hospital chief of staff at his side, waltzing into the room like he owned the place. He formally introduced his brother Milton from the states and his beautiful wife Valarie, whom he described as the beauty whose affections they both fought over, but the younger more handsome brother won out. A crying shame he said with almost believable sincerity. Valarie was clearly flattered by his easygoing boyish charm. I was impressed with his line of total B.S. I couldn't forget that this man, with his charm, wits and sheer determination, and yes----B.S., found me. Preston, ever thinking brought a lightweight crème colored cashmere sweater in extra large, as well as a pair of drawstring powder blue denim slacks that fit perfectly. He also included a pair of boat shoes, new underwear and no socks. I thanked him profusely for the clothes----but inquired about the lack of socks.

"Milton, you never wear socks when you wear your yachting attire, now do you?" Preston grinned and broke into a belly laugh adding, "Get dressed my brother the ship's about to sail."

With that I dressed and Preston informed the Chief of Staff to bill Milton, care of his office for the hospital stay and handed him his business card.

Preston, in a strong rich voice proclaimed----"to the yacht!" And with a flourish of his extended arm pointing direction, three stylish yacht people left the building with the hospital Chief of Staff looking on in some kind of awe.

Preston Hobbs had always been a bit much for British officialdom. He was fortunate or misfortunate depending upon whom is doing the considering----to be heir to an estate that reached back to the year 1096. It seems that was as far as they cared to trace it, in order to maintain their respectability. Preston, true to his reputation had a slate gray Rolls Royce waiting under the port cache. And along side in proper attire stood his faithful chauffer James, scene quite befitting mustard commercial.

We entered the Rolls and were whisked away like royalty. "Preston you really know how to live." I said with palms up and extended, as I looked around the luxurious automobile with its rich walnut trim and sumptuous gray leather, complete with thick wool carpets.

"I have no idea what you might be speaking of old chap." Preston responded with typical I was learning, aplomb.

The ride to the apartment was short----as a couple of miles from one side of Hong Kong to the other might be. The traffic was horrendous however Preston's driver was quite familiar with the terrain, and after a few zigs and zags we were motoring down a steep dark ramp leading under a building.

"We're home!" Preston said with pride as we entered this basement area with several cars parked against the far wall. Aside from the vehicles there wasn't much in the basement other than the standard landscaping tools and a ladder or two. There was nothing that indicated anything more than a second-rate building basement. "The elevator is over there. I guess we don't have much in the way of luggage, so let's go up. But before we do, here's a card key that opens the electric door we just went through at the top of the ramp. Here's the card key to the elevator we're about to take to the twenty-first floor. Oh yes, that black BMW over there is for your exclusive use, here're the keys."

"Nonsense, we can't impose on you like this."

"Chuck, the apartment is one of several I own here. The car is used when I don't want to be noticed on a case, as are the other two against the back wall. So you see this is no imposition. I rather enjoy having a Yank indebted to me. You never know when *I* might need a favor." He said with his trademark grin and a slap on my back.

"Just say the word." I responded with a smile.

Preston slipped the card key into the slot and the elevator door quickly opened. It didn't look like a freight elevator. Its walls were lined with highly polished teak, and the floor appeared to be of green marble. In any event this "service" elevator whisked them to the twenty-first floor. The door opened not into a hallway but in what appeared to be Preston's apartment. Standing in the entry hall was a smiling Chinese lady, her age impossible to guess. She dressed quite properly in a basic black, hemline just below the knee. She greeted her employer and showed us to the master suite with its twelve-foot ceiling, plush carpets, beautifully furnished in Chinese polished pieces, along with a king-sized bed overlooking the balcony and the harbor beyond. Valarie was speechless. She thought she was giving up John's beautiful hillside retreat, for a *practical* apartment where they could blend into the surroundings. In turn she discovered her change of venue was to perhaps one of the most beautiful apartments in all of Hong Kong. Valarie opened one of the two walk-in closets and discovered to her sheer delight that all of her belongings left at John's home were neatly hanging in the closet or placed in drawers. I discovered the same in my closet.

Upon returning to the entry area, the housekeeper indicated that Mr. Hobbs was waiting in the living room. Preston's apartment covered the entire floor, with the living room taking up about a fourth of the space. The furnishings were minimalist by design, which with the un-crowded look caused the room to appear even larger. The room featured two floor-to-ceiling window walls overlooking downtown Hong Kong and Kowloon in the distance. Preston was standing near the corner window gazing out at the city he obviously loved. "I assume this is one of your smaller places in Hong Kong." I remarked with tongue in cheek.

Preston looked at me, paused and said, "As a matter of fact it is. So you see you're not inconveniencing me in the least."

CHAPTER 49

Upon John and Art's return to the Sun residence, Art excused himself and went to his room to call his office. He needed to check in with his partner on aspects of the case he delegated when he left for Hong Kong. "Roberts." The familiar gruff voice boomed over the phone lines.

"Jimmy, what the hell are you up to? I thought you'd be sleeping in." Art kidded his partner of fifteen years.

"How come you're in such a great mood----any news on Chuck?" Jimmy asked----concerned.

"I'm happy to tell you that he's been found and he's fine." Art went on to say, "He was on a boat with a Chinese lady for a couple of days."

"I knew it, that son-of a-bitch, just like him to end up with a broad----on her boat. Someone had to drag him out didn't they?"

"Jimmy, as a matter of fact that's exactly what happened, can you believe that?"

"You bet I can, that guy has a way with the ladies. What did Valarie say?"

"Valarie was just glad to get him back. Let's talk about what you've found out on this case."

"OK. The cops in Portland haven't found the two missing guys----Jaxton or the other guy. I did find out what's going on with that Caribco thing in Las Vegas. Our guy you know----Tilly, retired Vegas P.D. Well, he used his contact and got a report for me on the account. Two million-six went in over the last four months. All but around a million bucks was withdrawn, spread over the same period. The balance was taken out yesterday in bearer bonds and a fifty thousand dollar wire transfer was sent to an account in Lisbon, Portugal. I have the account number in Lisbon and a name----probably a false identity, Mason Dixon. Yeah I know----the Mason Dixon Line. But I'm sure they don't have a clue in Lisbon."

"Good work Jimmy. You have Chuck's e-mail, send him this report on Caribco with names, account numbers, everything. Do it right away, OK? In the meantime get me everything you can on the Caribco registration with The Nevada Corporation Commission? I want to know who registered it, the incorporators, and officers, what address they gave, the method of fee payment, the whole nine yards---- please." Art ended with him and Jimmy's standard joke, a pause and a "please", when one partner is doing all the hard work and the other is "asking for results".

"OK boss." Jimmy replied with a good-natured jab to his partner.

CHAPTER 50

LAS VEGAS, NEVADA

John Foster called the cell phone as agreed in one hour and received the recorded message about the party leaving the service area and to try again. Foster was hoping the taller man had decided to go ahead, without waiting for evidence of a deposit wired from the Caymans to his bank, in Lisbon. He tried every fifteen minutes for an hour and a half, and finally, "Hello." The taller man answered from Victoria's house----her head close to his as they both tried to listen on the cell phone. "Where and the hell have you been? You said call me back in one hour. That was two-and-a-half hours ago." Foster asked unhappily.

"It's not important----the question is why doesn't Victoria want the money wired from the Cayman bank to Lisbon?" The taller man inquired again, this time for her benefit.

"I just talked to her this evening and she said we could get traced too easily and it isn't worth the chance. She really said she wouldn't do it because it can be traced to her. There's nothing we can do if she refuses to do it. Let's play her game. You can have your share wired from Switzerland. It won't hurt to wait a day or so. Let's just make sure we finish the job for KRL. Did you call your guy to find out when the money will be wired after you finish the work in Beaverton?"

"Yes, they have someone here right now to make the verification." The taller man said. "They'll wire as soon as he calls them."

"Great, call the service when the money is wired, OK?" Foster instructed him.

"OK" The taller man said and punched the end button. He and Victoria stared at each other----her in disbelief.

"Have you wired the funds yet?" He asked.

"Not yet, they were closed.   I need to do it in the morning."

"Good."

CHAPTER 51

HONG KONG

Mr. Lee dialed the home number of Billy Wong although he was apprehensive about calling such a man of great importance at home. He gave him the number at the beginning of the transaction with TechX, for what must be this type of circumstance----he hoped. "Hello." Billy Wong answered.

"Mr. Wong, this is Mr. Lee."

"Yes."

"I have just been contacted by my associate and I am informed that the last requirement has been met by our side. He is desirous that you please check with your man for verification and after which proceed to wire the balance of the funds as agreed. Is that acceptable with you?"

"If the job is done the funds will be wired and we are through with one another. Is that correct?" Billy Wong asked.

"Yes sir. May I check with you tomorrow to see when the funds will be wired?" Mr. Lee timidly asked.

"Yes, after 12:00 P.M. tomorrow." Billy Wong added, and ended his telephone conversation.

Mr. Lee was in sheer ecstasy. His dream of moving up in the world was two days away for him.

Shortly after midnight, Mr. Lee was unable to sleep so he lay in bed staring at the ceiling. Tomorrow would put the wheels in motion for his big payday. Two hundred thousand in US dollars would be Federal Expressed in an overnight package to his apartment----the day after the funds were wired to his client. He didn't hear the door unlock. He didn't hear the man dressed in dark clothing move down the hall to his tiny bedroom. He did see the man after it was too late. His eyes still open, staring, as he lay upon the bed, a soon to be rich man he thought moments earlier----never to think again.

CHAPTER 52

I called Art at John's home to check in and discuss strategy. John answering the telephone suggested that I should be resting and not thinking about the case. "Have a wonderful Cantonese meal sent down from the roof-top restaurant. I heartily recommend the food. You and Valarie need some time to yourself. That is an order from a new friend, do you hear me Chuck?"

"I hear you John, and let me say again how much I appreciate what you've done for me and Valarie, you are truly a friend."

I'll tell Art you're on the line." John said, and pressed the hold button.

Art Levy filled me in on the Caribco, Las Vegas account, and asked me to check my e-mail from Jimmy that should be there by now. We agreed to meet at my new digs for breakfast in the morning and would ask John to join us.

CHAPTER 53

It was early for Mr. Chi, who usually didn't arrive at KLR headquarters until after nine each morning. But today was the start of an important milestone for the company. He called Billy Wong an early riser into his private office and said, "I received word from my contact in the States that the last part of the TechX deal has been satisfactorily completed and we will need to wire the five million US today in order to finalize the transaction. Are we in agreement on this?" He asked Billy Wong.

"Absolutely, we can then immediately start implementing the software into our design programs and rapidly develop chips that far exceed the capabilities of anything on the world market, and will for some time." Billy Wong replied in a jubilant tone.

"What about Mr. Lee, we can't have him walking around with information on this transaction?" Mr. Chi asked as he slowly stroked his beard.

"It has been handled, last night in fact." Billy Wong said with a sense of pride in tying up loose ends.

"And this man Jaxton and the other man are they under close scrutiny?" Mr. Chi asked.

"Yes we have people in Las Vegas and Lisbon, Portugal. They will be eliminated after we recover our money." Billy Wong replied with confidence.

"You are certain your idea of wiring the last five million dollars to them is the best way to handle this. It seems a bit foolish to risk that much money when we could just withhold payment and only have to recover the first five million?" Mr. Chi inquired.

"Yes. We accomplish several things. First we have deniability if the police look into this. The worst thing they can say is that we bought stolen property, without our knowledge of course. We can demonstrate that we paid ten million US for the software to the company founder. No one will ever know that we recovered the money, which we will, rest assured." Billy Wong assured with a devilish grin.

"Then it is settled. I will instruct Mr. Kan in finance to wire the last five million this morning to the Cayman bank as agreed." Mr. Chi informed Billy Wong.

CHAPTER 54

Art Levy and John Sun arrived for breakfast at the apartment just after 8:00 A.M. Valarie was on the balcony, sketchpad in hand, recording the beauty and diversity of downtown Hong Kong stretched out before her. They were shown into the breakfast room where I was reviewing my notes, seated on one of six white iron chairs with comfortable seats and back cushions placed around an oval glass table. The room was decorated in yellows and subtle blue tones, with a wall of glass overlooking the now bustling city below. The table was covered with assorted fruit bowls as well as dishes of Cantonese specialties, along with scrambled eggs to satisfy Art's basic breakfast desires---- all steaming hot under glass covers. There was coffee and tea, as well as an assortment of sweet rolls. I ordered this from the rooftop restaurant the previous night and asked for a waiter to assist. I didn't want to ask Preston's staff to accommodate us more than they already had.

"Pretty fancy." Art said as he walked to the window to take in the astonishing view.

"Well it takes a little effort to remember just why we're in Hong Kong, however when I look in the mirror and see the cuts on my face and feel the lump on my head, I come right back to reality. Thanks for coming John. I knew Art would, he never turns down a breakfast invitation. That's not to say that your breakfast wouldn't exceed this. Art just likes me to buy him breakfast. It goes back to our San Francisco cop days."

"OK, that's enough of telling John all my secrets from the past----he already knows enough over the years." Art said with a smile while eyeing the huge dish of steaming scrambled eggs.

"By the way, I called Preston this morning and asked him to have his people talk with my saviors from the flotilla and tell them that saving my life has to remain a secret in order to collect the reward money. He said they previously mentioned this, but considering how word spreads among the flotilla residents, a second warning is in order. I intend to see them before I leave Hong Kong, and do something extra for them. I wouldn't be here had it not been for their kindness. Before we start, let's have our breakfast. I asked Preston to join us this morning. He provides a somewhat different dimension to our team. He can't make breakfast due to an earlier commitment however he'll be along shortly."

After trying all of the delicious breakfast specialties, Art decided that he could get used to the Cantonese fare. He thoroughly enjoyed the "mystery food" that only John could explain, and only in Chinese until after breakfast when he told Art the "fried bacon" he thought he was eating was really a form of fried eel. He decided that tomorrow he was returning to scrambled eggs and whatever else he could readily identify.

Art's cell phone rang. "Hello. What? OK Jimmy, I'll pass the word to him. I'm with him now, thanks." Art said to his partner.

"Chuck----that was Jimmy. He said Tom Claudius just called trying to get hold of you. It seems your cell isn't turned on and he tried mine but it was out of range or something. The TechX headquarters burned down in the middle of the night and it's totally destroyed. No one was hurt and they suspect arson. He wants you to call him right away."

"Unbelievable. I'll call him right now." I told Art with a grim expression.

The phone was answered and Betty put me right through to Tom. "Hello, Chucky?" Tom said with a sense of urgency.

"Yes----tell me what happened."

"The building was burned to the ground. I don't know if there's a connection with what you're doing, but the cops feel strongly that its arson. I sent Bill Esler from our office up this afternoon. I keep forgetting its morning in Hong Kong. Anyway, he's going to be acting CEO. He's a board member and stays on top of things from this end. He called the management of the office campus where the building's located, or I should say was, and they have space in a nearby building we can use until they re-build ours. I called Christine and she's getting the word out to the employees about the new temporary space. I told her to rent whatever was necessary from one of those furniture rental companies until we settled with the insurance company. Since you have a handle on the software and have had discussions with Bryan Cranston, please call him and find out what was not in the building in terms of software. I think it's time to forget about finding Jaxton and get started on the concept that you talked with Cranston about, that is him taking over the finalization of the software and getting this thing back on track. I told Esler that you would be talking with Cranston and getting him started, that is if there's anything that didn't burn in the fire. Let me know, OK?" Tom asked.

"What do you mean forget about Jaxton?"

"I mean, let's not count on him being around to help us any time soon, if ever. You finish your job and find out what happened and who's responsible, and just how deep this problem is at our company."

"I'll call Bryan now. I've got the list of cell and home numbers with me, and will get back to you."

"Well you heard my side of the conversation, any questions before I call Bryan Cranston the TechX Chief Engineer?" I asked the assembled group that now included Preston Hobbs who arrived while I was talking with Tom Claudius.

The gathered group, looking quite subdued, shook their collective heads while I dialed Bryan Cranston's cell phone.

"Hello." Cranston said.

"Chuck Winters, Bryan. I'm really sorry to hear about what happened at TechX."

"It was amazing, the place is virtually leveled. Not a thing of value left."

"Bryan, give me some good news. Tell me that you had your copy of the software and test results with you at home when the building burned!" I said in a hopeful, yet apprehensive tone.

"I always take my laptop home with me, and yeah it did contain the software and test protocols. After I learned of the fire I transferred everything from my hard drive to disc and took a complete set of discs to my safety deposit at the bank. I wanted to make certain they were safe and would never be lost or destroyed."

"Great work Bryan, Tom will be extremely pleased. I just spoke with him, and although Bill Esler's on his way to Beaverton to be acting CEO until everything is sorted out with Denton, he asked me to talk with you about taking charge of the project and finishing whatever testing is necessary to release the software to the market. When we last discussed this, you felt you could pull things together to do that. Do you still feel that way?"

"I do, however it'll take a few days to get rolling again. I understand Christine is coordinating the temporary facilities, as well as purchasing the necessary hardware to set up the engineering department. I've been helping her on that score a bit already. You better give me a week to pull things together and be moving on this."

"That's great, I'll let Tom know and he'll inform Bill Esler that you're heading up the project and to give you whatever support you might need."

"I'll get to work." Bryan said and hung up.

"Tom just called again and wants you to call him back right away. He says it's really important." Art told me.

I dialed Tom Claudius's number again and was put through to his office. "Chucky, I was just called by the Beaverton Police Department. They tell me that the fire department arson squad, while poking through the rubble came upon a body. They thought earlier that no one was in the building. It seems that the body was burned beyond recognition, however they found a wallet near the body that was not completely destroyed." Tom said, and paused.

"Well, whose was it Tom? I asked impatiently.

"Denton Jaxton's".

"You're kidding. Do they think it's him?"

"They don't know, but usually when you find a wallet with a body, one might think they go together. The medical examiner is trying to obtain his dental records. It's just too early for them to make a judgment."

"Is it possible Jaxton set the fire and made a mistake----killing himself in the fire?" I asked.

"Well they said they haven't ruled out Jaxton or anyone else as causing the fire. They did say that everything changes with the fire----which becomes murder if Jaxton is the dead man and wasn't involved. They have no information on Phil Hampton, even though he's officially listed as a missing person. We can't know for certain that it wasn't Phil that was the body in the fire. We just don't know, but the medical examiners should have something pretty quick." Tom said.

"Let me know if you hear anything. I'm going to finish sorting this out here and find out exactly who Knowledge Resource Limited was dealing with in trying to buy the TechX software. Keep in touch."

"Will do Chucky."

We hung up and I turned to the group, not speaking to anyone in particular.

"This is unbelievable, everything seems to be unraveling. Nothing makes sense. People are getting killed all over the place and motives don't add up. Now this thing with Jaxton----why would he want to burn down the building, he'd only be hurting himself and his future? If someone killed Jaxton and dumped him into the fire, what's the point? Where's he been during his absence?"

Preston interjected, "I'm the new man at this party, but from what I've been able to absorb in my short involvement, there's a whirlwind of activity that can become extremely distracting, and I think this is occurring on purpose." Nods of agreement were universal around the table. "Therefore, it seems to me that one should forget the distraction for the moment and focuses on a specific issue----in this case the question of who was trying to sell KRL the software. Then with that answer you can start to unravel this mystery. I think the distractions are in reality a diversion to buy time to complete the deal and disappear. They don't care who's in their way----they just kill them."

I responded. "You're right on target, Preston. Let's concentrate on finding out who's negotiating the sale of the TechX software----and go after him. We need to get the results from Inspector Li's visit to KLR this afternoon. In the meantime we need to follow the money, and thanks to the e-mail I received from Jimmy Roberts this morning, we know part of it went through Las Vegas to Lisbon, and into the account of a Mason Dixon. We have to find out who he really is and how to find him. Who has a contact that can get us into the Lisbon banking system, or particularly Le Banco Lisbon? We have an account number and evidence of a wire transfer of fifty thousand dollars from Las Vegas to the bank in Lisbon, yesterday."

Without hesitation, Preston answered. "I have a man in Madrid that may be able to help in Lisbon. He has deep contacts into banking systems and trades on information that very few others have access to. If you agree, I'll call him. It will cost five thousand U.S. for this kind of information, unless it's a problem, like something political or someone very well connected."

"Let's do it." I said. "How do we pay him?"
"I have good credit with him. Let him produce results and then we'll agree to send him payment. Is that acceptable to you Chuck?"

"That's fine. I appreciate that Preston."

CHAPTER 55

ZURICH, SWITZERLAND

Foster was sitting in his hotel room and had been calling the taller man's cell phone for the last several hours with no response. He was getting angrier by the minute and finally called Victoria.

"Hello" She answered.

"Hi honey, how're you doing?"

"Where are you? What in the hell got into you, asking him to burn the building down? Are you crazy? This was never part of the deal. Not only has there been a murder that I like a dumb fool discovered in the house. But you conspired to commit arson. Do you remember you said you had a simple little plan to sell some software to an offshore company and retire? A plan that you convinced me was safe----and went on to claim that the only fools that might suffer were the greedy fools in Hong Kong, and they could afford it. You assured me this would not harm the TechX firm, and it would continue on just fine. This was in effect an offshore trading deal, nothing more----nothing less, no murder, no arson, and no exposing me as a co-conspirator in this mess." She exploded with a sharpness he had never experienced before.

"I had no choice, things just got out of control baby. I'd never do anything to hurt you. I love you with all my heart. You know that. Let's talk about something productive. I'm in Europe where the bank is located, however they won't tell me if the money's in the account because they say I don't have access. Why won't they tell me about my account? I thought you were going to wire the first five million. Did you do that?" Foster rattled off questions in a tense distrusting tone of voice.

"No choice? Why did you order the building burned down? It's easy for you to sit there in Europe while I'm five minutes from a huge arson investigation, a murder, and two missing person searches, all connected to me in some way. For all I know I'm being watched by the police right now. I'm getting very nervous. Why didn't you get my input before you put me at further risk?" She asked angrily.

"I'm sorry honey. I only want to be with you and I just had to do enough to make that happen, nothing more, do you understand?" He asked in a tone dripping with honey.

"No I don't. But for your information, I did transfer the five million, and I've checked the Cayman account for the second five million and have just been informed that it's arrived. I'll send the documentation to wire that as soon as possible. Shall I wire your friend his money as agreed? Was that two million? You already gave me wiring instructions for the Mercantile Bank in Lisbon."

"No, I'll handle that?"

"The account isn't set up for you to write checks yet, or transfer funds. I need to do it, and I thought he expected the money. Are we going to have a problem with him too?" I just don't want any more problems."

Foster was fuming and concerned that he not push her over the edge further in order for her wire the money now into the new Swiss account, and further into his own bank----rather than rely on *her* future involvement to do so.

"I want all the money to be in the account before I disburse any more and I want to be able to handle the transfers myself. I first need to talk to him, probably in person, and have an understanding that his work is complete and he will not come back to me for more money. Do what you have to in order to get my authorization. OK honey----*today*?" Foster said in an attempt to sound loving and thoughtful, and still accomplish his purpose.

"I'll fill out the paperwork and fax it you'll have to sign it at the bank, unless you want me to send it to your hotel. Where are you staying?" She asked.

"Just send it to the bank, when will they have it?"

"If I'm going to meet you late tomorrow, I need to know where you're staying in Zurich. What's the big secret----you're making me nervous?"

He thought quickly, and recalled the hotel near the airport, with its name in his in-flight magazine. Opening it, he said, "Movenpick Hotel at Walter Mittelholzer Strasse 8", as he was looking at the letterhead of the Hotel Schweizerhof, a smaller elegant hotel, near the main railway station. "I won't be there until tomorrow. The hotel I'm in near the airport had only one room, just for tonight."

"Well if I need you before then, give me that name and number." She said.

"I don't remember the name. I do know I can't pronounce it, and there's no number on the phone.

316

Sorry, you won't need it, just send the documentation to the bank and I'll call you back later today to see that it was done."

"I have to go to my office and get the file. I'm planning on flying to Zurich tomorrow to be with you. Maybe it would be best if I just handled the financial transactions in person as the company lawyer, who they've been dealing with from the beginning. I told my firm that I was burned out and have decided to take a sabbatical, which I've earned and travel to the South Pacific to unwind and do some writing over the next three months. Little do they know that I won't be back. It's probably best that we handle the money when I get there, don't you think?" She said in a subtle, yet testing way.

Foster paused he was seething from her controlling attitude. There was no question in his mind that cutting her *and him* out of the deal was the right thing to do---- without any doubt at all. "No, I think we need to keep this low key and do it my way, do you understand?"

Being unable to control his temper, he further said, "Just do it----now!"

"OK, see you in Zurich tomorrow night sweetheart. I can't wait to see you." She said, knowing in her own mind that her suspicions were confirmed.

CHAPTER 56

Victoria arrived at her office and called Cayman Trust Ltd., Bank, where she previously set up the account. "Mr. Sinclair, please." She said as she asked to speak with the Vice President, who for a handsome fee set up her *specially handled account* as he called it.

"Sinclair here."

"Mr. Sinclair, this is Victoria Danville."

"Miss Danville, how can I be of service today?" He inquired in his most professional manner.

"I'm considering opening another *specially handled account* under a new account name. I assume there will be a fee associated with this. If so, can you tell me what that might be?" She inquired in a calm and professional manner.

"Of course, how large would the account be and where would the funds be arriving from?"

"This would involve ten million U. S., and it would just be a transfer from my other account in the bank." She said in a matter of fact statement.

"Since it's within the bank and you are a present customer, there would be an accommodation fee of ten thousand US, plus the normal bank charges for transfers etc." He said. "Is this acceptable to you?"

"It is. If you close the other account after the funds have been transferred, and if you do the same for this new account, after you receive instructions to transfer from myself only. Also and most important, you must eliminate any record of deposits received, or transfers out, anyplace within your bank or within your control. Is that understood Mr. Sinclair, not a shred of paper or a reference in any computer hard-drive or disk?" She said with authority, and continued. "I want you to close account # 347 which is in my name, and transfer all of the funds into a new account in the name of Falfah, Ltd.,

F-A-L-F-A-H, do you understand?" She asked. Thinking that the new account name was poetic justice and appropriate, standing for *free at last from ass-holes* !!!

"What will the new account number be?" She asked.

"Miss Danville, it will be account # 359, and it will be completed in less than ten minutes. If I am not here and you need access, please use the account number, the account name, and a P.I.N. number, which you must give me now."

"Make it 2020, for my new perfect eyesight. Sorry, inside joke." She said with a smile on her face.

CHAPTER 57

HONG KONG

John Sun received a call from Inspector Li, who through a confidential source determined that the two top men at KRL were out of the country, on business. The scheduled weekly meeting was going to be held by senior staff instead. As a result, Inspector Li elected to hold off the confrontation until their key suspects returned from their trip in three days. "We do have some information that could tie-in with the case you are working on. This morning we were called about a body that was found by a maintenance man in an apartment in the Central District. It turns out that the man, named Way Lee, was strangled sometime after midnight, and a search of his apartment turned up notes in a ledger indicating that he was to receive two hundred thousand U.S. dollars for his role in introducing TechX software to KRL. He was dealing with Mr. Chi and Mr. Wong at KRL. He was being paid by a man only known as Harper. I assume he is an American whose cell phone number we are trying to trace right now. His notes also say that his money is being sent by Federal Express in an overnight delivery. He was expecting his funds tomorrow, and we will be watching his apartment for a delivery if we are unable to intercept the package at the distribution center in Hong Kong." Inspector Li reported.

"Would it be possible to have this Mr. Harper's cell number in order for us to use our private contacts, on a non-official basis of course, see if we can develop information helpful to the case?" Mr. Sun inquired of his longtime friend.

Inspector Li, paused and said, "For you, I believe that would be acceptable, however, I must make one request, that the number not be called. I do not want to alert this person of interest that we are attempting to speak with him."

"That is acceptable, thank you. We will work under that condition."

"I do not have the number at the moment however I will e-mail it to you within the hour, along with a statement of our agreement of non-contact." The Inspector said.

CHAPTER 58

LISBON, PORTUGAL

"Is it done, there's a man waiting for his money in Hong Kong?"

"It will be within the hour, in the amount we agreed upon." She said.

"Thank you." He said, and pressed the end button on his cell phone.

CHAPTER 59

SHANGHAI, CHINA

"I just received word from Mr. Eng in Portland, Oregon. He said the Portland, Oregonian, newspaper, indicated that TechX is now operating in temporary facilities in Beaverton, and is expected to meet their new product release dates. He is e-mailing the article. It went on to say that essential development documentation was maintained offsite, and as a result no interruption in their development schedule will occur." Seething, Mr. Chi paused and continued, "I was assured by you that this product would be dead! It sounds to me like we spent ten million dollars on a product that anyone in the world can buy when the software goes to market, at a fraction of the cost. I want that product development stopped at TechX forever! I want Jaxton and his agent in Lisbon eliminated, permanently! I want our ten million dollars back from these criminals----do you understand Billy? I trusted you when you brought this *wonderful* opportunity to me." He spoke in such a way that Billy Wong thoroughly understood that his relationship with Mr. Chi and his future retirement in luxury, was in serious jeopardy unless he corrected all of the problems that occurred from this fast sinking venture.

"I understand, and will make the necessary corrections." He said without hesitation.

The two men were in Shanghai, sitting in Mr. Chi's extravagant hotel suite. His Hong Kong Police department source called him the night before warning him of the unannounced "interview" scheduled to occur the next day in their offices. He felt he needed time to sort out his response to questions on the TechX software.

He also needed to take steps to insure that his employees with knowledge of the TechX "product acquisition" would not discuss a word of it with the authorities.

"I want a list of every person in KRL that had even a remote awareness of TechX, or anyone involved in this transaction. I then want you to have a personal discussion with each of these people about their life expectancy and that of their spouses, children, parents, grandparents, cousins, aunts, and uncles. Do I make myself clear Billy?" Mr. Chi asked with a dead expression, one that made clear to Billy that he and his relatives were in the *most* danger if he did not or could not resolve these mounting problems.

"You do." Billy Wong said, fearing the daunting task ahead, one that precluded his daily daydreaming of his retirement with riches, his objective for the last several years.

CHAPTER 60

HONG KONG

The meeting I held at the apartment, ended with Preston following up on Lisbon with his Madrid banking contact. Mr. Sun agreed to use his telecommunication contacts in an attempt to trace the cell phone call to a man known as Harper by the now deceased Mr. Lee.

"Art, I'd like you to hook me up with Tilly in Las Vegas, and follow up on that Mason Dixon wire transfer to Lisbon from the Caribco account. I want to meet with him right away and track down what I think is a direct link to the principals in this case. We've been nibbling around the edges and they keep moving out while the page is always blank to us. I know Valarie would be better off staying here for a few days while I'm gone, but that's her decision and I need to speak with her about it. I know I don't want her to go home until this is wrapped up and the bad guys are in jail." I said to the group.

"I'll call Tilly right away. You know he's retired and not working in any capacity, and only helped as a favor." Art said.

"I understand that, but would he be willing to assist for a few days and be compensated for his assistance?"

"I'll ask, but in any case, I'm certain he'd be happy to meet with you and point you in the right direction."

"Chuck, if Valarie would be more comfortable not being by herself here, she's more than welcome in her room at my home." John offered.

"Thanks John, I'll pass that on to her."

"Chuck," Preston said, "Valarie would still have the staff here, and I'll provide twenty-four hour security from my organization if she would like to stay on."

"You are both terrific, let me talk with Valarie. I really appreciate your kindness and I know Valarie does as well."

"Chuck, I think I better fly back to the States with you. There's nothing that my two able friends here can't handle far better than I can." Art said smiling, "And besides, I can be more efficient when I have access to me files and contacts in my own office."

"Fine, I'll book the flights back to San Francisco right away. Are you ready to go now?"

"You bet."

"Excuse me while I have a little chat with Valarie."

Valarie was sitting on a comfortable wicker chair on the balcony, transferring the wonderful scene below to her sketchpad. "Hi honey." I said as I strode over to her and put my hands on her shoulders. "I have to follow up on a lead in Las Vegas and need to leave right away. I don't know how long it'll take, maybe a couple of days or longer. In any event, I need to know what you'd like to do. You have two men in the other room acting like teenagers vying for your presence in their homes. I'll be happy to have you join me, the only place I draw the line is you going home until we figure this thing out."

She looked up with a smile, took my hand and said, "What do you suggest? What would be easiest on you?"

326

"You being happy and safe is what I want."

"Well, I don't know if going to Las Vegas and sitting in a hotel room while you snoop around sounds like fun to me, even though you know I love being with you. On the other hand, would you need to come back to Hong Kong if I wasn't here?"

"Good question, the answer is yes. The KRL group is up to their necks in this thing and I need to get to the bottom of that. But the police are delayed because the principals are out of the country for a few days."

"OK, I'd like to stay right here where I'm very comfortable. I love being at John's, he's wonderful, however this is the heart of the city and I'm really making headway with my sketching. I have enough sketches of the harbor, and really want to capture the feeling of the city. I don't have a problem staying here. The staff is great, and I feel safe. I'll come out and talk with John and Preston. They're just wonderful. I can't thank them enough. When are you leaving?"

"I don't have a ticket yet. Art's going back with me to San Francisco and I'm flying on to Vegas. Are you sure you'll feel safe here?"

"I'll be fine." She said, smiling.

"Oh, I forgot to mention, Preston said he'd have security around the clock here at the apartment for you."

"Do you think that's necessary, I hate for him to do even more."

"Let him do it, he wants to and I'd feel a lot better, although I really don't think there's a risk at this point."

Valarie and I stepped into the breakfast room and encountered the smiling faces of her new Hong Kong friends, John Sun and Preston Hobbs, along with Art. "Hi, Chuck told me that he's going to Las Vegas on a gambling junket and I have two offers for room and board in Hong Kong during his absence. I'm so grateful to all three of you. With your permission Preston, I'd love to stay right here for a few days and do some more sketching of this beautiful city until Chuck returns from his vacation." She said smiling at me.

"I'm only too happy to be of service." Preston replied.

"Valarie, I'll be checking in with you to see if you'd like to join me for dinner, and I promise that we'll not be on water again." John said with a broad smile.

Before she could answer Preston chimed in, "John, you better be quick because my wife and I are going to spirit her away from this place for some fun and dining ourselves."

"I appreciate your interest in making me feel comfortable here in Hong Kong, you've succeeded. But now I'm only too happy to sit back and unwind a bit by myself. Should I become lonely, rest assured I'm not shy, and won't hesitate to call either of you and ask you out myself."

"This love fest is getting a little heavy. I totally concur with what Valarie said. You guys have been just great in every way. Art we need to get a flight out of here and get back to work."

CHAPTER 61

LAS VEGAS, NEVADA

I arrived in Las Vegas at 4:45 P.M. and was met at the airport by Gene Tilly, Art's retired friend from the Las Vegas Police Department. He carried a cardboard sign with Mr. Winters scrawled on it, like some kind of tour driver. After the introductions Tilly said. "We'll check you in at Bally's and then we'll go over how you'd like me to help you on this case."

Tilly was a pound or two on the north side of three-hundred and was dressed in navy blue slacks with his large stomach hanging over his belt. Shirttails hung from his white shirt, with stains from last week's breakfast clearly noticeable. His hair was thick and curly gray, complexion ruddy, with a bulbous nose that gave away a life of heavy drinking.

I checked into the huge and crowded hotel. It seemed safe to be back in the States surrounded by gamblers from middle-America, vacationing and having a good time. We went down to one of the many lounges in the hotel. This one a small quiet bar off the lobby. Its Western décor was surprisingly comfortable with only a handful of drinkers scattered around the room.

"Gimme a bottle of Bud." Tilly told the waitress----with his noticeable total lack of social skills.

I quickly decided I wasn't particularly interested in socializing with this guy. "May I have a club soda please?"

Tilly looked at me like I was from another planet and said, "Club soda, don't you drink?"

"Yes I have a drink now and then, but I don't care for one at the moment."

I wondered how Art Levy could even talk to this guy, let alone work with him on a professional basis.

"We might as well get right to it. Somehow I need to get find out who this guy is that controlled the Caribco account, what he was doing in Las Vegas, and how we can find him now."

Tilly stared at me and said, "Anything else?"

I didn't know if Tilly, as I was told to call him, was serious or facetious with the question.

"What do you mean----anything else?" I asked with a half smile.

"Just that Chuck, I can get you there---- I think."

"OK, how do we start on this?"

"I can get you a copy of the account records, signature cards, opening application, copies of checks, front and back and statements." Tilly stated confidently.

"What'll it cost, and when can we get it?"

"It'll cost you five grand for my contact, and two for me." Tilly answered without hesitation.

"When?"

"Tomorrow morning, or let's say no later than the lunch hour."

"Fine, I'll write you a check upon delivery."

"Five now----and the rest tomorrow when I deliver. I've got to give this individual at the bank cash on delivery." Tilly said in a matter of fact way.

"I don't have cash on me, but I can give you a check."

There was a big smile on Tilly's face when he said, "The banks don't get no bigger than the one you're sittin' in right here. Go to the cashier and cash a check, no problem, and you might as well make it for seven so you'll be ready for me tomorrow, OK?"

"OK, I'll go cash a check right now." I told him as I rose from the table.

"I'll be here. Hey, gimme another Bud!" Tilly shouted to the waitress.

I returned ten minutes later with seven thousand dollars in hundreds, and counted out fifty bills for Tilly's contact.

"Fine," Tilly said, "I'll call your room and leave a message when to meet me in this same bar tomorrow, OK?" Tilly said, swallowing the last drop of his second beer while hoisting his huge frame out of the chair that should have groaned in relief.

"That's fine, just call me. Oh by the way if this guy that's been using the Caribco account has been staying around town, is there some way you could find out about that too?"

Tilly turned as he was leaving the table, and said, "Sure, I can try, let's see what we get tomorrow," as he continued toward the door.

I waited until he left the bar and when the waitress came up to collect for the tab, I said, "May I have a double-Vox martini, up please?"

CHAPTER 62

ZURICH, SWITZERLAND

Foster sat in a chair by the window in his suite dialing Victoria's number and getting no response. He dialed her office and was told that she was on sabbatical and wouldn't return for three months. "Where is that bitch?" He thought. He then called the Zurich bank where the new account was set up, and spoke to an assistant director. He asked if they had received the documentation for MedTest, the corporation Victoria set up.

"She was faxing it from her office in the U.S. yesterday. She's our corporate attorney." Foster said in an attempt to demonstrate knowledge about the company and its account.

In a snubbing tone, "Mr. Foster is it?"

"Yes. Do you have the documentation?" He asked, doing his utmost to maintain control and not crawl through the telephone lines and strangle the little twerp.

"I am afraid that we have no information regarding a change that involves you. I might suggest however that you contact Miss. Danville directly and inquire." The man said in a matter of fact statement.

"I am not happy with this bank and you can count on this account being closed as soon as I transfer the funds out, do you understand?" Foster angrily asked.

"As you wish, sir." The man said, and terminated the call.

Foster threw the telephone so hard that the cord which was permanently wired into the wall, pulled loose as it flew across the room. Since the phone was inoperable, he moved to the bathroom and sat on the toilet to use the only working phone in the suite. Dialing the taller man's cell number, he received a recorded message that it was disconnected and no longer in service.

CHAPTER 63

SAN FRANCISCO

The city that Art Levy loved seemed just about normal to him, at seven in the morning. He could count on cool air with a thick layer of fog this time of year as he drove the last few blocks to his office. It was located on Geary Street in an older three-story building in a *mixed use area* as they called it, residential, retail, and office buildings. Art liked the ambiance, it allowed him to take walks in a real neighborhood with a sense of community when he needed to get out of the office and clear his head. He particularly liked to walk in *this* neighborhood, watching real people going about their daily lives.

Often he would sit on a stoop down the block next to Mr. Garcia a retired cable car "pilot" as he liked to describe himself. Jose Garcia had a grasp on what real people thought of life, kids, politics, crime and his favorite subject, the deterioration of the neighborhood and the morals of America. He didn't hesitate to tell Art exactly what he thought on each subject.

Art also enjoyed browsing in Chin's market across the street. Mr. Chin, his father and grandfather, had been proprietors of Chin's Market on this same corner since 1867. Upon entering the market, one experiences the rush of aromas that might be expected from hanging smoked ducks, fresh fish, and Chinese medicines, not to mention a beautiful produce section with many vegetables Art had never seen before. Although he was never invited into the back room, Art was certain it was a big-time gambling joint, complete with cigarette clouds hanging from the low ceiling, and lights directed over green felt tables. Or maybe it was an opium den, or a combination of the two. He liked to let his imagination transfer him from the puzzles of his daily reality, to a life of intrigue and romance in a bygone era.

CHAPTER 64

Art walked into his office and sat down at the large desk next to the window. The blotter was littered with correspondence and a backlog of messages. He started shuffling through the backlog from the last few days, pulling out those pertaining to the case. He started with Frank Hixon, of Hixon & Frontier in Portland, Oregon. Frank's message said nothing more than call me. Art dialed his home number, knowing there is no way Frank would be at the office before eight in the morning. "Hixon", he answered just like he was answering his office phone.

"Frank, Art. I've been in Hong Kong and just returned. Saw your message and decided to roll you out of bed this morning."

"I thought you might like to know I did a little digging about the guy that died eight years ago. You know the one that was found dead in Jaxton's house?"

"Yeah, what about him?"

"Well, I think he was in one of those spook units. You know, one of those units that didn't exist on paper. After he served in Nam, he apparently ended up in this type of unit and sort of disappeared from the radar screen. Then he ended up dead in Europe. I thought this was interesting and did a little checking. I got his unit in Nam and then checked on the members. I tracked down a couple. It wasn't too hard, because they still lived in their hometowns. It seems that this Peter Duvinchy, originally from Chicago, was half nuts. He called one of them a couple of times to see if he wanted to do some special work in explosives for him in the Middle East. The guy

337

said no, but this Duvinchy guy kept bugging him about joining up with his *team* as he called them."

"Frank, this is very interesting, but what's your point." Art asked.

"Well my point is simple the records said this guy has been dead for eight years. However this same dead guy called him again two years ago in another attempt to recruit him. He said he was working under contract on special assignments and could offer him a guaranteed hundred grand a year."

"Well----did he join up?"

"No, he thought the guy was scary, and no one could pay him enough to hook up with him."

"Where do we go from here?" Art asked. "We know he obviously didn't die when they said he did. The death information was phony."

"This Duvinchy guy said he was involved with a paramilitary group that hired themselves out to fight in military coups, or rebel organizations. They didn't care which side they fought for as long as the money was good. They also did some special assignments on private cases, which I got the impression were assassinations of some sort. My guess is that this little gang of hired thugs is the muscle for the TechX problems, and he gave me the phone number of the recruiting officer. It's a number in Lisbon, Portugal."

"Did you say Lisbon?"

"Yeah, why?"

"That's where a prime suspect is from. What's his name and number?"

"I don't know if it's his first or last name, but it's Mason."

"Mason?" Art said. "I think we have a direct hit here. Fax me a report on the entire conversation along with the phone number----and good work----very good work. Can you cross check the Viet Nam records of Duvinchy's unit and see if there's a Mason in it----first or last name?"

"I already did that. There was no Mason in his Nam unit that I could find."

"Thanks a lot Frank."

CHAPTER 65

Not expecting a call I reached for my cell when the jangle of its distinctive ring jolted me from my concentration. "Hello."

"Chuck, are ya winning or losing?" Art asked.

"Well, if you're talking about the tables I'm even. If you're talking about Tilly, I won't know until noon."

"Well I have some news. We have another hit on this Mason guy in Lisbon. It turns out the dead guy in Jaxton's house was not dead eight years ago like we guessed. Two years ago he asked a former Nam unit buddy to join his soldier of fortune group, and if he was interested to call a Mason in Lisbon and gave him a phone number. I'm getting details faxed to me within the hour."

"It looks like the noose is tightening. Do we need a visa or just a passport for Portugal?"

"First of all what's this *we* stuff? And secondly, I don't know if *you*, need a visa or not."

"Well, Preston thinks he can get me the bank information in Lisbon, and John's working on a phone number, you're getting a number, and Mason is the name confirmed by the Hong Kong lead----I think we're onto something, how about you?"

"I would agree with you but you didn't answer my question. Do you really think you need me in Lisbon?"

"The answer is yes. We won't be more than a day or two----is my guess." I said, hoping my request was convincing.

I checked in with Valarie and everything was going fine. "I miss you, when are you coming home---- I mean back? This is getting quite comfortable, all this pampering. I could get used to it." She said in her teasing tone.

"I miss you too honey, and if Hong Kong is starting to feel like home, then you'll understand that I'll be a few days longer before I can return. I need to go to Lisbon with Art." I said, expecting a response I didn't receive.

"OK, and be sure to take care of Art," she paused for a long time, and then continued "and you too sweetie----take care of yourself." She said with that typical bratty chuckle.

"Have you talked with John or Preston? I need to get updated from them."

"They've both checked in today, although I haven't seen either in person, nor have they discussed the case. They just wanted to know if I needed anything and that I was all right. Which I didn't and I was."

"Good, it's nice to know that you're well cared for and feel safe where you are."

"I'm fine----do you think you'll be back within a week? I just want to know if I should be making long range plans. You know----wardrobe planning, tickets to the theater." She said playfully.

"I'm really disappointed that you haven't found us a home yet----you've had nothing but time on your hands. You know what we want----view of the harbor as well as the city lights, lots of glass, private gardens and a nice pool with decks and lawns. Room for the servants, yes let's not forget the servants, make that staff. And don't forget the wet bar stocked with Vox and whatever----you know!" I said with delight.

We laughed and promised to talk daily. Next I called Preston Hobbs.

CHAPTER 66

"Hobbs Investigations." She said.

"May I please speak with Preston?"

"Hobbs here."

"Preston, this is Chuck calling from Las Vegas."

"I say old man, are you ahead of the game there?"

"It depends on the game Preston."

"Well let me tell you about our little game of find the bloke in Lisbon----do you remember that game?" Preston inquired with his dry humor.

"I do, where *is* the bloke from Lisbon, have you found him yet?" I asked hoping for facts, and not really interested in games.

"Not exactly, but my man in Madrid spent some of your money and learned the following about Mr. Mason Dixon. He received that $50,000.00 US into his account----and more, over the last several months. It seems that this account is only about three months old, and all of the deposits, totaling two hundred thousand dollars, up until the day before yesterday, were wired from Las Vegas, Nevada. The account came to the bank through a solicitor from London. It seems that the bank was told that Mr. Dixon would be receiving some sums from the States, which were to be used for acquiring property in Portugal. The bank officials never met Mr. Dixon, and everything was handled by telephone, wire and mail. Since the sums were relatively small in proportion to other of the bank's accounts, there was no---- how do you yanks describe it----red flags raised?"

"That's what they call it. I'm assuming there's more to this story Preston. Do we have a lead as to how to find this Mason person?"

"Let me move forward with my story. As I said, up until yesterday the transfers came from Las Vegas and were on the modest side. However yesterday, there was two point five million dollars US, wired from a bank in the Caymans, and the entire sum in the account was withdrawn in the form of a further wire transfer to a bank in Zurich, Switzerland. My man lost track of it in Zurich, not enough horsepower as you fellows might describe his ability to obtain information regarding numbered accounts. I can tell you the name and address of his solicitor, Mr. Günter Howard. This will do you no good, because the name is false as is the address. He is not a solicitor in London, nor did his address prove to be reliable. My thinking is that Mr. Howard and Mr. Dixon are one in the same, and that both names are false. It's interesting that Mr. Howard and Mr. Dixon were both signors on the account. As a result, Mr. Howard came to the bank on one occasion to establish the account and deposit twenty five thousand dollars US about ninety days ago. Mr. Dixon has had no occasion to contact the bank at any time, in any way. I am attempting to arrange a photograph of Mr. Günter Howard. My contact man said that our bank person is checking the security camera film on the day Howard came in and opened the account. They have the exact time that the opening deposit was made and where this Mr. Howard would be sitting in the bank. If we're lucky we may be able to obtain a shot of his face. The film is a new digital type, so they maintain the results on disk and do not erase every few days to save film or storage space, as in most security camera systems.

I was told that the bank person is taking the disk home tonight and will go through it on her computer. She will also make copies of the paperwork and send originals to Madrid in hopes that we might obtain a helpful fingerprint. We must promise to return the originals after we have checked." Preston explained in careful detail.

"Let's save some time on the photos and documents. Art and I will be in Lisbon tomorrow. Is there some way we can meet with this bank person and pick up the information ourselves tomorrow?"

"Well you are quite the world traveler. I will check with my man in Madrid, but I suspect the bank lady would not want her identity known, and may only arrange for delivery to your hotel----if that."

"I understand, then see if she'd deliver the items to The Carlton Palace Hotel, Rue Jau 54, Lisbon, as soon as she has something. How much do we need to pay her? I can pay her tomorrow."

"That will not be necessary, she is being paid around a half million Escudos, something over two thousand US dollars, directly by my man in Madrid. He will bill me and I will pass it on to you."

"Can you leave a message at the Carlton for me, regarding receiving the information tomorrow?"

"I will do that. Have a safe flight, and I will be watching over Valarie until your return."

"Great job Preston, thanks."

Next I dialed John Sun's cell phone. He answered as I expected in Chinese. "John, Chuck".

"How are you, Chuck?" John asked, in his usual polite professional yet friendly manner.

"I'm doing fine. The question is----how are you doing?"

"I am glad you called Chuck. I just received some information. The cell phone number in Lisbon for Mr. Fred Harper is 1099-030. It's been traced to a Lisbon cell phone dealer, a Mr. Santos who is located on Rue do Grila, 90. I have not spoken with him, because I thought you might want to make the first contact."

"I would. Art and I are going to Portugal tomorrow. Do you know if Inspector Li has uncovered this contact in Lisbon yet?"

"I do not believe so, because he promised to call me when he learned something, and I agreed to do the same." John added.

"It would be helpful if you held off contacting him until I speak with this Mr. Santos tomorrow. I'd like this to be a surprise to him."

"I have no problem with that, my promise was if I found Harper's location I would immediately turn it over to the Inspector."

CHAPTER 67

LISBON, PORTUGAL

The taller man sat on his master bedroom veranda overlooking the azure blue ocean. The sun was warm and he was wearing his usual attire while home---- white shorts, no shirt, blue baseball cap without logo and sandals to protect his feet from the hot crimson red ceramic tiles covering the nearly forty foot wide expanse of his private veranda. An American, he stood well over six feet, was fit by any standard, sandy brown hair streaked by the sun with wisps of blond, brown eyes and tanned to perfection, not by intent but by happenstance. He appeared to be in his early forties, but in actuality he was ten years older. He paid cash for this comfortable tiled-roof villa, high on a point in a desolate area just north of Lisbon. He had no phone service other than his cell, and the official records showed the home was owned by a Francesca Rialto. This of course was another attempt to distance his real identity from prying eyes. The name was fictitious and the real estate transaction was recorded by a local attorney. He was in fact, a part time attorney and a full time drunk. One that forgot the transaction that was supposedly being handled by the taller man for his aunt, after drinking his next bottle of hundred proof rum provided by the taller man.

Life was easy between assignments, and he only took the ones he wanted. He was now feeling comfortable financially, as he just added another two and a half million dollars to his retirement nest egg, now totaling over five million US dollars. He was thinking that his luck had been pushed enough and it was time to retire and go fishing. A hobby up to now he only infrequently had the opportunity to pursue. He never married, but had a current girlfriend who thought he was a diamond salesman and traveled frequently to places like Africa on his buying trips. He would often show her his diamonds and occasionally give her one. Her name was Anna---- Anna Santos. Her brother Rafael Santos sold cell phones and Anna worked in his store in Lisbon occasionally when she was not pursuing her singing career. The taller man met Anna several months ago while he was changing cell phones, which he did on a regular basis. It was his standard practice to go to a different cell phone retailer each time and use a different identity. He had a state of the art computer system in his home that allowed him to produce complete identities, including passports, visas, driver's licenses, social security cards and any other document he found helpful in plying his trade. He was also able to create photo identification while wearing assorted disguises, which he was an expert at creating. When he was on the road, rushed or cornered by circumstances, he turned to Hans his Zurich connection who early in his "career" carefully schooled him in the art of identity fabrication.

Anna knew him as Fred Harper, the name he fabricated as he prepared for his most recent cell phone identity switch. He had never before violated his professional work ethic of not associating in a personal way with any "thread" as he called them, to a clandestine activity. When he first saw Anna, he knew he couldn't resist her charm and beauty. She was twenty-five, had long black hair, a fair complexion and piercing emerald green eyes. She was tall and perfectly proportioned, and had earned college degrees in history and language. The fact that she spoke English, fluently, impressed "Fred Harper". That ensuing conversation with her was the start of his personal rule breaking. A situation that developed into one violation after another of things he knew to be dangerous to his own existence. As a result he

348

did not employ his standard procedure of threatening her brother with his life if he discussed with anyone, anything about him, his cell phone account, or even acknowledged that he ever met him. Fred Harper as he now called himself was infatuated, pure and simple, with this girl Anna.

Harper began thinking about Foster, as he called himself. What a joke he thought, him of all people taking an alias. Harper had not seen him for nearly ten years when he decided to contact him about a year ago, only on a whim, and also because he felt that pretending to be dead to the world was one thing, but to his own brother that was a whole different story. They agreed to meet on the condition that Foster would not tell a living soul about their relationship, and if he did there would be two less living souls around. They agreed to meet in Honolulu, an easy trip for Foster to explain away and a busy enough city for Harper, with flights in and out from all over the world. The reunion went surprisingly well. Foster brought his younger brother up on limited, general type details of his soldier of fortune life after working for the US Government in what they called 'Black Op.'s". This was primarily a group of Nam misfits with little or no family that could turn up dead for the record and take on a new identity, for special off the books work that the Government would deny any involvement with. And if caught, would disavow any relationship with these men. The pay was good and somehow it slipped through the income tax crack. Harper learned the ropes of assassination of government officials, creating unrest in third world countries, actually starting and then fighting in civil wars in some. He couldn't care less about the side he was fighting for. He was just interested in the money. He gained a very low-key reputation as a man to call if you needed some expertise in certain areas. He weaned himself away from the Government and became a freelancer, drawing on his old team from time to time as personnel needs dictated, but mostly operated on his own in order to insure security---- his!

Harper had given his younger brother a number in Paris of a friend who could contact him if he ever needed to get in touch. About four months later, Foster *needed* to get in touch. He needed his older brother's help, as things were about to blow up in his face if he didn't make a lot of money fast, and disappear. This was not at all of interest to Harper. It was risky and stupid, but he was stopped in his tracks when Foster said he would give him two million dollars to help him. The taller man, a.k.a. Harper, received his contacts by e-mail. He didn't keep a telephone number longer than ninety days, as it usually involved a specific assignment and not for social calls. He checked his e-mail this beautiful morning and was surprised to find that his friend in Paris was once again contacted by his brother. The message said, 'it was urgent that he call him right away'. Harper was curious, but suspected it had to do with the money, so he put on a blue t-shirt and sandals and went down to his garage, located under the villa. In his attempt to maintain a low profile, Harper drove a ten-year old Jeep Cherokee, however in case the need arrived, under the hood a supercharged V-8 was lurking, capable of matching or exceeding anything on the road. He wound his way down the hill to an area of retail establishments, restaurants and hotels. Pulling up behind a small, non-descript hotel, he went in through the bar. In the hallway outside the bar and close to the hotel lobby was a row of three pay phones. He pulled from his pocket an untraceable prepaid phone card, and called the number left by his brother. Harper didn't expect him to be there and was going to leave a message stating a specific time he'd call back, however the phone was answered. "Hello."

"It's me, what's your problem now?" Harper said in a not too brotherly tone.

"I can't find Victoria, she left and I think she took all the money." Foster said in the voice and tone of a man that knew the score and didn't want to admit it.

"I think Victoria is pissed at you. I wouldn't doubt it if she ran off with the money." Harper told him in a matter of fact way.

"Why? Did you talk to her?"

"You gave me no choice. I got the impression that seemed to be correct, that you were going to screw both Victoria *and me* out of our share. As it turns out we both got paid, and I guess you didn't. Too bad!" Harper said with a chuckle.

"What do you mean I tried to screw you?"

"Let's not go there. I wasn't born yesterday. You better find Victoria and make nice with her to get something out of this deal. The way you had this planned there wasn't going to be any killing, and it seems that's all there was. I don't think I was paid enough." Harper said trying to get a rise out of his little brother.

"Listen, it's not just the money, I think I'm being followed here in Zurich."

Harper went on alert. He knew this could spill over to him. "What do you mean; what have you seen that makes you think so?"

"When I went to the bank yesterday, I felt someone, or more than one person was following me. Every turn I took, first one person appeared to be following then another. I finally took a cab to a different hotel and then slipped out the back street and caught another cab back to my hotel." Foster said.

"Was this the bank that you were using in Zurich?"

"Yeah, I went to see if Victoria had sent documents for me to sign."

"What did these guys look like?"

"Asian. They both were Asian."

"My guess is the KRL group from Hong Kong wants to kill *you* and probably me and get their money back. Get out of Zurich----they're going to find you. It's just a matter of time!" Harper told his brother.

"But what about the money?"

"You're not going to find the money in Zurich, you need to find Victoria, but in the meantime forget about the money----you've got enough for now don't you?"

"I suppose, where should I go?"

"Fly to Paris and ask my friend Paul where to stay. He'll let me know. I'll call you. Do it now do you hear?" Harper instructed his brother in a tone that he understood.

He was confident that the Chinese were behind this effort to find the participants in the software sale and recover the money. It was most likely, he thought, their intention from the start, elimination of potential witnesses as well as recovery of the money they paid. He wasn't certain if they've traced the transaction back to him, but he was trained to assume such a situation and act accordingly. Now was not the time, when he was almost certain it was time to retire, to make a stupid mistake. Harper, now on alert, stayed in the phone booth until he had an opportunity to survey the hallway and determine if he was being watched. It was clear in both directions, so he carefully walked to the lobby and then out the door and around back to where his car was parked. He saw nothing suspicious and drove into Lisbon to make arrangements to fly to Paris.

CHAPTER 68

LAS VEGAS

Tilly called my room at 12:15 P.M. with the news that he had the information and to meet him in the bar with the final $2,000.00 in ten minutes. I agreed, and made my way down to the small cowboy bar where we previously met. The day was going to be a scorcher, the paper called for 105 degrees by mid-afternoon. I went into the bar and found Tilly sitting at 'our' table. He had a beer in front of him, and the sweet little waitress from last time came over and asked if the gentleman would like a Vox martini----while looking at me.

I, who looked like I'd been caught with my hand in the cookie jar said, "Just iced tea please."

Whereupon Tilly looked at both of us and said, I thought you didn't drink."

"I don't." I said to thoroughly confuse the man.

"You got the money?"

"Yes, what did you get?"

"I got everything you wanted. Signature card, application, statements since the account was opened, and copies of checks, front and back."

"Let's have a look."

"What about my dough?" Tilly asked suspiciously.

"I've got it, let's not play games OK?" I shot back----obviously not liking the guy.

Tilly shrugged his shoulders and moved ahead. He opened the large brown envelope and shook the contents onto the table. Out came the statements, cancelled checks, copies of signature card and application. There were only four checks and each was written back to the bank, with notations to acquire cashiers checks made in favor of John Foster totaling just over $1,500,000.00 dollars, and spread over the last four months. It appeared that Caribco was registered as a California assumed business name of John Foster. The mailing address was a post office box in L.A. The only signer was John Foster. There was a wire transfer totaling $50.000.00 to the account of Mason Dixon at the Mercantile Bank in Lisbon, account # B546-9832, and a bearer bond of just over one million dollars purchased when the account was closed.

Tilly received his money and we parted company. I headed for my room and called for a reservation to Lisbon for Art and me. I'll fly to San Francisco and pick up Art. A quick call to Art confirmed his grumbling agreement. Art Levy then called Hixon in Portland, thanking him for the e-mail with the complete report of his investigation on Duvinchy and the phone number of Mason in Lisbon. Hixon added that the medical examiner was no closer in identifying the body found in the TechX fire. They are confident it was arson, but have no clues they are willing to discuss, which meant to Hixon they had nothing. Also they have no clues on Jaxton's disappearance----if it wasn't his body found in the fire. Duvinchy, the dead man found in Jaxtons's crawl space is still a mystery to the police. Their official position on finding a dead man of eight years was a records snafu.

CHAPTER 69

LISBON, PORTUGAL

Art and I landed in Lisbon, Portugal at 9:30 P.M. The weather was balmy and the night skies were a landscape of glittering stars. The airport walkways were adorned with hanging baskets of flowering vines, emitting a fragrance that reminded me of my frequent vacations to my favorite Hawaiian island, Kauai. We picked up our luggage, cleared customs and found a cab for the ride to the Carlton Palace Hotel. The hotel was located on the ocean in a garden setting with abundant palms, flowering trees and plants. It appeared to cater to the tourist trade, as the doorman suspecting Americans greeted us in very passable English. Although I was fairly fluent in Spanish, I didn't think it would be very transferable to Portuguese. Our check-in was equally pleasant. Since the hotel was owned by a British group English turned out to be the prevalent language. Several key hotel positions were obviously filled by people from England. Art and I were taken to our rooms, which were across the hall from one another on the eighth floor. As our biological clocks were about nine hours behind Lisbon time, Art knocked on my door after he settled in his room and suggested that we go downstairs and grab a bite and have a nightcap.

"I could use a cool one about now." I told Art.

We walked down to the small bar off the lobby, which we learned not only served dinner from the hotel restaurant menu until 3:00 A.M., but the bartender was another transplanted Brit. As we happened to be the only patrons in the bar at that time, he was talkative and only too happy to be a one-man travelogue on Portugal. In order to keep things congenial, I said my friend and I

356

were taking a little vacation and were thinking of buying a condo because we heard the prices were reasonable. This turned out to be a mistake. Everyone is in the real estate business, and he knows a girl, etc. etc. He did help us on where to rent a car, and how to get to 'a friend of a friend's cell phone business, on Rue do Grila, 90. The bartender left us alone while he placed our dinner order for his recommendation of 'catch of the day', a fish variety we'd never heard of nor could we pronounce, however he assured us that it was baked with a lemon-herb crust that was out of this world.

"OK, we rent a car and drive up if we're lucky enough to find Santos's business with the bartender's directions, and say what---- we're from the government, and we're here to help you?" Art asked teasing.

"No, we're going to tell him the *truth*. We're there to obtain a cell phone and service to use while we're in Lisbon searching for a condominium." I answered with a broad smile.

"The truth----huh?" Art laughed. "Sounds as good as *any of your tall stories* ----but how does that find this Harper guy?"

"Simple, we're going to say a friend, Fred Harper sent us in, and see where that plays."

"I like it. We also should hear from Preston about the bank informant. Did you check with the desk for a message?" Art asked.

"Not when we checked in. I'd assume if there was a message, they'd have given it to me then."

"We're not in San Francisco, better check with the desk. Ask the bartender for his house line and check while we're waiting for the fish to be caught." Art kidded.

I followed Art's suggestion and called the front desk for messages, which there were none. Dinner was as advertised, excellent. We had another drink and decided a good nights rest was in order. For me, a quick call to Valarie ended the evening, after hearing how she's being wined and dined in the finest joints in Hong Kong----as she put it.

CHAPTER 70

Morning began with an early telephone call from Preston, apologizing for not calling the evening before. His man in Madrid had not been able to contact the bank informant until late, and just talked him. "She has the information and passable photographs. They will be delivered to the hotel sometime today. She does not want to say when, because she didn't want you watching for her. She is concerned about getting into some trouble for doing this."

"That's fine Preston, great work, this should be very helpful. How's everything in Hong Kong? I talked with Valarie last night----she's having a terrific time and getting quite spoiled from all the attention."

"Things *are* fine and Valarie's a delight. John talked with Inspector Li this morning, and the raid or as Li calls it---- the office visit is still on hold. The chiefs haven't returned to the office. I think they are in hiding, what do you think?" Preston asked me.

"You could be right. We need to stop any use of that software. Is there something we can do to push Inspector Li---- like file a formal complaint accusing KRL of possessing stolen software?"

"Let me talk with John about that, and if he agrees would you like us to file the complaint? I think we have enough information to put something together for their internal use to get them moving, though I think Li is more interested in solving the murders than worrying about your software."

"You're probably right Preston. Go ahead and do what you have to do to move this investigation forward. I really appreciate your help."

CHAPTER 71

Art and I ate breakfast on the veranda overlooking the beautiful ocean. It was early and we had some time to kill before going to Santos's business. Most retail businesses opened later than in the States, usually not before ten in the morning. I ordered the rental car from Eurocars before we went to breakfast and was promised that it would arrive at the hotel by 9:30 A.M., about the time we were finished with breakfast.

"Well, you ride in style don't you?" Art said as he checked out the new Jaguar XJL sedan.

"I thought that if we're anything but---- cool guys who are friends of big money, and slick operators, we'd be driving a Ford Taurus sedan working under a maximum allowance for auto rental reimbursement. Showing up in the Jag gives us credibility in buying a condo as well as being a friend of Harper, and not in any way on some kind of official business. Don't you agree?" I asked, looking at Art as he admired the shiny green automobile.

"Chuck, as I always say, that's why you make the big bucks." He laughed as he slid into the passenger seat and we drove away.

Surprisingly, the directions from the bartender at the hotel were amazingly simple and accurate. The green Jaguar pulled up in front of the Santos address at 10:15 A.M. The address was in a three storefront building. From the street it appeared to be a very modest business, probably occupying no more space than the small showroom and perhaps an office or storage room in back. It was definitely a one or two person business by outward appearances. We parked in front and noticed a light in the store, but couldn't see anyone. I opened the car door, casually looked around and walked toward Santos' front door, with Art following. We both wore casual slacks and short-sleeved sport shirts on this beautiful sunny day---- forecast to be eighty degrees.

"Good morning." I said smiling as we entered the store and stood staring right at a short heavyset man with a dark tan, handlebar mustache, and he himself wearing a smile that stretched from ear to ear.

"Americano?" He asked still smiling.

"Si." I said in my best Spanish.

The man motioned with a raised index finger and hurried through a door to the rear. The door re-opened with Santos leading a striking tall brunet with emerald green eyes. She smiled as she looked at us and asked, "Are you Americans?"

I was dazzled by her beauty and way to slow to answer. Art had to come to my rescue by responding, "Yes we are." She had a fair complexion and wore a sarong-type, dark blue dress showing a significant amount of her right thigh. "My name is Anna and my father asked me to help you. His English is rather limited."

Coming back to reality and business I said, "We need to get a cell phone and would like to pre-pay enough minutes for our business here. A couple of weeks should do it. Can you handle this for us?"

"We can do that. How did you find our small business?" She asked with a pretty smile.

"It's funny you asked, a friend of ours, Fred Harper recommended your brother's business." I said, waiting for a response----which I immediately got.

"You know Fred?" She asked with an expression of glee.

"Yes, do you?" I asked innocently.

"Well yes, we---- how do you say it in America, are dating?" She said in a shy and somewhat embarrassed response.

"You're kidding? Fred----well I'll be darned. He's a great guy. You couldn't do better." I said playing on her naïveté.

"We are together every chance he gets. He is always traveling you know, and it's hard with our schedules to see each other as much as we would like." Anna said, in a truly sweet and caring way.

"Hey, I think I have an old picture. I think he's shaved his mustache though." I said as I was digging into my pocket to retrieve the photo from the bank transaction. "Here, this was in a friend' business. Do you recognize him here? I think this is the right picture, I didn't bring my reading glasses."

"Yes, it is he. With a mustache----he looks funny in it. When was this taken?" She asked still studying it and smiling.

"Oh maybe a year ago, I forget." I said with relief, finally feeling I was making some headway. How sad it was that this killer could attract such an innocent young lady. "I guess we better get this cell phone business done.

We have an appointment downtown in an hour." I added with an intentional touch of indifference.

She spoke in what I assumed to be Portuguese to her father, and he responded.

"My father suggests that you purchase this phone," she said handing me a small cell phone, "and buy say five hundred minutes. If you need more you can buy what you need and the phone can be used in the States, so it isn't a waste."

"How much is it?"

"In U.S. dollars it would be a hundred and forty, including five hundred minutes. Does that sound acceptable to you?" She asked with a sweet sincere smile.

"That would be fine."

They did the paperwork and Anna handed me the phone and receipts.

"Just one more thing, I'm totally lost with map reading in Lisbon or anywhere to be honest. Fred told me how to get to his place and I can't figure it out with this map. Can you help me----where are we now? Just point me in the right direction." I said, with my winning boyish charm cranking at a thousand percent.

Anna giggled and leaned across the counter looking at the map while displaying her breasts in a way I was certain she did just for my benefit. As I had a most beautiful girlfriend in Hong Kong and this trip was one hundred percent business, my biological components were quickly brought into check and I went on with my charade.

"Now I see," she said, "see this road that leads to the top of the hill, Fred's house is at the very end on the left or the ocean side. When did you last speak with him? I think he's planning another business trip, and may be gone already or by tomorrow at the latest.

"Oh it's been a while, but if he isn't there we'll just leave a nice gift for helping us in Lisbon."

"I hope he hasn't left yet." She said.

"Me too, and I almost forgot, this is a big surprise. We weren't certain if we could come. Can you keep a secret and let us surprise him?"

"Yes, for sure, this will be fun. I hope he is still there," she said as she looked at the application and added----"Mr. Rose".

Art and I expressed our best sign language goodbyes to Mr. Santos, and smiled and winked at Anna, while allowing them both the opportunity to watch us leave and get into our big fancy gringo car from England.

"Pretty slick work Romeo."

"What do you mean Romeo? I was just doing my work?" I responded wearing my straight-face *stupid* grin.

"Well, we sort of have the address of this killer and extortionist. Not bad work old buddy!" Art said patting me on the shoulder.

"I don't think confronting him is the answer, although I'd like to."

"I think we need to maybe do a drive-by and see if it looks like anyone's home. I don't want him leaving the country before we can get some answers and maybe have him arrested." Art said in response.

"I agree, let's scope it out."

They followed the map Anna had marked and reached the dead-end road which Mason or Harper supposedly lived on. The house was on a bluff and was in my opinion worth at least a million dollars or more if in California in a similar setting. The man definitely had taste, and I'd need to reassess my conclusion that this killer was without depth of any kind. This revised consideration only made the man more dangerous, in my mind. As the road was a dead-end we didn't want to be seen looking suspicious and alert our suspect. The mailbox indicated No. 7, with the map showing it to be Azteca Rd. There was no sign of life around the house and the garage door was closed. I thought it best to leave the area for now, with the knowledge that we had finally made a direct link with one of the parties to the TechX case.

We turned around and headed back to the Carlton to wait for the information from the bank employee. We hoped to pull together enough of a case to go to the police with the cooperation and assistance of the Hong Kong and Oregon police investigations.

Upon arriving at the Carlton, we stopped by the front desk to check for messages and were told by the desk clerk that someone had left a large brown envelope for Mr. Winters.

CHAPTER 72

Fred Harper called Santos's cell phone shop and asked Mr. Santos if Anna was at the shop.

"Hello, Fred?" Anna asked in excitement.

"Anna, how are you?"

"Wonderful, I have been thinking about you."

"Really?"

"Yes I have some exciting news you will like but I can't tell you, it's a surprise."

"Well I was calling to say I have to leave on a business trip this afternoon, sooner than I thought." He said in an apologetic tone, as he knew she expected to see him before he left.

"Oh, that's too bad, I really wanted to see you, and about your surprise, I just don't know what to say now." Anna pondered.

"Well I don't know what to say about a surprise, and I'm not certain how long I'll be, but when I get beck we'll have a big celebration. Maybe we can go somewhere for a week or so."

Anna was silent for a few moments while she considered if she should break her promise to Mr. Rose----and finally said, "I have to tell you about your surprise----because if I don't, there won't be one." Anna explained in her confusing manner.

"OK, what is it?"

"Well, two men from the States came into the store earlier this morning and said they were friends of yours and wanted to stop by your house and surprise you. I showed them how to get there on their map." Anna explained in what she thought to be a nice gesture for her new friend Fred.

"You did what? You told these guys how to find my house?" Harper said with a suppressed anger along as well as significant fear and apprehension. "What time exactly was this?"

"You sound mad. I didn't do anything wrong. It was a couple of hours ago. They said you gave them your address----but needed help in finding it, so I just showed them. No big deal." She said in her defense-----she thought.

"What were their names? What did they look like?" He insisted in a somewhat elevated tone.

"One was Mr. Rose. His address was Los Angeles, California, and he paid in cash so we didn't need more identification. He was about six foot two or three, about your height, and he was in his forty's, longer brown hair, nice looking. The other man----I never heard his name, was older, short and had gray hair. They were both very nice." She said.

"I don't know a Mr. Rose. How did they get to the store?" He asked.

"They drove a fancy green car, I think a Jaguar." Anna said. "But if you really want to see what they look like, father has that silly security camera that records every thing that goes on in the store. He was held up once and lost a lot of equipment." She offered.

"What, your father has taped even me when I was there?"

"Yes, I think he keeps all the tapes for a long time and then uses them again."

"I'm coming down right now. Find the tape from April when I ordered my phone. Check your records. And get the tape from this morning, I want both of them."

"I'm sure my father will let you borrow them for a while. Is there a problem?" She asked with sincerity.

"No. I'll be down in thirty minutes." He said, and pushed end on the cell phone he used for special needs, his only phone that wasn't disconnected after ninety days.

CHAPTER 73

Art came up to my room and reviewed the information from the bank- informant. We immediately turned to the photographs from the security camera of Günter Howard, the man who opened the account for Mason. He wore a white linen suit and had close-cropped brown hair with a touch of gray, while sporting a large bushy mustache, probably a fake they concluded. Take away the mustache and he'd be easy to identify. The original application form was in a glassine wrapper, and would be sent by Federal Express to a lab in San Francisco for print identification, as well as the signature card and the two deposit slips.

"We can drop off our Federal Express package at the front desk, and then I suggest we figure out how to stake out Mason's house. We need to get a look at him----better yet a picture before we go to the next step with the police. I don't want the local police to botch this and allow him to run." I said to Art.

Art and I went car shopping at a low-end used car lot. We found a 1969 Volkswagen Combo van, the type used by hippies and beach bums to "do their thing" in the seventies. It was rusted through in a dozen places, covered with primer paint, bald tires but it ran----sort of.

I prevailed on the lot owner to come up with a beat up surfboard for an extra hundred dollars, and we'd be back in an hour to pick it up. Total purchase price including surfboard roped on the top, $475.00 equivalent U.S. It had small windows on the side that were cracked, however tinted to afford anonymous surveillance. Also included, and a must for any stakeout was a porta-potty and a bed. We hoped this non-descript, trashy ride would be taken for what it appeared to be, that of a surfer grabbing a nap or something else, while waiting to go back for that *perfect wave*.

I drove the VW back to the hotel and Art followed in the Jag. We parked both cars and went up to my room again.

"My only concern is that we don't have weapons, and this guy has no hesitation when it comes to killing. We could get a P.I. agency to join us with some firepower, but I don't think we have the time to check someone out." I said.

"Let's go without this afternoon and see if Preston's man in Madrid can suggest someone in Lisbon we can trust, and go back again this evening or tomorrow. We need a good camera with a telescopic lens and a pair of binoculars----make it two. I think I saw a camera shop in the lobby area, let's check it out?" Art said.

"Good idea, I'll call Preston since we've never talked with the guy in Madrid, and see what he can do for us."

A quick call to Preston with our latest request and we headed to the lobby camera shop to purchase a good camera with a zoom lens and binoculars.

"I think we're set. We don't look like surf bums, but hopefully we won't be seen and can snap a picture or two to verify that this is the same guy that set up the account at the Mercantile Bank in Lisbon. I think we better take both cars, because if we need to escape the scene I don't have a lot of confidence about trying to outrun anything in the van, including a good pair of Nikes. I'll drive the rolling bedroom and you take the Jag. We need the Jag close enough that if we have to make a run on foot we can do a little cross country to the next street down and make our getaway. After all, our total arsenal consists of a tire iron and some empty beer bottles in the van." I said as we made our way out to our transportation fleet in the parking garage and headed for Fred Harper or Mason Dixon's house on the hill.

CHAPTER 74

The taller man arrived at the cell phone shop and parked down the street. He walked cautiously, sensing his surroundings for any danger, continued past the shop and turned down the side of the building which was overgrown with weeds and discarded tires. He then proceeded around to the back door of the shop. The door was locked and he knocked several times before a surprised Santos opened it.

"Anna has some tapes for me." He said curtly.

Santos understood only one word that being "Anna". While the two men looked at one another she came rushing in from the showroom section to find her father with "Fred", as she knew him these last few happy months.

No greeting, just, "Where's the tapes?" He demanded.

"Here they are." She said handing two VCR tapes to Fred.

"I want to see them----now." He said in an unfriendly tone.

She inserted the tape showing Fred signing for his cell phone service, and then the tape showing "the two men" who said they were his friends.

"Are these the only copies?"

"Yes, father never uses these anyway. He hasn't been robbed since he installed the system."

"Have you shown these to anyone else?"

"No. I take them from the machine and store them in the box, father never looks at them."

The taller man left the building with the tapes in his hand, his small caliber silenced pistol back in his pocket, comfortable in the fact that the father and daughter would never be able to identify him ---- or anyone for that matter. He walked back to his car from a different direction and proceeded to the downtown commercial district where a number of large hotels were located. Parking in the public car park he walked to the Lisbon Hotel, an institution in the city that covered two entire blocks. He went to the desk and asked for telephone change as he had a number of calls to make. The taller man then walked through a large archway that was forty feet or more in height, along a thick-carpeted hallway to a row of ornate telephone booths. The booths were in fact small rooms measuring about six feet square, soundproof, with glass doors and wood paneled walls. They included exhaust fans to accommodate smokers and incorporated a built-in desk with writing papers, pens and telephone books. The taller man had often used these booths. The hotel was very busy and he could get lost in the crowd and unnoticed as he went about his business. His business this time was to find the green Jaguar and do the job he thought he had done in Hong Kong; kill Chuck Winters once and for all. He started calling car rental agencies to determine if they rented Jaguars. He found two agencies that rented Jaguars, and asked if he could rent a green one for his wife on her birthday. The first agency didn't have a green Jag in their fleet, and suggested he check with the other one that rented them.

"Europcars, this is Louisa, how can I help you?" The voice said in Portuguese.

"I am told that you rent Jaguars, is that correct?" He asked in his most pleasant manner----also speaking Portuguese.

"Yes we do, but we only have one left." The young lady said.

"What color is it? This is a surprise and I need a green one."

"The only Jaguar we have at the moment is a white one, our only green one is rented for a week."

"Oh, that's too bad, my wife is having a birthday next week and her dream come true is a green Jaguar. Since I can't afford to buy one right now I wanted to surprise her by taking her out in one for her birthday dinner. Can you verify when the car will be returned?" The taller man asked.

"It says he will bring it back next Saturday, by 9:00 A.M." She said in a helpful manner.

"This is perfect. I would like to reserve it now please."

"You understand if the gentleman wants to extend, he has the right to do so." She added.

"Yes, that makes sense. I just hope he doesn't do it though."

She took down his fictitious identity and stolen credit card, and gave him a confirmation number subject to the return by the current renter.

"Oh I forgot, my wife is heavy into astrology and I better have the license number before I go forward. She refuses to be associated with certain combinations of numbers. We had to take a boat on a vacation because our flight number was a negative number for her. It's really hard to make her happy. I appreciate your help in this and apologize for being such a pest. What is the license number of this green Jaguar?"

"We're not supposed to give out this kind of information in advance, but I suppose under the circumstances it would be all right, its 94003A."

"Thank you Louisa, I know that number doesn't work for her, please cancel my reservation, and thanks for your help." He said and hung up the receiver.

The taller man pulled out a cigarette and lit it while he waited to re-dial the Europcars number, knowing he could not speak with Louisa again.

He dialed the number, "Europcars, this is Raul."

"This is Sergeant Perez, Lisbon P.D. Who am I speaking with?" The taller man said.

"Raul Alvarez."

"Mr. Alvarez, one of your rentals, according to our records was involved in an accident----license number 94003A. It is important that we ask the renter a few more questions. Your car was not damaged. We need his local phone number----his name is Winters."

"We have a company policy against giving out information on the phone, Sergeant; may I have your badge number please?"

"Yes, it's #2483." He hoped it wouldn't be checked and was just a formality.

"Our policy is very strict----respect for our client's privacy is most important, but I'm new here and there is no mention about a police inquiry, so I will provide this and follow up with management. Mr. Charles Winters is staying at the Carlton Palace Hotel, 8548-932." Raul said.

CHAPTER 75

The unremarkable Volkswagen slowly crawled up the winding road from the sea, to the street I hoped would be the beginning of the end of this globetrotting saga. When we were within a few hundred feet of the house we slowed and looked for a parking spot that would not bring too much attention to our operation, yet allow for a good field of vision from the small windows on the side of the van. There were only three houses on this dead end street. Mason Dixon's or whatever his name was lived in the best house on the street. His was ocean side at the very end on the left. Another house was also on the left side and approximately two hundred feet from his. The best opportunity for our mission was the small shack-like house across the street but still about one hundred feet away from our target house. There was no sign of life from any of the houses, so we pulled off the road just past the driveway of the shack-like house. It would appear to most observers that the occupants of the VW were visiting the residents of the small house. We turned off the engine and crawled into the back. The only concern was heading the wrong way if we needed to escape quickly. However if it came to that we thought the Jag was one street down the hill and could be reached on a down hill run or slide, depending on the situation. Finding a spot for the Jag was not much of a concern to Art. It wasn't important what people thought when the Green Jaguar suddenly appeared on the road and parked midway between two fairly nice homes, both with expansive decks overlooking the Ocean. It would appear to most people that we were visiting one of the two houses, and to the occupants, they could easily assume that the Jag owners were visiting their next door neighbor or someone on the other side of the street.

We set up our camera on a tripod and checked out our new binoculars. Fortunately the small tinted windows opened, as did the sunroof, allowing air circulation. Although the temperature was in the eighties, it wasn't oppressive because the windows away from our target's house could be left opened without a concern of being seen. This waiting time was perfect for making cell phone calls to check progress on the various fronts.

I decided against getting Tom Claudius out of bed, so I thought I'd check in with Preston. "Cheers, Hobbs here." Preston answered in his booming voice.

With a chuckle I responded, "Preston, Chuck and Art reporting from our stakeout in the north Lisbon hills."

"Well old man, it's about time you're finally engaged in honorable work, like the rest of us poor blokes have to do on a daily basis." He replied laughing. "Are you in a tree or in some obvious rental car?" He asked, enjoying this interchange immensely.

"Actually, Art and I have become surfer bums, complete with our Volkswagen van and surfboard tied to the top."

"That a boy, Chuck." Preston broke into hysterics, so much that he couldn't stop laughing. "I want a picture----do you promise?"

"Yes Preston we promise, but I don't know if we'll be around long enough to even take a picture----armed only with a dirty ashtray."

"Chuck, your long lost *brother* Preston has solved your problems. I've been referred to a first class investigator in Lisbon. He's honest and knows the police if you need them. I've arranged for you and Art to be temporary staff members of his firm, and he's already obtained the gun permits in each of your names. I already had your resumes, and the owner, Harry Philburton another Brit rushed through expedited applications to the police department ----and has been granted approval. I suppose he could send someone out and bring you some artillery. It's up to you, but you are all set. His number is 6730-591. Philburton and Associates is the name of his firm and recommended highly by Madrid."

"That's just what we need, thanks Preston, I mean brother----you're the best."

CHAPTER 76

The taller man cruised through the parking g: the Carlton Palace looking for the green Jaguar. thought they were probably up at his place at that moment however he knew they hadn't gained acces because his alarm system automatically called his ce phone with a special code appearing on the screen if breech was attempted. If there was a successful entry then another code would appear and the taller man would know what action to take without calling the authorities----which he'd spent his life avoiding with a passion.

He parked the Jeep and walked into the lobby, then went to a house phone and asked the operator for Mr. Winter's room. The operator said she'd connect him and the phone rang until a voice mail mechanism answered. He hung up and went to the desk carrying an envelope with Charles Winters name written across the face. Inside was a blank sheet of stationary, taken from the desk near the bank of pay phones for the convenience of guests. He handed the envelope to the clerk and asked her in Portuguese if she would see that Mr. Winters received the message, and also if she could change a bill for him, which gave him the reasonable excuse to stand there and watch her put the message in the slot for Room 814. After receiving change he walked toward the elevator bank and stood alone as the door opened. He rode non-stop to the eighth floor, exited, and went directly to Room 814 where he was pleased to find that it was around a corner with no direct view from the elevator or stairs. He could hear the bell on the elevator as it approached the floor. He started to work on the lock, which he knew the hotel had modernized with a card key system. He held a small computer with a built-in card that was inserted in the slot. The start button was

code was cracked in less than thirty
press...ked into the room with his right arm
seco... and under his loose fitting shirt, firmly
beh...p of his .38 caliber handgun.

on

CHAPTER 77

I called Harry Philburton and took an immediate liking to him. He was friendly, cooperative and most important, didn't have an attitude. Harry agreed to personally spend the next few hours with Art and me in the van, in order to bring our weapons and see how his firm might be able to further assist in the case. He said he'd dress in one of the firms "costumes" and walk up to the van and get in after being dropped off a safe distance away.

During our approximate two-hour stakeout, we noticed that the mailman dropped off mail at every house *except* Mason's. Also, a white Mercedes pulled into the driveway of the first house on the left. A woman and two small children got out of the car and went through a door by the garage. It was probable that they were the residents of the house. Most importantly, they didn't appear to notice or look at the beat up old van we were observing from.

"Someone is on foot coming up the street. Looks like a large older lady, probably a domestic. Maybe she's going to Mason's house to work." Art commented.

We watched as she came closer to the van, which in itself wasn't threatening, as anyone would have to walk or drive by the tinted glass windows in the van if they were heading towards Mason's house. She was now within twenty feet of the van and she stopped and fanned herself with her big floppy straw hat. Just at that moment my cell rang.

"Hello." I answered quietly with my eyes on the old woman.

"This is Carlo from Philburton and Associates. My boss wants you to open the van door and invite him in. OK?"

"You've got to be kidding! Open the door Art. Thanks Carlo." I said as Harry Philburton struggled with his large body to squeeze into the van through the front door. Finding it impossible to hide my amusement and sporting an ear-to-ear grin, I held out my hand and said, "Harry, it is you, isn't it?"

"Yes good to meet you lads." Came the strong voiced Phiburton response.

"Well, that's some get up. You sure had us fooled."

"We have quite a costume center at the firm----- you never know when it's going to come in handy."

With that he reached into his full skirt, pulled out a rubber tube, pulled the stopper out and his three hundred pound frame escaped through the air hose melting to less than two hundred pounds. He was about six feet tall, mid-forties with a full head of red hair and a fair complexion after his makeup was wiped off with a handkerchief. Secured around his chest was a knapsack full of weapons and ammunition, consisting of two .38 caliber Smith & Wesson's, and two broken down, .3006 caliber rifles with sniper scopes.

"I can't believe this. You looked great---- and all this firepower, unbelievable. I'm impressed." I said, with Art nodding his concurrence as he started assembling the rifles.

"The best is yet to come." Harry said with a sly grin as he reached around his back and swung out a hanging bag attached to his now less than ample frame, producing three foil-wrapped packages and a thermos. "I have the best lunch you'll ever eat in Portugal----and I still can't pronounce it, but I eat them two or three times a week. It's a cross between a burrito and a taco and throw in a tamale. Anyway if you like those things, I know you'll love these like I do. Oh, I don't want to forget, there's fresh iced tea with lemon in the thermos."

Art and I filled in Harry on the case and why we were in Lisbon parked on this street. Harry reasoned that this man, if we were correct, had more than a passing experience in outsmarting all that have tried to catch him for his deeds to date. And he hadn't succeeded with such longevity by being stupid or a step behind his adversaries.

"The question is does he know about you being alive, and does he know you're on his trail in Lisbon?"

"I can't see how."

"How did you find his house? He must be more protective of where he bases his operations than to allow you to roll into town and find him within a day of your arrival."

"He broke a cardinal rule----he mixed business with pleasure in Lisbon."

"How so?" Harry asked with interest.

"He signed up for service with a small Lisbon cell phone company and become involved with the owner's daughter. We were there this morning and neither of them seemed to know anything about his real business. Mr. Santos's store is on Rua do Grila 90."

"Wait a minute I heard something on the news just before I left, let me verify it." Harry said with an obvious concern on his face as he punched numbers into his cell phone.

"Carlos----get me the details on that Rua do Grila news report we heard before I left. Call me on my cell right away." He instructed his investigator.

"What did you hear on the news?"

"I don't want to buy trouble Chuck, let's just wait for Carlos to call back."

Harry's cell phone rang back within five minutes. "Hello."

"Harry, it was Rafael Santos & Company----cell phones. He and his daughter Anna, ages about sixty and twenty-five, were murdered by one shot each to the head by an unknown assailant sometime around noon today. No suspects or clues other than an interest in speaking to an American, a Mr. Rose that purchased a cell phone earlier according to Santos's files." Carlos informed Harry, who remained silent during the report.

"Thanks Carlos, call me if you get something more." He said as he pushed end call on his cell phone.

"Well my guess is that he *is* on to you, considering he probably murdered Mr. Santos and his daughter around noon today." He added, looking at me with an expression of grave concern.

"That's horrible. They'd still be alive if I hadn't interfered."

"You had no way of knowing. Don't blame yourself."

"If he killed the Santos' then he most likely was told by Anna that we were looking for him. Since they didn't know our real names or where we're staying, I can't see that he knows that I'm alive and still involved in the case. Even if she gave him a description, he'd still need a photograph to even think that I survived the Hong Kong attack."

"Chuck, that's where you may be wrong, Carlos said that Santos had a security camera and they were going through tapes, however he heard from his friend at the department that the tape for today was missing. You and Art would be on that tape, and presumably this man Mason has it." Harry said with a continued serious expression.

"I'd like to get my hands on the tape when Fred Harper first went to the Santos's shop and ordered his phone and service. That should be easy to check from the files if they still exist. Do you suppose Carlos could talk with his friend at the police department and see if we can get a look at that tape?"

"I think we have to first deal with the Mr. Rose issue, and then they probably will be willing to work with us now that a local murder has occurred---- make that two murders."

"I don't have a problem with that, but I can't think how there's any way he would tie me or Art to the two guys looking for him today."

"This guy is smart and devious. What did you leave as evidence at the sight?" Harry asked, looking at each of us.

"We probably left some prints, and Chuck most likely left a print or two on the paperwork." Art said.

"I'm not talking about prints, there's not enough time for this guy to process that kind of evidence. I'm talking about what you may have exposed to the Santos's. How about your rental car, you certainly weren't driving this monstrosity to the shop this morning?" Harry asked as he pushed on with his questioning.

"Oh my God, you don't suppose----?" I paused.

"The Jag----it's got to be the Jag." Art said with a tone of disappointment.

"If you were driving a Jaguar rental, a novice investigator could have tracked that down and be in your room right now." Harry stated.

"Wait a minute, we have no evidence at all that he knows it's me." I said in a defensive tone knowing my bright idea to rent an unusual car could be placing us in severe jeopardy.

"That may not be true. He has the tape, and would know in an instant, particularly if he knew your face from photos or surveillance in Hong Kong." Harry said.

"You're right, and to assume anything less with a killer such as he would be deadly. We need to dump the Jag and change hotels. I have to remember that we're up against a ruthless, smart, and probably rich killing machine. Considering that my laptop's in my briefcase in

388

the Jag, I don't know what he might find in the room that'd be of interest. I kept the best picture of what we think is him, here in the van to compare with who might come up to the house today. What wasn't in my briefcase was Fed Expressed to a lab in San Francisco. I wouldn't put it past him to blow up half the hotel to get us out of his hair once and for all. Harry can you arrange to have the police go into my room with bomb experts to see if he's set explosives for our return?"

"I can after we clear up the Rose thing. Let's wrap this up here. He won't take a chance coming back, probably ever. He may be on an airplane right now, unless killing you is more important to him." Harry said.

I started up the Volkswagen and drove down to the house to turn around in order to head back to the Jag. Out of impulse, instead of turning around in the driveway I drove around to the lower level where the garage was, and parked out of sight from the street. To the amazement of my fellow passengers, I hopped into the rear of the van and pulled on the old lady skirt and shawl, along with the gray longhaired wig, a pair of latex gloves, and slowly opened the door.

"If you hear gunfire come in blazing, otherwise I'm the only lawbreaker in this gang." I said as Harry and Art looked on in disbelief.

Slowly I limped forward toward the garage side door that appeared to go into the main house, my hand on the Smith & Wesson in the folds of my skirt. Trying the handle I found it locked. I took the gun from my skirt and with the butt broke the glass and unlocked the door. I was confident there were alarm systems and perhaps booby traps, but time was limited and I needed to recover from the mistake I made with the Jag, as well as the grief

I felt from being the cause of the murders of two nice innocent people. The house was neat and orderly as I climbed from the lower level to the main floor. The furniture was tasteful and I couldn't help wonder what kind of man could be responsible for all the pain and suffering he has caused, while maintaining a lifestyle refuge that was elegant and comfortable at the same time. The walls were lined with artwork, mostly depicting ships and marine life, all quite fitting for a home perched on the side of a hill with a commanding view of the ocean below from most rooms as well as the wraparound deck.

I quickly moved to the kitchen in order to get a feel if the man actually lived in this house, or it was just a stopover location with a home base in another part of the world. The kitchen was modern with a fairly well stocked pantry. Opening the refrigerator, I found milk, orange juice, fruit and some salad vegetables. The freezer included what probably was wrapped meat or fish, along with frozen orange juice. The garbage pail under the sink contained nothing notable. I quickly moved down the hall to the dining room and into the living room. There was nothing out of place. Perhaps he hired a housekeeper, however from what I knew about this man he wouldn't take the chance of such close contact. Next to the living room was a den or office, with a teak desk clear of any papers or letters. The drawers contained writing tablets, pencils and pens. There was a telephone on the desk and I picked up the receiver intending to hit the redial number to check who he called last and found the phone line to be dead. What could be going on? I thought. There was a bookcase against the wall with an assortment of books that didn't make sense. There was poetry, architecture, old encyclopedias consisting of fifty or more books, again with no apparent clue as to the man's interest. There were no novels or non-fiction works usually found in a home library.

I sat at the desk and looked around, trying to understand this vicious man. Feeling around under the desk for anything that appeared out of order, I found nothing. Then I looked at the remote control sitting next to the TV, resting on a shelf in the bookcase. The TV was a Sony and the remote had no logo or other identification. It did have channel numbers and an off and on button, but was missing a volume control or mute button. I picked up the remote and hit the on button. Nothing happened. Maybe the batteries were dead. I then commenced to run through the channels just on a hunch. I was just about to give it up when I hit number 60 on the remote. The bookcase started to slide to the right, completely covering the doorway.

Behind the bookcase was an instrument panel that looked extremely sophisticated. I wasn't certain what the meters and control pads represented until I took a closer look and was certain I had uncovered an extensive routing system for originating phone calls from anyplace in the world and routed from country to country until any link was lost, making the identity of the caller impossible to trace. It also looked like there was a computer tie-in that displayed a small screen with blocks for name, address, telephone and cell numbers, social security, drivers license number, passport number, date of birth, description, etc. It seemed that if you plugged in as much as you knew, the computer, was tied in with some data bank or banks that searched records for filling in the blanks. I plugged in my name and year of birth and hit enter. The computer took about five seconds to return four Charles Winters born in 1955. It displayed all of the information on each. Two were deceased, one lived in New York City and the other was mine, showing-- --"before his recent death in Hong Kong he lived in O'Brien, CA." It showed every possible bit of information, including my unlisted home phone and cell numbers, address, which showed my moorage slip number, and PO Box number at the marina. I was totally shocked, but not as much as when I clicked on BIO. This created a biography on me from grade school to the present with "my death", and mostly accurate, except for the fact that I was sitting at a desk in a killer's house wearing a skirt. It even showed my parents current address.

"This man has to be stopped." I thought. I was visibly shaken. There was no time to attempt to determine what was in the computer memory, so I thumbed through the computer printouts that were in a tray next to the keyboard. I wasn't shocked but my chest pounded as I looked at page after page of news stories from Hong Kong, Beaverton, Oregon and Portland, Oregon. The explosion near the Black Orchid Restaurant in Hong Kong was included, indicating that American Charles Winters was killed, as well as two Black Orchid employees. There were articles about Sue Tang's death, Jaxton's disappearance, the dead man found in Jaxton's house, and the TechX fire. I also found a lengthy report on Knowledge Resource, Ltd., Hong Kong.

I was certain I had my man however I didn't know who was orchestrating these events and who was benefiting financially. I made certain everything was back in place. There's no question an intruder came into the house, but I didn't want it known that I'd found his hidden compartment. A quick swing through the guest bedroom and on into the master bedroom. I found nothing unusual, except that on the bed there was a bag packed with clothes. I found a passport under the name of James R. Deacon, of Boston, Massachusetts, having the same photo as the man in the bank pictures, however without the mustache. There was an American Express card in the same name tucked into the passport as well as an international drivers license, all assumed forgeries, but couldn't tell by their appearance. Under the clothing were several bundles of French Francs. Although there were no tickets or other indication of destination, he probably called in a reservation to Paris, and was paying with cash at the airport.

Checking my watch, I figured I'd been in the house fifteen minutes and better get out. I decided to make this look like a burglary for food, so I went into the kitchen and poured some orange juice into a glass, swirled it around and put the balance except for a quarter inch, down the kitchen sink drain. I then found a garbage-sack and took most of the items in the refrigerator and the meat in the freezer, a few noticeable cans from the pantry and left through the door near the garage where I'd entered.

"Are you nuts?" Art asked. "Besides breaking the law in this country, you could have gotten yourself, or worse us killed while you are burglarizing the house. You look like Santa Claus, make that Mrs. Claus coming out of the house with a big black sack over your shoulder not to mention the cute skirt."

"Funny? It had to be done! We've been working around the edges on this case without any concrete evidence of who's behind this mess. I found enough to circumstantially tie it to the guy living in this house. He has copies of articles from newspapers in Oregon and Hong Kong regarding the entire case. He's got a system in there to route telephone calls through dozens of countries, so much that his call could never be traced. He also has a computer system that breaks through all unlisted numbers and provides a biography as well as your credit card numbers and anything else that might help him find you or know everything about you. There's no question in my mind that he's the hit man carrying out the murders and strong-arm stuff. All we need to do is get the next guy up the ladder. I did find something else that distressed me. It looks like Mason is about to leave the country as James Deacon of Boston, Massachusetts. I found a packed suitcase on his bed with a phony passport, bundles of French francs, and an American Express card with the same name."

"Let's get the "Mr. Rose" thing straightened out with the police and see if they will help us with your hotel rooms utilizing their bomb squad as well as get a look at that tape, if it still exists." Harry said.

"That's' fine, but first I think I'll get out of this skirt though I'm getting pretty attached to it."

CHAPTER78

We drove down to the next street and picked up the Jag after carefully checking it out before starting the engine. We refused to underestimate this Mason person. Art drove the Jag while Harry and I followed to make certain he had no problem. We headed for Europcars rentals to turn in the car and decided not to rent another. We figured the Volkswagen and cabs were all we'd need for the few days more we may be in Lisbon. Harry called Carlos in his office and asked him to have his detective contact from the police department drop by the office. He told him he'd be there in twenty minutes with Mr. Rose of the Santos case.

Harry had a nice office on the second floor of a very old, authentic stucco and tile building. We parked the van around the rear of the building in the parking lot and went in the back door and up a flight of stairs to Harry's offices. There was a balcony surrounding an atrium in the center of the building. Harry occupied the entire second floor. Each office opened up to the interior balcony overlooking the lush garden below featuring fountains, beautiful tropical flowers along with small trees and shrubbery.

CHAPTER 79

"Good afternoon Juan," Harry said as he shook hands with the detective friend of Carlos who was waiting in the reception area. Detective Verto was introduced to Art and I, as was Carlos who joined the group as we moved into the conference room. The room was fairly spacious with a total of eight chairs on hardwood floors. At the end of the room there was a grease board that doubled for a screen, with a chalkboard alongside. I explained the background of the case from start to the present in great detail. Detective Verto was anxious to move this case forward. He felt it made sense that this man killed the Santos's, and he needed to move fast with a search warrant based not on my illegal entry which we didn't offer, but on the fact that the Harper identity was used at Santos's business by this Mason person who lived at this address. Detective Verto called the Santos investigating team and asked them to pull the Fred Harper file from sales records of about three months ago. They called back within minutes because sorting through his sales information was simple since he did so little business. The sales date was March 15th. Detective Verto then asked them to check the videotapes for that date while he stayed on the telephone. They reported back that the 15th was not in the box of tapes. After further checking and taking into account the normal days of operation of the store, the only tapes missing were the March 15th tape, and today's tape. Verto wanted a search warrant issued for Harper's house, a stake out and an all points bulletin for the arrest of this man of many identities, for suspicion of murder before he had a chance to leave Lisbon. He had to first speak with his Captain to approve his plan as well as authorize the bomb squad to enter our hotel rooms----and if disturbed to bring forensic people to dust for prints.

"I really appreciate the effort you're making Detective." I told Verto in all sincerity, considering he demonstrated the type of follow through and action I found rare among my own associates when I was involved in police work.

Verto had a relatively short conversation with his Captain and as I expected, being a well-respected detective on the force, his plan of action quickly received full approval. Art and I were to meet the bomb squad team leader at the hotel in twenty minutes. Harry asked Carlos to accompany us. Detective Verto was promised that his search warrant would be ready as soon as he returned to the station.

"Would you like a photo of the man we think is the killer?" I asked Verto, who looked at me dumfounded.

"Where did you get this?" Verto asked, as I handed him the print from the bank-informant.

"We got that from a confidential informant, and it was identified this morning by Anna Santos, as Fred Harper."

"I sure *do* want it. Do you have another?"

I asked Harry if he could copy the only photo we had, the one Anna identified, although the mustache was false. Harry had a state of the art graphics copier and made several copies. He even scanned it into the copier, and with a special program air brushed the mustache away and made several more copies, which Detective Verto took along to the station. I kept a couple of photos without the mustache as well as the original from the bank informant.

We left the van at Harry's office and hitched a ride with Carlos back to the Carlton Palace Hotel. The bomb squad was assembled in a meeting room on the main floor near the rear of the building. The hotel asked that the patrons be disturbed as little as possible, however the sergeant in charge explained that if the building required evacuation he was in charge----and the building "would" be evacuated. It would be his call. Art and I briefly provided information about the treachery of this man and cautioned them that whatever he did, if at all, it would be state of the art material and highly sophisticated. We were told to stay in the lobby and wait for their report. The bomb squad left with two bomb-sniffing dogs and headed toward the elevator and ultimately the eighth floor.

CHAPTER 80

Detective Verto, with a team of law enforcement personnel and two prosecutors drove to the house on the side of the hill at the end of the road. They sent a team through the front door and one through the garage door that I had earlier entered by breaking the glass. Since the front door was broken by the first group of officers there was little comment about the broken glass the other officers found as they entered by the garage. For all they knew it had been broken for a month.

The teams started their sweep of the house to determine if there were any occupants, armed or otherwise. When they searched the master bedroom walk-in closet they were surprised to find hidden behind the clothes a small Chinese man. He was armed with a semi-automatic pistol, a knife and a garrote. A further search turned up a second Chinese man hiding under the desk in the office where he had opened the bookcase. As the bookcase slid on a rail to cover the entry door it was natural for the search team to expect someone may be in the room. Once they shoved the bookcase aside far enough to squeeze in, they immediately found the computer and telephone routing system along with the details of the TechX newspaper accounts.

The man in the office was armed with similar weapons as the one found in the master bedroom closet. They claimed to speak no Portuguese or English. The man in the office had in his possession banking information involving account details from a Cayman Island bank. It wasn't clear if he brought the papers with him or discovered them there. Also among the papers found in his pocket, was the name and number of Billy Wong of KRL in Hong Kong.

CHAPTER 81

The bomb-sniffing dogs checked out the exterior of both Art and my rooms without an indication of a problem. The sergeant-in-charge decided that the city of Lisbon could afford to pay for a door or two, and drilled a hole in an upper panel and inserted a small camera to take a look around the room. With an arm that allowed it to extend its field of vision to project a close-up image, it traveled all around the door, top, bottom and sides, looking for minute triggering devices. The camera was then turned to inspect as much of the room as possible from its vantage point, including the ability to zoom up to a six-inch distance. The room had been ransacked, but the sergeant was still wary, even though at this point he could not see a trigger or a bomb. He decided to cut a hole in the door and send a small man through, rather than risk opening it and causing an explosion from a device they were possibly unaware of. The door was cut two feet wide, by three feet high, and a small man with twenty years experience in detonation device disarming, was selected for entry. But before he went through, they set up a platform that fit through the door like a diving board, and was suspended into the room. They were guarding against a pressure release type trigger that would go off the minute ten pounds of pressure was exerted, such as a man taking a light step across the carpet. The small man crawled out onto the platform and was suspended into the room six feet. He looked around and saw what looked like a thread of a wire that upon moving the door about six inches into the room would make a contact. He visually followed the wire and saw that it went to a paperback book lying on the floor. He knew it was not pressure sensitive and carefully walked over to the book and placed a large protective insulating pack over it, which was passed through the hole in the door and slid along the platform. It would not eliminate the entire explosive force of whatever material was incorporated, however it would reduce the impact should an error in disarming occur. The little munitions man carefully viewed the trigger and found that aside from its small size it would disarm just like all others he has handled. Within five minutes he was satisfied with his process and disarmed the device without incident. The bomb was placed in a special transport device, halls were cleared and the path to the street was evacuated. Art's room was given the same inspection and it appeared that it had not been entered.

The bomb squad moved the "book bomb" found in my room to a special lead container. It was designed specifically for forensic specialists to provide a semblance of protection during the highly sensitive process of attempting to lift fingerprints from explosive devices. This concept was developed when it was generally determined that the only place a print might be found was on the device itself. Most bomb builders, being a special breed with inflated egos, take such great pride in their ingenuity and confidence in their successes, that they generally do not wear latex gloves during the delicate assembly. In their opinion, print evidence would be lost in the explosion anyway. The inflated ego theory proved accurate in this case. The forensics specialist was able to remove a clean print, which was rushed to the various international agencies for a possible match.

I checked my room and found that everything had been tossed. My suitcase had been ripped apart, probably due to the fact that the perpetrator utilized suitcase linings for hiding *his* various identity papers as well as important documents and money. Considering I didn't leave anything important behind, I found nothing missing. Art's room was untouched. We didn't think

Mason or Harper or whoever, had a clue as to who Art was or that he was traveling with me.

CHAPTER 82

I arranged for messages coming to us at the hotel to be confidentially transferred to Philburton and Associates' office where we in turn would return the calls. We didn't expect many but the police needed a number to reach us should they have additional questions. In the meantime Carlos drove us through the parking garage, side entrance in his car and had another member of the firm drive the van back to their office for the time being. He drove down to the oceanfront along a tree-lined street to a small hotel on the water called Hotel Rosa. It had only fifteen rooms and was owned by an old friend of Harry's from England. It was truly charming with a center courtyard and walls covered with bougainvillea creating a mass of brilliant crimson. In the center beneath several small trees was a large free-flowing koi pond. And against the far wall a fountain flowed from a large metal sculpture, cascading to the rocks below. It created a pleasant ambiance for guests enjoying the tranquility while seated at one of the half dozen small round metal tables and chairs located in the shade of the second floor balcony overhang.

"Carlos, this is beautiful." Art said as I nodded in agreement.

"Yes it is, but Harry selected this for you with another thought in mind. The proprietor, Mr. Geoffrey Higgins is a long-time friend of his----but better yet, a retired member of MI 6 British Intelligence. Not only does he keep a secure hotel, he is a wealth of knowledge where international investigations and contacts are concerned. And he delights in being of assistance---- whether you ask or not. Just a small warning but well worth the bother if there is any need. One more thing, when Mr. Higgins retired he was a widower, so he moved to Portugal to buy a hotel and start a new life. It wasn't long before he met Rosa a Portuguese widow, a bit younger and a wonderful cook specializing in authentic local recipes. They married soon after he bought the hotel and he renamed it in her honor. Any opportunity to be invited to one of their meals should never be missed." Carlos explained with an obvious respect for the Higgins'.

We entered through the front door into a small lobby and encountered Mr. Higgins and his lovely bride standing behind the desk, smiling and obviously expecting us. The lobby looked truly English with antiques that were unmistakably removed from some British castle.

"I cannot help but notice you admiring the various pieces of furniture here in the lobby. It seems that when I moved from England and sold the family home I had more furniture than I knew what to do with. I couldn't part with any of it, as many of the pieces have been in my family for hundreds of years. As a result I came up with the brilliant idea that I needed a hotel in which to store them, so here I am----with my lovely wife Rosa." He said with a slight bow from the waist, his arm extended to her as they came from behind the desk to greet their new guests.

Higgins wearing a pair of khaki shorts, sandals and a lightweight white short-sleeved Latin shirt, was maybe in his mid to late sixties. He was ramrod straight without an apparent ounce of fat on his body. His hair was gray with flecks of black, a gray handlebar mustache, ruddy complexion and stood around six feet tall. Rosa was in her late forties, perhaps fifty, slender, also tall with long black hair and black eyes. She was nicely tanned and wore a white scooped, brocade peasant blouse and a full red and blue floral skirt.

"Your hotel is beautiful as are your furnishings. I only wish it was a pleasure trip, I could get used to this. I'd love to return with Valarie." I said in all sincerity to a smiling Mr. and Mrs. Higgins.

"Well we want you to be comfortable." Rosa replied.

"If you are all right now, I'll leave you and go back to the office. Don't forget, your van is at our office. Should you need anything please call me on my cell." Carlos said as he handed me a business card with his imprinted cell phone number.

"Thank you Carlos, we'll be fine. You've really been helpful." I appreciated being able to communicate in English.

"Carlos, Rosa and I will take good care of these gentlemen, rest assured." Higgins said as he ushered Carlos out the door.

"Harry filled me in on your work here, on a confidential and need to know basis of course. He may have told you----we go back a long way." Higgins said. "I believe I may be of some assistance. Should you need help with international authorities do not hesitate to ask. Quite honestly, I've been retired four years and I dearly miss the back and forth of a good real-life plot of murder and intrigue. It won't cost you a shilling. Sorry----make that a penny." Higgins said as we all laughed.

"Well, we have that in this case. I would consider it an honor if you would give us some ideas from time to time." I told a beaming Higgins. "Here's a photo of the man we believe to be involved in killing on three continents in this case." I said handing Higgins a copy of the airbrushed photo that eliminated the mustache. I don't expect him to show up here however I haven't expected him to show up where he has, so we can't be too careful."

"This man is here in Lisbon?"

"Yes, we were staking out his house on Azteca Road number seven earlier today."

"I take it he wasn't there. Did you get a chance to snoop a bit inside?"

I shot a glance at Art, who made an almost unnoticeable nod and said, "As a matter of fact, I did notice a broken door near the garage, and felt it was my civic duty to go inside and make certain no one was injured."

"What did you find old man?" Higgins asked with his charming British accent and a disarming smile,

I told him of the secret compartment and his high-tech telephone routing system, the false passport and French francs as well as the killing of the Santos' and the bomb found in my hotel room. Higgins listened with great patience and finally said. "I have a friend in Paris that owes me more favors than I might ask for in a lifetime. Let's see if he can keep an eye on this man when he arrives in France, if he does in fact. It's a simple matter of me calling him and then e-mailing him a memo with the information you saw on the passport along with this photo. We'll know if he crosses any border or lands at any airport and will follow him to his destination. If he tries to enter through an obscure border crossing where my friend doesn't have an investigator nearby, the customs people will delay him until one can be dispatched to the scene. What do you think----very low profile?"

"I'm amazed. I think that would be of great assistance, how about you Art do you agree?" I asked as Art nodded in agreement.

"Then it's settled, write down everything you can remember about the passport, name etc., and I'll scan the photo into my computer and
E-mail it to Jean in Paris."

"Not trusting my memory under the circumstances, I copied the information I saw on the passport at the time." I told Higgins, handing him the small card.

"Splendid, let me get this part moving while you settle into your rooms. When you're ready, come down stairs to the library which serves as my private office and we can have a drink while I will fill you in on my progress. Oh by the way, would you object if I made another low-key effort to try and determine where this bloke might be going if he were to fly out of Lisbon and not go to France? I don't want to horn in on your work however". Higgins said with his ear-to-ear smile.

"How could we possibly object to any of your help? I just hope we don't upset the Lisbon police's efforts."

"The Lisbon police couldn't find their fannies with four pair of hands. There are a few exceptions, but the higher up you go in the command level, the old American "Peter Principle" goes into effect. They have risen to the level of their incompetence. And that disease permeates the force here. That is probably why this bad bloke came to Lisbon in the first place, because the cops are incompetent." Higgins answered my concern.

"I'm for it if we aren't stepping on toes that have been helpful to us so far."

"They won't even know and they won't be doing what I propose." Higgins said in response to my concern.

"What *do* you propose?"

"Well, we need to know if this man has purchased a ticket on one of the airlines departing the country, don't we?" Higgins asked both of us.

""Yes, but how can you handle that? You're talking about reservations on twenty or more airlines at the Lisbon Airport alone." Art said.

"You are right. How can we do that? I'm not at liberty to tell you how or who can obtain this information. I can only tell you that I have access to someone that can look at any reservation in the world, for any flight leaving one country with the destination of another. The exceptions being, North Korea, and a few other small countries under dictator control, and effectively no normal scheduled flights to the Western world. Or should I say where no one we might be chasing after would be coming from or going to." Higgins said in a laughing response.

"If you can do this I say yes, we need to find this guy and who's directing him."

"Gentlemen, let me just say this, Harry knew what he was doing when he sent you here to me. He knew I would use my resources to help, knowing full well that the

local police are-----how do I put it kindly, a bit dense."
Higgins said still smiling, first at me then at Art.

"Go for it Mr. Higgins, see you in a few minutes."
I replied to this charming English, gentlemen who knew
his business and had already counted on our concurrence
to his involvement----probably before we arrived.

"Call me Higgins. May I call you Chuck and Art?
It's much easier when we're working closely on a case."
Higgins said while wheeling about and heading down the
hallway to his library before he could even get a response
from us.

CHAPTER 83

We climbed to the second floor on the broad curving staircase with hand carved banisters. I was given the key to room 7 and Art was in room 8. "I want to try and call Valarie and check in with Tom. Give me about twenty minutes. Better yet, why don't you just go down to Higgins' office when you're ready?" I said as I hauled my heavy briefcase and bag into the room. The room was surprisingly large with high ceilings, featuring an obvious bedroom suite from Henry the something of jolly old England. The four-poster bed with canopy was a dead giveaway. I only hoped that it had been a king size bed, but how could I complain with the help Higgins was offering. I wasn't prepared for what I saw when I walked to the French doors on the balcony. The ocean view was breathtaking. Opening the doors, I stepped out. The balcony was perhaps ten feet wide and the length of the room, about twenty feet. There was a table, three chairs and a chaise lounge with cushions. The balcony was shaded by the wide roof overhang, and was truly a beautiful setting. I tried my cell reception while sitting on the lounge and was pleasantly surprised that I had three bars, indicating excellent reception levels. I punched in Valarie's number in Hong Kong at Preston's apartment. It rang a number of times and a recording came on requesting the caller to leave a message, which I had to assume----because it was in Chinese. I left a message and told her I'd try again tomorrow.

CHAPTER 84

"Hello." came Tom Claudius' gruffly answered response to my call on his home phone.

"Hi Tom, what's going on with you?"

"Chucky, what in the hell time is it?"

"I don't know---- in Lisbon it's about five in the evening."

"Well, you woke me up. Since it's you, you're forgiven. Have you heard the latest about Jaxton?"

"No, what's happened?"

"Well, I'm sorry to report that the cops have identified the body in the company fire by dental records, and say it's definitely Jaxton's.

"You're kidding, God that's terrible. I'm so sorry Tom."

"I feel really bad about it. There's going to be a funeral service next Saturday. Since I can't make it, I'm sending a couple of people from the office."

"What's happening at TechX---- the Jaxton publicity?"

"There was so much coverage initially. We did everything possible to shore up the PR side, and with Bryan humming along and almost finished with the tests, the trade has been hand-fed more information about our progress than we would like, but under the circumstances it's working pretty well. That is not to say we're not really squeezed by the cash flow due to the thefts, but we're going to squeak by. We can't even make a claim for the thefts with the insurance until we know who did it and verify it with some indication of where the money went. Now it looks like Jaxton bought some software consulting from a company that doesn't exist. Our attorneys are working with Christine, trying to reconstruct how it all worked and it still points to Jaxton and looks like his signature. I guess I'll have to invest a little more in the company to see this thing through."

"Well, I should be able to help you get to the bottom of the money trail."

"There's more Chucky, the cops are trying to blame everything on Jaxton and close the case. That was until yesterday morning, when security, which we just added, saw a couple of men leaving the building by the back door. The security man was armed with a four-cell flashlight and was afraid to stop them, so he called in the Beaverton Police who had two cruisers in the area, and stopped the car at a light on Hall Boulevard. It turns out that the two were Asians, and had duffle bags full of arson equipment. By the looks of it, they were bringing back the stuff they didn't use. The police transported the two to the Washington County Jail, and the other two officers, with the help of the Beaverton Fire Department went to the temporary TechX building to inspect for possible arson activity. It didn't take long to find the timed firebomb device that was set to go off at four in the morning. The two Asians have yet to talk, but a search of their belongings turned up the phone number of a Billy Wong in Hong Kong. It took a while for the police to figure what they had, because Wong's name and number were written in Chinese characters. Isn't he one of the principals in KRL?"

"Yes, it looks like they're trying to finish the job they started. I think you need to beef up security."

"We have, and we still haven't found Phil Hampton. I don't know what the hell's going on. First Jaxton, then Phil, and did you know that Jaxton's girlfriend Victoria has left town?" Tom asked.

"No, I hadn't heard that, what happened?"

"Well, it seems that she told her law firm that she was taking a sabbatical somewhere, I don't know if I ever heard. Anyway she's gone and it looks like it was her own doing. She may have just gotten depressed with Jaxton missing, and then the fire. Even though they weren't sure at the time he was in the fire. The timing was interesting, because she left the day after the fire."

"That is interesting, but Phil Hampton's disappearance is even more so."

"You don't suppose that he's going to wind up dead too?"

"It's hard to say what's happening, but it's pretty clear to me that KRL is up to their neck in this thing. I think I've identified a culprit in the case here in Lisbon, one that's been killing people all over the world, the one that almost killed me in Hong Kong." I told Tom who was listening carefully.

"Who is it?"

"I haven't a clue. He changes his name almost daily---and is one smart, and I think, rich, son of a bitch. I had a chance to walk through his house today and saw some of the tools of his trade. He can route a phone call through so many cities and countries, that you have a snowballs chance in hell of tracing it."

"Wait a minute you say you took a tour of his house today? You're kidding me, how did you manage that?"

"Let's say it's off the record and I really didn't do it." I said with a dry little chuckle.

"I get it, what else did you find?"

"I found a packed bag with a different passport, a name I've never heard of----but with his picture."

"How do you know it was his picture?"

"That's a long story, another one that has to stay off the record. I'll tell you the whole sordid tale after we put this to bed, OK?"

"You've got it Chucky, anything else I need to know from you?"

"I don't think so. I'll tell you that Lisbon is beautiful, and the view from my balcony overlooking the ocean is fantastic."

"It sounds like you have it too good. Fancy hotel huh?" Tom kidded.

"Well old friend, I will say that it's an improvement over the one I left an hour ago. It had a bomb set to go off when I stepped into the room."

"What? Chucky, get your ass home----now! There's nothing I need that's worth your life, you hear?" Tom said with an angry voice.

"Tom, it's OK. I have this under control, and I'm careful, trust me."

"You better, but I don't like it. Thanks for calling, and be safe. You understand?" Tom exhorted.

"I hear you, thanks. Talk with you as soon as I know something more." I said, ending the call, as I had another call beeping in.

CHAPTER 85

"Hello."

"Harry here. How are you doing, all settled in with Higgins?" He asked as he laughed out loud.

"He's an interesting guy----is he real?" I asked, knowing that Harry wouldn't have sent us there had he been something less.

"Chuck, he is. I thought he could provide you with a wealth of resources, should you elect to use them. I might add, he really misses the service and is probably salivating at the chance to help you."

"I welcome it. He and Rosa are wonderful. Any report from the police on the house search?"

"There is. It's not so much what they found, even though that's a story in itself. It's what they didn't find that's very interesting. They didn't find a suitcase or passport or money. It was gone."

"Do you suppose he was in the house when I was there?"

"I don't know how he could have been there and at the same time be planting a bomb in your room, unless there are more than one involved here. The police found two Asians who are not talking, hiding in the house with papers in their pockets referring to Billy Wong and TechX."

"I think he'd have tried to kill me if he were there. He must have come back, grabbed the suitcase and took off again before the police got there. The Asians probably arrived after Mason left and before the police arrived. Bad timing on their part, or maybe it was good for them----and us."

"You could be right. Another thing, the bomb squad lifted a print and sent it out for identification."

"Well that's good news, but the missing bag tells me he soon will depart from Lisbon if he hasn't already. I better get downstairs and meet with Higgins. He promised to help on that score. I guess his help is needed now for certain. Thanks Harry, you're the best." I said ending the call.

CHAPTER 86

I changed into something as tropical as possible----
white shorts which I didn't think I would use but bought
anyway in Palo Alto on my clothes shopping spree, and a
short-sleeved green shirt. A knock on Art's door brought
no response, so I went down to the library-office where
Higgins said he'd be.

Art and Higgins were relaxing in two overstuffed
chairs, and when I walked in Higgins stood and extended
his arm to sit on the couch across form the chairs. There
was a decanter labeled "Scotch Whiskey" sitting on an
oval mirrored tray on the coffee table with one glass not
in use. By the looks of things, Art was totally under the
spell of Higgins, and knowing him, I felt he would be only
too happy to sit and listen to Higgins speak of his
investigative exploits for the rest of the evening----while
sipping on fine scotch whisky and sampling Rosa's
delightfully appetizingly appearing hors d'oeuvres.

"Well it looks like I missed the party." I said with
a wide grin.

"Actually, you're just in time for the party."
Higgins replied with his friendly smile, while Art raised
his glass in a mock toast.

"Let me fill you in on what I learned in the last
half hour. Higgins, some of this needs explanation and we
can bring you up to speed as we go, but let me run
through this first. Jaxton's dead, the police identified
him through his dental records. The temporary TechX
building was about to be firebombed when security
discovered a couple of Asians leaving the building at four
in the morning and called the police. They found the

name and phone number of Billy Wong of KRL, Hong Kong, in one of their pockets. Jaxton's girlfriend left on a three month sabbatical the day after the first fire. Here in Lisbon, the bomb squad found a print on the book bomb and sent it out for ID. The suitcase with the phony passport and French francs I saw at Mason's house is missing. It seems this Mason guy sneaked in and out of his house after the bomb plant and before the cops came. He's probably in the air now. The good news is the cops found two more Asians----probably working for Billy Wong and KRL, hiding in Mason's house when they searched it. They're being held at the police station and are being questioned now. That's my story anything new on your end?"

"Well that's a mouthful." Art said as he poured me a scotch and another for himself.

I commenced to answer their questions and explain my latest news in greater detail, while we all sipped Higgins' thirty-year-old Scotch whiskey.

After exhausting the questions and discussing the possibilities, Higgins moved in another direction. "With your previous approval I made the necessary contacts and will have all entry points into France secured within the hour. If a James R. Deacon went there we'll be able to track him. I also have the flight reservation data bank being checked as we speak. Hopefully he'll have a reservation, and we'll know that---before his flight leaves the ground." Higgins said with a smug look of satisfaction on his face. "Should he purchase a ticket just prior to boarding, we'll also have that information when it's entered into the system----in a matter of seconds."

"Great work Higgins, this really will be helpful. Any other thought that might help us find him or his co-

conspirators? Let me add----we do have documentation that he transferred over two million dollars in and out of an account at the Mercantile Bank in Lisbon in the last few days. It was transferred to a Swiss account and we can't trace it."

"I can probably do you some good on that account. Get me the information and I'll see if I can't pull the right string." Higgins offered. "Don't you just love a good mystery?" Higgins asked, causing my eyes to lock with Art's, while fighting to keep from going into hysterics as this little caper of near death experiences was hardly something to love.

CHAPTER 87

Dinner was served on the Higgins' private patio----
an invitation we knew better than to refuse. It consisted
of fish, chicken and pork in different dishes, accompanied
by a wonderful saffron rice dish, along with assorted
fresh fruits and home made breads. I wondered how
Higgins maintained his trim figure with Rosa's
mouthwatering cooking.

Higgins received a message from a hotel staff
person that he was wanted on the telephone---- a long
distance call. He excused himself and walked into his
quarters, returning five minutes later with the following
bit of news. "I just spoke with my contact on airline
reservations. It seems that a Mr. James R. Deacon
boarded Swissair flight SR693, not thirty minutes ago
and is heading for Zurich as we speak. It was a one-way
ticket paid with cash." Higgins explained and went on to
say, "I am not certain how much luck I'll have getting
help trailing the man, but I'll make a call or two."

"If we can hire someone to do that, I'll be happy to
pay for the services." I told Higgins.

"Let me see if I can get the gratis help----and if
not, I will insure the rate is fair."

"I'm not worried about the rate, I just want to find
this man and bring him to justice. It's now become
personal for me. I'm confident it was his finger on the
trigger in Hong Kong----nearly killing me."

Higgins moved behind the large mahogany desk
and sat down in his dark burgundy well-worn leather
chair. He swiveled around to face the ocean through the

French doors and commenced a conversation with his source in hushed tones. Art and I looked at one another and without speaking must have concluded that Higgins was now in his element----deep in the throws of foreign intrigue and conspiracy on an international level. After no more than three minutes Higgins gently placed the telephone receiver back in the cradle, paused and swiveled his chair around to face us, anticipating our expressions and waiting for a status report.

"Gentlemen, I am pleased to report to you we have one of our old friends, Oskar Andermatt, a thoroughly reliable chap on the job in Zurich. He will be at Terminal Gate A, Zurich International Airport to meet our Mr. Deacon's flight arriving at 1900 hours this evening. He has a female assistant to provide pass through surveillance. They'll both follow him using different cars and will be in communication by special radios with a range of seventeen kilometers. Upon our target passing through customs, the female team member will accidentally on purpose collide with him with such force she may just knock him on his backside with her large and heavy valise. In doing so, she'll place a small transmitter of a magnitude that is barely visible to the naked eye upon his clothing in an obscure location utilizing an adhesive so strong it can pull a Rolls Royce out of a trench." Higgins reported in delight, his smile of satisfaction radiating behind his bushy handlebar mustache. "Furthermore, our team will track the man to his hotel and will monitor his every movement until we remove them from their assignment. One other important factor----we will be provided with thirty-minute status updates via Oskar's wireless e-mail machinery. In addition it seems that Oskar is on holiday and his assistant is a highly skilled freelancer whom he uses for tricky surveillance work. He has promised that his charge statement will be minor and he guarantees his performance. A fine loyal soldier in this war against international corruption----let me assure you gentlemen. Questions?" Higgins asked as though he were attending a high level, top-secret gathering of British intelligence agents, discussing a mission involving the security of the free world.

"No, I think your man Oskar and his assistant have this situation under control. I do have that information for you on the transfer of more than two million US dollars from the Mercantile Bank here in Lisbon to a Swiss bank. I don't know the name of the bank. The record only shows routing information, which I assume represents the bank's identification number and general wiring information."

"That will be sufficient. Let me have a crack at this. I will e-mail it to my friend in London who is a wizard at uncovering funds in Swiss numbered accounts. In the meantime gentlemen, I think it is time for me to turn in after I send this out. Cheerio." Higgins said, grasping the bank information in his hand, as he left the room before Art and I could speak or stand.

CHAPTER 88

Wearing a lightweight gray summer suit, the taller man, AKA in this instance James R. Deacon, looking very much like a successful businessman traveling to Zurich on Swissair flight SR 693, was relaxing comfortably in his glove-leather seat in the first class section, sipping on a Coke in a crystal glass. Being very disciplined by training throughout his life, the majority self-imposed, he would never allow himself to relax at a time like this with an alcoholic beverage. He refused to diminish the self-preservation mechanism he worked so hard to develop and maintain. His thoughts turned to the events of the day and reflected on the mistakes that led to this hasty exit from the city he loved. His last four years in Portugal gave him the safe haven he always desired and had never previously found. One that allowed him the luxury of *relaxing* in a world he constructed for himself---- mayhem and death, with a battlefield of his making around every corner. Now he can never return to the home he loves on the hillside overlooking the sea. A refuge of calm and serenity would never return for him----at least in Portugal it wouldn't. Although the home was owned by his aunt who interestingly was not even living when she *bought* it with the taller man's money, he felt that it would be difficult to sell it for her anytime soon, and may have to arrange for a lawyer to take custody of the house rather than leave it abandoned.

He reflected on his mistake of dropping his guard and making a friendship with Anna. It was so easy. She was honest, open and of course beautiful----far different from the few other women he allowed himself to know in his chosen career of death and destruction.

Sadly, when it came time to eliminate the threat of Anna and her father---- forever, he felt no remorse when

424

he shifted his psyche from personal to soldier mode. It became strictly business, something he had done over and over before. He missed Anna and regretted her death as though she died in an auto accident, rather than the event he orchestrated personally and inflicted himself.

Along the way the taller man developed the ability to cope with the horrible terror he inflicted by learning to compartmentalize his actions and disassociate the results from personal accountability. His success in doing so allowed him to keep his edge. His mistakes were few, which was reflected by his bank balance and the fact that he carefully honed the ability not only to cover the tracks leading away from his actions, but to erase them entirely. His former stint with the US Government conducting similar "missions" as he liked to characterize them, afforded him the training and the discipline which served as a starting point. He learned the art of surveillance from both respects----following and being followed. This training and the years of practical experience applying the principles, made him as competent as any in eluding and or eliminating a surveillance team.

His greatest asset and the key to success in his chosen field was the ability to create new identities, complete with passports, driver's licenses and legitimate credit cards. He had a contact in Zurich, one he uncovered during his government service with the ability for a large fee to develop a new identity from a dead person of similar age. In most cases the depth of the new identity need not involve resurrecting a deceased person, as the taller man usually only needed documentation that would pass muster with custom agents and not so extensive that it would pass an in-depth security check. The work was flawless and had been tested in country entry points throughout the world. Funds were deposited with credit card companies on the guise of the necessity for advance payment due to extended travel. These deposits were all made by his Zurich contact and no direct trail could be made to the taller man or any other of his clients. His thoughts ran to his brother now in Paris and how his greed caused his girlfriend to bolt, probably with the money, and how his gambling addiction created a climate for possible exposure not only of himself but for all involved in the mission. He felt his brother was a loose cannon and decided that he would help him find a new location to live out the balance of his life, as well as a new identity. He was aware that the money his brother had available for his retirement could be gone in days if he persisted on gambling. If that occurred, the taller man decided he would sever all ties, and if his brother's actions deteriorated to a point that became destructive to he himself, he would end the problem----permanently.

An announcement came over the intercom that Flight SR 693, would be landing at Zurich International Airport in twenty minutes. The taller man went to the restroom, checked his appearance, returned to his seat and calmly waited for landing.

CHAPTER 89

John Foster sat in the Paris apartment that was arranged by his brother's contact. The ability to hide unnoticed and away from the scrutiny of police should they be searching hotels did not come cheap. The rate for such anonymity was the equivalent or two thousand US dollars a week for a dump as Foster considered it. He wasn't even running from the cops or at least he didn't think he was. The apartment was not far from the Eiffel Tower but it was up an alley and on the second floor. As there was no elevator it was necessary to climb a flight of stairs which were dark and musty smelling. The apartment itself had a living room furnished in "old motel" that overlooked the street in front which was in a light traffic area with a bakery and small bistro on the lower level. At night the sounds from the bar patrons spilled out onto the street with the louder voices floating up to his apartment----as if carried by balloons just for his benefit. As there was no air conditioning in the apartment he had to rely on open windows to cool the evening mustiness in his rooms. Through a small arched doorway off the living room there was a cramped kitchen and dining nook. The kitchen had a two-burner electric cook-top perched on a counter and a refrigerator the size of an apple box, which refused to make even a single ice cube. The bedroom with a double bed and dresser was down the hall and looked out to the alley and to the apartment building directly across. He was surprised to find a toilet after looking at the rest of the apartment, complete with an old tub and washbasin. The rooms probably were originally painted white but with obvious heavy smoking and little housekeeping, over time they had turned a yellowy cream.

This was his second night in Paris and although he was totally depressed with his accommodations he couldn't say he was bored with the situation. At five o'clock on his first night he went to the bistro below his apartment for a drink and to see if he would perhaps find it decent enough to eat there. Foster was dressed in a pair of jeans and a yellow short-sleeved cotton shirt along with a pair of white Nikes.

He walked through the right side of the double doors and found a busy bar with most of the tables occupied. He maneuvered his way to the long bar located along the right wall of the bistro. There was music coming from an old jukebox in a far corner with a small area in front should someone want to dance. The patrons appeared to Foster to be mostly working class folks, dressed not for the office but more for work as laborers and retail shop workers. About two-thirds were men with ages ranging from high teens to eighty or older. The place seated about forty with maybe a dozen at the bar. He found a stool between a woman in her late thirties and a man maybe in his mid-twenties. Not knowing enough French to find the bathroom let alone order something in this place where there appeared to be not a word of English spoken he reverted to the old standard of sign language----pointing to a bottle of scotch whisky behind the bar while pulling out a handful of French francs and placing them on the bar for the bartender to help himself.

The bartender was a skinny bald man in his fifties, wearing dark trousers and a white long sleeved shirt with a long white apron asked a question in French and Foster replied with----"English?" For which the bartender shook his head and turned away after taking his money and leaving change. Foster asked the pretty dark haired young woman wearing jeans and a green sweater sitting next to him if she spoke English, after she turned and smiled. The answer was a shake of the head from side to side. She then placed her hand on his arm and pointed to the woman sitting two stools down and said----"English"! Mary understood what was going on and said, "Are you an American?"

Finally Foster thought I can communicate. "Yes I am. Since I don't speak French I thought I'd have a difficult time trying to order something." He replied giving her a friendly smile.

"Well, speaking French doesn't make this crap any better." She said in an attempt at humor accompanied by a slight grin.

"It's that bad huh?" Foster asked still trying to be friendly.

"Nah, if you know what to order it isn't too bad." She said leaning back and talking around the two women between them. Finally the girl next to Foster said something to Mary and they switched bar stools so that they could hear one another, because the music had become louder and it was necessary to shout to be heard unless you were sitting right next to someone.

"Hi. I'm Tom!" He said as he extended his hand when she sat next to him.

She took his hand and said, "Mary."

Mary was dressed in a red dress that was a bit above her knees and rode up her thighs as she sat on the stool. She could tell that Tom's eyes were on her bare legs but did nothing to adjust her dress. Her hair was short light brown with streaks of blonde. Mary wore little makeup, just a light touch of lipstick and was not overweight but slightly Rubenesque with the top of her ample breasts slightly protruding from her dress with two buttons undone.

"Do you come here often?"

"If every night is often then the answer is yes." Mary said with a laugh.

"What is an American doing in this neighborhood?"

Tom thought that he shouldn't be talking about himself because it served no purpose other than to endanger his freedom and his life. However he was lonely and pissed off at life and a bit horny, so he decided to press on. "I'm doing some research on a book----for a writer friend."

"What a dumb place to do research----in this dump!"

"He wanted me to write some background observations on life in a working man's neighborhood near the Eiffel Tower." Tom replied almost believing himself as he had nothing else planned for his life and it sounded kind of interesting.

"Where are you staying?"

Tom gauged her question and tried to figure if it was just a casual friendly informational one or if it had something more meaningful behind it, such as to determine if he had a room that they could go to nearby. Or perhaps she lived with a girlfriend and couldn't take him home. Or maybe she was married or lived with a boyfriend and wanted a quickie before she went home.

There could be no harm in telling her where he lived. Why would she care, he rationalized. "I have an apartment in this building." He answered with another smile.

"Oh, that makes it easy for you."

"How do you mean easy? Tom asked, somewhat confused with her comment.

She touched his forearm that was resting on the bar and said, "I meant easy for you to come down here to eat and drink."

"Oh yeah, that's true."

"How did you learn to speak English so well?"

"I was raised in London and moved to Paris with my parents when I was twelve."

Tom signaled the bartender for two more and Mary said, "I'll have what you're drinking, Scotch isn't it?"

The bartender brought two more drinks, Mary switching from draft beer to hard liquor, probably because someone else was buying Tom thought.

"So is this a good place to eat or not?"

"There are better places, what do you like?"

"Oh, about most anything as long as I know what it is." Tom said and they both laughed.

"There is a great little Italian restaurant around the corner called Luigi's, if you like pasta."

"I do, but only if you'll join me for dinner."

"Well I don't know I have to work tomorrow, let me talk to my friends." She said as she whispered in French to the two women sitting next to her.

She turned to Tom, paused then said, "I'll have dinner with you but let's have another drink before we go, because they mostly only serve wine at Luigi's. Is that all right?" Mary asked smiling.

"That's fine, great!" Tom said pleased with himself and thinking things are looking up. This might not be such a bad place to hang for a while.

After two more drinks and both feeling a bit tipsy, Mary went to the jukebox and inserted some coins and pressed two buttons. The music started to play in a slow romantic beat and she returned to the bar, took Tom's hand and led him to the dance floor without objection.

"I hope you don't mind me dragging you onto the dance floor like this." She said as she pulled him close and slowly swayed to the music. Her breasts pressed against his thin shirt and he could feel her warmth through the material. She was now pressing her body against his groin, aware that it was having a material effect on him and obviously delighted by the results. After the two dances Tom wasn't sure if he could make it to the restaurant and was in favor of skipping the dining preliminaries and going right to his apartment instead.

"I'm starving, let's go." Mary said dragging him back to the bar to retrieve her purse while saying goodnight to her friends.

Mary put her arm through Tom's and swayed a bit through the bistro and out the front door and onto the sidewalk. Luigi's was a charming small restaurant seating perhaps thirty people and had the wonderful aromas of garlic, sauces and fresh baked breads upon entering. They were taken to a small booth and Mary pulled Tom next to her on one side. She ordered something from the waiter in French, and a moment later he returned with a bottle of Chianti and a plate of antipasto. The atmosphere was romantic, the weather balmy and the girl friendly, what more could a guy want Tom thought. They held their wine glasses up and touched rims in a toast, "to happiness." Mary offered.

"I'll drink to that." Tom said as Mary placed her glass on the table and turned to Tom, pulling his face to hers, kissing him in a long, deep and erotic manner, which again caused him to want to forget dinner.

"You're a good kisser." Mary said to Tom with a giggle, while holding his left hand in her lap and gently moving it across her bare right leg.

"You're not so bad yourself." He said as he kissed her again in a more passionate way to make a point that the evening was only beginning.

The ravioli was to die for. They finished their wine and topped off the meal with a dish of spumoni ice cream. After a cup of coffee, Tom paid the check and they got up and headed back toward the bistro.

"It's been a wonderful evening, thank you so much. I have to get up early tomorrow and need to get home." She said with an expression of sorrow.

Tom was aghast, fully expecting her to accompany him to his apartment----at least for a while. "Can't you come up to my place----for a while?" He asked in a disappointing tone.

She looked in his eyes, took his hand and said, "I can't, maybe tomorrow night." She said, and added, "for sure."

They kissed again and she promised to meet him at the same time tomorrow. She turned away and walked up the street while Tom walked back into the bistro.

Tom had no way of knowing how fortuitous it was that he was out of sight, as another emissary of Billy Wong's had successfully traced Foster to Paris. He easily found the luxury hotel Foster occupied in Zurich, and after bribing a clerk for a copy of hotel records came up with a message sent via facsimile that he failed to pick up confirming his flight to Paris the day earlier on Air France. Once in Paris, Wong's man, with the help of local associates commenced a concentrated search of hotels, starting at the top and working down to fleabag rooms with no success, but undaunted.

CHAPTER 90

The taller man embarked from Swissair Flight SR 693 at 7:16 P.M. He casually picked up his bag and moved toward the customs line. The customs agent first looking at his passport and then into the face of the taller man and asked him what the purpose of his trip was. "I am attending a business meeting and will be flying to Paris tomorrow." The agent then opened his suitcase which had nothing but a few outfits of clothing and a shaving kit. The French francs were in his suit inner pocket.

"Have a good evening sir." The customs agent said and moved to the next person in line.

CHAPTER 91

Oskar and his assistant Maria Karst waited near
the Swissair concourse on the terminal side of the customs
gate. They had carefully studied the photos e-mailed by
Higgins and quickly spotted the taller man, AKA James
Deacon as he passed through the gate. Maria carrying
her big valise headed toward him in a diagonal path that
would not cause a collision until she was within two feet
of him and made an abrupt turn toward him while
looking in the other direction while waving at an
imaginary person. They collided with such force that she
feigned losing her balance and in order to avoid falling to
the ground grabbed his arm and managed to tug him off
balance while her right arm circled around and affixed
the transmitter under his arm near the armpit of his suit
jacket. She apologized in French so vehemently that he
became embarrassed and not wanting to draw any more
attention than was already focused on the pair, politely
helped her up, smiled and handed her the valise. She
went on toward the customs gate while Oskar moved in
behind him with four people in between. Maria turned a
corner and quickly took off her long lightweight raincoat
exposing a sweatshirt and a pair of rolled up jeans which
she quickly rolled down. Next she pulled on her red
Chicago Cubs baseball cap, left the old valise and
raincoat on the bench and hurried to catch up with
Oskar. The taller man feeling comfortable with his
current anonymity moved through the terminal and
toward ground transportation. Before reaching the street
level he walked into a men's room and went into an
empty stall. He placed a sanitary paper ring over the
toilet seat and sat down fully clothed with his suitcase on
his lap. He opened the case and took out a tan long
sleeved lightweight sweater and a pair of blue denim
pants, canvas tennis shoes and a pair of white athletic

socks. He quickly changed his clothes and dress shoes, placing them in his suitcase. Before closing his bag he reached into a side pocket and pulled out a green nylon bag and an eyeglass case. He closed the suitcase and pulled on the nylon cover which fit like a glove over the suitcase changing the color from brown to green. The Taller man stood, slipped on a pair of heavy framed tortoise shell glasses with uncorrected thick lens and walked out. Although he felt certain he was not being followed he used this procedure in almost every airport, sometimes reversing the process and walking out with a business suit.

Oskar knew the restroom and the fact that it had only one entrance and exit and elected not to enter and be in such close proximity to his target. He sat on a nearby bench with a newspaper in front of his face with his eyes on the door. The traffic coming and going from the restroom was heavy since it was the last chance before leaving the terminal. After ten minutes, Oskar started to become concerned although from his experience he knew of many targets that would stay in a restroom for an extended period hoping to shake their followers. Oskar now decided that he should take a look in the restroom. This man was most likely too sophisticated to think he could wait out a person following him. He went in and found one man at a urinal and looking under the six stalls, found one occupied. He moved into the adjacent stall and with time being short, stood on the toilet getting as close as possible to the rear wall in order to look over the shoulder of the man and be less likely to be seen. He took a quick look over the top and found a short, bald, heavy man in his sixties and quickly moved out the door and spoke into his radio to Maria who was just outside the door on the street.

"I lost him in the restroom. Did you pick him up?" Oskar panted into the small microphone attached to his collar as he spoke to Maria.

"No he didn't come out here unless he's in disguise from the restroom. Did you see anyone leave the restroom that you didn't see go in?"

"I'm not certain but there was a chap in casual clothes carrying a bright green suitcase, who I didn't see enter."

"I see him out here trying to get a cab, the one with the thick glasses?"

"That's him. What do you think? I'm almost out to you."

"I think I better follow him because if it's not him we've failed in our visual effort at least. Can you pick him up on the transmitter?" She asked.

"Let me get in a secure area and I'll calibrate the receiver----one moment." He said as he reached in his pocket and pulled out what looked like a cell phone. He pulled up the antenna and put the earphone into his left ear. After tuning the calibration dials, the small screen showed a directional reading that was in the vicinity of the taxicab station at a distance of less than a tenth of a kilometer.

"Maria?" Oskar called into his lapel mike, now with an earphone in each ear.

"I hear you." Maria whispered into her lapel microphone.

"I picked up his location. He's out near the taxis. He must be the one with the green bag, do you agree?"

"Yes, the transmitter I planted on his jacket is in his suitcase now. I'll get in the cab behind him and you can get your car. I'll keep you informed as to our location until you pick us up. If I can, I'll get a quick photo. He's still outside the taxi talking to the driver." She said as she snapped off a few shots with her miniature camera and stepped up to the next cab in line and got in.

"I am heading to my car and will walk by him and get a look." Oskar indicated to Maria.

The two taxis rolled off into the warm Zurich evening with Maria offering her driver a nice bonus to keep close but not too close and not to lose the taxi in front. She explained that she worked for a divorce lawyer and the man is cheating with their client's wife. This was enough to get her driver hopping mad, promising to "follow like in the movies".

CHAPTER 92

The sky was a deep blue and the morning sun carried the expectation of a very warm summer day. From the balcony of my room I could see sunbathers starting to appear on the beach in front of the hotel. There were fishing boats on the horizon as well as a handful of surf fishermen casting lines from their long poles while standing on the beach. The white bleached sand and the sun's rays at this low angle cast a brilliant almost glittering reflection as I gazed out toward the horizon.

My thoughts however were not on the beauty of my surroundings but were focused on the turn of events that had occurred since receiving that early morning call from Tom Claudius just days ago. There have been murders and attempted murders throughout the world, arson and arson attempts, bombs set, not to mention grand theft, grand larceny and numerous other crimes---- a few I myself committed in an attempt to stop this tangle of death and destruction. Where would it end I wondered. I knew this Mason person was in Zurich now and if so I wasn't going to find the answers and cause the seemingly endless loss of lives to end unless I exposed this killer and properly identified him and the people behind him.

My mind wandered to Hong Kong and Valarie who I felt was safe for the moment. I didn't think she was close enough to the current activity to get caught in the crossfire. I did however think that KRL in Hong Kong was the focal point of all of the trouble. What I didn't know was if they were the focal point because they were the illegal buyer of the TechX software, or if there was from the beginning and continuing a joint effort between the parties in orchestrating this entire opera. I thought I needed an update on KRL in Hong Kong because that portion of the investigation had been dragging without any progress that I was aware of. I picked up my cell phone and punched in John Sun's cell number.

The call was answered as usual in Chinese and I responded, "John?"

"Yes." John Sun replied.

"Hi John this is Chuck, how are things?"

"Chuck it is good to hear from you. Are you all right?"

"I'm fine thanks. I'm in Lisbon. I tried to reach Valarie earlier but she didn't answer----is she all right?"

"Yes she is fine. As a matter of fact she was going out today with Preston's wife to some sort of gallery opening. I just talked with her she wanted to know if I had heard from you."

"That's good I'm glad she's keeping busy. If you talk with her please tell her I'll try to reach her later this evening----your time. What's the latest with Inspector Li's investigation on KRL?"

"I spoke with him yesterday and it seems that Mr. Chi met with him alone to discuss the police concerns. Mr. Chi said that he hasn't been able to reach Billy Wong since they arrived back from China. He denies any wrongdoing in regard to TechX saying that he was offered the product exclusively for ten million dollars by the president of the company Denton Jaxton, and they received the software. He also said, after a thorough testing KRL was satisfied with the product and wired the money. When asked about wiring the money to an offshore bank in the Caymans, he answered that Jaxton told him it was for tax purposes and Mr. Chi didn't feel it was his business to question the internal workings of a company they were buying software from. In regard to Sue Tang's murder, he of course denied any knowledge of the matter. It seems U.S. police authorities have asked Inspector Li about Billy Wong's involvement in this matter, in particular reference to the latest attempted arson at the TechX plant in Beaverton, Oregon. Chi acted shocked that his company was even thought to be involved in such unseemly activities. When Inspector Li told Mr. Chi that the arson suspects confessed they were supposed to report back to Billy Wong after the building was burned down he was speechless. Then when he was told that the suspects had Billy Wong's home phone number in their pocket when they were arrested, he became very defensive and indicated that if that was true he was not involved, nor was the company. Inspector Li also informed him that there was a complaint being filed that in effect would constitute an injunction or prohibition against the use of "pirated" software and that it would have to be returned to TechX and could never be used. According to Inspector Li, Mr. Chi then became livid. He said he bought it legitimately from the company's president and it was a legal sale. When asked to pick out the president from a photo of company personnel he was unable to. He did specifically say that the person he dealt with was not the person Inspector Li pointed to in a group picture. The person Li pointed to was Denton Jaxton."

"Wow that *is* interesting. Do you suppose Chi didn't know that Billy Wong was orchestrating this whole caper?"

442

"It is possible he didn't know Chuck but I really doubt it. Mr. Chi is a very smart and cagey man with a reputation for cutting corners and dealing in illegal ways. I will say he is very careful about insulating himself personally from illegal activities. I believe Billy Wong came into the firm a number of years ago just to play this role in over-the-line corporate dealings, giving Mr. Chi someone to blame if things went wrong. Considering Billy Wong had a background of shady dealings even when he was in your backyard in San Francisco, there's no reason to think that he wouldn't continue. Also there is no reason to think Mr. Chi wasn't fully aware of who and what his partner was."

"Great report, John. Let me see if I understand everything. Jaxton wasn't identified by Chi as the person selling the software from his picture only his name."

"That is correct."

"The Beaverton, Oregon police have a confession from the attempted arson pair sent by Billy Wong to burn down the temporary TechX facility."

"Yes, however they deny knowing anything about the earlier fire and were able to verify the fact that they were not in the country from their passport stamps."

"Billy Wong is missing. Do you suppose Mr. Chi made certain that he's permanently missing after he botched up the TechX purchase?"

"I would not doubt that possibility Chuck. There's no way for Billy Wong to plea bargain away his sentence by implicating Mr. Chi if he never turns up again."

Did you know that the police caught two Asians hiding in that fellow Mason Dixon's house yesterday? You remember Mr. Lee that was found murdered in his Hong Kong apartment and the police found among his things Mason Dixon's name and number in Lisbon along with notes on the TechX sale to KRL?"

"I remember Mr. Lee's name as well as Mason Dixon's but I hadn't heard about two Asians found in Dixon's house. Do you think they were sent by Billy Wong?"

"They had Billy Wong's name and TechX information in their pockets, but as far as I know they haven't talked yet."

"How did you do with the information Preston got from his man in Madrid, you know----the bank documents?" John asked.

"We're not sure yet. The documents we obtained that might have a print on them were sent to a lab in San Francisco. We also were able to get a photo that seems to be accurate. The most helpful information however was the name of the cell phone dealer and the name Fred Harper which you gave me. We're convinced Mason Dixon is one in the same. We were able to find his home here in Lisbon and get a positive ID from the daughter of the cell phone business owner. The sad part is that a few hours later, both the father and daughter were found murdered." I replied, with another bout of despondency.

"I'm sorry Chuck. It really hurts to know that had we not followed up on this lead they might still be alive."

"The only thing that keeps me going is my desire to stop this person from killing more people."

"What is the current status?" John asked.

"At this moment we have people connected with British Intelligence trailing him for us in Zurich."

"What are you going to do now?"

"I think I need to pick up his trail in Zurich and at some point soon have him arrested and either with his cooperation or without, sort out his TechX contact and end this madness."

"Chuck this man has left a trail of bodies around the world, most of which we don't even know of and he would delight in getting you in his crosshairs once and for all. Let the police finish this, it's far too dangerous."

"John, I know, but I don't have confidence that it'll be handled by the police----- in any country. So I just have to wrap it up myself, with the help of my friends of course."

"Just be very careful, do you hear me?"

"Maybe I can talk Art into tagging along, he's terrific backup don't you think?"

"Yes, if he's foolish enough to agree to go along."

CHAPTER 93

I called Art's room, received no answer so assumed he was downstairs with Higgins. Upon arriving in the lobby Rosa indicated that they were on the patio outside of Higgins' library-office having coffee before breakfast. I found Higgins and Art sitting at the round table with coffee, tea and a tray of fresh baked pastries. "Good morning, well look at this?" I said displaying my hungry smile as my mouth began watering over the pastry tray. I filled them in on the update from John Sun and answered all of the questions I could.

Turning to Higgins who sat comfortably in his white shorts and tropical print shirt, I asked, "Have you received a report from Oskar yet?"

"As a matter of fact I have. It seems that your man James Deacon as he now calls himself is a very careful man. He would have gotten away had it not been for the transmitter that was placed on his person shortly after he cleared customs. He apparently ducked into a restroom near the exit door and effectively disappeared altogether. It turns out the bloke walked in dressed as a businessman in his gray lightweight suit and came out as a casual fellow wearing summer clothes and a baseball cap, carrying a bright green valise.

Oskar and Maria, last name Kant, picked him up by deduction. The transmitter indicated his general direction however nothing else matched. So they followed him and his coat jacket that was stuffed in the valise to a smaller hotel in the Bahnhofstrasse shopping district----if you know Zurich at all. He is currently checked into the Scheuble at Muehlegasse 17. Unfortunately, unless he wears or takes his jacket, we'll not be able to assure that

446

his departure is monitored. Oskar did call the hotel and verified that Mr. Deacon had in fact checked in. He found it interesting that when he inquired if Mr. Deacon had checked in the desk clerk asked him if he was the party delivering a package. It appears that someone in Zurich has something for him and he expected it by the time he checked in. Oskar will keep a close eye for a delivery to the desk for Mr. Deacon. We also are quite confident that he doesn't think he's under surveillance because he used his passport name and hasn't made serious additional efforts to evade anyone that may be following." Higgins explained as we listened intently while sampling Rose's tasty pastries.

"It could be that Deacon, for lack of a better name is in Zurich to make arrangements for further disposition of the money that was wired from his Mercantile Bank here in Lisbon." I suggested.

"That's possible and with the French francs you saw in his valise when you searched his home it's still logical that he will be moving on to Paris soon." Higgins said with Art nodding in agreement.

"I'd like to see the authorities in Lisbon move forward with an arrest warrant for this Deacon, Dixon or whomever for the murder of Santos and his daughter and ask the police in Zurich to arrest him. That way we can stop him from more murderous activities and concentrate on uncovering the remaining conspirators." I said.

"Shall I call Harry and put him on the speakerphone?" Higgins asked.

"Yes by all means." I said turning to Art who nodded his concurrence. With that, Higgins reached around to the shelf by the door and retrieved the phone and called Harry Philburton.

"Harry, Higgins here. How are you old man?" Higgins said in his jovial way.

"Good of you to call, I was just about to call you chaps."

"Harry, I have you on the speakerphone, and have Chuck and Art here with me."

"I just received a report from Lisbon Police Detective Juan Verto. He said the lab was able to lift a good print from the paperback book-bomb found in your hotel room. It turns out the print matches the prints found in the search of Fred Harper's house on Azteca Road. They ran the print worldwide and are still waiting for results. In the meantime, they have enough evidence to charge the man with attempted murder----yours, breaking and entering, and hazardous endangerment, being the occupants of the hotel that might have also lost their lives should you have triggered the bomb he set. At the same time they want him for questioning on the Santos murders where everything points to him but hard evidence is still lacking at this point."

"Harry, this is Chuck. That's great news. Higgins here has done a magnificent job tracking this guy to Zurich where he has two associates keeping him under constant surveillance as we speak. Do you suppose we could get the Lisbon Police to do whatever the process might be with Portugal to execute the paperwork for the arrest and extradition of this Harper guy from Zurich?"

"I think they'd be only too happy to accommodate, particularly since you've done all the work by finding and following him. I know they really want to charge him with the Santos killings."

"What kind of red tape is involved in the paperwork and the diplomatic part of such an extradition process?"

"I don't know how Portugal works with Switzerland on this kind of thing or what their extradition requirements are." Harry told them.

Higgins listened to the conversation and said, "From my experience, the Swiss are not interested in white collar crime and will not work with anyone on those types of offenses, however they will cooperate on criminal cases, murder and the like, and I would put attempted murder and hotel bombs in a definite category."

"I'll call Juan right now, and he'll most likely want to come over there and discuss the status of your surveillance work and Harper's current location. I'll call you right back." Harry said and Higgins cut off the speakerphone.

While they waited for Harry's return call, Rose came through the open French doors carrying a large tray of scrambled eggs, sausage and bacon, an assortment of fresh fruit as well as a large pitcher of fresh squeezed orange juice. She placed the tray in the center of the table and with a pleasant smile asked if she could bring anything else. "Rose you're treating us like royalty. We really appreciate this, it looks wonderful." I told her as Art sat smiling in agreement as he surveyed the latest additions to the table.

"Oh it's no problem, and it's pretty standard fare for my wonderful husband." Rose said as she placed her arms around Higgins and gave him a squeeze, to his obvious delight and appreciation of this lovely lady he married.

"Thank you, love." Higgins said as he patted her arms and smiled. With that, Rose picked up the pastry tray, poured more coffee and hot water for Higgins' tea and quietly left the porch.

CHAPTER 94

The taller man awakened, showered and shaved with a safety razor. With his towel wrapped around his waist he opened his toilet articles pouch and pulled out his Remington electric razor. This was a very special razor as it only buzzed when turned on and could not shave a whisker. He recalled with pride the skill and technical expertise that went into "redesigning" this razor to work better, not for the purpose of shaving, but for the purpose of self-preservation. What he did was turn this innocent looking device into a highly sensitive surveillance "bug" detector. The rechargeable battery pack served as the power supply and the device was loaded with new state of the art electronic detection components, sufficient to sweep a room with a single push of a button. Upon detecting the presence of a bugging device he could follow the sound of the razor's ever-increasing detection tone right to the offending device. He made a practice of "sweeping" his room with this "razor" on a regular basis when traveling and while at home. He pressed one of two small obscure additional buttons on the side of the razor, causing a small green diode to light, indicating the device was active and fully operational. He then pressed the detect button located near the activation button and a red light illuminated along with a low continuous tone.

The taller man normally calm, cool and in control, became immediately tense. His face looked strained and became flushed. He knew that his space had been violated and sensed immediate danger. He turned the detector in a circle until the tone was loudest and moved in a manner that caused the pitch to get increasingly louder and louder until the shrill sounding device was touching his now open suitcase. Carefully he started

451

removing clothing, one piece at a time, until the razor-detector reached its highest pitch as it rested against the underarm portion of his suit jacket. He carefully raised the sleeve and with a trained eye detected the device that somehow became affixed to the jacket. He immediately recognized the type of device as it was similar to but not as sophisticated as the one he used in Hong Kong trailing Chuck Winters. The taller man did not avoid apprehension over the years by making mistakes. He carefully removed the electronic bugging device, placed it on a shelf in the back of the closet and sat down to consider his situation.

His adversaries could be the Chinese TechX people or some international police or governmental agency which finally connected him with one of his previous activities. It was also obvious to him that whoever it was, they either were not ready to move in on him or they didn't have sufficient evidence to prove a case. In any event he needed to complete his work in Zurich and get to Paris to resolve his brother's failing efforts and the disarray in his life and direction. All of which appear to have a direct effect on the taller man's ability to move around the world freely and conduct business when and where he chooses.

The package he received the previous night was brought to his room directly by his contact and not a messenger as previously requested, bypassing the front desk. The taller man as a method of operation, continuously changed plans at the last minute to frustrate any effort made by others to apprehend him or otherwise interfere with his activities. When he called on his cell phone to change the plans, he asked for the inclusion of a gray wig and a medium sized dark blue long sleeved shirt. He dressed in the new shirt and wore his gray suit pants and dress shoes. He carefully placed the gray wig on his head using the special wax he always carried with him, and affixed both the wig and bushy eyebrows he fashioned by cutting away a small unnoticeable portion from the back of the wig. He looked in the mirror, made some final adjustments and packed his suitcase. After closing the case he took the green nylon suitcase cover and turned it inside out exposing the black side, which he carefully slipped over the suitcase and zipped it closed, transforming the once brown then green suitcase into a sleek black anonymous appearing bag. He then took a towel and methodically wiped the room of fingerprints. Walking into the bathroom one more time he took a last look in the mirror and made a final adjustment. Satisfied with his appearance he walked out of the room leaving the small transmitter dutifully reporting it's location from the back of the closet shelf.

"Good morning sir." The cleaning man said in German as the taller man approached the elevator.

"Good morning. I am expecting a car, and the driver said he would pull in back of the building near the back door to avoid the traffic on the street. Is there such a door?" He asked with a friendly smile, while sliding currency into the man's hand.

"There is not an official exit however I can take you through the maintenance room which has a door leading to the alley in the rear of the hotel if you like." The man said while casually stuffing the currency into the pocket of his coveralls.

The taller man followed behind the old man as he shuffled along toward the service elevator, past the guest elevators and around the corner to the rear of the building. He stepped aside as the door opened and allowed the taller man to enter the elevator, which was dirty with stained canvas pads hanging from the walls. He pressed the button while the taller man stood to the rear, running through his mind again and again his immediate plan of escape and evasion. Once on the main floor the elevator door opened to a dark cluttered hallway littered with paint buckets and ladders leaning against the walls. The old man motioned for him to follow and they went down the hall and turned to the right where a large steel door with a slide bolt stood before them. He wrestled with the old bolt and pushed with the heft of his body to start the rusty bolt sliding to the open position. Obviously a door not often used, it creaked as it opened to an alley partially blocked with garbage cans and old packing crates. The hotel kitchen was located to the left about fifty feet away and had its own door for deliveries, which were in process as the taller man walked warily into the open. He demonstrated a certain casual gate and confidence, enforced by the knowledge that he had properly prepared and planned for this current situation. He paused and looked both ways, deciding to go away from the restaurant door toward a second alley to the right that ran along the right side of the hotel and perpendicular to the alley where he currently stood. Upon reaching the intersection he looked to his left and found that it exited one street over.

He casually walked to the head of the alley and saw a taxi waiting in front of a small hotel about fifty yards to his right and across the street. He turned right without crossing the street and walked up until he was opposite the hotel and taxi. He stood for a moment catching the eye of the taxi driver and nodded slightly with a slight upward lift of his suitcase, developing sufficient body language to communicate his desire to hire the cab. The driver clearly understood the unspoken language, started his engine and pulled across the street and down sufficiently to pull up along side the taller man who had moved further down the street to accommodate the driver.

The taller man opened the rear door, placed his suitcase on the far side of the seat and slid in beside it. "Ruetli, please." He said, asking to be taken to a hotel not too far away. He reached into his shirt pocket and checked his newly acquired passport which he hoped he could use for a while. He had however taken the precaution of purchasing yet another set of new identity documents, complete with assorted custom stampings showing moderate vacation destination travel sent by Federal Express, to his Paris contact. The Ruetli Hotel was on Zaehringerstrasse 43 and was small by most standards, sixty-two rooms, however it was located close to the bank he intended to visit and could walk the few blocks without bothering with another taxi. He paid the taxi driver and exited the cab. Carrying his black suitcase he carefully studied the entrance and decided to walk past it toward the park that was in the next block. He was very wary of possible followers and made frequent stops to window shop along the way. He walked into an alley that went through to the next street, turned right and walked a few steps to a bench appearing to be a bus stop and sat down. From his vantage point behind a shrub, he had a clear view of the alley entrance to the street and would watch for a few minutes to see if he could detect suspicious lingering by anyone coming out from the alley. He waited for at least ten minutes and a bus came and picked up the elderly lady sitting on the bench next to him. Looking around he could see that there was no direct line of sight to his bench from the shops across the street. There was a traffic directional sign that blocked a portion of the view to the front and a large potted shrub at either end of the bench giving him the opportunity to transform himself into Gerhard Schultz, a visitor from Munich, Germany. His German was near flawless, learned while in the military he could easily pass as a German, particularly with his rather stern, no-nonsense, sharp-featured appearance and demeanor. After checking his surroundings he bent down as if to tie a shoe and casually ran his fingers through his hair pulling the gray wig off in his right hand and with his left hand smoothly pulled off both bushy gray eyebrows. He casually pulled a comb out of his pocket and ran it through his hair, picking up any remaining wax adhesive. He then rubbed his eyes and eyebrows in a perfectly natural expression of tiredness to eliminate any tell-tail adhesive left behind. The wig and brows were stuffed casually in his right pants pocket and he stood, picked up his suitcase, looked around for signs of danger, finding none, strolled back towards the Ruetli Hotel.

CHAPTER 95

Oskar and Mary were sitting in Oskar's car on the far side and down a bit from the front entrance of the Scheuble Hotel. "Do you suppose he evaded us Oskar?" Mary asked her long time friend and associate.

"I don't think so. We know he hasn't left with his suitcase, the device is still transmitting from his room."

"Maybe one of us should make another trip up to his door, like you did last night to verify the bug is actually in his room and not in some garbage can somewhere else in the building." She said and added, "I'll be glad to do it this time."

"Good plan." Oskar said. "You do that and I'll watch the front."

With that, Mary stiff from sleeping in the back seat during her surveillance shift trade-offs with Oskar welcomed the chance to walk around. She smoothed her hair and took the receiver from Osker, placing it in her purse with the earphone positioned in her ear and strode across the street toward the hotel entrance. The night before, Oskar walked into the hotel when the night manager was busy checking in a guest, and unnoticed he slipped by to the staircase avoiding the elevator and any curiosity from the front desk. He then turned on his surveillance receiver and with the earphone in place, methodically walked each floor until the tone registered the loudest. It was clear the transmitter was strongest behind the door of room 416. Considering the time of day, Mary did not have to be concerned as the hotel lobby was busy with people coming and going as well as checking out of their rooms. She walked directly to the elevator and pushed the button to the fourth floor. Upon exiting the elevator she paused and checked to see that she was alone in the hallway, and was about to insert the earphone when the door to 417 flung open startling her. A very large man dressed in a suit that once fit him, moved through the doorway and walked slowly toward her. She smiled as she hugged the wall in an attempt to pass in the narrow hall. He smiled and nodded and continued toward the elevator. She went past 416 and lingered at the end, acting as though she forgot the room she was looking for. The heavy man was watching her every move as he waited for the elevator. He finally spoke in German.

"Who are you looking for?" He said with a deep gruff voice, one that gave Mary the shivers.

"I must have the wrong floor. Is this three or four?"

"This is four. Come on," he said with his hand extended out to her. "I will take you there."

"That won't be necessary." She said. "I'm early anyway and think I'll sit in the lobby until she comes back."

"As you wish," he said holding the elevator for her while she entered without much choice.

They rode down together, him leering at her chest and Mary almost vomiting from the horrible odor being emitted from his fat body. Not another word was spoken, however he moved to one side, which was a chore in itself in order to watch her backside as she walked out. Mary was thinking that if she didn't already need a bath she surely needed one now. She walked over to the newsstand and purchased a local paper, sat in a chair out of view from the front desk and proceeded to wait out this fat, smelly, slob of a man with saliva drooling from the right side of his droopy jowls. He lingered a few feet away still glancing at her while deciding what to do next, or who next to terrorize. It was nearing 10:00 A.M. and the smelly man after giving up on an opportunity to have another chance to see her bottom move under her jeans, headed out the front door and walked down the street toward Oskar. Mary walked to the door and checked on his location, seeing him waddling away she hurried back to the elevator and pushed the fourth floor again. This time the floor was quiet and she walked toward room 416 with the earphone in her ear, hearing the tone become increasingly louder as she approached the door, stopped and moved on. The tone started to diminish as she moved from either side of the room and was convinced the transmitting device was secure in his suitcase.

Chapter 96

The taller man was given his key to room 312 in the Hotel Ruetli and declined assistance with his suitcase. "We hope you enjoy your stay Mr. Schultz and please do not hesitate to ask should you need anything at all. The breakfast buffet begins serving at six thirty in the morning and ends at ten o'clock." The taller man took the elevator to the third floor and opened his door. He felt fairly confident he was not being followed and now is certain the woman at the airport was responsible for placing the transmitter under his arm. His room was clean and comfortable and quite close to his bank. He placed the suitcase on the bed, opened it and removed the suit jacket, but just to be certain he took out his *Remington razor* again and checked all of his clothing and suitcase for any possible surveillance or transmitting device. None were found.

Mary walked back to the car where Oskar was patiently waiting and watching. "What did you find?"

"Well I found a smelly fat man, or better he found me."

"I think I saw him roll down the street." Oskar said with a laugh.

"The device is still in the room. I can't say if he is though."

"It may be time to ring his room with a wrong number if he should answer. If for some reason he found the transmitter then we're finished on this assignment."

"Do you want to call from here?" She asked.

"I don't see why not." He said as he picked up his cell phone and dialed the hotel operator.

"Good morning, Hotel Scheuble."

"Mr. James Deacon, please." Oskar said with a casual confidence.

"One moment please." She said as she rang the room. Oskar heard the ring over and over again and finally the operator came back on the line and asked if he would like to leave a message.

"Is he still registered?"

"Let me check." She said and continued, "I believe he is. He was not checking out until later today or tomorrow morning according to our records."

"Thank you."

"What did they say, has he checked out?"

"She didn't think so. When he checked in he said he was staying until late today or tomorrow, and hasn't checked out according to their records. I just don't trust him."

With that Mary laughed heartily and said, "How could anyone trust him?"

"You are right there! I think I'll slip up there and see if my lock picking ability isn't too rusty, what do you think?" Oskar asked.

"I'm all for it, but I think he's gone however. I'll watch your backside and keep in constant radio touch, all right?"

"Right." Oskar said as he climbed out of his older Citroen and headed across the street.

"Do you read me Oskar?"

"Loud and clear, is there a problem?"

"Not yet." She said with a chuckle as she watched him move through the glass front doors under the hotel sign.

Oskar had no problem with being noticed by the hotel staff as he walked calmly to the elevator and pushed the fourth floor button. Upon arriving on the fourth floor he walked off the elevator and noticed a maids cart in the hall near the door of room 416. He walked up to it and saw that the door to the room was open. He tried to see that the maid was in the room alone and walked in saying, "I must have the wrong room this one looks unoccupied."

The maid looked at Oskar who looked quite harmless and said, "The guest must have checked out, are you sure 416 is the room you were looking for?"

Fumbling in his pocket, looking for an imaginary piece of paper that he couldn't find, he said, "I think I need to make a call on my cell phone. Is it all right if I make it from the room?"

"I still have to clean the bathroom make yourself at home." She said with a smile.

This was the break Oskar had hoped for. The maid went into the bathroom while Oskar, with cell phone in one hand and receiver in the other, turned it on and heard the tone in his ear. He moved around with the cell phone at his ear for cover with the maid and followed the increased intensity of the tone directly into the empty closet, where it became louder as he held it up to the top shelf where the noise level told him it was placed. He reached around and felt the small device in the left rear corner, removed it, placed it in his pocket and left the room in total despair. He knew that Higgins counted on him and he had failed. Oskar didn't even consider the excuse that he may have been following one of the more cunning killers in the world today.

Oskar immediately placed a call he didn't want to make. "Higgins, Oskar here." He said after hearing Higgins familiar and friendly "Cheerio!"

"Higgins, I am sorry to report that we lost him. He found our transmitter in his suit jacket, removed it and left it in his hotel room. He must have slipped out a back door because we were watching the only guest entrance and exit.

"Not to worry, we'll try and pick him up in France. My regards and thanks to you and your assistant. Please send me the charges for your time and I will forward them to the right party for payment."

"No, I couldn't do that. We had him. Let me do a little more checking, I have a bit of unfinished business."
"As you wish, and thank you Oskar." Higgins said as he ended the conversation.

Oskar turned to Mary and asked, "The photo you took at the airport, do you think you might have a decent likeness of him?"

"I took a three-quarter face shot and it should be good, particularly with this camera. Why do you ask?"

"It occurred to me that since this man was here on specific business and he had not finished his work, he needed to find another location before leaving Zurich, at least for a few hours if not a full day. Therefore he needed to get a taxi in order to relocate and escape our surveillance, particularly since he took his suitcase. Most people do not go too far on foot when they're hauling a suitcase on the street. Therefore he picked up a cab and moved to another hotel, this time probably feeling somewhat relaxed without our electronic leash on him. If he did receive the package that was expected, it may have contained additional disguises for the next portion of his business, either here in Zurich or on to France if Higgins is right on his guess, considering the French francs he had in his suitcase in Lisbon." Oskar said with a devious expression on his face.

"Oskar, how does all this help us find him in this city?" Mary asked with curiosity.

"Simple, the taxi drivers are assigned locations on the street by their companies. In other words at the Scheuble we saw the same group of taxi drivers come and go as long as we sat here. Of course they may have picked up calls en-route or on the street after delivering a fare, but as a general rule they migrate back to their assigned post."

"How does that help us?"

464

"The photo. We'll get a fast print made and canvas the taxi stands in the area, particularly on the street to the rear and close by. We'll offer ten Suisse francs to each driver just for talking with us and more if we get a bite. Our question will be----did you pick up or see this man carrying a suitcase in the last twenty-four hours, or did you pick up any man with a suitcase and take him to a hotel in the area?"

"I like your idea. Let's get this film developed and get to work before the trail gets cold." Mary said with renewed enthusiasm.

CHAPTER 97

The taller man sat in a chair by the window of the Hotel Reutli, cell phone to his ear waiting for his party to come on the line at Zurich International, a small bank where he was a numbered account holder. The account now had the equivalent in US dollars of two million, one hundred and fifty seven thousand dollars. He selected this bank because it could not tie him to the balance of his money and he didn't want a trail of any kind as he transferred this new money into his "retirement account" as he liked to think of it.

"Franz Drucker, here." He said in crisp perfect German.

"Mr. Drucker, this is account number 175491A. I'd like to stop in today and make arrangements for converting my balance into bearer bonds." The taller man said.

"Yes, that will be fine. Do you wish to also close the account?"

"No, I'll be adding a substantial sum in the very near future." The taller man replied, recalling his many dealing with bankers that when one closed an account, the cooperation level dropped to nearly zero and he couldn't afford any problems at this point.

"Very good, I will be happy to accommodate you. If you would like to expedite the process, I will need your personal authorization code."

The taller man provided the necessary personal code and said, "How long will it take to prepare the bonds?"

"I would say we can be ready by say two this afternoon, will that be acceptable to you?"

"That will be fine. Where do I go when I arrive at the bank?"

"Just go to the reception desk and ask for Mr. Drucker. You will then be directed to my office where I will have the documents ready for you. Your only additional requirement will be to provide your personal authorization code an additional time for confirmation. Are there any further questions?"

"No, I'll see you at two this afternoon." The taller man said.

He then punched in the number for his primary numbered account where he kept his retirement money and where he had a "personal banker". He would do special services for him, such as provide a Visa card with a one hundred thousand dollar limit that would be paid by a debit to his numbered "retirement account" upon reaching thirty days, or upon reaching his limit, which in effect resulted in no limit except for what he had in savings. The card was not a debit card, but a credit card that functioned like one and as a result avoided any direct link with his numbered account. When necessary, to reduce the balance, his personal banker transferred funds from his numbered account to a bank general account and in turn paid off the credit card obligation. His card was in the name of Euro Associates, Ltd., which allowed him to carry the card with any identity, and not have to worry about two different names at some customs checkpoint. His signature was always the same illegible scrawl, one that he used with every identification he carried, and one that could not be deciphered to mean any particular name. When someone would ask him about the signature, he would joke and say, "I should have been a doctor".

The taller man, always wary about being traced, would only use the Visa card for cash withdrawals from ATM machines to fund his travel and living expenses. His personal banker also arranged a Visa card at another Zurich bank, where he deposited on behalf of the taller man fifty thousand US equivalent dollars in the name of Euro Consultants, Ltd. This way, he could use the card to check into hotels if they required a card in lieu of cash, and would pay the bill in cash upon checkout. If for any reason that credit card was traced it would run into a dead end at the second Swiss bank, as there was only fifty thousand dollars on deposit with no direct connection to his main account or even to his bank. The only loose tie was that the Visa card was in the name of an entity that did not exist and was arranged by a second bank. In any event he knew that his "personal banker" would not divulge his identity even if he knew it, which he didn't. The main Visa card with the large balance was never used for credit just for cash withdrawals.

CHAPTER 98

"This is Euro Associates, Ltd. will you be available this afternoon?" He asked his personal banker.

"Well hello, it has been a while. Yes of course I will be in, when will you be stopping by?" He cheerfully asked.

"Sometime after two and before three this afternoon, I'll be bringing a sizable bearer bond and would like to add it to my account."

"Perfect, I will be expecting you."

He then called a third number, "Air France, all of our operators are currently busy, please hold for the first available operator," came the recorded message, repeated in a number of languages which he fully expected. After ten minutes, "This is Greta, how may I help you?" The Air France reservation operator answered.

"I'd like to make a reservation to fly from Zurich to Paris late this afternoon or early evening, first class if you have it."

"I have flight 2555, leaving Zurich at 5:55PM and arriving Paris de Gaulle at 7:10 P.M. I am sorry there is no first class offered on this flight."

"That will be fine. The reservation is in the name of Gerhard Schultz. I do not have a local number. I just checked out of my hotel."

"That total fare is 678 Swiss francs. Please arrive at the airport one hour and fifteen minutes prior to departure. Thank you for flying Air France."

The taller man changed into his business suit and without a disguise to conform to his photo in the new passport, walked down the stairs to the lobby, avoiding the elevator and went to the desk. He paid his room bill in advance with cash, telling the clerk that he had to leave early in the morning and wanted to take care of it today. It was 1:30 P.M. and the Zurich afternoon was as pleasant as the taller man had ever seen. The temperature was comfortable and not too warm. The white fluffy clouds that lingered overhead were truly beautiful, floating through the deep blue sky like a cotton candy train, rolling and swaying to and fro in extra slow motion. He was early and started a slow paced walk to the bank five blocks away. Although he could have gone in anytime, he was concerned that the documents wouldn't be ready and he didn't want to wait in the bank.

The streets were bustling and yet he was lost in thought, oblivious to his surroundings, as if walking down a deserted country road. He thought about the home he loved so much in Lisbon, and how a simple mistake, a broken personal rule involving a woman, caused the loss of a refuge that he felt now could not be duplicated. How he thought, could he have allowed his brother to draw him into such a sloppy endeavor, one that would forever change his life. A life he now has to be concerned about people tracking *him* and trying to apprehend or kill *him*. In this walking, personal self-analyst session, he was incapable of considering the people he himself had killed or the terror and suffering he has caused in the hearts of many. The money he thought, although significant, was not worth the cost. He would now have to find another home, not a house but a country where he could trust

470

enough to unwind and sleep without the fear of a silent figure slipping through a door or over a gate, climbing a staircase, entering his bedroom and ending his existence. Where would he go? How will he straighten out his brother enough to keep him from personal destruction or worse, to prevent his careless lifestyle and lack of responsibility from spilling over to affect he, himself?

The taller man felt he had lost control, was in a spin, when just weeks ago he was thinking about retirement. He was financially secure for the rest of his life. He had a home base where no one bothered him, where his neighbors kept their distance as he kept his, and he gave the local authorities no reason for cause in any way. His trail was covered. There were no manhunts by the law or others. He could finally at this point in his life relax, as he had fine-tuned his business and his personal life to the extent that he was a professional and didn't make mistakes----until now.

His life had turned upside down and people were after him, even here in Zurich. In some ways he liked the challenge if he was in control, as he always had been. But in this case he was not in control and he didn't have a refuge to return to after he plied his trade----he was on the run. He now felt adrift and a bit frightened, although he would never admit it to himself, in an ocean he once owned like a predator shark. He finally reached the bank and climbed the stairs.

CHAPTER 99

From mid-morning and through the lunch hour, Detective Juan Verto sat at the table where Higgins, Art and I had earlier taken breakfast. He was very disappointed to hear the latest report from Zurich involving the surveillance misstep of losing the current location of Fred Harper. Verto's Captain sent him over to document the current whereabouts of the suspect in order to expedite the governmental approval of the arrest warrant. Now that the Swiss government could not readily pick up the subject, the level of police investigative cooperation and interest from Zurich, not to mention now possibly Lisbon, became a significant unknown in the equation. Undaunted, Detective Verto assembled a very credible and impressive dossier on the suspect from our assembled group. He was hopeful that his Captain would gain an appreciation of the importance in taking the first step by any law enforcement agency to put an end to this man's worldwide reign of terror. As Detective Verto was finishing his documentation, Rosa breezed through the door wearing her now expected smile and whispered in Art's ear that he had a telephone call from San Francisco. He excused himself, not wanting to interrupt Detective Verto and followed her into the office to take the call at Higgins' desk.

"Hello."

"Art, Jimmy" came the voice of his partner.

"Hi Jimmy, what's up?"

"I just got off the phone with Frank Hixon in Portland. He's done a little more work on that dead guy--

-- you know the one in Jaxton's house, the one that's been *dead* for eight years?"

"Yeah, yeah, what's the deal?" Art asked impatiently.

"Well he came up with something very interesting. You asked him to check and see if this guy's Nam unit had a guy by the name of Mason or Dixon and he said he already checked it out and came up negative."

"OK, what?"

"He took another look at the list of guys in his unit and a name jumped out that he hadn't connected before."

"Jimmy, will you get to the God-damned point, please." Art said, losing his patience.

"He found a guy with a middle name of Mason and guess what his last name is?" Jimmy smugly asked.

"Come on Jimmy, tell me!"

"Gerard Mason Hampton. Does that sound familiar?"

"You mean Hampton, as in Phil Hampton of TechX?"

"Bingo. It is, or was his older brother. Hixon checked it out."

"What? Do you mean this guy Mason we've been chasing is Phil Hampton's brother?"

"That's what I said."

"And Phil Hampton's brother just put a bomb in Chuck's room?" Art said asking himself in disbelief.

"That's only the half of it, there's more, and you won't believe this." Jimmy teased.

"What Jimmy? Tell me now damn it!" Art said, tiring of the approach his partner was taking.

"You asked for it. Another name that meant nothing to Hixon, until he faxed me the list of Nam unit members will blow your mind."

"Who's on it----you?"

"Close, Tom Claudius." He responded and waited for the eruption.

"What, are you sure? Tom, from One Star? Oh my God!" Art replied in absolute disbelief.

"I thought you might like to know this bombshell. I'll leave it for you smart guys to sort out." He said kidding.

"Jimmy thanks, great work, fax me that list right away. You have the number here. By the way, can we compare the prints from the bank documents if the lab found any, with the prints on file with the military for this Gerard Hampton?"

"Not likely, the military seems to have misplaced his file, we're still checking on that." Jimmy said, and hung up from his end.

Art sat in Higgins chair and tried to collect his thoughts, after hearing the bombshells his partner just tossed their way. After a few minutes and still stunned he rose and walked out to the porch. "Chuck can I see you for a minute?" Art asked in a serious tone.

"Sure." He said and excused himself, following Art into Higgins office where they each sat in a leather wing chair.

"You look like you saw a ghost, is everything OK?"

"I think I *have* seen a ghost." Art replied and said, "Unless the Mason connection is a total coincidence this guy is Phil Hampton's older brother, which probably means that Phil Hampton orchestrated this deal. There's more. This'll really blow your mind. Tom Claudius and Mason Hampton served together in the same unit in Viet Nam. Maybe it's the ultimate inside job."

"What, who told you this? You've got to be shitting me." I said as I slumped into a chair. My body deflated like a balloon with a major puncture.

"Jimmy just called. He heard from Frank Hixon who took another look at the unit members in Nam where that dead guy was a member. It seems that Hampton's brother's middle name is Mason and was in the unit. Also, Tom Claudius was in the unit too. This all comes together, and now you know how Phil became involved with Tom and worked for him in several of his companies. Hixon didn't put it together originally, because Hampton and Claudius were names he hadn't focused on. He only discovered this connection when he took another look at the unit makeup in Viet Nam where the dead guy in Jaxton's house originally served."

"I can't believe that Tom wouldn't tell me about his connection with Phil's brother." I said looking at the floor.

"Chuck, why would he? It's no one's business why he hired Phil, and if Tom isn't involved in this mess, there's no reason for him to see the importance of this thing. But since Phil is missing and the dead guy from their unit in Nam was in Jaxton's house, things are starting to make some sense, at least as to who might be behind this thing from TechX. I don't know if Tom ever knew the name of the dead guy, or if he'd make the connection with someone he knew more than thirty years ago." Art said.

"You're probably right, we need to call Frank Hixon and see if he can find out from one of those guys he talked with about Mason, and verify that they were talking about *Mason Hampton* when they referred to the guy in Lisbon. Also exactly what was the connection between Hampton and Tom Claudius? I want to know that before I talk to Tom."

"Let's call him right now." Art said as he placed the call to Portland.

CHAPTER 100

Oskar and Mary produced a reasonable likeness of Harper from the photos taken at the airport the evening before, and made several copies to show the taxi drivers in the area. They went from taxi to taxi without finding a driver who recognized the man, until they reached a taxi in the street between two small hotels to the rear of the Hotel Scheuble. The driver looked apprehensive at first and finally when offered a handful of Swiss francs said, "I took him to the Ruetli earlier today."

"Are you certain?" Marie asked in German.

"Yes" came the reply. "I know it's the same man for sure. I was able to get a good look at his face and noticed it was too young for the gray hair and bushy gray eyebrows he was wearing."

"Take us there!" She said as she stuffed another wad of bills into his hand.

Oskar and Maria entered the taxi and rode to the place where the driver said he had delivered the suspect. The Hotel Reutli was located about eight blocks away and appeared to be somewhat smaller than the Scheuble. Maria and Oskar climbed the stairs to the small lobby and entered the hotel. They walked to the registration desk and asked the clerk, an elderly rather rotund lady if their friend had just checked in. They went on to say there was to be a wedding and the bachelor party was this evening. They needed to warn the groom that his ex-wife was planning on coming from the States to disrupt the wedding. "Buster" as they called him was certain to be around for her to find. She somehow found out he was staying here tonight. "Here's his picture taken at the airport, have you seen him yet?"

She looked at each of them carefully, and said, "That bitch, he seems like such a nice man, quite handsome you know. He left just a few minutes ago, wearing a very good-looking gray suit. What a shame hasn't she anything better to do than cause trouble?"

"Did he say when he'd return?" Oskar asked.
"No, but he paid his bill. He said he would be leaving early in the morning."

"Would you please see that he gets a message about this, may I have a piece of stationery and an envelope?"

With that, she turned smiling and pulled from beneath the desk counter the requested items along with a ballpoint pen. "You may write your note at the desk over there." She said pointing to a small writing table near the pay phone.

"Thank you so much." Oskar said as he and Mary walked over to the table where Oskar went to work on his warning. "Dear Hotel Guest, the management would like to personally welcome you to the hotel and would like to offer you a complimentary beverage of your choice at the hotel bar." He then folded the page and inserted it into the envelope, sealed the flap and walked back to the desk with a friendly smile on his face.

"I will see that Mr. Schultz, I mean Buster gets this as soon as he returns." She giggled as she wrote Gerhard Schultz on a post-a-note, affixed it to the envelope and placed it in slot 312, while Oskar carefully observed.

CHAPTER 101

The taller man, at the moment going under the name of Gerard Schultz, stepped up to the reception desk and asked for Mr. Drucker.

"One moment please", as she picked up the telephone and said a few hushed words, only to make him a little wary as he tried to listen to the conversation but was unable to do so. "You may take the last lift to the fourteenth floor, and upon exiting please announce yourself to the receptionist." She instructed with a pasty smile.

The taller man said, "Thank you" and walked to the elevator as instructed. The door was heavily laden with brass, probably from the nineteenth century when the bank was founded. Inside, the floor was carpeted in a deep burgundy and the walls looked like they were lined with teak, very expensive he thought, wondering whose account they rifled to outfit it. The ride to the fourteenth floor was quiet, unlike most European elevators whose useful lives had long since passed.

"Good afternoon." Came the sweet voice of the receptionist seated at a desk devoid of a single article, except a telephone. "You are here to see Herr Drucker?"

"Yes, I have a two o'clock appointment with him."

Considering that numbers not names are the common denominator in this type of bank, she did not ask for his name and said, "Please follow me."

He watched as she rose from behind the desk. She was young, in her early twenties he guessed, but quite nicely developed he thought. Her legs were long and her dark blue dress was short. She dressed quite simply, with white pearls and white pumps. As Hampton watched her bottom move under her dress as she walked, he adjusted and brought his thinking into line with a jolt. Remembering how he came to be in this place in his life without a home and on the run, mostly because of his dalliance with a beautiful young woman, starting in a place of business.

"Good afternoon." Drucker stood and came around his desk. As at the reception desk Drucker's was no different, devoid of all work materials only much larger. He wondered if they ever worked or whether this was only to impress their clients with the illusion that the only business they were interested in was theirs alone, thus no other files or distractions. The taller man however didn't care a wit about the desk or the office, he just wanted his bearer bond and to be away from this dangerous link to his freedom.

"Good afternoon, my account number is 175491A, do you want my security code now?"

"I know who you are, rather what your account number is." Drucker said.

The taller man taken back by the statement glanced warily around the office and said, "How do you know who I am?"

"Because you said you would be in my office at two o'clock and since you were my only appointment at that hour, I assumed. I would of course need your security code to complete our business." He said with a smile.

"It is 1486." Hampton said.

"Thank you, we can proceed now if you like." Drucker said. "I have prepared the bearer bond and only need your visual approval. They will be in your hands if accurate. Your account balance is zero at the moment, and as you say you will be adding a substantial sum in the near future. We will make an exception and maintain the account without a balance for you."

Hampton checked the total of 3,923,757.20 Swiss francs, which he had earlier calculated, representing the $2,157,000, US, that was transferred, plus a few days interest, as it was slightly more than he expected.

"That is correct." He said as he picked up the certificate. "Thank you." He turned and walked toward the door.

"Thank you, we look forward to your next deposit." Drucker said at a somewhat elevated voice level, as the taller man turned the corner and walked toward the elevator.

"What a joke, I'm never coming here again." He thought as he entered the elevator and pushed the button to the lobby. When he arrived on the ground floor, as a matter of instinct he surveyed the lobby systematically, checking every facial expression as well as accompanying body language before moving across the room to the front door. His next destination was his prime Swiss bank, The Zurich Industrial Bank, a short distance away. He had been to this bank a number of times in the past and felt very comfortable with his personal security when visiting, and their professionalism, when it comes to client confidentially.

CHAPTER 102

Oskar called Higgins, this time with better news. "Higgins, this is Oskar."

"Oskar, I'm sorry again that he managed to slip away from you old man, but don't take it personally he's made a career of doing just that."

"Higgins, I have better news than I provided on the last call. Maria and I canvassed the taxi drivers in the area with a fresh picture taken last night, found the driver and he took us to his new hotel. He's registered under the name Gerhard Schultz. My guess is that the package he was waiting for at his last hotel contained this new identity." Oskar reported with pride in salvaging his part of the case.

"Wonderful work Oskar. Where is he now?" Higgins inquired.

"Well my friend, I don't know but I do know he intends to return to his hotel to pick up his things before he leaves. He told the desk clerk he was leaving in the morning but I wouldn't trust anything he says. I can't risk using the same type of transmitter I used last time. I think I'll try to plant an intermittent device in his luggage, one that only reports when I call it up on my receiver. That way he can sweep his belongings and would never turn up my device, unless I happened to be calling it at the time. I believe if I'm careful I can avoid detection. Are you going to get the authorities involved now that we think we can track him?" Oskar asked.

"I need to get right back to you on that. Keep a close leash on him, and great work Oskar." Higgins said again with total respect for his old friend.

Higgins called me but my line was busy. He decided to walk up to my room in order to give me the latest bit of encouragement. The door was open and he saw that I was talking on the phone and Art was sitting in a chair on the balcony and motioned him in.

"How's Valarie?" Art asked.

"She's doing just great. I'll have to drag her away when this thing is over if it ever is."

"Well my friend, it might be getting closer than you thought a few minutes ago." Higgins said with a show of confidence that I needed at this point.

"What do you mean----what's happened?"

"Our bloodhound Oskar has performed a minor miracle. It seems he's once again proven himself to be the master sleuth I've known him to be. He and not to forget Maria, picked up the trail of our man in Zurich and have located his current hotel and room number. The trick now is to have some police intervention upon his arrival back at the hotel, before he has a chance to slip away again. Oskar is planting another bug in his clothes, this time a simple intermittent bug that transmits only on call, which will be difficult if not impossible to find."

"Great news Higgins, we need to get back to Detective Verta and see if his people can get moving on this, and fast."

"With your permission, I'll ring up Juan now." Higgins said, anticipating my approval.

"Please do, we can't afford to lose him now."

With that, Higgins pulled Detective Verta's card from his pocket and called his cell phone. Verta answered quickly and Higgins informed him of the most recent turn of events and the need to move quickly. There was a long pause, after which Higgins said, "Yes, thank you."

"Juan put me on hold and called his Captain. The last time he called him and told him that we'd lost the suspect in Zurich, he refused to call for emergency extradition procedures when they didn't even know if the suspect was in Switzerland at the time. This was entirely different because our on the ground operatives are currently tracking his moves. The Captain said he'd get back to him within the hour and gave strong instructions not to lose him again."

"Perfect, maybe you and I should hop a flight to Zurich and be there for the kill. I mean arrest." I said looking at Art, being unable to avoid a smile.

Art looked at me with one of his typical "are you nuts" expressions on his face and said, "You're not serious----are you?"

"Well as a matter of fact I am. Zurich's beautiful in the summer and I'll treat you to a fabulous dinner, like you've never experienced in your entire sheltered life." I answered with a devilish grin, running from ear to ear.

"I hate to see you go, but there's no more trouble you can get in here in Lisbon. Let me assure you, if I was a year or two younger you'd have to tie me to that tree out there to keep me off the plane to Zurich." Higgins commented with his normal good humor and a beaming face.

"What the hell----blow in my ear, fly me first class and I'll follow you anywhere." Art replied this time smiling after hearing Higgins' bout of envy.

"Settled! I'll make the reservations. Higgins, would you mind checking in with Oskar and see if everything is still under control?"

"Right away, it will be my pleasure." He said as he walked from the room to the stairs and down to his office.

I made the necessary arrangements for us to fly to Zurich at 7:15 P.M., while Art went back to his room to check on things at his office. Thirty minutes later he returned to my room.

"I need to call Tom Claudius and get this Hampton tie-in cleared up right away, but first I want that report from Frank Hixon as to how Tom fits in with this gang before I call though."

"If you want I can try and reach him to see if he's had a chance to follow up with that guy in his old unit."

"Good, that would help. If he can just reach him on the phone, he should be able to clear things up one way or another."

Art punched Frank's number in Portland. "Frank Hixon." Came the response on his direct line.

"Frank, Art. I'm calling from Portugal on the same case we've been working on. Did Jimmy call you back about this guy Hampton's tie in with Tom Claudius in Nam?"

"Yeah, he did and I made the call. The guy was at the store and they said he'd be back in about ten minutes----by now I guess."

"Frank, would you please call me on my cell number here? You still have it?"

"Yeah, I'll get right back to you. You want to know how this Hampton guy fits in with Tom Claudius----if he does at all, right?"

"That's right Frank, thanks."

CHAPTER 103

Higgins appeared at the door like a ghost. Art was certain he'd been in his element when he served England in her most secret agency. "Gentlemen," He said as Art looked up toward the open door in my room, "I have some news from abroad as well as here in Lisbon."

"Come in and give us the good news." I said in anticipation.

Higgins walked into the room with a look of accomplishment on his face, a face that always looked positive, or optimistic anyway, even when the news wasn't so good. "It is good news, considering what news we've received recently. I spoke with Oskar and he managed to slip into our target's room and successfully plant a device in the handle of his valise in a way that will almost with certainty avoid detection. He also placed an identical device in the heel of his casual comfortable walking shoes. He did so in case the target changed clothes upon his return and decided to leave without his valise, wearing casual attire. Of course should he decide not to come back to his room at all and just fly away, our goose is cooked. I don't suggest that will be the factual outcome, I'm only pointing to a possible eventuality that could turn into reality, God forbid." He stated, with his interesting approach in delivering a status report that was positive, yet provided the necessary cover to allow him to be a successful prognosticator in every possible outcome.

"Great news, anything else?" I asked.

"Yes as a matter of fact, I just moments ago received a ring from Detective Verta who wanted me to inform you that his Captain and the Chief of Police in

Lisbon have spoken with the necessary Government officials and have approved the issuance of a warrant of arrest for Hampton, AKA a list too long to possibly repeat. He named them all, most of which were provided by you gentlemen. The paperwork will be wired to Swiss and French authorities as well as Interpol within the hour. It seems that the Santos murders have become a major issue and hot item in Portugal, because it turns out Mr. Santos is the nephew of Ingrid Polares the deputy mayor of Lisbon. She ran on a law and order ticket and her own nephew and favorite grandniece were murdered in broad daylight and the police have not apprehended the killer." Higgins explained this latest twist to the apparent delight of his special audience.

"That's wonderful. I guess the attempted murder of a Yankee investigator was not sufficient to light the fuse on this investigation."

"Well, it looks like you fellows are headed for the grand finale----sure you don't need some help?" Higgins asked beaming with delight at the way things have developed for his two guests in the short period of less than twenty-four hours.

"Higgins, you are welcome on our team anytime, anyplace. In fact, if you would seriously like to come, you will be our guest. Every expense will be paid and you could personally introduce us to Oskar and Maria. What do you think?"

Higgins looked at me with a look of disbelief, his mind churning and finally said, "Let me talk with Rosa, I'll be right back." He hurried from the room and chased down the hall to the stairs, probably taking three steps at a time before reaching the main floor.

"Are you alright with this?" I said turning to Art.

"Are you kidding? This guy is great, and his contacts and experience in foreign matters of this type is a real find. I absolutely agree, and maybe he can play gin better than you."

"I don't know about that, but I bet he can find us a decent hotel and some fine Swiss dining, that is if we aren't on a stakeout somewhere in a Zurich back alley."

"Since you bring that subject up, this isn't likely to be a cakewalk. This guy Hampton is slick and very dangerous. My guess is we'll be looking for him in Paris before the day is over tomorrow." Art observed while I was contemplating the next move Hampton was likely to take, Higgins burst through the doorway with an ear-to-ear smile.

"Rosa says she can spare me for a day or so and pointed out that she runs the place anyway. She also said she hasn't seen me as excited with life for a long time, since I've been while dabbling in this case with you fellows. She said she'll also have a talk with you two, to insist that you get me back in one piece." To that he broke into laughter and said, "I do believe I need a ticket on this evening's flight to Zurich." Higgins added, still showing his excitement about being a part of a major investigation again.

"I'll book another seat. Should we make hotel reservations?"

"I'll speak to Oskar, you take care of my flight arrangements."

He left and went back to his office to call Oskar while I called Swissair and made arrangements for another ticket. Art's cell phone rang and he stepped out on my balcony to take the call.

"Hello."

"Art, Frank. I've got the information about Hampton during Nam."

"You talked to that guy in his unit?"

"Yeah, pretty interesting. It seems that their rifle squad got split off from their platoon during a heavy firefight north of Da Nang. It was nighttime and half of the squad was killed. Their platoon leader radioed to them to pull back. After they retreated to a safer position, Hampton asked where Claudius was. He said he was right next to him when all hell broke loose. Hampton said "I know exactly where he"----disobeyed his squad leader and took off into the night to find him. He found him in a thicket, covered with blood and unconscious. He put him over his shoulder and hauled him through enemy territory a couple of kilometers, to safety and a med-evac chopper. Tom Claudius survived and of course went to bat for Hampton who was in trouble for disobeying orders. Claudius' wounds were treatable, but had Hampton not gone back he would have died from loss of blood from his neck wound before the Kong would have found him. Tom Claudius said he'd never forget what Hampton did for him and my guess is that's why he gave his younger brother a job whenever he needed one." Hixon explained.

"Boy oh boy, this is really going to upset Chuck! Thanks so much Frank, great work." Art said as he cleared his cell phone.

490

CHAPTER 104

I was still talking to Swissair, and when I hung up I walked out to the balcony to sit with Art----and noticed the look on his face.

"What's up, you look like you lost your dog?"

"Worse. Tom's going to really be upset when you talk with him." Art said without expression.

"Why, what happened?"

"Hampton, or Mason saved Tom's life in Nam and of course he never forgot it. That's probably why Tom hired his younger brother and put him to work in several companies he controlled including TechX." Art went on to explain in detail what Frank Hixon told him.

"My God, Tom won't want us chasing after the guy who gave him a second chance at life."

"Well, that needs to be Tom's call doesn't it? The guy's a bloodthirsty, cold-blooded killer. What I don't understand is why Phil Hampton would bite the hand that fed him. It sure looks like these jobs came only out of a feeling of obligation to Mason or whatever he goes by." Art concluded.

"Is it possible that Mason didn't know that Phil worked for Tom this time?"

"It's possible, because it seems a little weird that a guy saves another and then turns against him."

"I need to call him, now. He needs to know that Gerard Mason Hampton is the guy we've been chasing around the world, and who's been trying to kill everyone that gets in his way on this case. He also needs to know that the only TechX inside suspect is his brother Phil Hampton. Everything points to him, but at the moment we don't know where he is." I said as I picked up my cell phone and placed the call, first to Tom's home number.

After a few rings. "Hello." Tom answered.

"Tom, Chuck in Lisbon. I need to update you on the case."

"Great Chucky, have you caught the bastards?"

"No, but the Portuguese Government has issued warrants for the arrest of one of the principals in the case, and through some help from an ex-patriot Brit, former intelligence guy, his friends in Zurich have him under surveillance as we speak. The Lisbon Police are asking for his immediate arrest and extradition back to Lisbon."

"That's great news, wonderful job Chucky. I knew I could count on you. I really appreciate what you've done." Tom said with total sincerity.

"We've got a problem Tom."

"What do you mean? It sounds like you've got this thing on its way to a finale?"

"Tom, that's the problem, you may not like the finale. It seems like the killer we've been chasing is a guy you know----and is pretty important to you."

"Chucky, who the hell is it? Come on, stop pussyfooting around, and just tell me!" He said with anxiety in his voice.

"Gerard Mason Hampton!"

Tom's end of the line was silent for the longest time while he digested this astounding news. Finally he said, "That's impossible because he was killed in Europe seven or eight years ago----his brother told me."

"I know that's on the official record. We got this from another guy in the unit, a guy Hampton tried to recruit into his nasty business of hired guns only two years ago ---- he ain't dead! I know first hand because he tried to kill me yesterday in Lisbon.

Bull shit, he wouldn't do this to me. We had a certain----bond. You just don't do that after all that went before." Tom said, ending with a softer tone, almost a whisper----his voice trailing off.

"Tom, I know the guy saved your life in Nam."

"How the hell did you find that out, we never discussed it again after I thanked him?

"We heard that from the guy he tried to hire."

"Unbelievable. I don't know what to say. Here I am sending you around the world to hunt down this guy and cause his execution----when he saved my life. How can I do that?"

"Well there's more to the equation. How close are you to Phil Hampton?"

"Well, I've known him for years and he's worked for me in several different companies. The first time he called me he said his brother saw something about me in some magazine or paper. I forget, and told Phil I'd see if there was an opening since he was looking for work. I of course would have hired him if he were worthless----because of the debt I could never repay to Mason. Mason never asked me for a thing. In fact, I never talked with him since I thanked him from my hospital bed for saving my life. I can't tell you how important that man is to me, and the character and courage he had, to go back and risk his life----expecting nothing but trouble from his commander for disobeying an order."

"What do you want me to do? Art and I are scheduled to fly to Zurich in a few hours. Also, every indication looks like Phil Hampton may have brought his brother into the scheme and orchestrated the whole mess. Was he any good in any of the jobs you gave him?"

"Well that's an embarrassing question and the simple answer is no. That's why I moved him around so much without giving him the top job. It didn't take long for his co-workers to see that he didn't have it. But I made a commitment to myself that as long as I was able, I'd find him work with one of my companies. That's the least I could do for Mason----and when I heard he was dead, I decided then that I had the self-imposed obligation to take care of him for life. That's the least I could do for the brother of a guy that gave *me* a chance for life, don't you think?"

"I understand what you're saying Tom, but do you know if Mason ever knew that you controlled TechX or that you gave Phil that first job?"

"You know, that's a good question. Since I never heard from Mason, I have no idea. I only hope he knew I tried to help Phil. Mason was too proud to ever ask for anything from me. He obviously knew I was successful when he referred Phil to me for a job. The more I think about it, I'd wager that Mason didn't know I was involved with TechX, because if there's something in his makeup that allows him to do horrible things like you describe, I can't imagine him hurting *me* in any way. You say he changes identities, what's he going by now?"

"He's going by Gerhard Schultz, supposedly from Munich."

"You say your people tracked him down and have he's under surveillance now? What's he doing?"

"He moved from one hotel to another and changed his identity. We think he obtained a new passport at his previous hotel."

"Do you mean he's cornered as we speak----in a hotel room?"

"No not quite, he checked into a second hotel and left a few hours ago, but our people expect him back."

"Maybe he's meeting Phil Hampton, I know Zurich pretty well. Where's he staying?"

"It's a small hotel called The Ruetli, do you know it?"

"No, it doesn't sound familiar."

"The balls in your court, do we let this thing go or do we finish this off and find Phil and get to the truth?"

"You say the wheels are in motion to arrest Mason in Zurich?"

"That's right, there's no way we can change that. The police will do what they decide to do."

"OK, go to Zurich and see if you can track down Phil Hampton in the process. It sounds like he's the bastard causing all this grief for me----and you too. And when the police catch up with Mason, find out if he knew about me in this mess."

"I will Tom, sorry to report this kind of information." I told my friend.

"Nonsense, everything works out in the end, it always does. Keep me informed----and thanks. I can never repay you for everything you've gone through trying to help me."

"You're right about that." I replied laughing as I punched the end button on my cell phone.

"According to Tom, he can't see Mason as he calls him, doing anything to hurt him or his investments. It must be that he didn't know that Phil worked for him, and if Phil is the driving force, he never told Mason about the link with Tom, knowing he wouldn't do it if it was known." I tried to explain in a convoluted way.

"Where does that leave us? Anything we do is going to hurt his savior Mason." Art said.

"Good question----simple answer. I say the ship has sailed on Mason, and besides, that the bastard tried to kill me twice and could have killed you too in my hotel room. We don't owe him a thing."

"I agree. I want to get him and also see that no good Phil Hampton is brought to justice." Art said with a frowning look of disgust.

"I don't know about you, but I could use a tall frosty beer----'bout now, how about you partner?"

"You're on. I bet Higgins can rustle us up a couple----right fast." Art said as they headed out the door and down the stairs to Higgins office.

On the way they found Rosa coming out of the kitchen and asked her where they might find a cool beer about now.

"You go right out to the garden patio----the door is at the end of the hallway. It has a wonderful view of the ocean. I'll bring you the beer and Higgins will join you in a few minutes. I have something special for you to eat with your drinks. Before I forget, take extra care that Higgins comes back to me in good condition from Zurich." Rosa instructed with a serious look on her face.

"You can count on that." I said smiling and hoping it was a true statement.

The garden patio was an area they hadn't seen before. It had low adobe slab walls with red flowering vines creeping over and back like a slow motion tennis game. The vines were old, with some trunks measuring four or more inches in diameter. On the patio were two round glass-topped tables, each with four metal chairs and padded cushions of yellow and white stripes. The ocean view over the low walls was as advertised----

magnificent to say the least. The late afternoon sun was low in the western horizon and the blue-green waves flashed with silver and hues of orange as the reflection of the sun tangled in the breakers as they crashed onto the white sandy beach----again and again in a mesmerizing action that left the brain and any thoughts in pause as more important things in life suddenly became small and insignificant. Art and I sat at the table nearest the ocean and quickly fell under its spell in a silent reflection until the moment was broken by----"Have you boys tasted real Portuguese beer?"

"Well as I a matter of fact I don't believe I have----you Art?" I replied to Higgins who stood with a silver ice bucket full of frosty brown beer bottles. Rosa was right behind him with her tray of goodies, which guaranteed a ten-pound, weight gain for anyone. I was curious to see if Higgins actually ate any of her treats, because his waistline didn't appear to indicate so.

I brought Higgins up to date on my call with Tom Claudius and he indicated he had more news from Oskar.

"Oskar said this time they wouldn't lose him if he came back to the hotel. Maria was stationed in a room across the hall from Mason where she managed to remove the small fish eye peephole in the door and replace it with a mini-camera that could rotate to afford a full vision of the hall from the elevator or stairs----all the way to the room. She hooked it up to the TV in the room to serve as a monitor. Oskar found a table in the lobby bar with a direct view to the stairs, the elevator and front desk. He and Maria were in constant radio contact.

CHAPTER 105

Mason Hampton walked into his primary bank and asked for Mr. Heinz. He was directed to the elevator as he always had been for the last eight years since he first opened the account. That was the same year he was pronounced legally dead from an automobile accident in Italy. It was a timely opportunity. He had taken on a contract to eliminate what he concluded was a bad person and needed to dispose of the body. He rented a car in his own name and placed his victim in the front seat after being careful that the cause of death would show only injuries that could be found in a serious automobile accident. On the deceased's finger he placed a ring that he wore from his military service days and managed to disfigure the victim so badly that dental records would be impossible to match. This extraordinary damage to the corpse would need to be covered up by an automobile plunge of major proportion off a cliff----one that he of course orchestrated.

The whole scheme of his personal untimely death worked to his advantage in two ways. First it eliminated any possible charges from past activities, allowing him to start with a new clean record and persona that would forever change to suit his needs. Secondly he was able to charge his client an additional sum to insure that the body would never be found again and would remain a missing person. He received the equivalent of $700,000.00, US dollars plus expenses. This tax-free sum was the start of his Swiss *retirement account,* which he established thanks to the proper introductions by his client in Italy.

"Good afternoon Mr. Euro Consultant's president." Hans Heinz said smiling, as he never knew his real name and under the circumstances Hampton didn't have a real name to offer. Hans was a small man with a hawkish face, long nose and rimless glasses. He was not yet forty but due to his Italian contacts, he had become one of the largest producers of new business for the bank. As his compensation was based on total deposits brought in, he earned a substantial living by Swiss banking standards, one that allowed him to own a villa on a hillside high above the city. Every workday morning he took a tram down the mountain and then a taxi to the bank.

"Good afternoon Hans, how's life treating you?"

"I am excellent thank you, particularly when *you* come to the bank with large deposits." Hans Heinz said with a slight upwards twitch of his rather thin lips---- which for him constituted a big smile.

"Good. I'm pushed for time this afternoon and need to be on my way. Here's the bearer bond I'd like added to my account."

"Excellent, I have prepared the necessary deposit forms. As usual it will go to a general bank account which will lose any trace of its disposition. Then I will transfer it into your Euro Consultants numbered account. Is there anything else I can do for you?"

"No, that will be all. By the way, will you be available at the bank over the next two weeks, or on holiday----considering you make so much money?" Hampton said, teasing his banker as he has done over the years.

"I intend to be here, however you know you can always reach me twenty four hours a day on my cell. So if you need anything, anytime, just call and it is handled no matter where I might be."

"I know that. Watch out for all those ladies who want your money." Hampton said as he always did when ending a conversation with his personal banker. His work completed, he stood and quickly made his way down the hallway toward the elevator for his return to the hotel and on to his flight to Paris to meet with Phil.

CHAPTER 106

Rosa brought Art a facsimile report received from Frank Hixon in Portland. It contained the information on the remaining members of Hampton's squad in Viet Nam. Of the four still living, aside from Tom Claudius and Hampton, two still lived in southern Alabama in their home town, a third lived in Detroit and was an autoworker close to retirement, and the last Paul Prill, was hard to run down because he has been out of the country for the last twenty years living in Paris. It seems that according to a source of Hixson's, his military record had recently been requested by the US State Department. After a dozen phone calls and calling in some favors Hixon learned that Mr. Prill is strongly suspected of arms dealing to third world countries. So far he's been too slick for anyone to prove anything, but they're now quite concerned that he's moved from small time deals and has substantially upped the ante and recently arranged for the sale of high-grade plutonium from the former Soviet Union to a Middle East terrorist. Frank also learned from the Alabama boy that Hampton and Prill were like brothers in Nam and talked openly about working together after they left the service. He has a legitimate business as a front----Euro Outfitters, selling military uniforms, boots, canteens etc. This allows him to openly call on these military organizations for their basic needs, while selling them illegal weapons out the back door.

"Very interesting", I said to Art upon reading the report. "Two-to-one our Mr. Hampton is heading for Paris and will hook up with his old buddy Paul Prill, why--- who knows?"

"We better gather up Higgins and head for the airport, are you packed?"

502

"Ten-minutes, see if Higgins is ready."

Hampton took a taxi to within two blocks of his hotel. It was getting late and he didn't have time to waste nor did he want to miss his flight to Paris. He carefully checked the street, making certain he wasn't being followed, then headed for the Hotel Ruetli. Upon entering, he had not intended to stop by the desk but the desk clerk called him over.

"Mr. Schultz, I have a message and a facsimile for you." The desk clerk said.

Hampton froze and quickly gathered his composure, casually sweeping the area with his trained eyes, looking for out of place people or things. He noticed a man in the bar glancing up toward him and then down at his newspaper. Sensing the man to be a threat to his life and existence, he went to the clerk, grabbed the message and fax, casually looked at his watch and walked back out the door and hailed the first taxi he could find. He told the driver to take him back to the financial district, and fast, as he left a package at his bank. He turned and looked out the rear window at the little man in his tweed sport jacket, scurrying around, anxiously trying to get a taxi.

He turned to the note with the name Gerhard Schultz on the envelope. It looked to be nothing more than a complimentary drink from the management, but he knew it was not from the management but from the little man trying to discover his current appearance. He then looked about again and did not see a taxi nearby and asked the driver to take the next left and go by a property a few blocks from here that he was 'considering acquiring'. That should lose his follower for a while he thought and opened the envelope, not before first checking for abnormalities such as an explosive or surveillance device and was confident there were none.

The facsimile letterhead said, "From the Desk of Tom Claudius".

Dear Mr. Schultz,

I am writing this to tell you that you will soon be having
company at the hotel from those that know most everything
about the TechX situation. I am surprised that you were
involved in doing this to a company I control, as I have over the years continued to do everything possible for Phil, even when
I heard you had passed away. I am telling you this in order to
give you a possible life-saving head start and maybe another opportunity to live, like you did for me. I consider us even now, although I know in my heart, I can never do enough.

Tom

Hampton's eyes glazed over, looking at the page in a rage, he began shaking and became furious. "That son-of-a-bitch! That son-of-a-bitch! That bastard, how could he do this to me, how could he?"

The driver turned and asked if he needed anything, and Hampton snapped no in a short, curt manner. He thought of his brother and how his greed

504

and gambling caused his own life to be altered forever, and now doing this to a guy that helped Phil over and over again because Tom appreciated something he did in Nam, not for money or praise but because at the time it was right, just the right thing to do. Hampton was so angry with his brother and the situation he didn't concern himself with the possibility of someone following his taxi. He decided he would have to think very carefully how he would handle this problem, as well as his brother Phil.

CHAPTER 107

Oskar lost track of his target immediately and his driver to take him to the airport. He and Maria whom he reported his current status to by radio, would just have to watch as many Paris flights as possible in order to try and find him, although they had no way of knowing he was going to Paris or France at all, except that Higgins told Oskar that the suspect was carrying a large amount of French francs. In the meantime he needed to call Higgins and inform him once again of their misstep in tracking this very elusive target.

"Higgins, Oskar here." He said, sounding short of breath and with scratchy cell reception.

"Oskar, how are you, any news?"

"There is and it isn't good this time. He walked into the hotel, was called to the desk for a phony message I left him for complimentary drinks on the management and walked out without going to his room. He seemed to be in a hurry and took a taxi waiting out in front and disappeared. Maria and I are on our way to the airport, only because we don't know where else to pick up his trail. I'm real sorry Higgins, I guess you fellows won't be coming tonight, right?"

"I don't know I need to talk with the chaps." Higgins said. "I'll let you know----all right?"

Higgins met me in the lobby with his bags and filled me in on the latest report from Oskar. "Higgins, have you heard back from your contact to see if Gerhard Schultz is listed for a flight out tonight? If so, we can change our flight to try and pick up his trail at his destination."

"I'll get on it immediately. I am surprised that he hasn't called. He's usually quite prompt about providing this sort of information." Higgins said with renewed enthusiasm for another chance to travel with the team.

CHAPTER 108

Tom Foster, the name Phil Hampton chose for his new identity, sat around his apartment all day brooding then went down to the bistro expecting to see Mary. Her friends told him she was sorry but she had to work that evening and might be in the next night. He ordered a beer, stared into the glass as if he was the only person in the bistro, and started up again with his *poor me* thinking. He was getting anxious to start his life and hated the circumstances that made him a prisoner in the shabby Paris apartment provided by Mason's friend Paul. He was after all a rich man with his bearer bond, but not *that* rich he decided. He couldn't get the "bitch Victoria" out of his mind. She stole his money----maybe eight million dollars. She was a common thief he thought. In all his mental gymnastics it never occurred to him that maybe *he* was the common thief and the money he thought was his would only be after he himself stole the money owing his partners in crime----his brother and Victoria, which he fully planned on doing, not to mention the fact that the entire amount was effectively stolen from TechX.

He drank beer after beer sitting at the bar amongst the steady clientele which he totally ignored even when someone struck up a conversation with him in English. He decided that he wanted his brother, a man with knowledge on how to track down people and get what he wanted to find Victoria and get his money back. Of course he thought he would have to pay Mason the amount he expected, but he didn't think Victoria was entitled to a dime after what she did to him. He knew he couldn't contact Mason and was upset that his own brother would leave him sitting in squalor----for days.

CHAPTER 109

Mason Hampton arrived at the Zurich airport still steaming at the stupidity and embarrassment his brother had caused him. He was so upset he temporarily lost his edge, his learned ability to sense his enemy and anticipate their moves. He soon came to his senses and checked in at Air France, told them he had no baggage and as he was over forty five minutes early did not want to go to Air France's gate areas. Instead he went to a bar near Singapore Airlines, a short distance away. After ordering a glass of wine, which he recognized was in itself a violation of every principle he knew that was designed to keep him safe, before raising the glass to his lips he pulled his cell phone out of the inside pocket of his suit jacket and placed a call to Paul Prill in Paris.

The phone rang a number of times and finally it was answered. "Hello."

Recognizing the familiar voice, "Paul----Mason!"

"Mason I've been expecting you. Where are you?"

"I'm at the airport in Zurich, and will be leaving in about forty minutes on Air France flight 2555, arriving Paris de Gaulle at 7:10 P.M."

"Good, Phil is in the bistro building apartment and probably climbing the walls."

"He should! I'm God-damned upset with him. He got me into something had I known the facts I would have skinned him alive. Now I don't know what I'll do with him."

"What did he do?"

"He screwed over Tom Claudius. After what we went through in Nam, my own brother fucks over a guy I risked my life to save----that's total bullshit. He really did a number on him, cost him millions and maybe ruined his company. A guy that gives him job after job and I didn't know he was still working for him. Can you believe that shit?"

"Calm down, do you think you're being followed?"

"Yeah I've been followed----probably to the airport."

"Where are you right now?" Paul asked.

"I'm in the bar at the Singapore Airlines gate."

"Good, sit right there. Forget the Air France flight. Within the hour there'll be a page at the Singapore Airlines gate for a Mr. Wilhelm. Go to the courtesy phone and answer. If the person says Paul sent me, do as he says. I'll have a private jet fly you to Paris. Just sit where you are and have a drink, I'm in charge now. Do you understand?"

"Thanks Paul, and for your information I'm traveling under the passport of Gerhard Schultz."

"See you in Paris, Gerhard." Paul said and the line went dead.

CHAPTER 110

Higgins was in his office for forty minutes while Art and I sat on the garden patio. He walked out and said, "I'm so sorry, my man had a family emergency and was delayed with my request. However, I'm pleased to report that he has the answer. Mr. Gerhard Schultz has a confirmed flight on Air France 2555, departing Zurich at 5:55 P.M. this evening for Paris. I then called Detective Verta with the update, and he said the paperwork was still in process and hadn't been signed by the Portuguese State Department official----which is required. Apparently he was not at work today and they are trying to find him and obtain his signature. Detective Verta said there's no way it can be processed before the flight leaves, so he'd put in a request to change the wanted party's last known location to Paris and will provide the French authorities with his alias as well as the Air France flight number."

"Excellent work Higgins, of course you're welcome to come as before, only to Paris. Is that all right with you?" I asked, knowing that his European contacts have thus far been invaluable in our search for answers.

"I'm certain that Rosa would be just as concerned with Paris as with Zurich, but I *can* promise her perfume and win her over. The short answer is yes, as is the long answer. Book the flights and viva la France." Higgins said with obvious delight.

Higgins called Oskar and informed him that the trail had once again been found and that the suspect was booked on Air France Flight 2555 departing at 5:55 P.M. He asked him to confirm that he was in fact on the flight, what he was wearing and that we would have someone pick him up at de Gaulle, as we'd reach Paris an hour after he lands. Higgins then called a retired Brit and close friend Albert Holmes in Paris to see if he could pick up the target on this short notice----until they arrived. As usual, Albert was home watching British football on satellite and jumped at the opportunity. Being a frustrated secret operative retiree, he maintained all of the necessary equipment should he ever be pressed into service, including a facsimile machine and a computer that was as fast as the speed of light, to hear him tell it. The photos were sent along with a brief recap of the case, and Albert was on his way to the airport.

I cancelled the Zurich flights and re-booked on Air France, leaving Lisbon at 6:00 P.M. and arriving in Paris at 8:15 P.M. As time was short we quickly gathered our belongings and Rosa drove the "Three Musketeers", as she delighted in calling us, to the Lisbon Airport in the hotel's Land Rover.

CHAPTER 111

Oskar and Maria without too much concern about being discovered reached 36 B, Air France Flight 2555's designated gate. They arrived thirty minutes before the earliest boarding's and felt confident that Schultz hadn't passed through the line. Had he arrived before them, with their good vantage point to observe the gate entry, he couldn't board without them seeing him. Their only fear was that he had arrived earlier, went into the restroom and changed his appearance, as he didn't have to resemble his new passport photo until clearing customs in Paris. This was a real possibility as he was out of their surveillance for more than an hour after leaving the hotel, and he could easily have stopped en-route and acquired different clothing. The last call for Flight 2555 was announced and the gate doors closed without in their opinion Mr. Gerhard Schultz on board.

Oskar placed a call to Higgins' cell phone but found it turned off, most likely due to regulations as he knew he'd be boarding the flight for Paris. He left a voice mail reporting his and Maria's surveillance and lack of a positive identification of Schultz boarding through the Flight 2555 gate.

CHAPTER 112

Mason Hampton was pleased with the arrangements made by his friend Paul Prill. The craft was a Gulfstream with a crew of three, including the flight attendant who offered him a cocktail upon boarding, however even with his current despondency about his brother's actions, he knew that his freedom and perhaps his life depended on clear thinking. He accepted a ginger ale and a plate of fresh iced jumbo shrimp. The plane was outfitted as an executive jet, with teak paneling, plush off-white carpeting, conference table and six oversized leather seats----far superior to anything he had experienced on first- class flights he had taken. The attendant introduced herself as Jennifer, and he knew right away she was British. She looked a young thirty, with trim figure, long legs and auburn hair hiding one of her green eyes.

"Mr. Prill said we should take very good care of you, as you are his oldest friend. That didn't come out right", she giggled, "not his oldest in age but oldest in years, you know----that he has known you."

Smiling, "you were probably right on the first count. Do you know Paul well?

"I have worked for him for three years and I love it. He is very kind and the greatest boss."

"Is this his plane?"

"Oh yes, but I usually fly the sister ship based in Paris."

"I had no idea he had these planes."

"He bought them just before I joined the company. They are usually very busy flying clients here and there. How long has it been since you have seen him?"

"About four years."

"Then that explains it doesn't it? He wanted me to tell you that his driver will pick you up at the plane when we arrive and the special customs agent will process you before you even *leave* the plane to eliminate red tape and unnecessary bureaucratic delays----as Paul says."

'As Paul says'----he might have a little more going than boss-employee I would guess, more power to him Mason thought. His business must be doing fine; two of these babies----even used cost twenty to thirty million each.

CHAPTER 113

We settled in on our flight to Paris. Higgins and I sat together and Art was seated directly across the aisle. Upon taking off I asked Higgins if it was time for a cocktail and he debated no more than a split second, "Scotch, if you please." He said, and we all ordered, and for the first time that day found the time to relax. Higgins was confident that his friend Albert Holmes would 'pick up the scent' upon arrival like the good tracker he was and call him on his cell phone as he followed Hampton from the airport. Higgins was also confident, Albert would bring along an ex-associate to assist.

Hampton arrived at 7:15 P.M. and was surprised that the customs official was so prompt and yet so relaxed for lack of a better word. A few questions and, "Have a nice stay in Paris, Mr. Schultz," as he stamped the passport and quickly exited the plane.

"Are they always this fast on private planes?"

"Usually, he is our regular customs agent and I think a friend of Mr. Prill's."

A friend is right, Mason thought. The limousine, a 500 series Mercedes with blackened windows was waiting on the tarmac at the foot of the Gulfstream's stairs. The chauffer climbed the steps after the customs agent deplaned to carry the bags, which in Hampton's case his work was easy. He moved to pick up Hampton's briefcase and was politely informed it wasn't necessary.

"I'll be riding with you. Mr. Prill wanted me to make certain you arrived safely." Jennifer said as she handed the chauffer her flight bag.

They walked down the steps to the tarmac with the chauffer following closely behind. He quickly, with one hand carrying Jennifer's bag, opened the passenger side door of the rear seat and Jennifer skillfully slid across the leather to the opposite side providing Mason with a nice view of her long legs and thighs, as she was a bit slow in adjusting her skirt. Mason settled in beside her on the soft leather seats. They were still moving off the tarmac when the telephone rang and the chauffer indicated that the call was "for the gentleman".

"Mason, how was the flight----everything OK?" Paul Prill asked.

"It was fine, you spoiled me. I'm not used to such special handling."

"Do you mean the flight, or Jennifer?" He asked, laughing.

"I meant the flight, but you are quite accurate on both counts."

"Where are you taking me----I need to find a hotel?"

"Nonsense, you're coming to my place. You'll be safe here and it'll give you a chance to catch your breath for a while and make some plans. I'm sorry you won't be able to meet my wife Sarah. She's visiting her parents in England for a few weeks. I'm happy to have the company."

"I didn't know you were married."

"Well, we don't usually have time for small talk. Sarah and I have been married for over three years now. It'll take about forty-five minutes to get here, so relax, have a drink----the bar's stocked, and don't think you can't have a drink because you're now under my protection and you don't need to be looking around every corner for signs of trouble. Is that a deal?"

"That's a deal, thanks for everything." Hampton said as he placed the phone back on the cradle.

The drive from the airport was slow until they left the busy thoroughfares and finally reached what appeared to be country roads.

"Where does Paul live?"

"He has a home in the country. He bought it when he and Sarah married. It was a large home on substantial land holdings, but in major disrepair as the property had been handed from heir to heir for the last several hundred years and the most recent heirs did not have the funds to maintain it. Paul bought the home and did a major renovation. The exterior looks the same but everything on the interior has been modernized and updated, as have the grounds. They invite me to stay there occasionally if I am flying out the next day and the car is at the airport anyway. There are plenty of bedrooms."

"It sounds nice."

"It is. Would you like a drink?"

Mason considered her offer and finally thought Paul is right, he has me covered and no one could possibly be following at the moment.

"That would be nice, what does he have in there?"

"Tell me what you like and I'll see if I can accommodate you. That didn't sound right----I mean what kind of drink." They both laughed and Mason asked for a Scotch neat and she joined him.

CHAPTER 114

The Air France Jet landed on time at de Gaulle Airport and "The Three Musketeers" as Rosa called us, cleared customs and stopped for a moment with bags in hand to check in with Albert Holmes when Higgins cell started ringing.

"Higgins here."

"Higgins, Oskar, he did not get on that flight. We checked every face boarding. We are certain. Maybe you can verify with your man on actual boarding documentation to check our surveillance."

"Thanks old man, we really appreciate the diligence you and Maria have demonstrated. Your check will be forthcoming."

"They said he didn't board in Zurich. I'll call Albert and confirm from this end."

"Albert, Higgins here in Paris, did you pick the gent up?"

"Higgins, I didn't see him. Are you certain he boarded this flight?"

"Albert, I believe he gave us the slip again. Our man in Zurich said the same thing. Thanks for your help. It was really appreciated. There will be a check forthcoming for your fine effort.

"Well, you heard my side of the conversation and that seems to say it all. I will call my man and have him check the actual departure record to verify if he did in

fact *not* board Flight 2555. Any other thoughts?"
Higgins asked.

"I don't know about you fellows, but I don't think
we can do much good at the airport. Higgins, as the
world traveler, suggest a good hotel where we can refresh,
relax, and plan our next move."

"I will do just that. I have a favorite, The Oxley,
not large, not too small, not too expensive, but not cheap,
with the finest restaurant this side of Rosa's kitchen and
located right in the heart of everything----and I might add
a wonderful bar, and oh yes the basics, great rooms."
Higgins suggested, grinning with anticipation.

"You're on. Let's do it. Do we need to call?"

"I have their number handy of course." Higgins
said as he reached in his pocket for his address book and
punched in the number.

Speaking in French, the only word that was
recognizable was Pierre, but according to his body
language, Higgins managed to accomplish his mission.

"Well, are we booked?"

"Not only are we booked, we are booked in style.
Pierre cannot do enough for us. It seems that he has not
forgotten the many bookings I made on behalf of British
Intelligence. He informs me they still are his best
customers and the bar turnover since I started the
alliance has been tremendous.

"I can't imagine that Higgins, I didn't know you
drank." Art said.

Higgins looked at Art for a long second----and broke into laughter, "Drink, man? I have yet to show you a true drinking man, one that can drink a snoot-full without the slightest sign of impairment. I have a reputation to uphold in the Oxley Bar, for all I know I hold the record, or some record, who the hell knows. I was drunk at the time." Higgins said, still laughing.

Art and I couldn't help but laugh with our new British friend with that wonderful personality and genuine charm. It was definitely time to re-group and plan the next step which appeared to center around Paul Prill and Euro Outfitters.

Upon settling into the taxi for the ride to the Oxley Hotel I suggested, "There are other options here---- Hampton may have charted a private plane out of Zurich to Paris or flew from another Swiss city, maybe Geneva or Bern, and then on to Paris, or even a different French city."

"Also, what we don't know is whether Hampton changed his identity one more time and left on a flight to Paris or even the same flight under a different name---- and a serious makeover." Art added.

"We should call the Reutle Hotel in Zurich and see if he's checked out. For all we know he may have returned to the room. If you could call your guy and check on the possibility of changing his reservation to another flight, and also see if his reservation was cancelled on 2555 or if he was just a no-show." I asked Higgins.

"I'll ask Oskar to check on the hotel, and then call my man."

"Higgins, can your man get a record of private flights and charters departing form Zurich to Paris, from say 4:00 P.M. to now? One more thing, can you ask him to check all flights into Paris in the last week, for a passenger named Tom Foster or Foster with initials of T either first or middle name?"

"The charter and private plane information was always important to British Intelligence and I've prevailed on him a number of times to get just that information, but it is time consuming and therefore a bit costly. I can ask him to search for the name Foster in his computer and fax us a report."

"Please ask him to do both. I want to get this thing wrapped up soon.

CHAPTER 115

The Mercedes limousine carrying Mason Hampton and flight attendant Jennifer rolled up to the electronic gates at Paul Prill's home just before 8:00 P.M. It was dusk, however Mason could see the high stone wall and the beautifully crafted iron gates, each curving upward in a graceful arch beginning at the height of the ten foot wall and joining in the center at a height of at least fifteen feet. The wrought iron design consisted of a pattern of long-stem arching floral arrangements, which to a trained eye appeared to be that of craftsmanship found in the early seventeenth century. The wall extended in both directions as far as the eye could see.

A man in a dark suit came up to the gate from what appeared to be a gatehouse tucked just inside and to the left. He conversed in French with the driver and the gates slowly and silently moved inward, allowing the limousine to move forward and onto the entry drive. The smooth cobblestone drive was lined with trees at least fifty feet tall and spaced every twenty feet. Through the trees one could see huge expanses of lawns and gardens that one might expect to see in photographs of the castles of Europe. The entry drive continued for perhaps a mile and then broke into the open where Mason saw a huge stone mansion perched on a rise, with grand porches encircled by railings of stone balustrades and fountains with frolicking nymphs, a setting befitting a grand former era of nobility, entertaining with lavish garden parties and formal grand balls.

The car pulled around a circular entry and in the center a large fountain spurted an umbrella of water, illuminated by a dozen or more tiny spot lights built into the base of the fountain, causing the effect of thousands of crystal glass prisms cascading in and endless stream of glistening facets into the pool below. The covered main entrance with wide sweeping granite steps led to the front door. Paul was standing on the landing with a broad grin on his face, as he for the first time was having the opportunity to show his old friend a symbol of his success----far exceeding the Gulfstream that transported him from Zurich. Paul wore a pair of jeans, white polo shirt and a pair of moccasins----no socks.

"Welcome to my humble abode." Paul Prill said to Mason as he was climbing the stairs with Jennifer a few steps behind.

"Well, you always had a talent for roughing it in style. Do you work here?" Mason said in jest, smiling and looking from right to left, taking in the grandeur and magnificence of the mansion.

"Yes in a manner of speaking---- actually I stole the place."

"Well I assumed that----are they still looking for you?"

"Very funny, come in and let's have a drink. Hi Jen, thanks for taking care of my partner here."

"No problem boss." She said with a wink.

"Join us in the library Jen."

"No thanks Paul. I think I'll settle in and take a nice hot bath. Regular room?"

"You bet----Sarah wants to put your name on the door since you use it so much."

"I think I need to see my apartment a little more, but I love your hospitality. Do you suppose Rene can fix me a snack, I haven't eaten since breakfast?"

"No problem, give him a jingle and tell him what you want."

"Thanks. Nice meeting you Gerhard." She said as she turned to the left after entering and disappeared down a hallway.

"Paul, I can't believe this, it's absolutely the most beautiful place I've ever seen." He said with sincerity.

"It's a higher profile than I wanted, but what the hell, the feds are all over me anyway so I thought I'd give them something to talk about. I'm very secure here and sweep the entire house and grounds daily for electronic intrusions. I'll have Dave take your bags to your room."

"It seems that I had to leave in a hurry, so I am without bags, I only have my briefcase and laptop." Mason responded still grinning.

"No problem, since we're both the same size you won't need to worry about clothes. Do you want to change out of that suit?"

"Nah, later, I'll just take off the jacket and tie." Mason said as he followed Paul down a wide, very high ceiling, and granite-floored hallway to the library.

CHAPTER 116

The Oxley Hotel was everything advertised by Higgins. It was a block from the Ritz Carlton, so any time they felt the need to hobnob with the rich and famous, they could walk the short block. The Oxley displayed a brass logo at the entry indicating that it had been established in 1827, and had been in continuous operation since. The feeling was comfortable and quiet, with dark paneled walls and thick carpets of royal blue trimmed with gold. The high lobby coffered ceiling was even further heightened by a balcony on the mezzanine surrounding the entire floor. Off the lobby was the small bar Higgins was so fond of. It was in keeping with the rest of the hotel, richly furnished with comfortable appearing leather chairs, high ceilings with antique chandeliers, sofas conveniently placed near a large stone fireplace which was not normally used in the summer and a piano bar, probably a favorite spot for Higgins.

We decided to meet in my room after everyone settled in. Upon entering the room, I was just opening my suitcase when my cell phone rang. John Sun was calling with an update.

"Chuck good to talk with you. I told Valarie that I would try to reach you on your cell, and she asked that you call her when you get an opportunity. She said she is fine and not to worry----but misses you."

"Thanks John, I've been on the run and just arrived with Art in Paris an hour or so ago."

"You *have* been traveling. Let me fill you in on KRL, Mr. Che and Mr. Wong. Mr. Wong was found floating in the harbor near the Central District. He was strangled and had been in the water for several days. The police have no suspects. Mr. Che blames Wong for any problems and claims he made a legitimate business deal with TechX and knows nothing about Sue Tang's murder. Che has been having trouble explaining how a legitimate business deal would involve wiring funds to an offshore bank, in the Cayman Islands. Inspector Li suspects that Billy Wong was murdered to keep him from talking and implicating Mr. Che in the sordid mess. Inspector Li requested that TechX file a formal complaint against KRL for possessing stolen property, namely pirated software. TechX agreed and signed a formal complaint. KRL could be made to pay substantial fines, and this approach may uncover, according to Inspector Li, the missing evidence to charge Mr. Chi with murder and conspiracy to commit murder, among other crimes, such as arson in Oregon, etc. Billy Wong's men involved in the attempted arson plot have confessed that Wong hired them, now that he is dead and they have no one to defend them."

I filled John in on Mason Hampton and the connection with Phil Hampton, and how we are now in Paris hoping to pick up Mason's trail and eventually lead us to Phil Hampton. I also asked if he wouldn't mind calling Preston and giving him an update.

"I'll try Valarie now and if I miss her please tell her I'll try to call as soon as I have a break, also that I miss her and hope to be back in Hong Kong in days not weeks."

"I will do that. Be very careful Chuck and do not forget this man is a cold- blooded, calculating murderer."

CHAPTER 117

In the library, Paul and Mason settled into soft deep burgundy leather chairs. This was for them an almost mystical view, one not in keeping with their backgrounds or the chosen careers of these two men, however the pair easily accepted the moment. They gazed through leaded glass windows, observing a broad expanse of lawns, hedges and gardens, boasting a plethora of color and grandeur in the fading light. They seemed to slide easily into the surroundings, which over the centuries this same room was most likely steeped in both moments of grandness and despair, but probably not criminal activity. They were served drinks in crystal glassware hardly noticing the arrival and departure of the butler. Most people could only experience such privilege in a movie scene.

"Tell me about Phil, have you heard from him since he went to the apartment?" Mason asked.

"No, I told him you would be in touch as soon as you arrived and to sit tight."

"There isn't a phone there is there?"

"No, but I'm sure you can reach him on his cell phone."

"I'll go see him tomorrow. I also have to decide where I'm going to live now that my house has been---- how do I put it, compromised."

"Where would you like to live? Why don't you work with me?"

"Paul, I think it's time for me to retire. Nothing as luxurious as you, but I have enough in my retirement account to live pretty well for the rest of my life----and maybe one or two more." He said smiling, feeling the need for his friend to understand that he too was successful and quite satisfied with his present financial strength.

"I'd like to slow down, but I have so much going and so much overhead, I'm not sure I could maintain my lifestyle if I quit now."

"Did you ever think that maybe you could scale back a little and relax?"

"I've thought about it, but my business is really starting to percolate."

"That's when things are toughest to handle."

"I know, but I have some really big deals on the fire and if they go through, I could quit with the brass ring."

"If you don't get caught you mean."

"That too." Paul admitted.

"When you're flying around the friendly skies in two Gulfstreams and live in a house like this, you're on everyone's radar screen----period!" Mason warned.

"I know but fuck'em----I cover my bases."

"I hope so. I'll tell you one thing, if you ever need me, any time any place in the world, I'm there for you man." Mason said, looking directly at Paul.

"Mason, I know that. If you hadn't bailed my ass out a dozen times or more, we wouldn't be sitting here right now, and your brother wouldn't be in that safe house in the city." Paul said as he came close.

Mason nodded in agreement.

"So Phil's got you in a bind and did a number on Tom. Unbelievable, I thought he understood that you had a special feeling for the guy you saved and risked your sorry ass for."

"Well, considering he's given him every job since his first job that he fucked up, and got his ass fired on."

"He didn't tell you that he was still working for one of Tom's companies?"

"Hell no, if I'd known I would have kicked his ass big time. I thought he actually got off his ass and got a real job on his own. This was during the period I was dead----remember?"

"Right, and have you been resurrected yet?" Paul asked smiling.

"Hell no, I'm still dead and I like it that way. Do you think I want the IRS and who knows who else on my back?"

"Did Phil think you were dead too?"

"Yeah, I guess. I didn't call him and say don't cry for your brother----because I don't think he would cry for anyone. He probably wondered why he wasn't called by some attorney to be told he was inheriting my huge estate. Fat chance!" Mason said with a devious chuckle.

"You have a little attitude going against Phil----am I right?"

Before Mason could answer, the butler slipped silently into the library and brought two fresh drinks, exchanging for the first two, although both were in various stages of completion. Mason just looked in awe and wondered if he could ever give up so much control to another person that he himself was not making the simple decision of do I want to finish this drink, and do I even want another?

When the library door closed quietly again, Mason answered, "I do have an attitude about what he did and I'm trying to figure out how I'm going to set things straight with Tom."

"How did you find out Tom was involved?" .

"He sent me a fax this afternoon."

Paul sat up straight in his chair and leaned over the arm getting closer to Mason, and said, "bullshit, how would he be able to fax you in Zurich, when you're doing your Houdini routine, changing your identity and escaping whoever is after you as often as you take a piss?"

"He's hired some guy to catch me, not knowing until yesterday that the guy he wants to get is *me*. So he found out from his investigator where I was in Zurich and what name I was using, and sent the fax to the hotel. I picked it up at the desk and hauled my butt out to a cab as fast as I could, because these bastards have been on my ass at every step."

"He sounds pretty damn good, maybe we should hire him."

"Forget it, this guy Chuck Winters has more bucks than you and I combined and he's not for sale. He's only doing his buddy Tom a personal favor."

"How did you figure that out?"

"When I was trying to stop him in Hong Kong and Lisbon, I researched his background and found out he used to be SFPD until he developed some software, and although I didn't put it together at the time, Tom must have taken him public. Winters owned most of the company, sold out, and socked away zillions and retired before the market took a dot-com dump."

"He sounds like trouble for you----and maybe me. You need to get Phil on his way wherever he's going, because if this guy found you, which is a miracle, he's going to find us here in Paris." Paul said with a hint of worry in his voice.

"Don't worry, I'll be gone in the morning and Phil will be gone too. I'm not going to let my troubles rub off on you or affect our friendship." Mason said in a stern, serious tone.

"Hold up Mason. I don't want you to leave. I only want you to be careful. This guy seems to have contacts----the likes that you and I haven't run up against before in the private sector."

"He is good, but I'm on alert now and recognize that I have to be a few steps ahead while I'm straightening out this thing that Phil has done. If you don't mind I need to check out some things on my laptop and will go to my room and call it a night."

"You haven't eaten yet----let me have Renee bring you something. What would you like----put him to the challenge. You name it and he'll have it? He hasn't missed yet for me."

"I'm not very hungry Paul."

"Mason, you need to eat----now I sound like a mother or a wife."

"OK, how about a Chicago type, deep dish pizza." Mason said with the first hint of his chuckle Paul had heard in this most recent exchange. "That should take care of things. I won't be bothered then----will I?"

"Mason, you underestimate me. Renee has the authority if he doesn't have the ingredients, to fly to Chicago on the Gulfstream and bring you back your deep-dish pizza. But I don't think it'll be necessary. I'll tell you what----I wouldn't mind in the least to taste a few slices of a good old Chicago pizza along with a cool frosty one to boot. If Renee performs, I'll join you, OK?" Paul asked.

"You've got a deal----do they have Dominos in Paris?" Mason asked as he stood. "By the way, where's my room?"

"In answer to your first question I think so, but trust me, Renee won't be pulling that one. In answer to your second question it's next to Jen's room, I'll show you."

They walked down a long wide hall to a grand staircase where they climbed to the second floor. There were doors after doors on both sides of the wide hallway. At the end of the hall on the right, Paul opened the door to a beautifully decorated suite, complete with a bathroom that was larger than the bedroom Mason left behind. The floors were black veined marble as was the shower, tub and double sink vanity. The faucets appeared to be gold- plated, and fresh-cut flowers adorned almost every flat surface in the suite.

"This doesn't look like any Motel 6 I've ever stayed in. What's the nightly rate?" Mason said as he opened the *his and hers* walk-in closets, where he found an assortment of men's clothing----all in his size.

"Don't worry about it, the management has comped the room. And the stuff in the closet----not a problem, I'll never miss it. You'll notice it's all your size." Paul said smiling.

In a lower voice Mason whispered with his thumb pointing to the room next door, "what's the deal with Jennifer? It's none of my business, but is something going on there?"

"No way, she's just as close to Sarah. Do you think I'm nuts? Wait until you meet Sarah, then you'll understand." Paul said with a huge grin. "I actually insisted she come here thinking that maybe you two might get along, but I can see now you have heavier things on your mind."

"That's true, but thanks just the same. Another time another place, she looks like fun, but not now." Mason said as Paul left him alone in the room.

Mason opened his briefcase and removed his laptop computer and cell phone. Carrying the cell he went over to the terrace, opened the French doors and stepped out. He had a view that overlooked the tennis courts and by his estimate a swimming pool of Olympic sized proportions. He sat on a cushioned, wrought iron lounge, and in the dim light escaping the room pressed the familiar numbers that would ring Phil's cell phone.

After eight or ten rings, "Hello", came Phil's familiar voice.

"Where are you?"

"I'm in Paris at the apartment. Have you forgotten you were going to meet me here? Where in the hell are *you*?"

Mason checked his emotions, determined not to let on what he learned for Tom until the right time. "I'm in Paris. I want to see you tomorrow morning. I won't meet you there. Go to the Ritz Carlton Hotel and sit in the lobby as close as possible to the reception desk. Do you understand?"

"Yes, but what time?" Do you remember how old you were when you got Spike? Don't say it on the phone, but I want you to meet me there at the hour represented by how old you were."

"OK, I'll be there, but what's up with this cloak and dagger stuff?"

"We'll talk tomorrow----be on time." Mason said and cut the connection. He wondered if Phil would remember that he was nine years old when his parents gave him that ugly looking bull terrier mutt.

CHAPTER 118

Mason stood and walked into his room from the terrace and sat at the desk with his laptop open and the phone cord plugged into a house line which he could see by the phone buttons there were at least three. He inserted the recently updated disk he retrieved from his house after he returned from his bombing attempt at the hotel. This was the program that allowed him to trace telephone call records from most cell phone service provider companies throughout the world. It had been invaluable and worth the more than a hundred thousand dollars it cost him to buy it from a cell phone tracing expert hired by the CIA to develop a method to find cell phone subscribers and then tap into the billing software to determine not only their call record but their original application and payment documentation. This was available to Mason because the developer, a contact he used in setting up his own system for computer surveillance and background tracing, broke so many privacy and other laws that even the CIA backed off and cancelled the contract before he could complete his massive hacking effort. Most of the cell phone service providers were in the system, and for a fee new providers were added as they became known. Mason counted on the fact that the majority of cell phone users were affiliated with major telephone companies, and as a result he could cover most of the bases with the system. When he needed to find someone, as long as he had a number or a name they were currently using, unlisted or not, and an active cell phone provider account, he could run the information through the "search mode", and usually find his target. He punched in Victoria Danville, confident that her old cell phone was not being used. He knew that she didn't have the resources to have concocted a new identity yet, so she more than likely would be using her name, thinking that a new cell would be impossible to trace. After fifteen minutes of programmed searching and a number of Victoria Danville's, which for one reason or another he quickly discounted, there was what he considered a good hit in Toronto Cellular Service, LTD. He looked at the account application form and saw that Victoria Danville was retired, and paid a five hundred dollar deposit with a debit card issued by a bank in the Caymans, not the bank she set up for the initial KRL transfer but a different one, Cayman Insurance Trust. As Victoria was in a billing cycle that ended three days after she acquired the cell phone, her first few calls were on the record. She made one call to Oregon and two to the Caymans. She also made several calls to Toronto numbers. There was a post office box for her address, as she probably told the cell company she was looking for a place and would be living in a hotel for the time being. Mason picked up his own cell and called the Oregon number.

"Hello." A woman answered.

"Is Victoria in please?" Mason asked.

"No, she doesn't live here, who is this?" She asked.

"This is Mr. Harper, she just opened a new account with us and the number she gave us never gets answered. She left this number as a reference number. I do have the right Victoria don't I----the attorney?" He asked politely.

"Yes you do, this is her mother. However she is traveling on sabbatical from her law practice, which you should already know." She said with a slight impatience.

"Sorry to bother you ma'am, everything is fine." Mason said as he cleared the call.

He then called the Cayman telephone number which she had called twice in the first few calls she made from her new number and heard a recording stating hours of the Cayman Insurance Trust Bank on Grand Cayman Island.

A knock on the door and Renee entered with a deep dish Chicago style pizza, steaming hot, with three iced mugs of beer, three plates and two dinner guests directly behind him----Paul and Jennifer.

Mason looked at the large silver tray Renee placed on a side table, and salivated over the golden brown high-sided crust, filled with gooey mozzarella cheese, tomato sauce, sausage, onions and topped with thick slices of fresh tomatoes with generous sprinklings of fresh basil, oregano, and parmesan cheese. "Well, well, well Paul, it looks like Renee really outdid himself, and I have to say you're a very lucky man having his talent right in your home. Give him a big raise before you lose him---- to me!" He said laughing.

Paul stood back grinning, with an arm draped around Rene's shoulder as Jennifer broke in, "Can't you see why I never turn down an invitation to come here? The only problem is Renee spoils me with his pastries, since he knows I have a weakness for sweets. A day at Paul's house demands a week of workouts at the gym---- but it's worth it."

Renee turned to Paul and said, "Sir, will there be anything else?"

"Renee, this is great, thanks so much, great job. Won't you stay and share in this feast you've prepared?" Paul asked him.

"No thanks sir----I never eat my own cooking." He said smiling as he backed out of the room.

Paul suggested that they eat at the table on the balcony as the night air was still comfortable. Jennifer had changed into a pair of jeans and a dark red silk blouse. Her hair was down and loose and she fit quite nicely into her jeans, exposing her very shapely figure. Mason felt the body language between Paul and Jennifer was no more than that of a healthy employer-employee friendship that went no further as he had previously indicated. Mason thought Paul had personally mellowed with his business success of late. He seemed to have dropped the edge and arrogance he noticed the last time they met about four years ago. He was glad that his best friend was happy with his life, and it sounded as though his marriage was good.

They ate every piece of pizza, savoring the flavors and drank their beer while making small talk.

"Where do you go tomorrow?" Mason asked Jennifer.

She turned to Paul and looked for a sign of approval and received a nod. "We are flying to Cape Town, South Africa and will be back in three days."

"I'm going too, but you stay as long as you want, use the limo or take one of the cars in the garage----no problem. If you need to fly somewhere, the other

540

Gulfstream will be on the ground for a couple of days, so just call me on my cell and I'll set it up."

"I'm not going to impose on you. I'll find a place in the morning. I just appreciate what you've done so far."

"Mason, stay here it's better for you to be here----understand?" Paul told him.

"You'll be missing out on Renee's yummy cooking." Jennifer said in an attempt to use her gastronomical logic to convince Mason to stick around while they went to South Africa.

"Thanks, I appreciate that. Let me see what's going on tomorrow."

Jennifer and Paul stood and walked from the balcony back into the room and headed toward the door. "You must be tired, we'll be eating breakfast about 7:30 in the morning if you're up, come down and join us in the kitchen, otherwise I'll see you when we return later in the week." Paul said as he closed the door behind him.

CHAPTER 119

Art and Higgins sat in the overstuffed chairs in my suite and enjoyed a cocktail from the service bar while I filled them in on the Hong Kong news and outlined the mysterious death of Billy Wong as well as the charges filed against KRL in the illegal acquisition of their software. Although much of this was new to Higgins, he proved as I suspected a quick study, allowing him to make significant observations and ask intelligent questions.

"If we assume Billy Wong sent his emissaries to Lisbon and were found in Mason Hampton's house, even though *they* haven't admitted as much, what did they want?" Higgins asked.

"That's a good question. If KRL already had the TechX software and they already paid their ten million dollars, why would they be in Beaverton, Oregon and Lisbon?" I asked rhetorically.

"Maybe they were pissed at the way the deal went down and were trying to get their money back. Did you think of that?" Art asked.

"That's the only thing that makes sense. The burning of the TechX facility was probably part of the plan to put them out of business permanently and the attempted arson on the temporary building by Wong's men was a furtherance of that scheme, once they discovered that TechX was back in business and their ten million bucks didn't buy an exclusive right to anything."

"How do you suppose that this----what is it KRL----?" Art corrected Higgins, "KRL."

"So be it, how do you think they were going to get the ten million dollars back?" He asked no one in particular.

"The same way this gang of thieves gets anything. They kill you to get it or threaten to and then do so after they get what they want. What makes this case so difficult is that we are involved with two separate gangs of killers and caught in a cross-fire between them. In addition, these people have money and the best contacts, compared with the majority of kill-for-money schemers." I said to a subdued Art and Higgins who sat and nodded in agreement.

"Oh, by the way, I just talked with Jimmy in San Francisco and he got the lab report on those prints from Mason Hampton's Lisbon bank. The prints found on the application were definitely his, even though they did go into the "he's been dead for eight years routine." Art told us.

"We need to find both Hamptons and we don't even know if they're even in Paris. Higgins, can you check with your contact and see if he's had any luck finding a possible private flight out of Zurich to Paris this afternoon or evening?"

"I'll call him immediately." Higgins said as he flipped open his cell phone, punched a speed dial code, and waited.

CHAPTER 120

Billy Wong's Paris operative apparently didn't get the word that his boss was no longer of this world and continued his methodical search, with the help of local assistance for "Foster". Wong's man was able to obtain a good security camera photo by bribing a guard in the Las Vegas casino where "Foster" gambled away the TechX funds he embezzled. He and his thugs circulated the picture in nearly every hotel, bar and restaurant in Paris, offering cash for information. When one of the local Asians working for Jo Chin, Wong's man, thought he had a "hit" on the photo, Chin quickly caught a taxi to the address of the bistro where he was waiting with the bartender. At about 11:00 P.M., he arrived at the Bistro and walked in, looking the part of a tough character with a shiny black suit, black turtleneck and a shaved head. Chin was thirty-two years old and looked older. He had a fu-man-chu beard on his round face, stood about five-foot four, yet was tough, fast and trained in the martial arts.

The bar patrons usually looked up when the squeaky front door opened, particularly when the crowd had thinned, as was the case this time of evening. It was apparent to the patrons whose attention was drawn to the stranger that he didn't belong in the place. His demeanor was offensive and his look menacing. He walked up to the bar where his associate sat nursing a beer. They whispered a few words and motioned the bartender over. Chin showed him the picture of Foster and nodded, not speaking enough English to carry on a negotiation such as this for ratting out a customer. When he needed assistance he looked around and saw one of Mary's friends sitting at a table. He went over with the picture and asked where the guy lived.

In French, Claudette said, "I wouldn't tell you if I knew----because the Chinese guys look like a couple of thugs and they have no business in here in the first place."

Dejected, the bartender went back to the bar and shrugged his shoulders, pointing at Claudette and shrugged again.

Chin and his man went over to Claudette and showed her the picture. She started yelling at them to get away from her and said she would call the police, all in French. Her loud yelling caused the patrons to look her way, and three regular customers, well built dock workers got up from their table and walked over to Claudette saying, "Are you being bothered by these men?"

Before she could answer, Chin and his partner muttered something in Chinese as they strode toward the door without looking back. Once outside they looked around at the neighborhood, and before starting on a door-to-door search, decided they needed an interpreter. Chin pulled out his cell phone and made a call. Within fifteen minutes a taxi arrived at the corner near the Bistro, and a European appearing man in his early thirties, trim with black longer hair got out and walked over to Joe Chin and his associate. A few words were spoken and the man, dressed in dark slacks and a light tan sweater took the photo leaving Chin and the other man walking over to a bus stop bench, while he strolled casually into the bistro. He found a stool at the bar and sat down. When the bartender came over, in French he ordered a glass of beer and waited for an opening, which came within a few minutes.

"I haven't seen you in here before." The bartender said in French.

"No, I am a salesman and just was assigned this part of Paris to my territory."

"What do you sell?" The bartender asked, just trying to make conversation on a slow evening.

"I sell furniture to hotels and some furnished apartments." He answered. "I was a little concerned about the neighborhood and wondered if it was safe to even be here after those guys gave me such a difficult time out front."

"What guys----what do you mean?" The bartender asked with interest.

"A couple of Chinese guys blocked my path into here and shoved a photo in my face, asking me if I knew this guy. I knew they weren't the police."

"What did you do then?"

"I told them I have never been in the area and just wanted a beer. They still blocked my path and shoved the picture in my hand and then let me by."

"You have the picture?"

The "salesman" casually sipped his beer and responded, "Yeah, somewhere." He shoved his hands into his front pants pockets and found nothing, then tried his right rear pocket and pulled out Fosters wrinkled picture.

"Can I see it for a minute?"

"Sure----do you know him or something?"

"Yeah, he's been coming in here the last few nights, but I haven't seen him tonight."

"You think he lives in the neighborhood?"

"Yeah, in one of the apartments but I don't speak English and couldn't tell those guys anything."

"They said they would pay for information but they made Claudette mad---- over there," pointing to her small table where she was seated with a girl friend. "She told them to get the hell out or she would call the police. If you could talk to her, maybe she would tell you and you and I could maybe split the money if they're still around." The bartender proposed.

The "salesman" smiled, told the bartender to buy a round for Claudette and her friend and when it was delivered, the bartender nodded his way. They smiled and nodded to him. He casually stood, picked up his drink and strolled over to their table.

"Hi," he said in French, "the bartender said you were roughed up a little like I was by those two Chinese guys." He said, pulling a third chair from another table and sitting down without objection.

Claudette and her friend smiled and Claudette said, "Thanks for the drinks, are they still outside?"

"Yeah, they were when I came in a few minutes ago." He said in a disinterested way.

"We should call the police and have them taken away." Claudette said.

"Why, do you know this guy or something?" The "salesman" asked in a disinterested manner as he took another swallow of beer.

"He's a friend of Mary's, but she hasn't been in here tonight. I think she had to work late again."

"So they were right he does live around here, you just didn't like those guys, right?" He said with a sly grin like they were sharing a secret.

"You could say that. They looked slimy." Claudette added.

"Do you think someone should warn him, these guys look bad?" He said.

"Probably, he hasn't been in tonight, but he lives in the apartment right above the bistro."

"You know those guys look pretty scary to me and I don't think I should put my nose in someone's business I don't even know. I have to get up early ladies, for an appointment. Let me buy you another round and if I don't show up tomorrow night, tell the police I've been shanghaied." He said, and they all laughed. He stood, went back to the bar, ordered another round for the girls, paid his tab, told the bartender that they were no help and walked out the door toward the bench where Chin and his man were sitting.

"He lives in the apartment upstairs."

CHAPTER 121

At 6:00 A.M., there was a knock on Mason's door and it opened slowly. "Mason?"

Mason stirred from his sleep as Paul came over to the side of the bed and said, "I just got a call from the apartment building supervisor. I have some bad news for you. Phil was found murdered a short time ago in his room. A girl was also murdered she was with him, apparently in bed." Paul said with a sorrowful look on his face.

Mason looked overwhelmed with grief, even though his brother had caused him so many problems recently; he was still his little brother he thought. "What, who called you?"

"Well, the building supervisor did at first and then the police called and wanted to know more about him. I told them that he was the brother of an old friend of mine that passed away a number of years ago and I was giving him a place to stay while he was in Paris. They still think his name is Foster and I doubt they will check prints, but one never knows.

"What happened, do they know who did it? Who was the girl?"

"The girl was Mary Justine, formally from London. They called the management of the bistro below and got the bartender out of bed. He told them that Mary met Foster in the bar a few days ago. He also said two Chinese tough guys had a picture of him and were asking where he was earlier in the evening."

"Those bastards, I should have gotten him out of there last night. He counted on me for everything, those bastards. Damn it!" Mason said, near tears.

"I can't claim the body. Will you ask that he be released to you so you can bury him here in Paris? Please tell them he has no family."

"Sure, I'll take care of it. What are you going to do now?"

"I don't know. I need to think. My guess is they were trying to get their money back and this was a KRL, Hong Kong deal. Phil had about a million bucks in bearer bonds on him at the time and I suppose they got those and are looking for me now. For sure they'll make the connection to you, because of the apartment and will think they can find me through you. I need to leave right away, but I need to get a new identity. I don't want to travel on this one that everyone knows about."

"Come to Cape Town with Jen and me----you'll have no trouble with your Gerhard Schultz identity there. Call your guy in Zurich and have him send whatever you need by Fed Express, to our hotel in Cape Town. You'll need the few days to think----and its best you get out of France."

"Thanks Paul, you'll have your attorney follow up on making arrangements for Phil?"

"You bet. You get ready, take a suitcase from the closet and pick out any of the clothes you want and I'll call Leo and have him handle the funeral arrangements."

"You're a great friend Paul."

"You'd do the same for me."

"Yeah, I would."

CHAPTER 122

Higgins called my room at 7:00 A.M. "Hello", came a sleepy voice that bore a resemblance to mine. It was understandable as Higgins took us to the Oxley bar and closed the place at 2:00 A.M.

"Good morning old man, how are you feeling this fine morning?" Higgins said with too much joy in his voice.

"How can you drink all night and be this chipper?" I asked with a moan.

"It's all a matter of training my friend, and I've had more than you." Higgins informed me.

"I guess!"

"I have two bits of very important news. My special contact on air travel just called me, and it seems that Mr. Schultz cleared customs on a Euro Outfitters Gulfstream early last evening here in Paris. This I believe is the same company you indicated our Mr. Paul Prill owns."

I came to life and sat up on the bed. "Higgins you're right, great work, where did the flight originate from?"

"He said it left Zurich at about 5:34 P.M., yesterday."

"Bingo, that's our man. He's probably with Prill right now."

"I have another even more important piece of news. I walked down to the newsstand a bit ago and picked up the late edition. On the front page is a late breaking story of an American and a British woman found strangled in bed this morning." Higgins said, and paused.

"So, how does that affect us?"

"Well, there's a passport photo of him, and the name listed is John Foster."

"You're kidding? No I suppose you're not."

"No, there isn't much in the article, but I am certain it's our man." Higgins said.

"Can you come to my room with the paper? I'll call Art and ask him to meet us here."

"I'm on my way."

I called Art who arrived about the time Higgins did, as he apparently was up and already dressed. They looked over my shoulder at the paper as I sat at a round table in the suite. Considering the paper was in French, Higgins with an adequate understanding of the language served as interpreter. There was no explanation as to the relationship of the dead woman, nor were they able to provide much about "Foster", other than his passport indicated he was from Las Vegas, Nevada.

"I better call Tom Claudius and inform him that another of his people is dead."

"What say we take a run to the apartment and see what we can find out on the ground?" Higgins said.

"Maybe have a little chat with some of the locals. It was not a hotel but an apartment, uncovering some information from nosey neighbors might be jolly, worthwhile."

"Good idea. I don't imagine that his brother will be having any conversations with the Paris Police very soon. He probably has little reason to stick around now. Higgins, can you alert your airline man that we're looking for Schultz to leave Paris, maybe today for a destination unknown."

"I will call him now hopefully Mr. Schultz has not been replaced by a new identity."

I picked up my cell and punched in Tom's number while Higgins walked back to his room to call his airline contact.

CHAPTER 123

"Tom, Chuck."

"Chucky, any more bad news for me?"

"Well, I'm sorry to say there is. Phil was found murdered in Paris early this morning. I don't know much more about it, but when I do I'll let you know."

"This is unbelievable, first Jaxton, then the news about Mason and now Phil dead. Who did it? How did it happen?" Tom asked in a breaking voice.

"We don't know yet, but apparently he was strangled. There could be more, but we haven't found out yet. We only first knew about it fifteen minutes ago."

"What are you going to do now? Where's Mason?" Tom asked.

"I thought we'd tie up the loose ends and make certain no one is still out there trying to sabotage TechX or any of the folks associated with it, like you or me. As to Mason, we knew he landed in Paris on a private jet last night, but I doubt he had anything to do with Phil's death.

"I don't know what to think. Yes, by all means finish up what you think needs to be done to wrap this up----once and for all."

"Oh I forgot to ask you, did you know that Paul Prill is here in Paris and apparently is a good friend of Mason's?"

"Well it doesn't surprise me. They were always pretty tight in Nam. Does Prill have something to do with this whole mess?"

"I don't think so. But he did give him a lift on his Gulfstream last night."

"Pretty fancy----his own Gulfstream?"

"Not just one but two, both registered to his Paris headquartered, Euro Outfitters. Our initial look at him and his company hinted that the US Feds were looking at him for gun running, among other things like maybe plutonium sales to third world countries. They haven't charged him with anything yet, he must be too slick."

"Keep in touch, and thanks for everything. By the way TechX is doing great with the new release work and has all the testing done. We're looking at a release in six weeks."

"Terrific, then this whole effort will prove to be worth while, except for the lives that were lost as a result of greed."

"Amen Chucky!" Tom said as he ended the call.

I looked at Art and said, "This is still personal with that bastard Mason. I want him brought to justice. He wouldn't lose a moments sleep if he'd blown me away, or you too in that Lisbon hotel." Art sat opposite me slowly nodding in agreement. "Killing that Santos girl because we asked some questions damn it and calmly flying off to Zurich, probably to count his money. That bastard. I won't rest until I see him caught."

556

"Chuck, I don't know if we'll ever catch him. He's spent his life honing his skills of disappearing and blending with the background. If something gets in his way, he thinks nothing of destroying it. He doesn't play by the rules. Just think about the times he's tried to kill you, and only because you represent an obstacle, not because you're a bad person or you've done something to him, just because you're in his way. I understand how you feel. But do you think it's worth it?"

I looked at Art for the longest time and finally when I was about to speak, Higgins charged through the door and said, "The Gulfstream's in the air and headed for Cape Town, South Africa, however we don't know if Mason is on board and won't until he clears customs----if he does at all when they land."

"Do you want to go after him or go down to the apartment and see if we can learn anything from the neighbors first?" Higgins asked.

"I think we should learn what we can here, because we won't know if he's on that plane for hours."

"I agree." Art said.

"Let me hop in the shower and I'll meet you two downstairs in the restaurant, for breakfast."

"Fine." Higgins said with Art nodding.

CHAPTER 124

Mason sat on the plane looking out the window thinking and brooding about the what-ifs that would have saved his brother's life. If only, he thought, had he met Phil as soon as he got in and gotten him out of the apartment, but that wouldn't work because there would be no logical reason to leave the apartment that night rather than the next day after they discussed plans. He also thought of the things he considered doing to Phil when he saw him, or if he decided his case was hopeless---. It sickened him to think that he himself thought of the possibility of killing him. Now he wondered how he could ever think that way, and convinced himself that he hadn't meant it, even if he did think about it. He decided that this exercise of feeling sorry for his brother was in fact an effort to feel better, as he was in reality just feeling sorry for himself, as well as feeling guilt, an emotion that he never experienced in the past----for anything, ever.

Mason Hampton came to his senses and picked up the flight phone and dialed a number that went to a forwarding device, which went to another and another until any trace of this call he was about to make would be lost forever in cyberspace. He then punched in the number of his identity maker in Zurich.

"Hello." He heard in German.

"Franz, this is Euro, I need to meet some new friends, one from the US, Florida would be fine, and another from Canada, British Columbia if you don't mind. Would you put an emergency rush on this and see that they are at my hotel, the Hotel Pacific Sea, 743 Ocean Avenue, Cape Town, South Africa, by tomorrow or day after."

"Done." Franz said and hung up.

CHAPTER 125

After showering and shaving, I dressed in a pair of casual beige slacks and a blue long sleeved shirt, open at the collar and wore a pair of tan loafers. I walked into the dining room twenty minutes after they left my room. Art and Higgins had already ordered breakfast and were eating melon when I came to the table.

"You look a lot better." Art said as he surveyed me in my fresh attire.

"I am, but I really need a cup of strong black coffee. Either that or a double shot of something."

"We've looked at a map of the area where Hampton and the woman were murdered. It isn't too far from here, about a twenty minute cab ride." Art said.

"I wonder if the Portuguese arrest warrants are being followed up here in Paris?" I asked.

"I could check with Detective Verta and see if he has some word back from the French." Higgins offered.

Good, if you do that I'll call Euro Outfitters and see if Mr. Prill is in town or in South Africa." I added.

"Higgins, do you have any sway or I should say any contacts with the Paris police officials that you might be able to learn if Phil Hampton AKA, John Foster had any bank documents or money in his possession when they found him?"

"I just may be able to dust off an old contact or two and get some information."

I thought a moment and said, "What do you fellows think of helping the Paris police by telling them that he's Phil Hampton?"

"I can't see how that could hurt us, and besides, that kind of assistance would go a long way toward getting something in return from them." Art said.

"I must agree." Higgins added in.

"Higgins, maybe we should hold that information for the cops working the case which will make them look good, rather than have the information as to the true identity come for "upon high". I said with an all-knowing grin.

"Right-O. It should get us a substantial amount of cooperation from the men on the street." Higgins said. "I'll make a call or two to find out what the status is on the warrants, and then if you like, and considering I am the only French linguist in the group, get in touch with the Inspector named in the article I found this morning that provided the information to the newspaper."

"Perfect, now we're moving forward with a plan. In the meantime, we'll want to stay on top of the Cape Town customs clearing and see if Mason or Schultz enters the country."

"I'll handle that as well." Higgins indicated to the two men. "I think I'll run back to my room and make the calls and meet you back here?"

"Good, I'll finish my breakfast and Art can watch me eat."

Higgins returned after I finished my breakfast and had a third cup of coffee. "Gentlemen, I was able to reach an old contact here in Paris and he gave me the name and number of the party to call in order to obtain a status report on the warrants originating in Portugal on Mason Hampton. I called the chap, and after an excruciating effort to establish exactly who the hell I was, I managed to mention a name that meant something to him and we were swimmingly on our way. He said, after putting me on hold for a period, that the French police had the documentation however did not have a line on whether our man was in the country or not, and if so he said they had no idea where he might be. He did say that he would prod them a bit and call me back on my cell if he had some additional information. Now in regard to the local dual murder investigation, I called Inspector Ferrar the gentleman who made the statement to the press regarding John Foster and his friend's death and had to establish my credentials before he would even take the time to say one word about the case. After I took care of that business, I told him that we would like very much to have a moment of his time at the crime scene, a proposal that he immediately discarded. I went on to say that the true identity of this man Foster is something that could prove beneficial to their case effort and we would be only too happy to provide that information----but would like a little update for the courtesy. He immediately jumped at the opportunity and set up a meeting with us at the site in thirty minutes." Higgins said with a proud of his work smile on his face.

"Excellent." I said. "I don't know how the British are surviving without your contribution these days."

Higgins laughed and said, "Quite nicely I am certain."

CHAPTER 126

The morning sun suspended against the deep blue sky masked the terror that occurred a few hours earlier. The street was crowded, police were still working the neighborhood and the locals were gossiping about the terrible happening that occurred "in such a quiet and safe neighborhood".

Our taxi pulled up directly in front of the bistro and we got out on the sidewalk side. No sooner had we stepped onto the sidewalk, a short, slight, pale-faced man, early forties, black slicked-back hair and wearing a small pencil mustache stepped up and asked----"Mr. Higgins?"

"Yes sir----Inspector Ferrar?"

"That's right." He said in English, which by the expressions on our faces, it was a welcome revelation.

"Let's go in here and talk a moment." The Inspector said.

He held the door while we filed through and into the darker space. While our eyes were becoming accustomed to the change in lighting intensity, the inspector had already found a table and was seated. As the bistro opened for breakfast, there were several tables occupied, but nothing close to the number of patrons that filtered in throughout the afternoon and into the evening hours. He sat without talking, probably waiting for someone to speak. Finally, after speech was not forthcoming, he broke the ice and said, "Mr. Higgins tells me that you can identify the dead man as someone other than who we were led to believe."

"That is true." I said, and without divulging our bargaining chip, explained the history of our interest in him and asked for an update, as well as asked him to answer few questions.

"Mr. Winters, before we get into a question and answer session, I would appreciate you providing any information you have on the true identity of this man," the Inspector stated as he reached into his pocket and showed them a photo of the dead Phil Hampton. Not wanting to anger the Inspector, and hoping to find out everything about the crime scene, I said, "His name is Philip Hampton, an employee of TechX Corporation in Beaverton, Oregon, USA. He is also a resident of the same city."

"Why would he be going under the name John Foster?"

I paused and finally said, "We believe he has been involved in some improper company financial transactions and left the country under the alias you mentioned."

"What kind of financial transactions are you talking about?" Inspector Ferrar asked.

"We believe he and his brother were involved in selling company proprietary software to a Hong Kong company."

"Why was he here in Paris and where is his brother?" The Inspector asked.

"We think he was on the run and was maybe meeting his brother here. His brother flew in last night,

564

but we don't know where he is. Now that we've told you all we know, please tell us about the crime scene and what you found in regard to his possessions."

Inspector Ferrar sat for what seemed like an eternity staring into my eyes and finally said, "I will bring you up to date with our information on the condition that you make yourself available to answer additional questions as they arise, honestly and completely."

I was incensed by the Inspector's approach, bringing myself under control I politely responded, "That has always been our intention and don't forget, *we called you* to assist with the true identification of the murder victim."

"Fine, the victims were both murdered by strangulation. Initial observations indicate the use of a wire or garrote. The heads were nearly decapitated. We searched the personal effects of the two victims and found that the woman had only a purse, contents of which were strewn on the floor. The small amount of paper money she appeared to have among those contents was left at the scene, indicating that this probably was not a random robbery gone bad situation. It was quite clear that she did not live in the apartment. The bartender that works here in the bistro verified that she met him several days ago. She was a regular customer and would meet her girlfriends in here after work. We also learned that two Asian men came into the bar last night with a photo of this Foster, you say Hampton, person, inquiring as to his whereabouts and offering a reward for information. We will have our sketch artist working with him to see if we can generate likenesses to circulate to the press. He also said these two men stayed around the Bistro out in front for a while after leaving, when two of Mary's friends refused to give them information and threatened to call the police if they didn't stop bothering them."

"How did they know to talk to Mary's friends?" I asked.

"Well apparently the bartender couldn't speak Chinese or English and the Asians did not speak French, and considering the bartender knew this Foster person had come to know Mary, he sent them over to the girls."

"Have you interviewed these girls yet?" Higgins asked.

"We are locating them down right now. The bartender said that Foster did not come in last night as he had for the last three nights." The Inspector indicated.

"How did Foster happen to be in that apartment, did he rent it?" I asked.

"No, it is rented on a long term basis by a French corporation. We do not know what connection this Foster had with the corporation and the landlord never saw him. She said, to her knowledge the apartment was used infrequently by the corporation. I can't imagine why any corporation would send someone to that dump. The bodies were discovered by a boy from a neighboring apartment, seeing the door ajar, out of curiosity he pushed it open to take a look. We have no reason to believe this was a sexual attack, although the medical examination is currently under way."

"What corporation leased the apartment?" I asked.

The inspector thumbed through his note pad, looked up and said, "Euro Outfitters, Ltd."

"That doesn't surprise me."

"Why is that?" The Inspector inquired.

"The owner and Foster or Hampton's brother served together in Viet Nam and were apparently close.

"Are you referring to Peter Prill?" The Inspector asked.

"Yes, have you spoken with him yet?"

"No, I called his office and was told he was out of the country but their attorney called and asked that after the medical people were finished with the body, Mr. Prill wanted to arrange for a private internment here in Paris, as he was a friend of the family."

"Did Mr. Prill's office tell you where he was?"

"I asked them that question and they said they weren't quite certain where he was at the moment as he was making a tour of several countries. I told them I wanted to talk with him and asked that they have him call me when they make contact." The Inspector said.

"What was found among Foster's personal effects in the apartment?" I asked.

The Inspector looked at his notepad again and answered, "There was a briefcase, with papers strewn as though the killers were looking for something, a cell phone, wristwatch and a file folder that was in a kitchen drawer, probably because he didn't want it out for maybe the girl to see. It was clear that the killer or killers did not see it."

"Was there anything else, like money or banking records of any type?" I further inquired.

"That was all."

"How about his wallet?"

"Missing too." The Inspector said.

"May we see the file?"

"Our lab people have it, but I asked for a copy, you can have a look at that when I get it."

Getting a little frustrated, I asked, "Can you tell us generally what it contained"?

"I can tell you that there were some e-mail copies between Hong Kong and Oregon." He again rustled through his notepad, "here it is, between a Mr. Denton Jaxton of TechX Corporation and a Mr. Billy Wong of Knowledge Recourse, Limited."

"What did they say----if you can remember?" I asked politely.

"They just talked about completing some testing and sending the software, something like that, quite innocent sounding to me." The inspector added.

"Do you remember what e-mail account Jaxton used? I mean like AOL or something like that."

"I do, as a matter of fact, it was MSN Hotmail." The inspector said.

"I really need copies of those for my case, do you suppose that would be possible?"

"It would if I am satisfied as to who you are and what right you might have to that information."

"I'll get the owner of TechX to send an authorization allowing me to have copies of all of the business papers of his employee Foster or more accurately, Phillip Hampton."

"That would be fine."

The Inspector rose and signaled the end of the discussion. He then asked for names and local addresses as well as home addresses and telephone numbers for each of us.

"Inspector, can you tell me when I might stop by for a copy of the journal contents, assuming I provide you with a faxed authorization from the majority owner of TechX Corporation?"

"I will call you at your hotel when it is ready. If you have satisfactory documentation regarding your authority, I will give you a copy."

"Thank you," I said as we walked out of the bistro. "By the way, would it be possible to take a look at the apartment?"

"I think our people are finished by now, let me see. Please wait here and I will come back and let you know."

The Inspector said as he headed toward the alley street leading to the apartment lobby entrance.

"Well what do you think?" Art asked.

I looked at Higgins and said, "I think that Mason Hampton is long gone after he found out Phil was murdered. He either feels this episode is concluded now that his brother is dead, and walks off into the sunset not to be heard of again, or he's looking for vengeance and heading for Billy Wong, not knowing that he's dead, and maybe after me, because had I not been chasing him and his brother, Phil might still be alive. I think we need to find out if he cleared customs in Cape Town, because I intend to find him even if it means following him around the world." I said in a tone that probably sounded like it had an edge to it.

"I understand how you feel old man, he's been ruthless in his heavy handed approach against you personally and you need to know that he's not out there somewhere----or you won't have a moment's peace." Higgins said as we walked toward the door to wait outside.

CHAPTER 127

The Inspector came from the alley and said, "You can go up now, however please do not touch anything. It remains a crime scene and our people may need to do some additional work there.

We followed Inspector Ferrar up to the second floor apartment and walked past the policeman stationed at the door and saw a ransacked mess.

"Was this done by the police or was it like this when you found the bodies?" I asked.

"Our people are very thorough at searching, but not so thorough at returning things to the status quo." The inspector said with a sheepish grin on his face.

Art chimed in to soften the moment. "Our people in San Francisco are the same way."

Aside for the total destruction of the basic furnishings, the place looked like a hideout for third-rate criminals, not a place where thieves involved in multi-million dollar capers might hole up. It was starting to appear to me that something had gone very wrong with Phil Hampton's plans----*and* those of his brother.

After looking at the several rooms, the Inspector excused himself and left. I said, "It doesn't look like Phil received the big money he had schemed for. KRL admitted they paid ten million US dollars for the software. Mr. Che claims he thought it was a legitimate purchase. The question is, if Phil received the lion's share, then why was he living here in this tacky little apartment provided by his brother's friend, and who got the money?"

"Maybe he did get the money and his brother suggested he hide out here rather than go to a hotel where he might be easily discovered." Art offered.

"I don't think so, I bet his brother ended up with most of it----he was obviously in control. For that matter, we don't know that he didn't arrange for Phil's death in order to keep it all." I offered.

"Easy there, I think we need to step back a bit and look at this whole thing with a fresh look." Higgins chimed in.

"You're probably right Higgins, let's go back to the hotel, have lunch and see if your man knows if Schultz cleared customs in Cape Town."

CHAPTER 128

The ride back to the hotel took them by the Eiffel Tower, a sight that Art and I had never seen, and turned out to be truly impressive against this unusually clear, midday blue sky. Cars, taxis and trucks played tag in the heavy traffic, all jockeying for a foot or two of advantage, and giving it up once again by choosing the wrong lane. After arriving at the hotel, Higgins checked at the desk for messages, and found that "Mr. Schultz had safely landed in Cape Town, South Africa".

Higgins went directly from the front desk into the restaurant where we were looking at menus. The room was crowded with late lunch diners and our table was off to the side, towards the rear. A large basket was in the center of the table with three baguettes of French bread and a silver bowl of fresh butter resting in a dish of shaved ice.

"Our man Schultz has landed in Cape Town and has cleared customs. Where he went from there is anyone's idea." Higgins reported.

"Well, at the least we should let the Portuguese authorities know that they need to send their arrest documents to South Africa if they're going to bring this man to justice for the killings he committed in their country." I said looking at Higgins.

"I'll call Detective Verta immediately and inform him of the new information. If you don't mind, please order me a bowl of soup and a pot of tea." Higgins said as he rose from his chair and walked out of the restaurant in hopes of finding a quiet location conducive to placing a cell phone call.

I nibbled on a hunk of crusty French bread while I pondered my next move. "I need to go to Cape Town. I fully understand that Jimmy is short handed with you being away from the office so long and I wouldn't blame you if you decided to return to San Francisco."

"It'll do him good to sweat a little. I've always wanted to go to Africa and if I have to settle for "south", then so be it, I'm in." Art said smiling.

"What about Higgins, I don't think we need to impose on him any more, do you?"

"Well, if you think about where we'd be right now without him, I don't see how we can't bring him. We really need this guy who can hack into airline bookings as well as custom authorities." Art concluded.

"You're right, and considering that Tom told me to do what I had to do to get to the bottom of this case, I think I should at least ask him if he wants to come."

Higgins returned just as his big steaming bowl of tomato bisque arrived. He delighted in pouring a cup of hot tea and breaking off a large hunk of bread, then expertly slathering it with the rich creamy butter.

"Higgins, I'm going to ask you for a favor, however I fully understand why you might turn me down."

"If the question is would I like to join you in Cape Town, the answer is yes. If the question is anything else, I need to hear it." Higgins said as we roared with laughter.

"Then it's settled! By the way Higgins, do you have any contacts in Cape Town?"

"As a matter of fact I have and I've been there many times on government business of course."

"If you like, I'll reserve three rooms in a nice hotel in Cape Town. Do you have an idea how long we might stay?"

"Higgins, your guess is as good as mine, but if Paris is an example, it won't be long."

"I did speak to Detective Verta in Lisbon. He thanked us for the information, and I told him where his suspect is, or was a few hours ago. This shifting of bureaucratic gears is like trying to make a u-turn with the Queen Mary. I have a hunch we'll not have the Cape Town police chasing after our slippery friend anytime soon. "

"We need to find him fast before he can change his identity, if he hasn't already. Once that happens, it's like shooting in the dark trying to find him. We do know that Paul Prill is helping him and he's probably staying where *he* is at least for the moment. We'd be better served to find Paul Prill and work backward to Hampton. We need to canvas every hotel in and around Cape Town for Mr. Paul Prill of Euro Outfitters. Does anyone know how we might efficiently go about that?"

"I've got a guy in San Francisco, that's a P.I. specializing in finding people by canvassing. He has watts lines, a crew of trained callers and makes a zillion phone calls until he hits pay dirt. This shouldn't be too difficult the hotels are listed on the Internet." Art said.

"Call him----get him on Paul Prill, Euro Outfitters, and Gerhard Schultz."

"I'll get on it, are you going to make the airline reservations?" Art asked me.

"I'll do that as soon as we get the check, do you want the rest of your sandwich?"

"No thanks, I've had enough." Art said as he rose and left the dining room.

CHAPTER 129

Peter Prill, Jennifer and Mason rode in the limousine that met the Gulfstream on the tarmac. Since Prill made his first illegal nuclear weapon sale he changed his lifestyle from riding in filthy taxis at busy airports that took him to budget hotels in order to sell combat boots, surplus fatigues, canteens, M-1 rifles and bayonets to dangerous men with fistfuls of money, mostly stolen in some manner from the US Government in order to fight their grimy little incursions into some neighboring country or region, to riding in style both on land and in the air. He never landed either of his two Gulfstreams without having a chauffeured limousine meet him under the wing of his plane. He rented suites at the finest hotels he visited and entertained his clients royally. He always was of a mindset that *success breeds success.* Along with *you have to fake it 'til you make it.* It became so difficult to fake the success that he had to forget that one----and concentrate on doing a deal that would allow him to look successful. That happened three and a half years ago, and now that he thinks he's "arrived". Paul Prill is spending like the super rich.

The Hotel Royal Sunset was an oceanfront marvel with lovely ocean views, and to the rear the Cape Town Bowl area and in the distance Table Top, a beautiful natural sandstone mountain with a flat top.

Peter waltzed up to the front desk and was immediately recognized by the staff, and without the need for registration was escorted by the manager and several bellmen pushing carts of baggage, presumably samples of his sales merchandise, to the elevator.

"As you requested Mr. Prill you have your usual Royal Dutch suite, complete with two additional bedroom suites for your guests." The manager stated as he opened the tall floor to ceiling double doors leading into the opulent suite.

"Thank you as always Frederick, everything looks great. Oh by the way, my associate Mr. Schultz is expecting a package from Zurich. When it arrives, please be certain to let us know."

"Well, you really know how to travel Peter." Mason said smiling, as he looked at the richly paneled room with high ceilings, exotic wood paneling and elegant, yet comfortable furniture. The floors in the living area were a dark highly polished hardwood, enhanced with the proper number of Oriental carpets. As he stepped into his bedroom from a doorway off the living room, he found the floors covered with wall to wall, thick wool carpeting that cushioned each step as he walked past the richly decorated walls of grass cloth and teak paneling to the far end. Tall double French doors led to a wide balcony overlooking the rolling waves crashing on the shore under the blazing African sun. He gazed out toward the horizon and reflected on how his life had changed since becoming re-involved with his now deceased brother. From a life with order and control in a business of deception, larceny and murder, he was now a wanted man on the run, in a country he had never been, without a home, yet with a mission of unfinished business. If he could only get his package from Zurich he would be able to set some things right, at least in his own mind. Although he never was very close to his younger brother, he blamed himself for things getting out of hand and the ultimate death of Phil. Hanging around in Cape Town was not something he wanted to do, even if he was in the company of Peter and Jennifer. He felt the police and TechX people were on his trail, although he wasn't worried so much about being followed because he knew how to disappear as soon as he finished his work. His exposure was greatest here in Cape Town until his new identities arrived, and he could slip off unnoticed like a ghost in the night he thought.

"Hello, anybody home?" Jennifer said as she knocked on Mason's door.

"Yeah, come in." Mason said, as she walked into the room wearing a pair of bright yellow shorts, cream colored short-sleeved silk blouse and a pair of white deck shoes.

"Peter has a meeting with a client and will be tied up most of the afternoon. Do you want to take a look around Cape Town with me?"

Mason hesitated a second or two and thought it was probably much safer being away from the hotel while he waited for his new identity. "Sure, I'd like that, what did you have in mind?"

"Peter said to take the limo and enjoy the afternoon. The driver is out front and would probably be best at picking the sights of Cape Town, what do you say?"

"Sounds good, let's go, but first I think I need to play the tourist role too. Wasn't there a gift shop in the lobby with shorts and stuff?" Mason asked, thinking that a couple on vacation looked quite unremarkable, a status he desperately needed right now.

CHAPTER 130

After making reservations for Cape Town, the earliest flight available was the following morning at 10:00 A.M. When I finished, my message light was on. The recorded message was from Inspector Ferrar indicating I could come down to the station and pick up a copy of the documents found by the police if I had the authority from TechX, as it appeared to all be related to a transaction involving the company. I called Tom's office, and asked Betty to fax me an immediate authorization to accept any documents in the possession of Philip Hampton on behalf of TechX Corporation. Also included would be a copy of Tom's TechX stock certificate, along with documentation filed with the Delaware, Corporation Commission, demonstrating his majority interest in the company. Betty said the documents were on hand and would be faxed in the next ten minutes to The Oxley.

"I have an appointment with Inspector Ferrar." I said as I stood at the reception desk. The office didn't look much different from the San Francisco P.D. offices, except the receptionist was definitely an improvement over offices where I had worked. The other difference was that she didn't speak English and had to bring over another quite attractive young lady to translate. In a few minutes Inspector Ferrar arrived at the desk, smiling, quite unlike his somber appearance demonstrated at the crime scene. I wasn't sure if the new demeanor was meant for me or the two young ladies who may not know his real persona.

"Please come with me Mr. Winters", he said as I followed him down a hallway to a conference room with a table and four straight back chairs.

"I assume you have some evidence of your authority on this matter", he said as I handed him the freshly received faxes from Betty. He looked them over and smiled.

"I would say this man is entitled to the information, and you as his representative are entitled as well."

"Thank you, do you have the copy?"

"I do of course. But first I would like to learn a little more about the background of this man as well as how his brother and Mr. Prill fit in." The Inspector said with a somber look, a face I remembered from the crime scene.

"I've told you what I know about Phil Hampton and I don't know how Paul Prill fits in. I do know that Prill flew Mason Hampton from Zurich to Paris on his company plane. If they have business together, I don't know. From what I've been able to learn, Mason Hampton is an ex-undercover special operations type from the Viet Nam period. I understand that he works on his own and is not involved with the US Government. I think he's a soldier of fortune type, willing to go anywhere and do anything if the money is right. I believe he was deeply involved in helping his brother steal software from his company, as well as kill or attempt to kill anyone who got in the way of their plan. I know because he tried to kill me in Hong Kong and again in Lisbon. I was very lucky both times".

"How do you know so much about his travels?"

"Mr. Higgins, as an ex-British official has contacts from that association that he occasionally consults, who have the ability to find out this type of specialized information." I answered, hoping that I could skate by with the answer.

"What is your objective and who do you work for?" He asked with a rather hard look.

"My friend Tom Claudius asked me to assist him in finding the president of TechX, who was missing at the time. Since he helped me in business, and I was an ex-San Francisco police detective, I said I would do what I could."

"Is he paying you for your work as a private detective?" The inspector asked.

"No, I am not working for pay he is only covering my actual expenses. Why do you ask?"

"I checked your status with the stated of California and they said you are not licensed."

"Why would I be licensed, I'm retired?" I replied, my face reddening and getting more upset with this man by the second.

"No reason, I just wanted to assure myself that you were not directly involved with this crime, in any way."

"Are you satisfied?"

"If these documents are valid", the Inspector said as he shook the sheaf of papers in his right hand, "then I would say we have no problem."

"Inspector, are you going to give me that copy of the TechX documents or do I leave and go back to my hotel?" I asked looking directly into his eyes.

"After I make one phone call, will you wait here for a few minutes?"

"What choice do I have?" I said as he watched the inspector leave the room and close the door behind him.

Higgins and Art were sitting in Higgins' hotel room, while Art was checking in with the telephone canvasser in San Francisco. He went right to work and called every hotel in Cape Town and was successful. "Peter Prill and Gerhard Schultz are staying at Hotel Pacific Sea." Art told Higgins.

"Well done old man." Higgins said as he saluted Art who smiled with a feeling of satisfaction after Higgins had been instrumental in getting the needed answers in the last few days. "The question for Chuck will be, do we tell Detective Vertos where this man is in Cape Town in order that the warrants from Portugal can be acted upon, or do we try something ourselves on the ground in Cape Town, whatever that might be----I wouldn't know?" Higgins asked Art.

"I think this is Chuck's call, but it makes sense to have the local police arrest him on the outstanding warrants."

CHAPTER 131

Jennifer and Mason stepped into the gleaming black Mercedes limo parked at the hotel front door. Mason had purchased a pair of tan shorts, a cotton short-sleeved white shirt, a pair of comfortable sandals, a dark blue baseball cap and a pair of sunglasses. He looked fit and tanned, and could easily pass as a tourist seeing the sights of Cape Town with his younger attractive girlfriend or wife. Their driver Frederick, took the lead and assured them a grand tour of the city and surrounding tourist sights, but Mason informed him without Jennifer's objection that dropping them off at the first stop, St. George's Mall, would be just fine and they would find a taxi for their return trip to the hotel later in the afternoon.

"What do you have in mind? I thought this was your first time in South Africa." Jennifer said with an "I'm up for anything" smile on her face.

"To tell you the truth, I thought we might get a room somewhere." Mason said, waiting for her facial expression to change to a look of *I hardly know you*-----it didn't come!

"Really? All right", she said blushing.

"It's not like that----really." He said with a hint of a grin in recognition that she was ready and willing to sleep with him.

St. George's Mall, once a busy congested street was closed and turned into a pedestrian mall with sidewalk cafes, coffee shops and a plethora of shops that attracted not only tourists, but locals as well. It was a great place for people watching and just relaxing under the shade of an umbrella, sipping a cool drink or enjoying any variety of coffees.

Mason took Jennifer's arm guiding her to a sidewalk café and found a secluded umbrella table behind a potted tree.

"Jennifer, I don't know what Paul has told you about me." Mason said and waited for a response.

"He told me that you were his oldest and closest friend, and not unlike himself, your business is not one that you discuss with anyone, nor can you." She answered with a slight smile.

"I would say that pretty well sums it up. You have gathered I assume, that my brother was involved in, let me just call it a situation, and it got out of hand, thereby causing his death. I was helping him, now I have a number of people trying to find me so I'm asking for your assistance, although I am flattered that you might consider spending some private time with me." He said with a devilish grin.

"Tell me what I can do to help you and I will see if it feels comfortable to me. Is that all right with you?"

"I have no doubt that my pursuers will soon be in South Africa. I want to stay a jump ahead of them and don't want to cause Paul or you any trouble. I'm waiting for some papers that will probably arrive here tomorrow. They'll allow me to fly out of here unnoticed and complete my unfinished business. Does that make any sense to you?"

"It does, but how does it affect me?"

"Since these people know the name I'm traveling under, I need to move to another hotel this afternoon to avoid any problems that certainly will follow me here. I'd like you to get a room in your name so there's no connection with my identity. I just need to have the package address changed to this new hotel care of yourself and simply wait for it to arrive."

"Is it illegal?"

"Not checking into a hotel in your name. I'll make it worth your while. He said.

"I am not interested in money I just want to make certain I don't have a problem."

"It'll be fine, will you do this?"

She watched him as he gazed at the crowds moving in every direction across the pedestrian mall while stirring his iced tea. He appeared to her to be calm and in control, the kind of strong confident man she always desired and yet somehow always managed to end up with the exact opposite.

"All right, let's do it." She said hoping she wasn't making a big mistake.

He looked into her green eyes and saw a smile that could cause him to let his guard down. He had to be especially vigil and under control, leave the emotions carefully bottled up, he told himself. Mason dropped some bills on the table and stood, moving around to Jennifer's chair, casually pulling it away as she rose and placing it back in position after she stepped aside. She noticed his courtesy and wondered if the general warning about him from Peter was serious, or rather his not so unnoticed desire to keep her uninvolved. Although he had not overtly shown an interest in her, she sensed he had feelings for her and thought better of acting on those as he appeared to by serious about making his marriage work.

"Let's find a taxi and see if the driver could suggest a hotel. Considering we have no luggage and we will be picked up in the center of town, he'll suspect that we might be having an affair and direct us to a not so public accommodation. So if you don't mind, maybe we can do a little role-playing that might lead him to that conclusion. Is that OK with you?"

"Well considering I have no experience at running off in the middle of the day with a man I hardly know to find a hotel room----I'll give it a go." She said smiling in agreement.

Jennifer slid her arm through his and moved close as they walked toward the street, all the time acting like a moonstruck teenager. Mason glanced at her as they walked, and for the first time took careful notice of this beautiful woman, one that was knowingly in the company of a man whose business they could not discuss and who had the unusual judgment not to pry, at least so far she did. He noticed her long tanned legs nearly as dark as his own, reminding him of the many relaxing hours spent in the Lisbon sun on the deck of his home, which after events in the last few days was now only a memory.

They walked across the cobblestones toward a street where Mason thought they might find a taxi. Out of habit and from behind his dark glasses, his piercing eyes darted from face to face looking for recognition of any sort or suspicious movements, finding none they

587

continued on to the street where a number of taxi's stood patiently waiting to rescue the tired feet of mall tourists. The street was busy and four lanes wide. The taxi driver first in line was leaning against his front fender waiting for a fare as Mason and Jennifer walked over, her still hanging on his arm as though he might get away if she didn't. The driver was a man Mason judged to be in his mid-fifties and based on his girth rarely did more than drive and eat, and perhaps drink.

"Are you available?" Mason asked knowing the answer.

"I am sir, where to?"

"You tell me. Would you be able to suggest a nice quiet hotel?" Mason asked with a phony smile on his face.

The driver looked at Mason and then turned to Jennifer who was clinging to Mason in a manner that the only way he could miss their intentions was to be blind. "I know a very nice place----the Protea Hotel on Bantry Bay, it's not too far from here." He said with a sly grin.

"That'll be fine."

Sitting close in the back seat, Mason pulled out his wallet and gave Jennifer four thousand South African Rands in large bills, acquired at their hotel upon arrival, the equivalent of five hundred US Dollars.

Mason whispered, "When you check in, I don't want you to use a credit card unless you need to show it for identification. We'll pay cash. This is enough for several days."

CHAPTER 132

They drove up to the circular entrance of the Hotel Protea which was on the ocean with views not unlike Paul's suite. A bellman opened the door while Mason paid the driver. They walked up to the entrance and Jennifer pulled Mason's arm and directed him to a bench to the right of the front door.

Jennifer sat down and pulled Mason down beside her and asked, "How long am I staying here?"

He laughed and said, "I think you are staying in Paul's suite aren't you?"

"I don't know, Paul is going to be very busy and I only need to be available when he's planning on flying out, otherwise my time is pretty much my own." She said, arching her eyebrows, giving him a devilish, teasing look.

"You are unpredictable Jennifer." He grinned, "Stay if you like, get a two bedroom suite if you like, I just need to keep a low profile until my package comes and I can't change that until I have an address besides the other hotel. I think you better go to the registration desk alone, and after you check in, tell them you will be expecting a Federal Express Package and to please let you know the minute it arrives. By the way, now that we're getting a hotel room in a strange country, it might be nice if you introduced yourself to me, I don't even know your last name." Mason said smiling.

"Does it really matter----I have no idea who you are and haven't inquired, have I?"

"Touché. I'm Mason Hampton, at least for a day or so."

Glad to meet you Mason Hampton, but I already knew that. I am Jennifer Alice Heath."

"Well Jennifer Alice Heath, how about getting us a room?" Mason asked still smiling.

"It would be my pleasure, sir." Jennifer said as she turned and walked through the large double lobby doors.

CHAPTER 133

I returned to the hotel with a set of papers found in Phil Hampton's apartment. After the excruciating effort of getting possession of the mysterious papers, I found he had five e-mails that were between Jaxton and Billy Wong, discussing the sale of the software and the need to wire ten million dollars to a Cayman Bank. They included concerns about the testing and protocols and delays in receiving the agreed upon documentation. There was also a mention of the need to permanently eliminate the ability of TechX to continue in the manufacture and distribution of the product after the sale was complete.

The phone rang in Art's room where he and Higgins were waiting for my return. "Hello."

"Art, you wouldn't believe what I had to go through to get a few e-mails, which were really nothing more than we suspected but serve to prove a lot of our suppositions."

"Come on up, Higgins is here and we have some news."

Higgins opened the door after hearing my knock. "Welcome back, I hear the inspector gave you a difficult time."

"I think he delighted in working me over." I said as I walked into the room and sat on an overstuffed chair by the window not far from where Art was sitting on the bed leaning against the headboard. "He seemed to be on some kind of power trip, and what he finally gave me was not all that new or interesting. I'm certain that Phil Hampton with the muscle and killing assistance of Mason

Hampton. I'm also convinced that KRL in Hong Kong thought Phil Hampton *was* Jaxton and he was unhappy with the way the company treated him and willing to sell the software to them for ten million dollars, screwing his employer----TechX. I'm almost certain that KLR didn't know that Phil Hampton even existed. They did somehow find out about Foster, probably through the first payment made to the Cayman bank, thinking that that was the name Jaxton was using. Billy Wong, who of course is dead now, probably sent his stooges after Foster, AKA Phil Hampton, in order to retrieve the ten million dollars they lost in the stolen software deal after the Hong Kong police confronted them with it. All of the e-mails supposedly written by Jaxton were from an MSN Hotmail account that anyone can get, so there was really no easy trace for KRL, but I intend to use a source of mine to track down the computer that sent and received the e-mail. Jaxton had an AOL account, and my guess is that he was already dead when some of this mail was exchanged, besides, how would Phil Hampton have his hands on these if he wasn't a party to the scheme. I think I'll fax it to John Sun in Hong Kong and see if it might help the police in their case against KRL. Now what's your news Art?"

"My guy in San Francisco traced Prill and Gerhard Shultz to the Hotel Pacific Sea in Cape Town, South Africa. The question we have is do you want to turn it over to the Lisbon police and let them follow through, or try and do something on the ground in Cape Town, whatever that might be?" Art asked, looking at my face which at the instant happened to be a blank stare.

"I don't think we have time for the Government of Portugal to go through their hoops. I'm going to go there and somehow bring him down."

592

"Don't you remember how dangerous this man is? If he's cornered, look out!" Art reminded me.

"Look, who's to know if he won't come after me and maybe Valarie if I just quit and say this is a finished case. Phil Hampton probably spent most of the embezzled money in Las Vegas, it's gone and not coming back. As to the money KRL paid him, who knows and it was their money anyway. Phil Hampton is dead, so there's no case to bring against him. KRL will not be using the software now that the Hong Kong Police are bringing charges against them for software theft and Billy Wong is dead. Denton Jaxton was a good guy after all who didn't need to be murdered by most likely Mason Hampton. That takes us full circle to Mason Hampton, he's a threat to me and maybe you Art, but in any case I'm going to find him and figure out a way to stop him---- period." I responded with anger on my face, one that Art hadn't seen for many years since we worked together as detectives in San Francisco.

"OK, I agree----and I'm with you all the way." Art said.

"I am as well my new friend." Higgins added.

"I hesitate to allow either of you to go and be put in danger when this case has become very personal for me." I said, looking each square in their eyes.

"Nothing's changed, and if you think you're going alone you're nuts, do you understand?" Art said with a tone I hadn't heard either for a long, long time.

"We don't have the same history, but I can take care of myself. I've been doing it against some of the worst jackals in the world, even the original one." Higgins said with a wry grin.

"If you are certain we leave at ten in the morning. Higgins any contacts that could help me get a weapon----or two or three?"

"As a matter of fact I do know a chap that stayed around when our party ended there. I'll ring him up and see if he's still up for a little fun. Why don't you write down your, how do you Yanks say it, 'wish list' of weaponry and other items, while I run up to my room and see if I can find his number?" Higgins said as he headed for the door.

"Thanks guys, you're the best. I don't know about you, but I could use a drink."

"I'll meet you two in the bar then." Higgins said closing the door behind him.

CHAPTER 134

Mason watched Jennifer check in while he stood on the far side of the lobby next to the gift shop. As she was walking away from the desk with a smile on her face, Mason assumed there were rooms available and she succeeded in obtaining one on a cash payment basis. She saw where he was standing and casually moved toward the gift shop stopping near the entrance and turned, "Now I have two rooms"; she said with a teasing look on her face, "whatever shall I do with two rooms----do you have any suggestions?"

Mason laughed and said, "Let's take a look and see how well you did."

They walked to one of the four lobby elevators and Jennifer pressed the sixth floor button. Room 617 was to the right and down the hall of plush green carpet. "May I help you with your bags sir?" She asked as she handed Mason the card key.

"Thank you but no, my girlfriend and I always travel light." He said laughing as he slipped the card into the slot, and upon seeing the green light appear, turned the handle and pushed open the door. The room was quite large with a king-sized bed, sitting area, a bathroom with double vanities, marble surfaces and a telephone conveniently placed near the toilet. Mason walked to the draped window and pulled the cord, exposing a magnificent view of the ocean.

"I would say this is just about right, wouldn't you?" Jennifer said.

"I would. Now I need a minute to take care of some business on the phone." Mason said as he stood before Jennifer.

"That's fine I'll just powder my nose." She said as she went into the bathroom and closed the door.

Mason pulled his cell phone from his pocket and pressed the numbers of his Zurich contact. "Franz, this is Euro again. Have you shipped my order? Fine, will you change the shipping instructions to read Jennifer Heath, at the Protea Hotel, Alexander Road, Bantry Bay, Cape Town, 8060, ZA?" Mason paused. "Excellent---- tomorrow for certain! It sounds like my timing was perfect."

Jennifer walked from the bathroom, her auburn hair pulled back in a sort of ponytail, looking even younger than she is and said, "Are you through with your business for a while, I'm starving?"

Smiling Mason replied, "as a matter of fact I'm as free as a bird. Let's find a great restaurant and have something South African."

"I'm not certain what that might be, but let's talk to the concierge and get his recommendation." She suggested.

"Fine but you do it. As I said I want to keep a very low profile----do you mind?"

"Not at all, I understand."

What have I gotten myself into? She thought. It must be quite horrendous if he's afraid to make contact with even the concierge.

They rode to the lobby in the elevator and Mason fell behind as Jennifer found the concierge's desk and posed the question. She discreetly handed him some bills and walked toward Mason who appeared to be looking at a rack of brochures, advertising tours and other special interest locations in the Cape Town area.

"He said the Island Restaurant is the very best---- serving wonderful seafood entrées, and best of all we can walk to it. It's in the next block. What do you say?"

"I say lead the way."

CHAPTER 135

They walked out of the hotel and down Alexander Road toward the restaurant. Even in shorts and light shirts the heat was almost overbearing. The walk under the warm sun was worth any discomfort as they watched ocean waves crashing against the low bank shoreline. Small seabirds rode the incoming swells and appeared to be frolicking as they tumbled over and over, disappeared from sight and popped up again to repeat the process.

The Island Restaurant's walls consisted of bright white stucco and were ablaze with fiery-red blossom covered vines climbing on trellises reaching to the roofline, where at least a dozen large blue pennants flew from white poles in the soft afternoon breeze. As they reached the front door's well-worn handle made from the wheel of an old sailing ship, they immediately experienced that hard to describe feeling, an intuition of confidence or lack of same before one sets foot inside. In this case it was confidence. It involved a sense of the overall attention to detail and cleanliness one observes from fresh paint and immaculate landscaping coupled with signs of use. Inside the carpets were dark blue. From the door they could see the tables arranged in a semicircle each against the oceanfront curving wall of glass.

A tall man, mid-forties with sandy hair and beard, wearing black slacks and a white shirt with black bow tie was standing at a podium near the door when they walked in.

"Good afternoon, welcome to the Island Restaurant. Is this your first time?" The maître 'd asked.

"Yes it is." Mason said, not wanting to divulge even in an innocent way they were staying in the hotel next door.

"Wonderful, I will find you a special table that allows a spectacular view of the ocean, and incidentally most of our seafood originates from these very waters in front of you, we pride ourselves on its freshness."

He pulled the chair for Jennifer and opened her linen napkin placing it on her lap, turned and did the same for Mason. Upon indicating their waiter Charles would be with them shortly, he handed them each a large menu and asked if they would like something to drink. Both Jennifer and Mason selected ice tea, after which Mason discretely slipped the maître 'd the equivalent of a ten-dollar bill. Mason learned long ago that a proper gratuity worked wonders and continued to benefit mostly when someone later comes around asking about you. In many cases the memory becomes very short.

"Enjoy you're lunch, I will be checking back with you to make certain everything is to your satisfaction." He said as he turned looking for Charles.

"This is just beautiful." Jennifer said as she looked out at the ocean waves rolling onto the rocky shore below the restaurant.

"It really is, thanks for helping me with the room. I really appreciate it." Mason said smiling at her.

"You can pay me back by entertaining me while I'm here. I know Paul has a dinner meeting and I'd be on my own, most of the time anyway. I don't usually mind but as long as you're in the same position with time on your hands we might as well not be bored."

"I'd like to spend time with you, but don't forget, when I get my package I'll need to leave shortly after that."

"I understand, but in the meantime, if you don't mind let's keep each other company. Is that all right with you?"

"Of course, what are you hungry for?" Mason asked as he opened the menu, thinking his timing is always wrong. Here is an intelligent woman, one that understands that he and in a lesser way Peter is involved in business that cannot survive the scrutiny of law enforcement. In fact almost everything he does is a maximum penalty offence, either life in some filthy prison or execution, depending on the laws of the particular country he has broken. Although he would very much like to consider the possibilities with this woman, logic and experience tells him----don't get involved!

"I'd like to know what their seafood special is today----and then make a decision." Jennifer said, studying the man she suddenly had become quite attracted to, and being a realist, knowing his life couldn't possibly include her.

"I agree, let's see what the chef is promoting." He said. "On another subject, I was thinking I need to get my stuff from the hotel. I only have a briefcase and my laptop, the other clothes are borrowed from Paul. I don't know what he wants me to do about those. I suppose he can have them tossed on the Gulfstream and taken home when he returns to London."

"Would you like me to get your things after lunch----it would be no trouble and you wouldn't have to go back?"

"Would you?"

"Of course, then you would have no excuse about doing some things with me this afternoon." She answered with a girlish smile.

"That's a deal. I'm starving, where's Charles when you want him?"

Just as the words left his lips a young slender waiter came up with slicked- back black hair and a wearing small pencil mustache.

"Good afternoon my name is Charles and I will be serving you this afternoon. Are your drinks all right, or would you like to order a bottle of one of our fine wines from the cellar?"

"The drinks are fine and we may have some wine, but first tell us about your seafood specialties." Mason said with a sound of authority.

"You are very lucky, we received a wonderful marlin this morning, caught about five miles off this very section of coastline. It is prepared with an herb hazelnut crust, sautéed in lemon juice, butter and white wine. The vegetable is asparagus, and also included is a house special green salad with our secret island salad dressing recipe, unless you would prefer one of the more traditional choices."

"That would be fine." Mason said as he looked and received a nod of concurrence from Jennifer. "What white wine do you have that is fit for a meal such as this?" Mason asked----and stopped to listen to his own words, which to him sounded as if he was talking and acting like someone whose sole purpose was that of courting a lady rather than a hired and sometimes freelance killer dealing with immediate survival.

After a lunch that under normal circumstances could be the start of an exciting new relationship between two handsome, intelligent, compatible people, each knew without speaking that their time together would be short but seemingly worth the risk of sorrow and misgivings that surely could develop after their lives become separated by geography as opposed to desire. They caught a taxi that would drop Mason off at the mall area they left earlier to shop for new luggage and necessary clothing for his new identities he hoped to receive from Zurich the next day. As planned, Jennifer continued on in the taxi back to the Pacific Sea Hotel to leave a message for Peter and pick up Mason's brief case and laptop computer. They would meet back at Jennifer's room in the Protea Hotel later that afternoon. On the way to the hotel she wondered why she was subjecting herself to risks both legal and of the heart for this man she just only met, knowing that their lives and history were so different and her involvement with him could only bring trouble.

CHAPTER 136

Higgins walked into the hotel bar and found us in conversation at a table in the corner next to a window, allowing a view across the lobby to the reception desk.

"Well, what's the word from Cape Town?" I asked Higgins.

"Once again we're in luck. It seems that old George has actually gone into the arms business on a sporting level only, representing a number of British manufacturers of hunting rifles, pistols as well as knives and safari outfitting. He's only too happy to be of service and asked that we call back with our needs and he will supply them post haste."

"Very good Higgins, we'd be lost without your assistance. I've made up a list of things, some that I'm certain are not of his normal stock in trade, but maybe we could ask him to, for a fee obtain these items in order to have this a one-stop situation tomorrow." I said handing him the list.

"Let me see here, one to three Glock 9 millimeters with silencers. Which is it, one or three?" Higgins asked.

"That's your and Art's call. I'm not going to ask either of you to get more involved than going with me and being there for moral support."

"I told you I'm in," Art said, "besides I don't want another Hong Kong incident without me being there to save your ass." Art said with a chuckle and a grin.

"Right, just how would you have avoided the explosion?"

"Fellows, this discussion is one without resolve, now or probably ever. Let me say, as Art I am willing to stand beside you fully armed in this noble effort. Let me continue with your list. Wire, duct tape, chloroform, cloths, radios---- walkie-talkie type, binoculars, the best rifle he has with night vision scope, black jogging type outfits, night camouflage for face and hands, ropes, maintenance coveralls, empty tool box, two mini TV cameras and monitor, men's wigs, one gray longer hair, brown average length and a close cropped black wig, and-----a private jet plane willing to fly with a passenger that may not have proper credentials, not to mention against his will." Higgins stated. "All right----this sounds exciting, what is your plan, if you are prepared to share that with us?"

"It is not too complicated. I want to find him, kidnap him and deliver him to the Lisbon authorities for prosecution."

Art and Higgins looked at each other without comment and both nodded concurrence, understanding how this "simple" plan was fraught with danger, considering the target of their objective was a ruthless killer with a track record of avoiding his enemies against significant odds.

CHAPTER 137

Mason sat on the balcony of Jennifer's room at the Hotel Protea and was lost in thought, mostly about Phil's death and the associated guilt from not protecting him. He acknowledged that Phil's problems were mostly his own doing, and that had Phil been on his own, arranging for his own escape from his old life, he probably would have been found sooner by the Chinese, but that didn't change things from a blame standpoint. In all his adult life he never felt the need to accept blame until now----when it involved his little brother. Mason heard the door to the room start to open and he went on full self-preservation alert, until he saw Jennifer trying to manage the door while loaded down with the heavy briefcase containing his laptop and some sacks that appeared as though she went shopping. He rose, said hi and went to her aid.

"Well it looks like you've been shopping----and thanks for the briefcase, I know it's heavy with the laptop."

"No problem. I left a note for Peter and said I would call later and that you had made other arrangements and really appreciated his support and assistance but had to go it alone for a while." Jennifer said with a smile on her face while setting the bags on the table and then walked over to the bed, kicked off her sandals and stretched out with her head on the pillow.

"This feels wonderful, come lie down with me." She said as she patted the right side of the bed.

Mason looked down at her, and he too took off his shoes and stretched out beside her. She leaned over and

gently kissed him on the mouth and Mason pulled her
down and rolled her over as he continued to kiss her
passionately, giving leave to his emotional turmoil and
concentrating on his feelings for this woman who appears
willing to accept him, despite his baggage. He gently with
her help, removed her blouse as she tugged at the buttons
on his shorts, finally freeing them to the point they
slipped off along with his underwear, down his legs and to
the floor, while Jennifer with her other hand, at the same
time was sliding off her shorts and letting them also drop
to the floor. Jennifer wore no bra and his mouth moved
to her full breasts while she anxiously reached for him, he
slipped off her panties and she slowly guided him into her
warmth. They made love until they lay exhausted, side-
by-side holding hands while the afternoon sea breezes
washed their naked bodies with a fresh desire.

CHAPTER 138

The Air France Jet landed at the Cape Town Airport shortly after three in the afternoon. My two cohorts and I were met at the airport by a large van, complete with all of the requested items that Higgins called in. Josh Hooper, his former British Intelligence associate was at the wheel as they headed into town. Hooper was about Higgins' age, under six-foot tall, wiry looking and in as good shape as Higgins. His hair was short-cropped and gray and his eyes were emerald green.

"Well, I was able to get the jet faster than the damn wigs, what are you doing going to a costume party?" Hooper joked.

"You might say that. I haven't had a chance to properly thank you Josh; I really appreciate what you're doing for us and understand what kind of position this puts you in."

"Nonsense, I am in business and there is nothing I have provided you that is against the law or in violation of my licensing agreements, except maybe those damn wigs----I may be violating the South African Hairdressers Alliance, if there is such a thing, for practicing without a license. By the way, Higgins didn't know if you needed ground transportation or not, so I rented this van in case you might. If you want to keep it, it's yours, I can catch ride back in a taxi." Hooper said smiling.

"That is perfect, we'll need it. I didn't hear if you managed to get us rooms at the Pacific Sea?"

"I did, and did so under the pretext that I was putting up some clients and booked the rooms in my company name, African Sportsman, Ltd."

"Great, if we're going to find this guy in his hotel, it's a lot easier to explain our presence if we're staying there. Before we get there, Art and I need to put on our wigs. I know this guy can easily recognize us and I don't want to help him."

"Excuse me. Did I hear you right? I suppose you expect me to wear a dress too?" Art inquired with a playful scowl.

"It worked for me in Lisbon----didn't it? If I needed one to save my life or get this guy I'd wear one, in fact I'd wear pink tights and a tutu if I had to."

"OK! Higgins, what's that smirk on your face, don't you think you should wear one too----we have three you know?" Art teased.

"As a matter of fact I would, but I think I need to make a memorable impact on this sad excuse for a human first, before I might need one."

"I'll wear the gray one and you wear the more traditional brown wig. It might be an improvement, and if you just have to have it, consider it yours." I said with that special grin saved for my old buddy Art.

"Thanks loads you old hippie. Let's see it on you----you'll fit right in with the Rolling Stones!"

Sitting in the second seat, I pulled out the gray wig and carefully put it on my head, making certain that all my real hair was under the skullcap. I then slid to the center and looked in the rear view mirror.

"Perfect. Kind of makes me look like a cross between Willie Nelson and Keith Richards."

"I think you look just about the way you always do, and that description is just about right." Art said as he struggled to adjust his brown wig.

"Now there's a scary sight." I countered. "You look a lot like Harpo Marx---- now only if you didn't talk."

"Very nice, now I understand why I'm you're only friend, and that status might be in question." Art said as he turned to look at me causing us to both break into laughter.

"Well no one will think we're very threatening, just stupid maybe." I added.

"Well I would think my Rosa could find you a couple of nice older unmarried Portuguese ladies that would think you're quite handsome----in your own way." He said laughing at us.

"I have you registered and picked up the keys to your rooms this morning, so there is no need to stop by the front desk. You can leave the bags in the van and casually saunter around the hotel lobby and when you're ready, take the elevator to the fifth floor, numbers 514, 516 and 518. They're on the same side with two rooms adjoining. I'll see that the bags and your gear are brought up to 516, the middle room and you can distribute them from there. Any questions?"

"Were you able to determine what room Peter Prill and Gerhard Schultz are staying in?" I asked Hooper.

"I did when I registered this morning. I casually asked if the Royal Dutch Suite was available or did Peter Prill beat me to it. The reply from the friendly assistant manager was that he did. It was a good guess, but I do know some weapons manufacturers that sell to him and know that he always stays in that suite when he comes to Cape Town, number 601. There are three large bedroom suites within the main suite, and I am certain that Schultz is in one of them."

"Why would Schultz register if you didn't have to list us individually?" I asked Hooper.

"I would assume that he's expecting a package or a telephone call and he didn't want any confusion by not being registered."

"As usual, brilliant thinking Josh." Higgins replied with a look of admiration for his old friend.

"Yes that does make sense, and my guess is it's a package and when he gets it he's gone, this time without a trace. He must have new identification coming." I said.

"That would be my guess. After all, he left Lisbon in quite a hurry and didn't have time to hang around for transformation into a new person and an entirely new life." Art said.

The van approached the Pacific Sea Hotel and drove up the circular drive at the entrance, past the front doors and pulled into a short-term parking space. Out of view of the front entry, Art, Higgins and I stepped out of the van and walked toward the front entrance. Me in my stringy longer gray hair, looked much like a seventies type who never grew out of the period. Art on the other hand looked fine just different, and I suspect secretly kind of liked the look as it erased the middle age graying look that accompanied his expanding waistline.

As we approached the front door, we walked through with an outward look of indifference, but with an alertness that far exceeded our appearance. I was most concerned about an accidental confrontation in the lobby, elevator or hallways, without being prepared, although the wigs provided a degree of disguise, we were up against one of the most diligent adversaries we had ever encountered. The lobby area was relatively crowded, with the registration desk on the far right and an assortment of lobby shops on the left. We could see a restaurant overlooking the ocean to their front that was several steps down from the lobby floor. There were potted plants and abundant flower filled vases placed on glass tables, with a color scheme of yellows and blues tastefully decorating the walls. The windows were fitted with white plantation shutters, the approximate four-inch wide wood shutter that looks like an oversized Venetian blind.

I led the way to the elevator where we joined an elderly couple with the man carrying a small poodle in his arms. Higgins smiled and said "Good afternoon" to the couple.

"Good afternoon, where in England do you live?" The man replied with his unmistaken English accent.

Not expecting to announce his presence in any way, Higgins responded he was from London and added, "Are you visiting?"

"The woman replied, "We are visiting my cousin and her husband who are celebrating their fiftieth wedding anniversary."

"Congratulations to your cousin and her husband and have a wonderful time." Higgins said warmly as the elevator stopped on the third floor to let them off.

"It's a good thing you're here to bring some civility to this gang." I said with a chuckle.

"My pleasure sir." Higgins added as the elevator opened on the fifth floor.

They walked down the wide hall to room 516 where Hooper promised the bags would be brought. The room was large and nicely furnished and was more in the category of a suite than a standard room. Maybe Hooper took a cue from Higgins I thought, that cost was not a factor, therefore he must have assumed we were not accustomed to second-class accommodations. No sooner had they walked to the window to check out the view, there was a knock on the door, and upon opening I saw Hooper along with a bellman pushing a large brass cart filled with all of our personal belongings as well as the newly acquired 'special list' containing weapons and ammunition among other tactical operational items. "Come in Josh. You really made good time. I can't thank you enough."

After the bellman left the room, Hooper responded, "It's my pleasure Chuck," as he handed me the keys to the van. "Had it not been for Higgins here, I wouldn't have wanted to be involved. Your list looked more like a Peter Prill deal, only rumors of course. I have no first hand knowledge of the gentleman."

"Well in any event I thank you. Now what do I owe you?"

"Higgins suggested I bring an invoice and you can pay any way you like." Hooper said as he handed me a single spaced itemization of the items provided including a $10,000 deposit for the private jet, which will remain on call for three days. The first night's hotel accommodations, weapons, night vision scopes, ammunition and assorted materials, two mini-surveillance cameras and remote monitor, not to mention wigs, coveralls, and other tactical items, came to $9,757.35, or a total of $19,757.35 in US Dollars, which at the outset Higgins suggested he base his charges in order to make it simpler for me.

"Help me understand the jet deposit. If we don't need the jet for the first three days, then the deposit is charged against the cost of grounding the plane for three days and it's used up at that point?"

That's the way I understand it. Is there a problem with that? Because we can do something else, I didn't have guidelines when I reserved it?" Hooper asked.

"There is absolutely no problem whatsoever. I just needed to know what they expected in terms of timing. Who is the contact person?"

"It's a lady named Doris Sweet. She can be reached at the number on the bottom of the invoice----you see right after her name. She needs two hours advanced notice, as she must bring in her pilots as well as file a flight plan."

"Have you been in the Royal Dutch Suite?"

"I have several times."

"Would you mind sketching out the floor plan for us, or would that exceed your interest in personal involvement?"

"No not all. In order for me to agree to provide this material to you, I asked Higgins to brief me in general terms to satisfy me that I was not helping the wrong side, a position I might regret later. I was satisfied, particularly when I learned that this man is a cold-blooded murderer, with a total lack of conscience."

Hooper sat at the desk, opened the stationery folder and with the use of a postcard as a straight edge, drew an exceptional scale drawing of the Royal Dutch Suite No. 601.

"That is outstanding." I said as Hooper handed me the drawing.

"When I was working with Higgins I specialized in transferring images from recollection onto paper with the requirement of accuracy to within a quarter meter. Since I was in that very suite two weeks ago meeting with a munitions manufacturer I surveyed the suite, partly out of curiosity, partly out of habit, and mostly out of sheer boredom as the gentleman I was seeing was talking to London most of the time I was there. Since no one else was in the suite, I just used the bathroom and took the occasion to snoop around, and while doing so, I memorized the dimensions and layout of the rooms."

"How would I get a card key to the suite?"

"Well that is breaking and entering, and I don't deal in that. I could give you the number of a gent that specializes in helping people gain entrance to their rooms when they have misplaced their card keys." Hooper said with a hint of a grin.

"I believe that is the man I want to meet. Is he available now?"

"Here's his number, ask for Jake."

I wrote Hooper a check for the billing which he accepted without hesitation, considering had he received a credit card, the processing cost to him would have ranged from $500 to $1,200 or more depending on the card----and Higgins vouched for me.

Hooper left the room and I dialed Jake's number. After a long period of rings, a gruff voice answered. "Hello."

"I just left Josh Hooper and he gave me your number saying you might be able to get me a card key to a suite at the Pacific Sea."

"I might, what do you need it for?"

"Something has been misplaced and I believe I can find it in Suite 601 and return it to the proper authorities. That is all I'll be doing. I'm not stealing anything or intending to hurt anyone." I told the man called Jake.

"It will cost you four thousand Rand." Jake responded with an indifferent voice and attitude, one that I thought was a sign of someone I didn't want to do business with or for that matter even meet, but under the circumstances I needed access to the room. I did a quick mental conversion and knew that he was taking five hundred dollars and replied, "Fine, when can you get it to me?"

"How's tomorrow sometime?"

"No good I need it today."

"I'm kind of busy with another job right now."

Knowing this game I responded, "How much?"

"Another thousand, I'll have to delay another client."

"Yeah, yeah, just get it done in two hours, do you hear?" I told him in a cold voice.

"Meet me in the lobby by the gift shop in exactly two hours and bring cash." Jake said and hung up.

I unpacked the assorted items purchased from Josh Hooper and outlined plan A and B to my cohorts. Exactly two hours later at 7:00 P.M., I went down to the gift shop to meet Jake. I found a scrawny, weasel-like looking man, wearing dirty tan shorts and a dark green tee shirt, sporting a baseball cap with some kind of logo, probably representing a prison softball team I thought.

"Jake?"

"Yeah, you Josh's friend?"

"Yeah, got it?"

"Yeah, got the five thousand?"

"Yeah, how do I know it works?"

"You won't until you try it. If you don't want, it fine." The weasel-like man said as he turned to walk away.

I grabbed his shirt and pulled him back, hearing a tear as I pinned him against the wall behind a potted tree, out of sight of passer bys.

"Don't screw with me, do you hear?" I said as I twisted the tee shirt around with my fist full of cloth shoved under and pressing against Jake's throat.

"All right but look what you did to my shirt, I can't go out in public looking like this." Jake said in a whining voice.

"Stand right here." I walked around the tree, entered the gift shop and returned in less than two minutes with another green tee shirt, only this one said "Dirty Old Man", that I thought was perfect under the circumstances.

"Put this on and give me that card key and if it doesn't work I'll take the time to hunt you down, do you hear me?"

Nerves fraying, I pressed the little man against the wall again after he put on his new tee shirt and handed him the money, with my hand out taking the card key.

"Hey, this is short 80 Rand." Jake grumbled.

"Business expense, you just bought a tee shirt." I said as I shoved the man away and headed back toward the bank of elevators wearing my shabby appearing long gray wig.

"That was fun." I said as I arrived back in room 516.

"What happened?" Art asked.

"Nothing really----he just brought me flashbacks to the old days dealing with street scum in San Francisco, no big deal let's get to work."

"We're ready." Higgins said.

"Higgins, are you certain you want to take this first step? I feel guilty about dragging you into what has turned out to be a personal thing for me?"

"As I said, I'm with you all the way."

"Unfortunately, Art and I are not too swift with an English accent and that's what's required in this first step."

According to plan, Higgins picked up the pair of medium sized blue coveralls and slipped them over his clothes. He put on a navy blue baseball cap with the gold embroidered word "MAINTENANCE" on the front and slipped his silenced revolver through the gap in the side of the coveralls and into the top of his belted trousers. He put two extra ammunition clips into the tool box along with the special adhesive and a miniature TV camera. I fastened the second miniature which was the approximate size of a pencil eraser to the handle of the toolbox.

"You look great let's check the camera, how are you coming with the monitor?"

"Just a second, is the camera turned on?" Art asked.

"Yes, did you press the camera button?"

After a bit of adjusting, Art said, "That's it I have a great picture now, move the box and let me focus it."

"We'll be able to monitor your movements and rush up if you run into a problem. First you need to call the room and ask for say Mrs. Collins and use the "sorry wrong number", excuse."

"I'm ready, let's give it a go."

He picked up the telephone and dialed 610. The phone rang at least ten times before the recorder picked up and transferred to the hotel room voicemail, which caused Higgins to hang up.

"It looks like nobody is home." Higgins said with a smile. "I'm on my way. I understand there is a TV maintenance problem in 601----duty calls gentlemen." Higgins added, slipping the new card key in his pocket as he headed for the door, hoping to avoid any hotel personnel.

Art and I watched the monitor as Higgins made his way to the elevator and entered. He did a good job keeping the toolbox facing forward, allowing the camera to have the best field of vision for his backup team in room 516. Higgins reached the sixth floor and moved out into the hallway. Room 601 was the only door on the right hand side of the wide hallway. The entry consisted of double doors perhaps nine feet tall, with a large gold and red crest to the right that identified the Royal Dutch Suite.

Higgins, utilizing his years of intelligence experience with the British, casually walked up to the door and knocked. He waited and knocked again. After the third time and waiting at least three minutes he felt certain no one was going to answer, so he used his card key and opened the door. From the monitor in the room one floor below I was happy to see that Jake's card key actually worked.

CHAPTER 139

Higgins stepped into entry of the lavish suite and called out----"maintenance" and received no response. He then walked into the suite and went from room to room pointing his toolbox and on full alert for danger. He knew only too well how many times "targets" would consider an unexpected, unanswered telephone call to a hotel room, a signal that the room would soon be entered and searched, causing them to set up a death trap for anyone entering. The suite was silent as Higgins moved quietly with gun in hand as he entered into the large living room. He stopped after taking a step into the room, listening for movement or noise from any of the closed doors leading from the main room. He stood silently for a long period, moving his toolbox in a sweeping motion for our benefit in the room below. Sensing that he was alone, at least in the large living room, he crept to the first door, listened for a few seconds and turned the handle. The room was a large bedroom suite with some women's clothing on the bed and a few items hanging in the closet. There were no personal items, purse or suitcase in the room. The bathroom looked similar, like the occupant might be staying somewhere else he thought, perhaps with someone in another bedroom.

Higgins left the room as he found it and went to the next room. It was clearly a man's room with a suitcase and only a few items of men's clothing. There was nothing to indicate that it was Peter Prill's room, so it must be Mason Hampton's, AKA Gerhard Schultz's room, however it didn't look much like it was being lived in. The bathroom was devoid of anything personal, not even a toothbrush or shaving items.

Higgins heard a noise sounding like the front door opening. His heart raced and thumped in his chest. He silently glided toward the closet door and pulled it almost closed behind him, leaving a small crack to observe anyone entering the room. He stood waiting, with his right hand tightly gripping his drawn gun. Finally as it seemed like hours rather than seconds, there was a knock on the bedroom door and it burst open. To his surprise, standing in the doorway, was a rather overweight hotel maid carrying fresh towels for the bathroom. After tending to that duty she came toward the closet, walked past and moved to the bed pulling down the bedspread and turning down the sheet. She reached in her pocket, placed a gold foil packet, presumably a small piece of chocolate, on the pillow and moved to the other rooms providing similar treatment to complete her evening assignment.

Higgins stood still shaking, all along praying that he would not have to get into a lethal confrontation on this trip that Rosa was not too happy about. After he heard the front door close with a thud, he waited and listened, then went to the last door and walked in. He felt confident that had someone been in the room there would have been some conversation with the maid and he would have heard that. There clearly was not, so he walked confidently into the last room. Walking to the dresser Higgins found papers, letters and brochures on guns, many with the name Peter Prill on the cover sheets. He looked in the closet and found a wide assortment of men's clothing. Feeling confident that he was in Peter Prill's room, Higgins decided to install the two mini-cameras before anyone returned to the room. It only took a minute to position both devices----one in the living room and the second in Mason's presumed room, where he found locations on the wall sconces that easily hid a mini-camera. He then decided a quick look around for evidence was in order as long as he didn't stay longer than two or three minutes.

Higgins went back into Prill's bedroom, walked up to the nightstand and noticed a folded sheet of paper with the name Peter written on it. He opened it and read the simple two lines. "Peter, Mason asked me to get him a room in another hotel for security purposes. I did, but hated to leave you alone and wouldn't had I not known that you were entertaining the Prince and his entourage this evening and didn't need me. Mason didn't want me to tell you the name of the hotel----but if you need me to fly at an earlier time I would never let you down, so call me at Hotel Protea. Mason wanted me to tell you how much he appreciates your help and has changed his package shipment to arrive under my name at the new hotel. He feels safer. See you tomorrow. Love, Jen."

Higgins didn't want to disturb anything in the room, so after making a mental note of the contents, left the bedroom and headed for the main door. He twisted the handle and confidently strolled from the suite without being noticed and headed toward the elevator. The trip back to 516 was uneventful, and upon returning to the room his teammates were congratulating him on his cool response to the maid coming into the suite, as well as the note they were able to read from the monitor as he positioned the toolbox to read the letter from Jen.

"Great work Higgins. It looks like we need to take a trip to the Protea Hotel and get *him* before his package comes tomorrow and he disappears." I said.

"This is a lot trickier. We need to figure out who this *Jen* is, but I suspect she is Prill's assistant or stewardess or something of that nature. We just don't know her last name. For that matter we don't really know her first name. It's either Jenny or Jennifer, or something like that. Any ideas?" Art asked us.

"She probably isn't registered at this hotel. There was nothing in the room that gave you a clue?"

"No, she really didn't leave anything of a personal nature behind other than a few items of clothing."

"Let's go to the airport and check on Euro Outfitters' Gulfstream. There must be a record of the flight crew or some documentation that would give us the names of those landing on that plane, if nothing else for customs purposes." I said.

"Maybe I can call Josh and see if he knows a way to get the names of the flight crew. It might save us some time." Higgins suggested.

"Good idea, call him."

Higgins called Josh Hooper and asked for his assistance which he readily offered and said he would call a contact in customs that was a holdover from the old days in his British intelligence work and call them back.

"While we wait for Josh, let's talk about a game plan for apprehending this guy." I said as I sat in a chair near the window.

CHAPTER 140

"Mr. Prill!" Frank said.

"Is there something wrong with the plane?"

"No sir, but I thought you ought to know that my friend at customs----you know the one, just called me and said a supervisor called and asked him to verify from his work sheet those who landed in Cape Town on the Euro Outfitters' Gulfstream. He said he had to give him the names although he didn't know why they needed them tonight, since his supervisor could access the information at his office from the official custom files in the morning."

"Thanks Frank, did he ask anything else? No, he really seemed interested in Jennifer, asked for a description and residence address."

"You did right by calling, thanks again, we'll be leaving in four days, enjoy your stay here."

The telephone rang several times and reached a voice mail as Jennifer and Mason left the room shortly after seven for a dinner reservation at a restaurant overlooking the city called the Cliffs. Peter hesitated as he wondered whether he should leave a message with any detail, yet he didn't want to allow this information to be so diluted that the importance might be missed, so he said, "Jennifer, Frank called, his friend at customs received a call from a supervisor who was interested in you and your description, maybe he wants to take you to dinner----thought you and your friend should know this." Peter said as he ended the call.

They were discussing various alternatives for the capture and abduction of Mason Hampton from the Hotel Protea, when the telephone rang. I reached for the phone and handed it over to Higgins.

"Yes, yes, I have that, thank you very much Josh."

"How are we doing?"

"Very well, Jennifer Heath, 32 years old, red hair, five-foot nine inches tall, one hundred and fifteen pounds and lives in London. If we need one, we can get a photo tomorrow."

"We need to call the hotel and asked if Miss Heath has checked in yet. After we confirm that, we'll have to figure how to go about finding her room number. Any ideas?" I asked Art and Higgins.

"I suppose we could send her flowers and follow the delivery person, but then she would be alerted." Art said.

"We could accept the fact that they would be alerted and just move in right then after the delivery guy leaves." I added.

"I think we need to take a look at the hotel, even get a room in order to have a staging area and a place to keep our quarry until it's safe to transport him to the jet." Higgins suggested.

"OK. Let's call for a reservation and go over there. I guess *you* could get the room Art, and show your identification, I don't think your name is on his radar screen."

"That's fine, I'll call now. What's the number?"

I found the telephone book in the bedside table drawer and thumbed through the pages until I found Hotel Protea and gave the book to Art while pointing at the number. Art punched in the hotel number and waited for an answer.

"Good evening, Hotel Protea." The voice responded.

"Yes, can you tell me if Miss Heath has arrived yet?" Art asked in a relaxed pleasant voice.

"Let me check sir."

"Yes she checked in this afternoon, may I connect you now?"

"No thank you, we have an appointment in the morning and I just wanted to be certain she has arrived." Taking a chance, Art followed up with, "One more thing, I didn't call for a reservation in advance but do you have a single available for tonight and tomorrow night?"

"As a matter of fact we do, and if you like I can put you on Miss Heath's floor."

"That would be fine but if you should happen to see her, I would like to surprise her." Art said in a pleasing tone of voice.

"I fully understand, your room number will be 616. I need your name, address, and credit card please."

Art gave her the information and said he would be there within the hour and hung up the phone.

"What's the story?"

"She's on the sixth floor and so are we. I have a room for the next two nights. The operator agreed it was our secret and promised not to tell her should she speak with her."

CHAPTER 141

Jennifer and Mason had a leisurely dinner and took a stroll afterward, looking at the view of the city below and the ocean beyond from the hillside restaurant gardens. They sat on a bench with a sweeping view of the twinkling lights below and talked about life in general, places they both had been, and their likes and dislikes---- just as any couple might while getting better acquainted. Jennifer was beginning to like this mysterious man even though she sensed danger; she seemed to thrive on the excitement. She took his arm as they walked back up the garden path to the restaurant front door where they found a waiting taxi for the return ride to the hotel.

Upon opening the door to their room they noticed the red message light flashing on the telephone sitting on the desk. Jennifer picked up the phone and pressed the message button. The voice was Peters and her face drained. After hearing the message, with a shaky voice she handed the receiver to Mason saying, "You need to hear this."

Mason stood expressionless, thinking, never showing emotion. He pressed the button that caused the message to replay and absorbed every word, carefully, after which he erased the message.

"I thought you weren't going to tell him where you were staying." Mason said, staring unemotionally at Jennifer.

Worried and embarrassed by her misleading him, she said she only did so in case he wanted her to fly out sooner than expected.

Mason looked up the Pacific Sea telephone number and called Peter. "Hello." Peter replied.

"Peter, this is Mason. Thanks for the warning. When are you planning on leaving Cape Town?"

"Not for three more days, I have an unavoidable appointment. What do you need?"

"I'd like to rent your plane for twenty four hours, to fly to Hong Kong. They can turn around as soon as they land. Under the circumstances, I don't know another way to safely get out of the country. I'll pay what ever you want and put it on my high-credit Visa card." Mason said.

"I won't charge you a damn thing."

"I won't feel right----let me pay for fuel, at least." Mason said.

"OK, give Jennifer your credit card number and when we know how much the fuel cost is, we'll bill that much to the card."

"Can I leave at say noon tomorrow?" Mason asked.

"No problem, I'll call Frank and let him know."

"You'll see that Phil is taken care of? Charge my card for all expenses, you hear?"

"OK Mason, but I don't want too."

"I really appreciate this Peter." Mason said and hung up.

"There are some people on my trail and are so close they may be in the hotel right now. I have to move on but I need you to get that package that's coming here tomorrow before I leave the country. I'm also going to need to find another place to stay tonight, and you should too. We should leave now." Mason said to Jennifer who appeared to be in a state of total shock, thinking that she would at least have a last romantic night with him in this beautiful ocean front room. Now they were scurrying like rats leaving a sinking ship.

"Who are these people?" Jennifer asked with an edge in her voice and a look of anger on her face.

Mason looked at her and assured himself once again, that his recent problems have occurred because a woman, without thinking, said something to someone that led his adversaries to him. He thought it had to be Winters again, as the police would not have been so subtle in dealing with the flight crew about occupants of the Gulfstream, and he proved how clever he was when he managed to avoid the bomb in his Lisbon hotel. With the police surely on his trail and Winters probably ahead of them, he couldn't delay.

CHAPTER 142

We loaded up our necessary gear into the van and after obtaining directions to the Hotel Protea drove the several miles north along the coast to the hotel driveway, passing by and circling around to the parking lot on the north side of the building. Art walked around and through the front door, this time without his wig and went directly to the registration desk. He signed in and was given directions and his key and indicated he would retrieve his own bags that were still in the car in the lot. He proceeded through the lobby, down a long hallway that led to the side parking lot. Higgins and I saw him coming out the hotel and picked up the two heavy canvas bags of weapons, surveillance equipment and the miscellaneous disguises and assorted items provided by Josh Hopper. Their clothes and other personal things remained at the Pacific Sea Hotel.

"Let's you and I get up to the room Art, and see if we can figure out Jennifer Heath's room number. Higgins if you don't mind, I'd like to station you in the lobby to watch the front door and registration desk. You have her description and have seen the photos of Hampton. Use the radio to call us in the room if you see anything. We'll call you if we're able to figure out the room number. If by chance you get friendly enough with one of the hotel staff to extract the number, give us a call. OK?"

"Perfect, I will move into position right away and check in every few minutes."

"Good." I said as we lugged the heavy bags to the elevator and pressed the sixth floor button.

CHAPTER 143

Earlier, while Art was registering, Mason and Jennifer walked out a lobby door on the opposite side of the building and moved down the path to the street where they caught a taxi. Jennifer carried her small overnight bag and Mason his laptop and new luggage filled with the wardrobe purchased earlier in the afternoon. In order to go underground until he left the country, Mason decided he would select a place to stay where he could easily use an alias, register as husband and wife and pay cash.

"Good evening." Mason said on his best behavior as he opened the door for a still shaking Jennifer. "We are looking for a small motel for the night, nothing fancy as we have an early flight in the morning. Do you know of such a place?"

"Sure, there is a small quiet place up the coast a few miles and closer to the airport that should have a vacancy." The driver said, thinking that they don't look like husband and wife.

The motel was as requested, not fancy but probably catered to those that didn't want to be noticed, particularly by their spouses. Mason paid the driver and gave him a reasonable tip not enough to be memorable and not too little to be memorable, just enough. He asked him to wait for a moment to be certain there was a room available.

They walked into the dumpy office, where a large woman was sitting on a chrome-legged dinette type chair, probably on a plastic cushioned seat which one might be able to see had it not been for the fact that the seat became invisible as her massive body engulfed it along with the top third of the now fragile looking legs. She was middle-aged and her stringy thinning brown hair with streaks of gray was hanging down her face, partially blocking the view of the flickering black and white TV on the stand in the corner of the office.

"Good evening," Mason said, pouring out his charm to this sad looking woman, "My wife and I have an early flight in the morning and we would like a room if you have one."

She looked at him, with a blank stare and finally said, "It will cost you four hundred cash, four-twenty if you use a credit card."

"I'll pay cash." Mason said with an indistinguishable sigh of relief.

He pulled the bills from his wallet and signed the register as Mr. and Mrs. Donald Coleman, from New York City.

"Number six," she said as she tossed a key on the counter, attached to a turquoise oval tag reading five, and a big 6 scrawled over it with a black marker pen.

Mason picked up the key and said, "Thanks.", as he turned to see Jennifer standing in the doorway with a look of "what on earth have I gotten myself into?"

They walked to room six and found everything as perceived. The bed was a double, with a sag in the middle under a white chenille thread-bare bedspread. There was a bathroom that could best be described as basic, with brown water stains under the faucet and a shower that no one would want to use. A TV sat in the corner of the room on a small wooden table.

Mason turned to Jennifer and said, "I'm so sorry you are here in this awful place, if you like I can send you back to Paul's hotel, but I think you're probably safer here."

"Why do you say that? What have I done that puts me in some kind of danger---- and from whom?"

Mason paused and said, "You've done nothing wrong, except that some desperate people are after me and there's no telling what they might do to find me." Mason said knowing he was lying about Winter's state of mind, and the only person in jeopardy was himself. His only goal was to keep an eye on her until she retrieved his new identities at the Hotel Protea tomorrow morning.

"All right, I'll try and make the best of this hell hole." She said as she walked to the bed and lay down---- looking up at Mason.

CHAPTER 144

Art and I were at a loss as to which of the fourteen rooms beside our own was occupied by Jennifer Heath and Mason Hampton. We finally decided on the direct approach. Art would feign drunkenness and with his card key in hand, stumble against each door knocking and muttering until someone opened it and then he could excuse himself as having the wrong room.

"Higgins, any luck?" I asked as I called him in the lobby on the small radio transmitter.

"No luck here, anything on your end?"

"Art's going to knock on each door and act like a drunk in order to see if we can't at least eliminate most of the rooms."

"Sounds like a reasonable plan. I've had no opportunity to get close to any staff on this end."

"Higgins, why don't you come on up here?"

"Directly!"

Art walked to the first door, 601 and tried his key making a racket and pounded on the door a few times, saying "Martha, open up". The door opened and a middle-aged man appeared, to which Art apologized in a drunken act and moved down the hall to the next room. The system seemed to work, because of the fourteen rooms, he was able to eliminate nine, leaving five to narrow down the search. It was clear that the hotel was not full and several of the five could be vacant. Art went back to the room where I was waiting.

"Well, I narrowed it down to five." Art said, "Any ideas?"

"Yes, I want you to call the front desk and tell them you are trying to move five fellow business associates to this hotel from another and want to know if there is enough rooms available on the sixth floor so they could be close to each other."

"Good idea, I'll try it."

Art pushed the hotel desk button on the phone. "Front desk."

"This is Art Levy, I checked in earlier this evening and I'm trying to convince five of my associates that are staying in different hotels to come here and stay on my floor so we can easily meet and get together. Do you have any vacancies on this floor?"

"Yes we have three and two more on five."

"How close are the rooms to mine in 616?"

"We have 614, 618, and 602 available."

"Great let me talk with them and I'll get back to you if I can convince them to move." Art said, as he disconnected. "It's 612 or 617."

"OK, we need to eliminate one, any ideas?"

"Let's try the door knock program on these two. As soon as we get one response, we have our answer." Art suggested.

"Do you mind Art?"

"Not if we get this thing going, I don't."

"I think we should take the last mini-camera, the one attached to the tool box and mount it in the hallway, so we can watch both doors without sneaking out in the hallway or leaving the door open to see who's coming and going." Higgins offered, looking at me.

"Let's do it before Art does his door knocking, that way we can be certain he's all right."

"I'll mount it." Higgins said, as he opened one of the big canvas bags removed the camera from the toolbox and set the monitor on the table. He took the adhesive tube and the mini-camera with him and walked out of the room. The hallway was unoccupied and he turned toward the elevator in order to mount the camera in such a position that he could establish a field of vision looking back down the hallway. Higgins selected a location just below a seashell shaped wall sconce, a location that would easily disguise the small lens. The hallway still quiet, he placed a small amount of adhesive on the rear of the camera and carefully positioned it against the wall. He then rushed back to their room to see if it was properly aimed. Seeing that the monitor was able to view the entire hallway and could cause the picture to zoom from the monitor controls, Higgins was satisfied with his work and closed the door completely.

"It looks like your turn Art, with your very effective drunk act." I chided him playfully.

"Thanks old buddy. Don't forget, I've seen you rehearse this role a time or two, yourself."

Art caused his clothes and wig hair to be in as much disarray as possible. Before leaving the room and although the surveillance camera was operating, just in case he thought, he cracked the door a little to see if there was anyone in the hall. Opening a bit further, he was satisfied that he would not be seen leaving the room. He went into his act knowing that Higgins and I this time could watch him on the monitor, so he picked up his routine in his first televised acting debut. Art swayed and stumbled and did a spin, bouncing off the walls, while back in the room Higgins roared in delight as I just shook my head, grinning at my friend of many years. Art stumbled over to 612, bounced off the door and held out his card key and started fumbling with the card slot, making enough noise with the plastic card to alert someone if the room was occupied.

The door burst open, and standing before him was a little gray haired lady holding a very large, heavy looking green glass vase in her right hand, raised slightly above her head. "What exactly is it you want sir?" Came the response to Art's fumbling act. Art came to his senses immediately as he was not certain he wanted five pounds of glass breaking over his head.

"Madam, it is my mistake. I see that this is not 616. I apparently became disoriented on the way up. I have trouble with heights you know." He said with a smile.

"Sir, your trouble originated in the pub not the elevator." She said with a scowl, momentarily lowering her weapon, after deciding that this man was no trouble to anyone but himself----or a wife if he had one.

"Sorry ma'am." Art said with a bit of a bow as he made a rapid retreat to room 616.

Upon opening the door, Higgins and I could not contain ourselves. We were doubled up in laughter. Without discounting the seriousness of the mission, we felt comfortable allowing some humor to creep into the process.

"That was your finest hour Art. You deserve an academy award----at least a nomination." I said, still laughing.

"Art, I thought you were magnificent in the finest tradition of British Intelligence. You would be a welcome addition to our group, let me assure you."

"All right knock it off you guys. It was serious and dangerous work, I didn't see you two out there making a fool of yourself for the cause."

"Of course, you're right. But never fear, to prove your devotion to duty in this case, Higgins found the record button on the monitor and recorded your performance for posterity, and Jimmy too."

"Give me that tape."

"There isn't one, it's on the hard drive and we can't erase it. Seriously Art, you did a great job and we know the room is 617. Would you knock on that door again, and do your thing. We just need to know that it's not occupied at the moment, and somehow gain access to it?"

"I will, if I can break that damn monitor when this is over."

"You've got it." I said as Art left the room, card key in hand and stumbled against the door to 617 without a response. He then after fumbling with the door started knocking and after at least a dozen knocks and hearing nothing, went back to his room.

Without further comment from Higgins or me about his acting ability, Art said upon entering their room, "that does it. We have the right room and nobody's home. I'm not certain what the benefit to getting inside is, but lacking another plan that seems to be it."

"What do you think Higgins, should we be waiting in the room when he comes back and jump him there?" I asked turning to Higgins.

"Well it depends on how paranoid the man is. We don't know if he left some device attached to the door to see if someone has entered. This man has survived for many years on probably every continent in the world, and he didn't do so by being sloppy. He may in fact have left his own mini-camera watching the room and will play back the tape before he comes even close. The monitor could be in a closet on the floor below."

"It's getting late and I doubt if he's out partying when he's most likely trying to escape as soon as possible. He must think things are closing in or he wouldn't have moved here. I think we need to take the chance that he might figure someone has looked at his room. If he's moved out again, we'd be sitting here looking for a man that won't be back. We need to know that." I said.

"You're right." Art added. "I don't know that we have time for your pal Jake, however if he could get here in say a half hour it would be worth the wait to avoid knocking the door down and drawing all kinds of attention."

"I agree," Higgins threw in.

"I'll call him now." I dialed Jake's number.

"Yeah."

"Jake this is Chuck Winters again."

"What's the matter didn't the key work?" He asked suspiciously.

"No, it worked fine. I have an emergency job, same thing, different hotel---- double the money if you can get here in thirty minutes or less."

"I'm on my way, where am I going?"

I gave Jake directions to meet in our room and placed the receiver back on the phone saying, "If nothing else we'll know if we should be sitting around here. I do know one thing, if it looks like they've gone to another location, we need to set up a surveillance watch on the front desk here for packages going to Jennifer Heath or Gerhard Schultz, which I suspect is the only identity available to him at the moment. We'll need to find when the Fed Express and other overnight type trucks pull in, and where they usually park when making a delivery. My guess is he won't show his face around here. If he did leave, he must suspect that either we or the authorities on his tail. It might be worthwhile to have a photo of Jennifer, if we can get one before the morning overnight's come in. Can you check with Josh and tell him we'd like to take him up on his offer, but need it probably before 9:00 A.M.? Higgins, will you ask Josh to include a tranquilizing gun, complete with enough potency to put a man out safely for six to eight hours? We don't want to kill him, just control him, OK?"

"Good idea, I'll call him now."

CHAPTER 145

Jennifer and Mason were lying in the lumpy bed, nude with only a sheet loosely pulled over them. There was little conversation except for the repeated request to discuss for the third or fourth time the plan for tomorrow morning. Jennifer was getting frustrated with the repetition, but repeated her role----"I go to the hotel at 9:30 A.M., ask for the Federal Express package I am expecting. They will say Federal Express doesn't arrive until about 10:00 A.M. I will say, 'I will not be in my room, so be certain to hold it at the desk'. I will check back and pick it up around 10:00 A.M. or shortly thereafter. Mason, I understand what to do. Then with the package, I take a taxi to the same coffee shop in the mall where we stopped. You will be waiting with our luggage there. You will go to the airport and fly out in the Gulfstream and I will go back to my room in Peter's suite like a good little girl and life will be beautiful."

Mason thought in silence for a few moments and turned to Jennifer, looking at her face as the moonlight streamed through the dirty motel window. Not knowing her feelings and facial expressions, he could only guess that she felt both disappointed and used, not emotions a man such as himself would have, but one he could imagine she might----if that was possible for him. He reached under the sheet and took her hand and gently squeezed. She turned her head towards him and looked at his eyes in the moonlight and caused her mouth to show a slight smile. He gently moved toward her and brushed her lips at the same time saying, "I'm sorry. I've tangled you up in my problems without thinking how you might feel." Mason not really into this felt he needed to reverse the bad feelings he was sure she had about the latest turn of events, as well as about him at this point. His only goal was to get his package and he didn't care how he did it.

"I understand you're under pressure." She said, thinking that maybe he might ask her to go with him tomorrow, or to meet him someplace when he settles.

Jennifer turned and kissed him back, this time with passion as each got into their role playing for reasons of their own. They made love for the second time that day and fell asleep in each other's arms.

CHAPTER 146

Jake knocked on the door at 11:30 P.M. I opened it and allowed weasel man to come in. "Do you have the ten thousand?"

"You're twenty minutes late----I'm paying you five thousand, take it or leave it, besides, you're so late the guy will be back shortly and I won't even need you."

"All right five thousand." Jake grumbled as I peeled off half the bills and pushed him out the door.

"Wait a minute, you only gave me half."

"That's right, the other half when the card works." I said, exacting a small amount of vengeance on this nasty man.

Three minutes later Jake knocked on their door and held out the same generic looking card with a magnetic strip that hopefully would allow the door to 617 to open as if it were opened by the key provided by the hotel. I motioned Jake to follow him and they walked to room 617 and tried it. The green light came on and knowing that the door had unlocked, pulled the card out of the slot and motioned Jake to follow him back to the room, where Art and Higgins had been watching the monitor, following their movements. I handed Jake the remaining twenty five hundred Rand and watched him slink out of the room toward the elevator. While Art and Higgins watched the room on the monitor to be certain no one entered, I called room 617 and let the phone ring until the recording came on and hung up, although if someone were in there they probably would have heard the card key unlock the door.

"I think its show time gentlemen. Lets get equipped." We put on their coveralls with the deep pockets filled with the necessary paraphernalia for the mission, complete with loaded weapons as well as replacement clips.

The three of us walked across to 617. I knocked on the door one more time then slid the card key into the slot and the green light appeared on the locking mechanism. I slowly turned the handle, right hand on my silenced Glock and opened the door while standing to the side. Most of the room was visible except the bathroom. I walked to the half open door and pushed it aside, gun at the ready and pushed the shower curtain with the muzzle of my weapon. Empty! I walked to the closet and peered inside as it was more than half open, shoving it all the way, finding nothing. I went to the bed and found a pedestal arrangement to prevent guests from leaving clothing or for that matter garbage behind. The room was empty, yet the bed had been used. A closer examination indicated that the relationship was other than platonic.

"These people are gone." I said. "Not to return----ever."

"Now what?" Art asked.

"We watch the front desk. First, Art you ask when an overnight package might arrive as you're expecting something and you aren't certain if it's Fed Ex or another currier. Ask where you could pick it up because you won't be in the room. Then ask for those two other rooms and tell them to add it to your tab, and you go down and get the card keys. Higgins and I can at least have a bed while we wait for the morning show. The fact is that's a good time to inquire about your "package", they can even show you where it's held if not delivered to the room when you pick up our keys."

"I'm on it, and when I get back up I want to see some snacks delivered by room service and a bottle or good Scotch----- right Higgins?" Art asked.

"Right-O Art, I do agree."

"Don't worry about that stuff. I'm hungry and thirsty too, not certain about which order though." I said as I scratched the side of my head, grinning.

CHAPTER 147

It was seven in the morning and Mason had quietly allowed Jennifer to sleep, while he showered, shaved and dressed in casual clothes, khaki trousers, pale yellow knit shirt and white Nike shoes. When he picked up his suitcase to finish packing, Jennifer stirred and opened her eyes without saying anything, but looking around, refreshing her memories of the good and the bad of the previous evening.

"Hi, were you going without me?" She asked with a devilish smile, apparently thinking that after their lovemaking again last night, Mason wound never do such a thing.

"You know better than that, I just got up early to plan my morning before I meet you at the café. I need to pick up some things, and thought I would check the telephone directory. If you want to shower, we can have a nice breakfast and then split up and go about our morning business."

"That would be nice. I wonder if we can leave our bags someplace, so we don't have to drag them around." She said.

"Good idea, I'll ask the lovely lady at the desk if we can leave them here until later this morning." Mason said as he walked out the door and headed toward the office.

In the office, Mason arranged for storing the bags and asked to see the telephone directory. He sat in the only chair, while "gracious" stuffed massive quantities of chocolate doughnuts into her unfriendly mouth.

Mason asked for a piece of blank paper so that he could write down the places he needed to visit for supplies. When he finished he asked where the pay phone was and requested an assortment of change for his calls. He thanked the woman after handing her the equivalent of twenty dollars, US, and walked out the door and across the parking area to the curb, where a pay phone sat on an iron post. He called each of the numbers, spoke with a vast degree of knowledge about his field, "mining", and after gaining the confidence of the personnel from each company, he set up an appointment for picking up his purchases.

"Hi." Mason said smiling, as he walked in on Jennifer standing in her panties and in the process of putting on her bra. "Do you need help?"

"I bet you are better at taking these things off than putting them on, am I right?" She said smiling.

"You've got me there, but I'm willing to learn." He said, grinning.

"I bet you are, but I think I have this job finished. How did you do with your girlfriend at the office?"

"I'm afraid I didn't make her the same offer, but she will hold our bags."

"Sounds like you had to make her a better offer." Jennifer said teasing.

"Not hardly, it took cash. Are you hungry?"

"I'm famished; I'll just be a minute. I'm through with this bag, you can drop it by the office if you like and I'll be ready when you return."

Mason picked up her bag as well as his, walked out of the room and across the gravel parking area to the office.

The taxi arrived in less than ten minutes, and looking quite out of place, Mason and Jennifer left the grounds of the seedy looking motel and headed downtown. They decided that they might as well eat at the same coffee shop in the mall that they intend to meet after completing their mutual assignments.

Upon sitting down at a table alongside the pedestrian mall area, Jennifer asked Mason a question that had been gnawing at her for hours, "will I ever see you again?"

Mason looked at her, uncertain how he should respond. He liked her as a woman and he liked her sexually. He just felt that entanglements were the source of his problems, yet if he said the wrong thing, he would risk getting caught without the necessary forged documents he needed her to retrieve. She was looking at him not as a demanding woman, but as a person that seemed to care about "them", and had certainly bent over backwards to help him, for no good reason.

"If it is OK with you, when I get settled, which will be soon, I'd like to send for you to come visit and spend some time, kind of play it by ear. Is that all right; would you like to do that?" Mason asked, the words even surprising him.

"I would like that, but under one condition." She said with a serious look on her face.

"What's that?"

"That it be soon." She said, broadly smiling.

"Madam, you have a deal." Mason said as he rose and gently kissed her lips, astounded as to how this lady had the effect on him that she does.

After a leisurely breakfast, Mason and Jennifer walked to the street bordering the Mall and each took a taxi in a different direction, agreeing to meet at 11:00 A.M. back at the coffee shop.

CHAPTER 148

We rose early and agreed to have breakfast in Art's room watching the monitor, being fully aware that it was a waste of time. By 9:00 A.M. a knock on the door produced a messenger with a large brown package addressed to me. It was the photo of Jennifer Heath, which happened to be eight and a half by eleven inches in size, and along with it a dart gun with a number of darts of varying strengths, and specifications for the safe use of each. There was also a note form Josh, saying, "This is on the house, good luck".

With the photo, Higgins removed the mini-camera from the hallway and re-positioned it across from the lobby, focused on the reservation desk. This way they could watch from the room until the time drew closer, and at the same time Higgins was sitting in the lobby near the front desk with his radio for communications to the room.

At 9:30AM sharp, Jennifer walked casually into the hotel and stepped up to the reception desk. She looked very attractive in tan shorts, a pink silk blouse and leather sandals. Her hair was pulled back in a ponytail and she looked much younger than her early thirties. Higgins picked her up immediately and called us in the room. We rushed to the elevator to join him.

Jennifer conversed briefly with the desk clerk and walked away toward the coffee shop. Higgins walked a discreet distance, looking at a newspaper as he stopped near the gift shop. He felt confident that her background would not give her the innate ability to notice everyone within her field of vision, while noting any irregularity or unusual action. She was, according to the records provided, a member of Prill's flight crew and probably not much more. She glanced at her watch and sat at a table for two in the rear of the restaurant.

Art and I saw Higgins as we exited the elevator and walked into the gift shop. Higgins, feeling that she was safely positioned in the restaurant, quickly joined us while constantly watching the restaurant entrance through the glass window in the gift shop. Holding a newspaper I said, "There's no question, she's willingly assisting him. I don't know if she knows his background, or if Peter Prill just glossed it over as a friend from the Nam days. I don't think we should strong-arm her. Because of her apparent innocent background, I think we can successfully follow her to Hampton, unless he's somewhere around here watching as we speak. I'm confident he'll have no trouble picking us up as "out of place", no matter how hard we try in this setting."

"The Fed Express and DHL arrive at 10:00 A.M. and 3:00PM. An overnight should be here at 10:00 A.M. unless they wanted a less costly delivery, which in this case is unlikely. My guess, she'll walk back to the desk a little after 10:00 A.M. or when she sees the Fed Express guy, pick up the package and head for the door and either meet Mason on the street or at a prearranged site." Art said.

"We can pick up his trail when Jennifer hands off the package to him. I don't think he'll use a third party. I think we just might have to use the dart gun with the relaxant, kind of like bringing down a bull elephant." I said.

"I think we need to pack our stuff in the van and be ready to roll when she gets the package, assuming today's the delivery date. Give me your card keys and I'll get a bellman to take whatever's in the rooms and put it in the van. If we have to fly out quick we can have our stuff shipped from the Pacific Sea." Art said.

"I can get Josh to oversee that, not to worry." Higgins added, as Art headed toward a bellman standing near the reception desk.

Higgins and I decided the best place for observation was the coffee shop where Jennifer was waiting. They could sit there without looking suspicious and leave when she does. At ten minutes to ten Art walked back into the lobby, looking around, seeing Jennifer at her table reading a newspaper he quickly found Higgins and me sitting not too far from her. I saw him and motioned him to join us.

In a quiet voice he said, "Everything's in the van and I moved it to the circular driveway so we can leave at a moments notice and follow her cab---- whichever way it goes."

"Good, thanks Art. I've been thinking, why don't you casually walk to the desk the same time she does, and ask if your Fed. Express letter has arrived yet. The moment she stands take off toward the desk, she won't get suspicious if you get there first. You could hang around and say how important it is, yadda, yadda, yadda, and she could join you in looking for her package. Maybe you could even bond." I said grinning.

"Yeah, yeah, yeah, why do I always have to charm the ladies? At least she isn't old with a vase in her hand." Art said with a forced smile.

"Because you're the handsome one, and oh yeah, you already asked about an overnight letter."

We sat there, making small talk as the minutes dragged by at an excruciating slow pace.

"She's up----go Art!" I said, as Art smoothly rose and strode to the entrance and reached the desk with too much time to spare, since she stopped to pay her check at the restaurant cashier. Noticing the problem, Art engaged the desk clerk in assistance with directions to the airport, as he 'was driving and not familiar with the area'. As soon as he saw Jennifer approaching he said, "I think I have it. Now most importantly, I'm expecting a Federal Express package this morning. Has it arrived yet?" He said just as she reached the desk, and loud enough for her to hear every word.

"We are expecting that delivery any minute now. They are usually quite prompt and arrive very close to ten." The clerk said.

"I'm waiting for the same thing. You say it should be here any minute now?"

"Yes ma'am. Under what name?"

"Jennifer Heath." She replied smiling.

"You sir?"

"Arthur Levy." He said, not being concerned about any connection to the case with Jennifer Heath.

"If you would care to sit for a minute he should be right up." He said as he pointed to the couch at the end of the counter.

"Thanks." Art said as he stood back and motioned with his extended arm for Jennifer to precede him to the couch, which she did.

"I'm Art." He said as he extended his hand to shake hers as the two sat side by side on the couch.

"Jennifer----I hope he's right and it doesn't take long. I have an appointment."

"Me too, you English?"

"Yes, you sound American."

"Good guess, but I'm sure it's pretty obvious."

"Vacation or business?"

"A little of both----you?"

"Oh, mostly business, but it's my first time and I'd really like more time to see things." He said.

"I know." Jennifer politely added.

"The desk clerk is waving, they must be here." Art said as he rose.

They walked side by side to the desk and the clerk said, "Miss Heath, I have a package from Zurich for you, is that the one you were expecting?" He asked.

Not knowing the origin of the package, it threw her for a moment and she regained her composure and replied, "Yes it is."

"Mr. Levy, there wasn't a package for you. Are you sure it was Fed Express?"

"Yes, they must have missed the deadline, I'm certain it will be in tomorrow, thanks." Art said as he turned to Jennifer.

"I guess I have to wait, do you need a lift I'm going downtown?"

"That's all right, I can take a taxi. I'm just going to the Mall area to meet someone." She said thinking that was stupid, it's a good thing

Mason didn't hear her talking to a complete stranger and telling him where she was going to meet someone.

"Well good luck, enjoy your trip." Art said.

"Thank you so much, you too." She said as she headed toward the door and the taxis lined up at the curb.

Higgins and I were already in the van when Art walked out the lobby door. I was at the wheel and motioned for him to get in as Higgins was watching Jennifer and making note of the number of the taxi she was entering.

"She's going to "The Mall". I think it's a shopping area in the center of the city." Art said.

"Josh, where's "The Mall?" Higgins asked on his cell phone. "Thanks for everything."

"It's right in the city center. It's comprised of several streets, closed off and converted into a shopping area. This road will take us directly to it. Just follow that taxi, no problem unless we lose it." Higgins said.

CHAPTER 149

Utilizing my surveillance driving experience from my detective work in San Francisco, I was confident Jennifer had no idea she was being followed. We were able to move in directly behind her taxi without a problem and were right behind her when I stopped as she was getting out.

"Art you stay with the car and keep your radio on, we may need some help picking up their trail if they give us the slip, besides we don't want her to make you, it might spook her."

Art took the wheel, Higgins and I started following her. I lagged back thinking Mason might recognize me, however Higgins moved up very close and I could tell he was a real pro at surveillance. He was able to move in and out of vendor's booths and stores without being more than twenty feet away from her. She soon reached her destination, a coffee shop that served food as well. She went in and took a table in the rear looking around for her appointment date. After fifteen minutes a waiter went to her table and whispered something in her ear. She sat a few minutes, stood with the package in her hand and went to the back where the restrooms were and entered the ladies room. Higgins watched the door from a close vantage point as women entered and left. After fifteen minutes, Higgins and I were convinced she left through another door in the restroom, when she suddenly appeared and walked out without the package.

"Art, can you hear me?" I asked as I spoke quietly into the small radio transmitter.

"I hear you, over."

"She passed it off to someone in the ladies restroom." I said as I watched Jennifer walk by. Waiting a few seconds until she was out of earshot I continued. I turned to Higgins who was by my side. "It won't do us any good to pounce on her because I don't think she knows a thing, but I would like to talk with that waiter who told her to go in there. Art, can you still hear me? She's heading your way if you are still double-parked where we got out. Try and follow her and call me on the radio if you've picked her up again."

"Got ya." Art replied. I see her coming now, out." Art said as he signed off.

I had the equivalent of one hundred dollars US, in my hand and waived it in front of the waiter's face. "What did you tell that red haired woman sitting at that table back there?"

The waiter was perhaps twenty years old and looked scared. "I told her that her friend was in the ladies room and needed assistance. That's all, honest."

"Who told you to say that?"

"A lady gave me a tip to tell her and she left. I don't know where she went or who she was."

"Did she go into the restroom?"

"I don't know. When she asked me to tell the lady----I didn't watch where she went."

"Can we take a look in the restroom?" I asked still waving the wad of bills at him.

"I can clean it now and then you can go in. I need to have one of the waitresses see if it's empty first." He said, as I handed him the currency and waited.

"Sir you can go in now, he said."

There was a sign that said "cleaning" on the door, with a broom propping it open. Higgins and I walked in and looked around. There were two stalls and a small window high up that looked difficult to climb through. The wastebasket contained the standard towels and tissues with no sign of any Federal Express packaging. Whoever was waiting in the restroom took the envelope, hid it in her clothing and left unnoticed.

"Well, we knew he was slick. Any ideas?" I said as I looked disappointedly at Higgins.

"The only thing I know is that he's still close by within the Mall, and if he has what we think he has, he's flying out of here today with a new identity----to God knows where in this world, doing God knows what to whom." Higgins said.

662

"Chuck, come in, over." Art's voice squealed from the small radio in my hand.

"I hear you Art, what's up?"

"She's in a cab about two cars ahead driving toward the beach I think."

"Good, stay with her and if you lose touch with us try and call my cell, I'll leave it on and you do the same. In the meantime we'll grab a cab and head your way, out toward the Pacific Sea Hotel. If we lose you meet us in the lobby of the hotel. You can also page us in the lobby. We'll hang out there until we hear from you. She'll eventually go back there and leave with Prill---- unless she's meeting Mason at the airport."

"Roger that old buddy, out."

CHAPTER 150

Mason was pleased with his new identities, and after successfully obtaining the items he had requested, made his last stop of the morning at an office supply store purchasing an expensive snake skin briefcase, complete with a combination locking devise. He also purchased sufficient lead sheeting to hide the contents from x-ray intrusions. He of course knew that Frank or his co-pilot would never open the case. Before going to the airport he had one last stop----his luggage. The taxi pulled up at the dilapidated motel and the driver's face expressed surprise that he would stay in such a place however nothing was said by either. He asked the driver to keep the meter running as he'd be only a few minutes. With that Mason carried his new briefcase, his other purchases which fit in one shopping sized bag, as well as his old briefcase into the office.

She sat swigging coffee which looked like a vanilla shake, considering the amount of cream and sugar she shoveled into the cup. "It's you again?"

"Yes, and I see that check-out time is noon and I have an hour to spare. Would you be so kind as to return the key to me so I can change and freshen up?"

"You look fresh enough to me." She said, while Mason considered that she didn't know the meaning of the word.

"I'll be happy to make it worth your while," as he again slipped her the equivalent of a twenty-dollar bill US, while she slid the key across the counter.

Mason, still carrying his old briefcase containing his lap top computer, picked up his bag and the one belonging to Jennifer, along with his newly purchased items and juggled his way out to the cab, dropping off Jennifer's bag as well as his own, then walked back across the gravel drive to the depressing room they stayed in last night. For lack of a table, he spread out on the bed his very familiar purchases and began sorting and doing what was required.

Twenty minutes later, Mason left the room with the briefcase, a bag of garbage and his old briefcase. He stopped by the office, dropped off the key and heard, "you don't look any fresher to me", from the *happy* manager. Without a word he climbed into the taxi with his briefcase and his garbage.

"Do you know where the private plane gate is at the airport?

"You mean on the far side of the field where all the politicians and big shots land?"

"I guess that would be it, but that ain't me." Mason said with a cackle.

"Yes sir, I know where it is." The driver said as he sped off.

665

Before long the airport directional signs came into view as the driver pulled onto the north road leading to the west end of the main terminal buildings. The private terminal was just beyond that in a metal building with its own parking area and security gate. The driver pulled through the gate with a nod from the security guard and stopped in one of the five minute parking places for loading and unloading.

"Would you mind dropping this suitcase by the Pacific Sea Hotel and see that it gets delivered to Miss. Jennifer Heath, suite 601?" Mason asked as he fanned through a large handful of Rands. Eying the money, the driver replied with a smile, "No problem at all."

Mason gave him a good tip as well as sufficient fare for the delivery of Jennifer's bag. He carried the bags into the building, all except the new snakeskin briefcase to which Mason responded, "I'll take that."

The driver thanked him, walked out to his taxi and drove away while Mason stood on the landing watching the car while deep in thought as it disappeared from sight around a turn in the road.

The sun was warm and the sky a deep blue without a cloud, a perfect day for a flight to Hong Kong.

Frank was finishing his paperwork in the terminal office when he noticed Mason and walked over.

"Mr. Schultz, I understand we're flying to Hong Kong, one of my favorite cities. Mr. Prill alerted us and we are ready to leave whenever you are. I'm signed off here."

"I need to make a quick phone call, where do I meet you?" I can wait for you or you can just go through that door, we're right outside."

"Great, I'll meet you at the plane." Mason said smiling.

He punched in the cell number on a pay phone in the lobby of the terminal. "Hello." Came the voice of Peter Prill.

"Peter, Mason."

"How are you?" Peter asked.

"I'm OK Peter. I just wanted to thank you so much for helping me with this flight. I can't tell you how much your friendship means to me." Mason said and paused.

"Mason, it's nothing, the plane was just sitting there and now it can be put to a productive use. Let me hear from you from time to time, and you might give Jen a jingle sometime, she's really worried about you. Are you sure you're all right?"

"I'm just fine, really. I sent Jennifer's bag over in a cab to your suite, should be there in a few minutes. I'll be in touch with both of you."

Mason placed the receiver on the hook and lifted it again to clear the line.

Cleared by the tower, the big Gulfstream took off to the south cutting into the clear blue sky under the blazing hot sun----like a graceful bird heading home. She slowly turned, setting a westerly heading as it gained altitude toward its cruising elevation of 38,000 feet.

CHAPTER 151

"Well, how was your day?" Art asked Higgins and me as we sat just inside the lounge door with a cold beer in front of each of us. From our vantage point the front desk was clearly visible, as was the front door.

"Some people know how to do surveillance and others spin their wheels. How did you do?" I asked grinning.

"I lost her in worse traffic than San Francisco after a 'Niners game."

"While you were cussing, Higgins and I were sitting here sipping and waiting for out quarry to walk into our trap."

"She's here?"

"Yup, in 601 right this minute. Now if we bring that TV monitor in from the van we might be able to find out what they're talking about up there."

Higgins and I walked out to the van with Art and helped bring in our things as we had the rooms for the night. We went up to my room and set up the monitor. We could see the living room where Peter Prill we assumed was talking on the telephone about some order that was past due. Jennifer was probably in her own room without a camera and Mason's room looked empty and appeared to be unoccupied.

"I think we need to shake things up a bit in 601."

"How do you propose we do that?" Art asked me as Higgins looked on with interest.

"I say one of us walks up to the room and ask for Mason Hampton. We can watch their expressions and listen after whoever does it walks away. We can follow up with something like we had an appointment to meet here at say one o'clock, which is about now. We can also say he made the appointment yesterday morning."

"I like it and I'll do it----that is if it's all right with you fellows." Higgins offered.

"Go for it." Art said. "My acting days are over."

"Higgins left the room and rode the elevator to the sixth floor. Upon arriving at the door he rapped with authority.

Peter Prill answered in his stocking feet and said, "Yes?"

In his finest most proper English, Higgins said, "I have a one o'clock appointment with Mr. Hampton----Mr. Mason Hampton."

Prill looked speechless, not knowing whether to acknowledge that he even knew Mason. Finally, he responded, "I'm afraid you have the wrong room, you might check with the desk."

Higgins, enjoying the awkward situation added, "You are Mr. Prill, aren't you?"

Hesitating, he said "yes, but there's no one here except my assistant."

"He said he would be staying in your suite." Higgins added.

Peter Prill was getting red and agitated and Jennifer had slipped from her room and positioned herself behind the door and where Peter was standing.

"Just who are you?" Prill asked pointedly.

"A friend from the service." He said as he headed back toward the elevator leaving Prill standing at the door----his mouth agape and Jennifer now not hiding but standing next to Prill, watching the elevator door close behind Higgins who pressed "Lobby" for effect.

Art and I were crowded over the monitor and hushed Higgins as he came in talking. The performance by Higgins was first rate. It provided them with a dialog devoted to Mason for the next twenty minutes.

"He wasn't from Nam, I knew those guys and besides he has an English accent."

"Well, you know a lot of our Brits were fighting right alongside you Yanks."

"I know, I'm sorry but I knew the guys with us and he wasn't one of them. If he was, he would have wanted to talk with me he knew my name, that's why I know he was a setup."

"Maybe we should call him before he lands in Hong Kong." Jennifer said.

"He's jumpy enough I don't want to worry him anymore by calling the plane. Whoever that guy was, he doesn't even know he's on his way to Hong Kong. If he did he wouldn't be messing with us here."

I was truly shaken, my thoughts were for the safety of Valarie, whom I hadn't spoken with for days but was confident she was OK with John Sun and Preston Hobbs----until now.

Do you know how to reach him in Hong Kong?" Jennifer asked.

"No, I think he's disappearing again, no one will know where he is until he decides it's time."

My first call was to John Sun who added Preston Hobbs to the call, filling them both in on Mason Hampton's destination and his concern for the safety of Valarie. Both agreed that she had been in the same place too long and would be moved immediately and would keep me informed.

I then dialed a second Hong Kong number. "Hello".

"Honey, I'm so happy to hear your voice, I miss you so much."

"Who is this?" Valarie said, and then after a long pause began laughing and said she missed me too and has been terribly worried.

Art nearly pulled me off my chair and yanked me to the table where the monitor was flickering the image of Peter Prill standing next to the telephone table.

"Hold on honey." I said as I turned up the audio of the monitor.

The audio feed turned up to its maximum, screeched "They said what? Repeat yourself word for word. You just got a call from some South African flight control center. And they got a call from Australia? Whatever! What did they say? The plane went down----when----where? When will they be there? Oh my God. Call who you have to----but get me factual information." Prill said as he placed the receiver back on the cradle.

The room was silent as they crowded around the monitor----listening.

"What happened Peter?" Jennifer asked with a sick look on her face, already knowing the other side of the conversation.

"Frank, Billy and Mason apparently crashed in the Pacific, about two hours out----miles from everywhere. They disappeared from radar without a word, and the US Navy, reported sighting some floating debris in the general area. Rescue planes are on the way, but it doesn't look good."

"That's horrible----Frank had three children and a loving wife. Billy was so young, God's gift to women. I don't know about Mason, but no one deserves to die that way."

"My, how things change in this case." I said as I explained what we just heard to Valarie. "I think it's time that we had our own vacation----together, you think about where and I'll be there probably tomorrow. I'll call you before I leave. Love you."

"Sounds great, can't wait. I love you too, and miss you." Valarie said as we hung up our phones.

"I'll believe it when I see it." Art said with a skeptical tone.

"Well it's easy enough to verify the crash on the news, and it does sound like Peter Prill and Jennifer both believe he was on the plane. They were not doing an acting job for us because I'm convinced they don't know about our mini-camera in the suite." Higgins said in his normal, logical approach to evaluating a situation.

"I agree, they think he went down with the plane----if it did." I said.

"Let's turn on the news. There should be something at least locally on the crash----it did originate from Cape Town." Art said.

For the next two hours the three watched television and ordered up some appetizers and cold beer. There was limited news coverage of the missing Gulfstream, however it did mention Peter Prill and Euro Outfitters as owner of the plane. Releasing names of passengers and crew was being withheld at the moment, until more information had been received.

"I know this sounds bad, particularly for the flight crew, but if that plane really did go down, we have one less bad guy to worry about and our work is pretty much finished." I said to Art and Higgins as the latest news segment had just finished airing.

"If he's out of the picture, I think you and Valarie are finally safe. There wasn't anyone connected with KRL that had an axe to grind with you, even though you did mess up their deal. I think they were more upset with Mason and Phil, don't you?"

"I agree, I think if Mason's swimming with the fishes, we're OK and life can get back to the real business like dropping a hook with a fat worm off the back of the houseboat, while nursing a cold one."

"Gentlemen, I have to admit I really enjoyed my time with you fellows and hate to see it end, although I know it needs to." Higgins said.

"Let's have a farewell dinner tonight, without the worry of what Mason Hampton is doing or planning at the moment." Art suggested.

"Great plan, let's find the best restaurant in town and have a good last night in Cape Town. I'll make flight arrangements home for you fellows. I hear there are only first class seats available, do you mind suffering along with the rich and famous?"

"Why don't you book me to London----I'd like to look around for a few days before joining Jimmy in the work-a-day grind. I can fly along with Higgins that way, unless there's a non-stop to Lisbon that he might prefer." Art said.

"No, as a matter of fact I might just like a couple of days layover myself, and look up some of my old cronies. Let's say three nights in London and on to Lisbon----if you're acting as my travel agent." Higgins said with that trademark grin, as he stroked his mustache.

"As long as you're scheduling vacations, make mine three nights too----OK?"

"You've got it, and with your permission I'll also set you both up at the Oxley, and I'm telling the hotel that your money's no good." I added with my famous smile. "That's the least I can do for you. In regard to your time and whatever expenses you've incurred, I want you to e-mail the amount and I'll send you a check by return mail----from wherever the hell I might be, who knows?"

"I told you I don't expect anything for my time Chuck." Higgins said in protest.

"That you did my friend. If you don't comply with my request, I'll do it on my own."

"Then you'll have to, because I'm not expecting anything for work that was fun for me----really!"

"I have one last request. Can you call someone that might be able to provide us with an accurate status on that Gulfstream? I don't think the press gets this kind of information on a real-time basis and I would feel a lot better having some certainty on the matter." I asked Higgins.

"I think I can get some accurate information from my friend that helped us with the Jennifer Heath identification. I'll call him." Higgins responded.

Just then the audio portion of the monitor in Peter Prill's suite, which had been turned up to its loudest setting picked up Peter Prill answering the telephone.

"OK Shelly, go slow." He said as he listened with a strained look on his face.

"You say some international flight control agency called the office and asked for the owner of the plane. OK, and they said that the US Navy picked up some floating debris and the wreckage they retrieved appeared to be parts of seats covered with expensive tan leather, and they'll check with Gulfstream for possible identification. You told them that

both of our planes had tan leather seats in the
cabin. Uh huh. Shelly, call the insurance
company----you know that guy Philippe, yeah the
goofy guy. Get him out of bed, I don't care, just
tell him we want our money or another new
Gulfstream----do you hear?

OK!" Prill slammed the phone down and
went to the wet bar and poured a large glass of
something----and sat down looking out the
window.
"I think *our* news source is better than any
other." I said.

Peter then turned in his chair and shouted
over his shoulder----"Jen?"

Jennifer came out of her bedroom looking
bedraggled and said, "yes?"

"Would you please get the home and
emergency numbers for Frank and Billy, I need
to speak with their families."

"Well, he isn't all bad----after all." Art said as
I sat there in thought.

"I just spoke with my friend and he said the
wire reports are saying that evidence at the scene
indicates a non-commercial luxury flight crash,
with first appearances indicating explosion, due
to the widespread wreckage area."

"That checks with Prill's reports. It certainly looks like the plane went down with our boy on it." I said.

"I need a shower before our big night out." Art said as he headed for the door.

"That sounds like a splendid idea." Higgins added.

"I need to take care of some TechX business----suppose we meet here in about an hour."

CHAPTER 152

I retrieved my laptop from my brief case, plugged into the phone line and looked for the insurance files sent from Tom's office in Palo Alto a couple of weeks ago----which seemed like years to me. After a few minutes I found the right sections and fired off a lengthy e-mail to the agent of record, handling TechX's business insurance.

I felt like the weight of the world was steadily being lifted from my shoulders as news of the apparent air disaster came filtering in. Although horrible as it was for all involved, it seemed to eliminate the problem that had become a fixation for me over these last few weeks----Mason Hampton. I walked over to the mini-bar and selected a small two-ounce martini bottle, although not my favorite Vox it was good enough. Pulling a glass from the shelf, I scooped it full of ice from the bucket, unscrewed the metal cap and poured the clear liquid over the glistening shards of ice. Walking over to the balcony, I stepped out and sat down on one of the cushioned wrought-iron chairs, watching ocean waves crash against the rocky shore retreating only to gain new life and strength to repeat the endless process.

Sipping, I felt life was much the same, providing one doesn't despair from events that parade along the path, preventing them from moving forward as we all journey through this precious trip called life. My thoughts turned to my feelings toward Valarie. I loved her company and loved her, but before I became involved with the TechX problem, I thought getting serious could come later; after all I just recently retired. After thinking about how I was almost killed twice in the last two weeks and possibly Valarie as well, I started thinking about what really is important, not the destination but the journey. I couldn't think of anyone more important to make that journey of life with than Valarie.

I finished my drink and was pouring a second when the familiar rap, rap, rap, "Hey Chuck open up", came from outside the door.

Art walked in followed by Higgins who came out of his room after hearing Art's commotion in the hall.

"Let's party." Art said----somewhat out of context for the San Francisco private investigator.

"It looks like you hit the mini-bar too." I said smiling at Art.

"Actually, I'm looking forward to total relaxation in London, starting tomorrow."

"Oh, you weren't relaxing here in Cape Town?" I chided.

"Do you call chasing a serial terrorist killer a vacation?" Art responded as he headed to the mini bar behind Higgins who was in the process of pouring a mini-bottle of scotch in a glass.

"Putting it that way, I have to agree with you. Have you called Jimmy to tell him you're finished?" I said watching and expecting Art's expression.

"Are you nuts? If he knew that, he'd have already booked a tenth class ticket on the red-eye tonight, so I could get be in the office tomorrow to pitch in." Art answered with a snarling expression on his face.

Higgins and I broke into laughter at Arts response, and soon the three of us were laughing and toasting one another on ending the case.

EPILOGUE

Art and Higgins flew to London, first class as promised and were squired around town by an entourage that could only be assembled by Geoffrey Higgins, everyone's best friend---- and rightly so.

I flew to Hong Kong and was met at the airport gate by a welcoming party consisting of Valarie and of course John Sun and Preston Hobbs clinging to each arm.

After a welcome back dinner party at Preston's home, Valarie and I retreated to the "home" that she had become so accustomed to and we very passionately renewed our love for one another.

The next morning, Valarie showed me some brochures of a little get-away spot on Bali, where we could rent a magnificent villa on a white sand beach, complete with guaranteed afternoon tropical breezes rustling through the thatched roof.

"Done." I said. "Let's call and see if we can get it for a couple of weeks----what do you think?'

"Done!" Valarie said, "I already rented it."

The next morning on the way to the airport, John Sun said, "I received a call from the Inspector early this morning and it seems that Mr. Che from KRL was murdered outside his home sometime after midnight. The police feel confident it was the same people who killed Billy Wong. I guess the case against them will probably be dropped, unless there is some continuing civil damage claim to be brought against the company."

"Interesting." I said as I thought about the implications. "We're going on a vacation and can't go to the funeral, please send my condolences." John smiled at the comment.

I tried to reach Tom Claudius prior to leaving for the airport, but Betty said he was fly-fishing in Colorado for the next three days and was in an area where his cell had no service. I asked her to have him call my cell number when he returned.

The villa was gorgeous as was Bali, where neither of us had been before. Days were spent just relaxing, either in a hammock or snorkeling among the endless varieties of rainbow colored fish in an ocean where visibility reached fifty feet or more.

Tom called the following Monday after returning to his office. "Chucky, how the hell are you?" Tom asked in his usually good-natured way.

"Tom, I'm fine, and I called because I owe you a report."

"Well now, I can't imagine you owing me anything after getting a call from the insurance company this morning telling me TechX, thanks to your formal request, is getting a check for the "key man" loss of $12,500,000. Ten for Jaxton's death, and two and a half million for Phil. I had no idea we even had that coverage in the policy. It's the same boilerplate provisions I've used for every startup. I never had the occasion to even consider a death claim before. How did you know about it?"

"One late night, a long time ago, when I was considering your offer to fund my project, I looked at the insurance requirements where you included a draft policy. In reading the fine print I decided the easiest way for you to make money off my deal was to collect on the ten million bucks the CEO coverage called for. That's why I asked Betty to e-mail me a copy of the TechX policy early on and I found it to be exactly the same. What happened to the employee theft portion, they should have covered that too?" I asked.

"They would have had I not informed them that TechX received a wire transfer from a Cayman bank yesterday for $2,750,000, which looks like the approximate principal and interest repaying every cent taken by Phil Hampton." Tom said without divulging the fact that he also received a note in a plain envelope bearing a Toronto postmark dated three days earlier saying only;

"We're not even anymore----.
Sorry it happened---- I didn't know it was you."

The Miami yacht dealer stood watching at the dock as the tall trim well tanned man who looked younger than his fifty-plus years, sporting a red Yankees baseball cap, stood at the wheel of his new $527,000, sixty-foot ocean going Premier yacht. With both powerful engines gently idling, as if lying in wait for their next prey, a taxi pulled up on the dock and an attractive woman wearing a floral print dress, sandals, a yellow wide-brimmed floppy hat spilling out just a hint of either dark red or brown hair, carrying an overnight bag, jumped from the cab and hurried without a word or look as she breezed past the dealer and crossed the waiting gangplank.

Once onboard and holding her bag in one hand said, "You told me to travel light because no matter what I need we can always buy it!"

"You're right about that, welcome aboard. Dan, it looks like we're ready to go, will you untie the lines, please?"

"This is truly beautiful."

"Thanks---- all set?" He said smiling. "We have a man to see about an island."

686

13465127R00406

Made in the USA
Middletown, DE
17 November 2018